A NOVEL OF NEW FRANCE

BRAVING THE DAWN

PEGGY JOQUE WILLIAMS

Black Rose Writing | Texas

This is a work of fiction. Names, characters, businesses, places, events, and incidents are either the products of the author's imagination or used in a fictitious manner. Any resemblance to actual persons, living or dead, or actual events is purely coincidental.

ISBN: 978-1-68513-698-7
PUBLISHED BY BLACK ROSE WRITING
www.blackrosewriting.com

Printed in the United States of America
Suggested Retail Price (SRP) $22.95

Braving the Dawn is printed in Book Antiqua

Dedicated to
my mother, Genevieve,
my grandmothers, Ida and Blanche,
and all my many-times great-grandmothers
who came before them

PRAISE FOR
BRAVING THE DAWN

"Peggy Joque Williams captures readers with a gripping frontier saga of love, loss, and struggle—proving even the wilderness of New France isn't far enough away from the mother country to escape the long arm of the Crown."
–Cam Torrens, bestselling author of the *Tyler Zahn suspense series*

"Peggy Williams is one of the best historical fiction authors I have ever read, easily comparable to Philippa Gregory. With painstaking attention to historical detail, she weaves entrancing stories that blend fiction with fact and makes it impossible to put down her books... In Braving the Dawn...the author's exceptional storytelling abilities and her well-developed characters had me heavily invested in this exciting, emotional, and totally engaging novel."
–A.J. McCarthy, author of the *Charlie & Simm mystery series*

"I loved her first book in the series - I love this one even more! Braving the Dawn is a historical romance, but SO much more."
–Deb Heim, co-author of the *Spirit Song: Rebels Rising series*

"I'd be hard pressed to say what I enjoyed most about this smartly crafted historical novel: the well-drawn characters; the twisty, action-filled plot that kept me in suspense; or the intriguing love quadrangle that had me pivoting on who to root for. A terrific read!"
–Ruth F. Stevens, award-winning author of *My Year of Casual Acquaintances*

Exiled to the backwaters of New France, Sylvienne discovers the true meaning of family and what she will do to protect it.
–Marie W. Watts, award-Winning author of *Tough Trail Home*

"Even if you're not into historical fiction, I would highly recommend that you check out Williams' *Braving the Dawn,* a well-researched and beautifully written novel."
–Jacquie Herz, author of *Circumference of Silence* and *Hannah Bloom*

"Romance, intrigue and adventure await on every page of Braving the Dawn. Follow strong-willed Sylvienne as she voyages to Quebec during the early years of the fur trade, where she'll find danger, make new friends and enemies, and discover whether true love endures. Captivating and memorable!"
–Marilee Dahlman, author of *Mall Goddess*

"With the rich historical detail of a Phillippa Gregory classic and a heroine as compelling as any you'll ever meet, *Braving the Dawn* is a mesmerizing, must-read triumph of transformation and courage."
–Joan Fernandez, author of *Saving Vincent, A Novel of Jo van Gogh*

"For those readers of *Courting the Sun* by Peggy Joque Williams, you are in for a treat. *Braving the Dawn* is a continuation of Sylvienne d'Aubert's journey from the court of King Louis XIV to New France (Canada). Even if you haven't read Williams' previous novel, this story stands on its own. This meticulously researched novel, based on real events, has an authenticity not usually found in historical fiction. Sylvienne's inherent goodness thrives as she adapts to the new world. As she meets other new immigrants and First Nation people, she is thrown into a community unlike any other she has experienced. The plot and characters are fascinating, and the twisty ending a surprise. Curl up with this book and have a wonderful read."
–Iris Glazner Leigh, author of *Liza's Secrets*

"*Braving the Dawn* follows Sylvienne, suddenly banished by Louis IV, as she sails to New France. Once a favorite of the Sun King, Sylvienne is now uncertain, terrified, and pregnant when she joins the French settlers establishing Quebec. She must call on every shred of courage, wits, and gumption to survive in the harsh, beautiful wilderness. Peggy Joque Williams' careful research as a descendent of several of Louis' Filles du Roi and her vivid storytelling make this novel a compelling delight."
–Anne Davidson Keller, author of *Empty Chairs*

BRAVING THE DAWN

Paris, France, June 1672

Ma Très Chère,

You will never believe who paid me a visit this morning!

De Lorraine and I were still in bed, both of us quite naked. Of course, that is neither here nor there, except it put me in a rather awkward position after I complained of his ungodly snoring and farting and had to send him from the room. I lay sprawled across the silk sheets, eyes closed, savoring the morning breeze on my skin, when I heard the key turning in the door. I thought it was de Lorraine returning and sitting on the end of the bed. Except, when I opened my eyes, it wasn't him at all, but rather your beloved shoemaker! Fully clothed, of course, and pointing a pistol at me. You can guess my reaction.

Once over my shock, I asked him, how did you get in here? I quickly yanked the silk sheet over my princely member, which rose unbidden to salute his handsome physique. The brother of the King must show some dignity after all.

He said, I have to know. What happened to her? They say the King spared her from the blade. Is that true?

He did, I assured him, feigning casualness. For all the good it will do her. You know, you'll hang in the public square if they catch you in here.

I'll hang no matter where they catch me, was his reply. He stood and began to pace, shuffling his pistol from hand to hand, mumbling, saying, I should never have left her there…she begged me to flee, but I shouldn't have listened. Mon Dieu, she saved my life!

I must say I was quite astounded. Saved your life? I asked. Are you saying what she told us is true?

What does it matter now? he said. Oh, ma chère, the despair in his voice nearly brought me to tears. Except de Lorraine chose that very moment to rattle the doorknob. At which point your young man panicked and dashed back to the open window. With one leg over the sill, he begged, Tell me…if not beheading, what fate befalls her?

*What could I tell him but the truth? The King gave her a choice —
either the convent or New France.*

Which did she choose? he asked.

*I told him, You know her better than anyone, my friend. What do
you think?*

And then he was gone.

*There is other news, of course, the usual court gossip. But I've
neither the time nor energy to go into detail. Except for my own
woeful news. Louis has chosen a wife for me. The badger-faced girl.
You saw her portrait. I am distraught beyond words, but he refuses to
change his mind. You will write to me, won't you, ma chère? And tell
me of life amongst the Natives and the wild animals? Have you seen a
bear yet? Or a moose? I still weep for you.*

Bien à Vous Pour Toujours.
Philippe

CHAPTER ONE

The sea breeze stung my eyes as I gripped the gunwale, scanning the dock and the shoreline, hoping at the last moment he would appear. Rescue me from this ship. Or scramble aboard to journey with me into my new life.

But there was no sign of Etienne as the ship was tugged from its berth by a single boat with four rowers. The lines were detached just before the wind caught our sails and we lurched out into the harbor, the murky water between France and our ship growing wider. As we sailed out into the bay, I watched the sentinel towers of the fortress at La Rochelle grow smaller, the land of my birth receding from my life, along with dear Maman, my friends, and the only true love I had ever known. I knew not whether my beloved lived or had died at the hands of the King's guards. All I knew was the King had put a price on his head.

Glancing down into the water, I wondered what it would feel like to end it all. To climb over the gunwale in a single motion and drop into the waves, letting my skirts and petticoats pull me under. Would that be preferable to the fate awaiting me across the ocean? My muscles tensed, knuckles white on the rail.

"Mademoiselle! You must join the others," a voice spoke behind me.

Jolted out of my melancholy, I swung to face the ship's boy, his face so earnest on my behalf. "I'm coming."

I turned one last time, the towers barely visible now against the horizon. *I'll find a way back,* I vowed. *I'm not leaving forever.*

Our ship moved out into the bay. The sailors hustled about their duties coiling ropes, climbing the masts, setting the sails.

With a resolve meant to keep despair at bay, I turned my back on the tableau of my past life and glanced up at the twin masts of *La Nativité*. Behind them, the angry glow of a contrary morning sky settled into a soft rose. Ocean waves grew as we headed out onto the open sea, setting up a gentle rocking that soothed my damaged soul.

A cool breeze caught me by surprise, loosening a tendril of dark hair from under my white linen coif and settling the nausea that threatened. I closed my eyes and savored the sweet salty wind on my face.

"*Demoiselles!*" a ship's officer called out. "Gather round, and I'll assign your quarters."

I opened my eyes to survey the other girls. While we were all of marriageable age, not one of us had reached our twentieth birthday. Clinging to the side of the ship, some wore the glow of anticipation, for others, shadows of trepidation filled their eyes. Together we made our way across the deck and clustered around the bearded ship's officer. Next to him stood two women of the cloth and a priest, Jesuit by the look of his robe.

"Demoiselles," the officer said again.

To be referred to as an unmarried woman took me by surprise. Without thinking, I fingered the gold band on the finger of my left hand before reaching through an opening in the folds of my skirt. My fingers checked to ensure the small silk pouch was still sewn to the waistband of my underskirt. Inside the pouch were two other rings. One was an engraved silver band given to me as a memorial gift by the King's brother, Philippe, upon the death of his young wife, Henriette. The other was a braided gold band given to me by King Louis himself.

"Your belongings have been stowed below deck where you will make your berths. You may be up here on the main deck as much as you like between dawn and dusk, as long as the weather holds and the sea is calm. But do not get in the way of the sailors. And you must remain in the company of your chaperones at all times. If you will follow me." He turned to speak to the priest and the nuns before heading down below.

"Sylvienne?" A voice called out. "Sylvienne d'Aubert, is that you?"

I swiveled to face a girl my own age. A familiar face. "Claudette?"

It seemed a lifetime since I had last seen her. Since she had reported me to the Mother Abbess at our small convent school for having visited the home of a supposed witch. Thus causing me to be expelled from the school.

"Why are *you* here?" she asked. "I thought you had a position at court."

Clasping my hands together, I slipped the gold band from my finger. Hoping she wouldn't notice, I slid it into the pocket of my skirt.

"Are the rumors not true? Were you not maid of honor to one of King Louis's retinue?"

"Hush!" I grabbed her arm and pulled her away from the group moving toward the steps. "You mustn't say anything. I beg of you."

She winced and pulled her arm away. "Then it is true. Why keep it a secret? Won't your rank be obvious if you have quarters next to the captain?"

"I am quartered below deck like everyone else. My past is exactly that—the past."

She studied my face with an oddly familiar gaze. Perhaps she was gauging the extent to which she could take advantage of my vulnerability.

"And you?" I said. "Were you not betrothed to the son of one of your father's business partners?"

A momentary look of pain crossed her eyes, but she straightened her shoulders. "He turned out not to be a worthy match. I am here because I seek adventure, travel."

"In New France? An untested colony?"

"They say there is opportunity to be had. I travel toward my future. I am not…" She gauged me. "Running from my past."

I straightened my shoulders. "I wish you good fortune."

"Come on, demoiselles!" the officer shouted at us. "I can't be waiting all day." The others had all disappeared down the hatchway.

"Perhaps you will need luck more than I." Claudette offered an arch smile before strutting away. She took the officer's hand to steady herself on the first step down and fluttered her eyes at him. I hurried to catch up.

"I'll carry your bag, mademoiselle." Snatching my satchel, the boy gave me an ingratiating smile and trotted off.

"*Merci*, Hannibal!" I called after him.

Whistling a little tune, he disappeared down the steps. The first to welcome me when I came aboard earlier that day, he couldn't have been more than twelve or thirteen. One of the busiest people on the ship, he ran errands across and between decks for the captain, helped passengers who seemed lost, and made himself available to anyone who needed an extra hand.

"Mind your step on the ladder, mademoiselle," he called out as I lifted my brown wool skirt and followed him down into the murky darkness of the hold.

"This way!" he urged.

I followed him across the crowded hold. The sleeping quarters below deck were stuffy and dismal. A single lantern swayed erratically from a center post casting a dim, uneven glow. Other girls had already claimed berths mounted like shelving along the wall. A single bed remained, luckily for me on the opposite side from where Claudette stood inspecting her own berth.

Hannibal set my bag on a thin straw-filled pad which would serve as my bed for the next two to three months. He bowed before running back up the steps. I took a moment to survey my new quarters. We would be sharing the space with a family of goats, several pigs, and a large crate of chickens. The dank, fetid air only served to increase my nausea. Slop buckets were placed at strategic intervals. When we used them, it would be our responsibility to haul them up for the sailors to dump over the side of the ship.

We had been allowed to pack a bag with a change of clothes and a few personal possessions to be kept at the foot of our bunks. Our trunks were stowed in the bowels of the ship. The male passengers—our priest, several merchants, a carpenter, and two soldiers—would sleep in similar berths at the opposite end of our deck, divided from us by a thin wooden partition. The sailors, Hannibal later informed me, slept on hammocks hung from beams on the level below us.

"It's only a half-level, actually," he said and demonstrated how the seafaring men had to stoop to get to their sleeping accommodations.

When the time came for our first meal, to be taken up on the main deck under a hazy midday sun, I fetched a few items from my travel bag. Like the others, I had packed several days' worth of rations: bread, apples, and meat wrapped in a bakery crust. However, unlike some, I was careful to eat very small amounts, for when those reserves were gone, I would be reliant on whatever was served by the ship's cook. Limiting my portions turned out not to be a problem because, regardless of how rough or calm the waves were on any particular day, nausea became my constant companion.

The first week of our voyage we enjoyed calm seas and balmy air. The sun played hide and seek with billowy clouds, allowing us to spend our days above deck. The men stood at the gunwale gazing out to sea or watching the sailors at work, while we women clustered in small groups chatting and getting to know one another.

I learned the other girls were recruits, volunteering to go to New France, to the land some called Canada, in hopes of finding a man to marry. Several told me the King's representative had promised them they would be able to choose their husband. I realized this was the same journey my dear friend Perrette had taken several years earlier, after she had had an unfortunate encounter in Amiens with a man who took advantage of her, leaving her potentially unmarriageable in France.

"The King has paid our passage," a pretty redhead, Jeanne, said. She was from Paris. Most of the recruits, I learned, had come from Paris, many having lived at the Hôpital-Général, an asylum for foundlings and the poorest of the poor. Several came from the farms around Rouen. Claudette was the only other girl from Amiens.

Jeanne was the daughter of a fish merchant. "My father supplied cod, mackerel, and sturgeon to the royal palaces," she said, a wistfulness in her voice. "Before he died."

"I'm so sorry." I reached out and touched Jeanne's arm, wondering if I had eaten some of his cod and mackerel when I was at court.

"I would love to see the inside of one of the King's palaces," another girl said. Françoise, her voice dreamy.

Claudette perked up. "Sylvienne lived at Versailles."

"Truly?" Françoise said. "What was it like?" She sat close to another girl, Geneviève, who I learned was her sister.

An older girl, Madeleine, eyed me with suspicion, a challenge in her voice. "What did you do there?"

When I hesitated, Claudette jumped in. "She served as maid of—"

"Yes," I said, cutting her off. "A maid. Not a very glamorous job, I'm afraid."

"Tell us more," Jeanne pleaded.

Claudette seemed to smirk as she gazed at me.

"There is nothing to tell," I said. "A maid is a maid. I expect some of you held the same job in different houses. Madeleine, what did you do? Did you live in Paris?"

Caught off guard by my question, Madeleine seemed to soften. "Like you, I was a maid. But in the home of a wealthy banker."

My effort to change the subject worked. Madeleine seemed elated to be the center of attention, recounting her life in a Parisian mansion.

Later, alone at the rail, I looked out over the never-ending expanse of water, pondering the fate that had brought me to this ship, on this journey, with these girls.

"Why are you so secretive?" Claudette asked, startling me from behind. "What is the harm in telling them of your life at court?"

"It will do me no good with these women if they believe I hold airs above them," I said. "My life is among them now." I turned to watch the sailors scurrying over the deck and up the masts, adjusting the sails, checking the rigging.

"It won't matter once you marry," she said. "Their lives will be common. Surely you will marry one of the King's administrators or a wealthy merchant."

"I don't plan to marry at all," I said, keeping my voice low.

"Why ever not? Why else make this voyage?"

I had no answer for her. It hadn't really occurred to me before this moment. All I knew was that I was weary of having my heart broken.

Claudette filled the silence. "Do you plan to join the convent once we get there?"

I couldn't suppress a rueful snort. "When the Mother Abbess kicked me out of school, I vowed I wouldn't set foot inside a convent again. So, no. I will find another way to get by."

"You've always been an odd one," Claudette said. She headed to the hatch to join the group below deck, giving one of the sailors a broad wink on her way.

I wasn't ready to leave the fresh air. So, I moved to the other side of the ship even though I knew the view would not be any different. All one endless sea.

A sailor shouted, "Mademoiselle! Watch that rope there. Mind you don't trip over it."

Too late. I tripped anyway, grabbing for a post to keep from falling. But to no avail. As I landed on my backside, one of the several pouches I had sewn to the inside of my underskirt broke off and fell to the deck.

"What's this?" The sailor grabbed me by the arm to haul me back to my feet, his eyes fixed on the pouch as if he'd found treasure.

"N-nothing," I stammered, reaching for the small bag. "Keepsakes, that's all."

To my dismay, he snatched up the pouch before I could. Tugging on the drawstring, he spilled the contents into his hand. His grin of anticipation quickly turned to disappointment. "Stones?"

"*S'il vous plaît.*" I held out my hand, but he cursed and tossed the bag and the stones onto the deck before striding off.

Dropping to my knees to retrieve them, I groaned in frustration. Of course they meant nothing to him, but to me they were precious, gifts from my mother, one from Etienne, others I'd picked up along the way. Gathering them up, I knew without counting I was missing one. As I stood, weary and frustrated, Madeleine held out the missing stone. I hadn't seen her approach.

"Do you read them? The stones?" she asked.

"No, I…it is my mother who deciphers them."

"Will you read for me? I need to know…" She put a hand on her belly, and I realized she had a slight swelling. There was something about the look in her eyes, a combination of despair and hope.

Immediately, I thought of my own predicament. I pictured Maman, reassuring the women who came to her for words of hope and encouragement. I would sit at her feet as a child, wide-eyed as she instructed them to throw the stones, close their eyes, and choose three, or six, or five randomly. I had begged her to teach me, but she said it was not something that could be learned. The gift was given by God.

I had no gift. But I knew how Madeleine must feel—cast off, abandoned, alone, frightened for herself and the tiny one she carried. "Come, tell me about your baby."

We sought a shady spot away from where the sailors were working. With relief, she sank down onto the deck next to me and immediately began talking, spinning a story of unrequited love. The master of the house in which she had worked, so handsome, so charming, pursued her until…

I knew how the story would end. Without thinking, I emptied the contents of the pouch into my hands. When, finally, she sat silent, I realized I had been fingering the stones the whole time. "I need to know," she said again, pointing toward them.

Reluctantly, I handed her the stones. She rubbed them between her palms then let them drop onto the deck between us. I looked at them. Their colors. Their position. What was it my mother saw in them? "Close your eyes and choose three," I said. The remaining stones lay there, unspeaking. I looked into her eyes again. The yearning so evident. "I don't know if it will be this one or the next, but you will have a healthy baby boy."

"A boy?" She held a hand to her cheek, heartened.

Inwardly, I hoped so, but in the end, I doubted it would really matter when the time came. "When we land, you will meet a man who will love and respect you. He will provide you a home to fill with boys and girls."

She leaned over and hugged me tightly. Whatever else happened to her, I knew she would go forward with the confidence needed to make the future her own. After wiping away tears of relief, she slipped a coin from her dress pocket and held it out.

"No," I protested. But she insisted, putting it into my hand before hurrying away. I pocketed her coin, remembering the small, lacquered box in which Maman kept her offerings. And her words: *They must believe the reading is worth something. If it's not a sacrifice, they won't heed the words.*

"Will you tell mine, as well?"

I looked up to see another girl waiting, a tall girl with a mole under one eye. Beatrix, from a village near Rouen.

Before I could protest, she slid into place next to me, thrust a coin into my hand, and began to tell me her story. Resigned, I invited her to throw the stones, close her eyes, and select three. Again, the remaining stones said nothing to me. But when I gazed into Beatrix's anxious eyes, I knew she feared the future. Could this be the secret of my mother's gift?

It wasn't long before word got around. Claudette was the only one of the girls who didn't approach me to have the stones read. I wasn't surprised.

Several days afterward, the ship's boy sought me out. "Mademoiselle, is it true you tell the future?"

"No, Hannibal, I—"

He held out a coin, his eyes lit with anticipation. Against my better judgement, I patted the deck next to me for him to sit. His eyes grew large when I poured the stones into his hand.

"Throw them down, then close your eyes and choose three."

His fingers touched each one before picking up the shiny black stone with the two white stripes, a pretty amethyst, and a speckled river rock. He opened his eyes to gaze at the ones in his hand.

There was something about him I couldn't discern even though I'd studied his face all the while he chose his stones. I knew from previous conversations he came from a large family in LaRochelle. His father owned a tavern. Hannibal had been offered to the captain as an indentured servant when he was ten. He said he loved being at sea and hoped to become a sailor and a ship's officer one day.

"What do they say, mademoiselle?"

"That you and the sea are as one in spirit."

He broke into a grin. "Will I ever captain my own ship?"

Looking into his eager eyes, a sudden shiver of dread passed through me. I shook it off and smiled. "If you work hard, your future is yours to determine."

A gruff voice interrupted us. "Hannibal! What are you doing, you lazy oaf? Go get the food tray from the captain's cabin."

"Aye, sir!" He jumped to his feet. "Merci, mademoiselle. You are most kind." He ran off to do his chores.

We were at sea for just over a fortnight and had settled into a routine of sleeping belowdecks and eating and taking the air above. I had tucked two of my beloved books into my travel bag, but the light was too dim to read on my berth. And even above deck, I dared not read, for the very act of it on the rolling sea set off the nausea I worked so hard to keep at bay.

Likewise, I had packed paper, quill, and ink, but a recap of my journey for Maman would have to wait until my feet were on solid land and I had a table in front of me.

After three weeks of mostly pleasant skies, the weather changed. The wind blew markedly colder, coming out of the north. Squalls of rain chased us from the deck during the day, forcing us to eat our meals below in the increasingly fetid confines, shaking off water dripping from the planks above, shooing away rats and mice. Lightning flashed through the portholes at night, all the more eerie as the single lantern candle was put out during storms for fear of fire. The ship rocked wildly, and I clung fiercely to whatever I could grasp to keep from rolling out of my berth. I couldn't sleep. I couldn't keep anything down. I felt so exhausted and weak, I began to fear I would not survive the trip.

Then, suddenly, the storm was over. The sea calmed. Eager to go above deck and suck in fresh air, I readied myself to join the passengers already hurrying up the stairs. Moaning from the berth next to mine caught my attention. Madeleine. She was lying on her side with her legs curled up.

"What's wrong?" I asked.

She pulled back her skirt to reveal a bloody cloth shoved up between her thighs.

"Oh, Madeleine. I'm so sorry," I whispered.

"Don't tell anyone," she pleaded. "Just say my monthly is heavier than usual."

She had managed to conceal her condition as I had. But her "condition" hadn't survived the storm. I fetched a bucket of water and helped her clean up.

"The next one," she said.

"The next one?" I asked, confused.

"It will be a boy. I know it. And I will find a husband. And he will never know what happened to me. He will love me and respect me, just like you said."

"He will." I stroked her hair. "I'm sure of it."

Finally, she fell asleep. Night had fallen, and the others began making their way back down the stairs. I helped clean up the mess on the floor created by the storm. One by one, my co-travelers climbed into their berths, the soothing rocking motion of the ship lulling them to sleep. I took advantage of the loud snoring of our chaperones to sneak up the creaky stairs to breathe the fresh air above deck myself. The lone sailor high in the crow's nest was too busy scanning the dark horizon to notice me on the deck.

Leaning against the portside gunwale, I gazed in awe at the moonless heavens above. I had often looked up at the vast expanse of stars back home, but never did they seem so close or so numerous as they did here out on the ocean. The swath of milky light they called *la voie lactée* hung low over the water.

Etienne. Where was he now? Could he be gazing at these very same stars? Or had he been arrested and imprisoned? My heart ached to think we would never be together, that I would never again feel the thrill of his touch, the warmth of his lips. I had managed to keep one pair of the slippers he had made for me, tucked away in my trunk, now deep in the hold.

The day we first met—I must have been ten, he twelve—he had been delivering shoes to my uncle's lover and found me sitting in a tree spying on them. How we loved climbing trees. And swimming. We didn't discover the joy of each other's bodies until I was already at court, when it was too late to do so without being furtive, without betraying my vows to my husband.

A tingle ran along my arms when a shooting star brushed across Cassiopeia, named for the queen in Greek mythology who boasted about her beauty. Maman had tried to warn me court was not the fairytale life I imagined it to be. I wished now I had listened to her.

My hands instinctively cradled my midriff. I couldn't deny it any longer. A seed was growing within me. I wouldn't know who had fathered it until the first time I gazed into the babe's eyes. Would they be hard and cold as steel like those of my late husband, the Duc de Narbonne? Or would they possess the mirth-filled warmth of Etienne's blue eyes? Or perhaps they would be like my own, green, in which case I would never know who had fathered it.

CHAPTER TWO

We were four weeks at sea, and I was spending as much time above deck as possible to get relief from the stench below.

A month without a proper wash meant we were all rank and itching and beginning to scab over. The mites and the lice housed in our worn mattresses were nearly unbearable. I noticed the other girls furtively wringing out bloodied rags in buckets of seawater. For better or worse, that was one small inconvenience I had been spared.

The food provisions had grown sparse, the captain rationing the gruel and hardtack. The one highlight of each day was the cup of sweetened lemon water we were given to drink. The captain insisted it would keep us from getting scurvy, a deadly disease that afflicted sailors and passengers alike on many voyages. I couldn't imagine something as simple as lemon water could make a difference, but I enjoyed the taste and didn't complain.

One of the merchants traveling with us scraped his ankle on an exposed nail while trying to locate his traveling chests in the hold. Days later the wound festered, and before long, his muscles became rigid, including his jaw. He couldn't eat or even swallow water. Within the week he was dead. The sailors wrapped his body in linen, weighted it with a brick, and, after the priest said prayers, sent the dead man over the side of the ship.

Then word spread that Hannibal had taken to his hammock with a fever after being drenched in yet another squall. His condition worsened and he became delirious. The captain ordered him put to bed on a pallet in his own cabin. The boy had become dear to me, so I knocked on the captain's door and begged to be allowed to care for him. The look in the captain's eyes told me he thought my help would be useless, but he consented with a curt nod.

For three days I wiped the boy's brow and body with wet cloths, dribbled lemon water and broth into his mouth. Prayed. Despite my ministrations, Hannibal's fever raged, his breathing grew increasingly labored. On the morning of the fourth day, the captain pulled the sheet over Hannibal's sweet but emaciated face.

Standing with the others on deck, I shivered in the cold breeze. The sun crested the horizon, sending ribbons of light toward us across the uncommonly calm water. The priest intoned his prayers over the boy's linen-wrapped body. A dull ache tightened my chest. When the priest finished, the seamen stood at attention as two sailors carried Hannibal to the side of the ship. A third sailor tied the brick to the boy's wrapped feet. With a stoic set of his lips and a curt sniff, the captain nodded. The men let the boy go. His body slipped into the welcoming water with barely a splash. My sweet Hannibal sank quickly beneath the swell, becoming at last one with the sea.

We lost three more people in the weeks to come—two soldiers and Claire who had ingested something foul and developed stomach pains, a fever, and uncontrollable diarrhea. For fear of dysentery, the captain ordered her quarantined in a small boarded-off area of the hold.

I couldn't find it in my heart to abandon her, so I took turns with the two nuns, sitting with her, mopping her forehead until, too weakened to feel pain anymore, she took her last breath. The priest said quick prayers, but there was no ceremony when she was sent over the side to her final resting place.

During the seventh week of our voyage, the sailor on watch high in the crow's nest shouted "Land! I see land!" Another sailor yelled for the captain to be fetched.

A rush of passengers jostled to claim space on the starboard side of the ship, several attempting to shoulder me out of their way. I held fast, gripping the iron rail, straining to see what the lookout had spotted. But all I could discern was the unending expanse of water.

Chatter immediately arose over the prospect of our journey's end and our new lives beginning. I was torn. As much as I wanted to be off this dismal ship, I dreaded the thought of what lay in wait on land. Savage people? Hairy woodsmen? Wild animals? Everything I had ever read about and feared. Including a future that held…what? I had no idea. I closed my eyes against the growing apprehension in my gut. And what of my dream of returning to France one day? I mustn't let it fade.

Our excitement, it turned out, was premature. What lay ahead was a large island called *Terre-Neuve*, or Newfoundland as the English called it. Heading into the Golfe du Saint-Laurent, we still had nearly two weeks to go before reaching the river settlement of Québec. The other passengers dragged themselves below deck to scratch and moan and complain. I preferred to stay above despite the sharp bite of the frigid air.

Touching my hand to my stomach, I noticed a slight swelling despite how thin my frame had grown during my time on the ship. Or maybe it was because of my gauntness. I was grateful the worst of the morning sickness had abated, though a rocky sea could rekindle it at any time.

"Mademoiselle, look!" a sailor called out.

I lifted my head in time to see a behemoth leap out of the water, arc, and dive back in, tail fins slapping the waves so hard I could feel the splash before it disappeared into the depths.

"Was that a whale?" I asked. I had read of such creatures, but thought them to be mythical, like unicorns and dragons.

"A humpback, most likely," he offered. "Keep your eyes open and you'll see more."

What other mythical creatures would I encounter in this new place?

Once past *Terre-Neuve*, we could see only water again, no land.

"Have we missed New France altogether?" Jeanne asked the captain.

"What? Do you think we've gone back out to sea on the other side of the world?" The captain laughed. "Patience. You'll see land again soon."

The sailors, amused, repeated her words every time a woman was near, calling out to each other in jest, "Have we missed New France altogether?"

The first week of August we saw land again. The brininess of the ocean air gave way to an earthiness carried on the breeze. The captain announced we were on the Saint-Laurent. Great green mountains rose in the distance on both sides of the river. We came to a confluence of the Saint-Laurent and another river which I learned was called the Saguenay. Nestled along the shore were a dozen or so crude buildings.

"Tadoussac," the captain informed us.

We dropped anchor. A contingent of sailors rowed the ship's longboat to the village to replenish enough barrels with fresh water to get us to our final destination.

"Sylvienne, look. Are those *sauvages?*" Claudette peered over the gunwale, her voice tinged with eager anticipation.

A dozen or so partially clad men, their skin glistening, some with feathers in their black hair, paddled birchbark canoes away from the cluster of huts and up the Saguenay River. A shudder of dread ran through me. The stories I'd read were true. New France was filled with savages.

When our men returned in the longboat, I felt a palpable sense of relief for their safety. An unfamiliar Frenchman came back with them. The captain announced he was a river pilot who would help guide our ship the final leg of our journey, as the river was challenging to navigate from this point. Once the water barrels had been hoisted onboard, the captain ordered the anchor raised and we were on our way again. The sails billowed out as the ship fought against the current.

Three days later, just as dawn was breaking, the captain sent word for us women to change into our best dresses. We had been advised to pack only three for the entire trip—one to wear, one for when the first dress got drenched during storms (hoping it dried out in time to change if the second one got wet), and one to save for our arrival.

Eager to get out of the filthy dress I'd worn the past three weeks, I slipped into the green satin skirt and pulled on the matching bodice with lace edging I had saved for this moment. To my dismay, the dress hung loose over my shoulders and hips. None of the girls' dresses fit properly after the long voyage. But there was nothing to be done about it. I tucked my dirty hair, dry and brittle from washing in sea water, under a clean coif, then scrubbed my face with water from a rain barrel.

After helping several of the others with their bodices and hair, I tidied my berth, making sure everything was packed and ready to go. Satisfied, I hurried up top to find a spot along the gunwale to witness the moment we arrived at Ville de Québec. Butterflies flitted in my stomach.

Up ahead we could see the enormous outcropping of sparkling rock the sailors called *Cap-au-Diamant*. Under it, a fort kept watch over the village nestled at the base of the promontory. Québec appeared to be nothing more than a primitive collection of buildings, not unlike what Amiens must have looked like hundreds of years ago.

As we drew closer, I could see men lining the shore. We dropped anchor in the middle of the river, and a chorus of cheers and whistles erupted from their ranks. The other girls perked up at the sound of our welcome committee, but trepidation filled me. These men were waiting to find wives. That was why these women had agreed to this journey. What would be the consequence for someone who had no interest in marriage?

The sailors lowered the ship's longboat. A flotilla of row boats, barges, and canoes filled with eager men made their way against the current to help ferry us and our belongings to the river's edge.

"How will they get our travel chests onto land?" Claudette asked the quartermaster.

"Don't you worry, mademoiselle. They will load all the cargo onto barges. Once on shore, the men there will carry them up to the convent for you."

She frowned, looking down at the barges and other craft lining up next to the ship. I understood her worry. When all your worldly possessions are contained within one single chest, you would not wish to see it end up at the bottom of the river.

I took my place in line to climb over the gunwale and make my way down the precarious rope ladder in all my finery and into the waiting longboat. Once settled, my gaze shifted to the half-dozen other ships anchored in the river. Were any of them heading back to France? Was there any way I could sneak aboard one? I scolded myself. What folly to even think about experiencing that dreaded voyage again so soon.

The longboat took us to a small landing, and as we drew near, I groaned inwardly at the sight of the ramshackle wooden buildings clustered along the shore. They resembled nothing less than a collection of tinder boxes positioned to go up in flames at the slightest spark from flint and steel. Was this to be my new home?

A group of men crowded the small pier, eager to help us out of our longboat. *"Bienvenue, belles demoiselles!"* they called out. They reeked of sweat and unwashed wool clothing. Their hair hung in limp strands over their shoulders, their beards had foodstuff caught up in them.

Two men grabbed my arms, pulling me out of the longboat and set me onto the pier. When they let go to reach for the next passenger, my legs began to wobble, and it seemed as if the pier were swaying madly. Nausea threatened briefly.

The swaying sensation continued as I made my way onto the rocky land where two sisters of the cloth waited for us. Ursulines. I recognized their black garb and white wimples from my days as a student at the convent in Amiens. They hugged the two sisters who had accompanied us, bowed to the priest, then turned to welcome us, the recruits.

"Bonjour! Bienvenue au Québec," one of the nuns said. "I am *Sœur de Sainte-Agnès*, the abbess of the convent here." She looked young, not more than thirty. Nodding toward the other, even younger nun, she said, "And this is Sœur Gabrielle. We have a steep climb up to the convent."

"But what of our trunks?" Claudette looked back at the ship, her eyes registering uncertainty as she watched the cargo being unloaded.

"I promise you," Sœur de Sainte-Agnès said, touching Claudette's arm in a gesture of reassurance. "We have never lost one to the river."

"There is always a first time!" Françoise said with a wink toward me.

Claudette's jaw tightened. I had thought to chastise Françoise for being unkind, but I had no wish to take Claudette's side.

Sœur de Sainte-Agnès's eyes twinkled, and she suppressed a smile. "God willing, *les poissons* that swim in the river won't be subject to any of your underthings. Shall we go?"

I reached for my travel bag, but a young man dressed in a patched doublet and well-worn breeches grabbed it before I could. The feather on his dilapidated, wide-brimmed hat fluttered in the breeze. "*S'il vous plait*, permit me to carry it for you, mademoiselle? The path uphill can be a challenge."

I hesitated, uncertain, but all around us men were seizing bags and other items to carry. He smiled shyly and headed off after the nuns. I chased after him through a clutch of wooden houses to where a steep path led upward. By the time we reached the top my legs ached, and I gasped for breath.

"We are almost to the convent," my porter said. "By the way, my name is Michel Leblanc. Perhaps we will meet again at *la grande réunion*."

"The grand reception?"

"Oui! The nuns hold a reception several weeks after a ship arrives. So the ladies can meet eligible gentlemen. You should know, I am building a house. It will be a very nice house. Though perhaps not nice enough for someone as pretty as you."

I barked out a laugh. I felt anything but pretty after spending more than two months at sea. My skin was pale, my hair drab, I was thin as a reed. However, I was flattered. "I'm sure it will be a very nice house."

He grinned as I pushed aside a lock of black curls escaping my coif and tickling my cheek.

"We are here!" He set my bag down on a plot of grass in front of a thick wooden gate.

I glanced up, puzzled. The walls around the convent were made of wood pilings not stone. "This is the convent?"

"Oui! I helped build the palisade myself. Well, I didn't build it. It was done some years ago. But I do help with repairs."

A groan escaped my lips. I'd had enough of convent school life in my youth. I had chosen to come to Québec to avoid spending the rest of my life cloistered behind stone walls. And here we were, about to be ushered into a wilderness convent with only a timbered wall for protection from wild animals or…sauvages.

"I will bid you *au revoir* now." Michel swept his hat from his head, flourishing it as he bowed. "I hope to see you again soon, mademoiselle."

Mustering what I hoped was an appreciative smile, I offered a weary, "Au revoir, monsieur."

As my plucky new friend trotted off after the men, I picked up my bag and followed the nuns and the other recruits through the looming wooden gateway.

CHAPTER THREE

Despite the primitive nature of the outer palisade, and in contrast to the wooden buildings clustered down near the river, the convent was a sturdy, stone structure with ten windows on each of the two floors. The building was topped by several massive chimneys. Gardens and an orchard within the large courtyard bustled with young nuns in black and younger girls clad in red, feeding chickens, working in the garden, hanging clothes on a line.

Sœur de Sainte-Agnès led us into the building, past the chapel, a room where a chorus of young voices recited a catechism lesson, and to a large parlor filled with chairs and stools. There she invited us to sit.

"Welcome to the convent school of Saint Ursula," she said. "Our mission is to educate the young girls, both Native and French. And you...you are all so brave to undertake such a long and arduous journey to settle here in *Nouvelle-France* and, by the will of our Heavenly Father, marry and start families. How many of you are there?"

"We numbered nineteen when we left La Rochelle," Madeleine said. "But Claire sickened on the ship." Her voice thickened and she choked back tears. "We...we gave her up to the sea."

"I am so sorry." The nun touched her forehead and shoulders in the Sign of the Cross, then clasped her hands in front of her. "Our foundress, own dear Mère Marie de l'Incarnation, recently passed to her heavenly glory as well. My sisters and I will pray to her to look after the soul of your traveling companion." She brightened. "But only one? You are quite fortunate. We must thank our Heavenly Father for that."

Bowing my head and crossing myself, I thought of poor Hannibal, the merchant, and the two sailors whose fortunes were not as favorable as our own.

Sœur de Sainte-Agnès continued. "You have been recruited and carefully chosen to help grow His Majesty's colony. King Louis has seen fit to sponsor each of you. You have come on a unique mission to marry and have families. We have rooms prepared for you here in the convent to stay until you choose a husband. Sœur Gabrielle will give you your room assignments. But first, I must caution you. Please do not wander about the village without adequate chaperones. There are many more men here than women, some of them quite rough. I do not like to have to say it, but it is not safe for a single, young woman to be out and about alone."

We nodded in assent, the situation no different from home.

"When will we meet the eligible bachelors?" Claudette asked.

"In due time," Sœur de Sainte-Agnès said. "But first, we must clean you up, don't you agree?'

We followed her and Sœur Gabrielle to the wing of the convent that housed the kitchen and dining room. In the kitchen sat a large cedar cask filled with water.

"Oh, Blessed Lord!" Claudette exclaimed. "Is that a bathing tub?"

"It is, indeed," Sœur de Sainte-Agnès said. "And there is another in the pantry."

We shrieked and clapped in delight.

Sœur de Sainte-Agnès spread her hands expansively. "Monsieur Ducharme, a local barrel maker, graciously fashioned the tubs for us several years ago. We have been welcoming young recruits such as yourselves for nigh on a decade. We are delighted to have such fine washbasins for your use."

Two other nuns, Sœur Seraphine and Sœur Julienne, helped by several girls in simple red tunics, hustled to finish filling the tubs with buckets of hot water from the kitchen hearth.

"May I go first?" Jeanne asked, her eagerness evident as she rubbed a scabbed-over arm.

"And me," Claudette said. She was already heading toward the pantry.

"Let's get your room assignments taken care of, then the two of you may come back down to bathe," Sœur de Sainte-Agnès said.

Sœur Gabrielle ushered us up a narrow set of stairs to the sleeping quarters where she assigned us four to a room. I was relieved to learn I would share with Jeanne, Madeleine, **and** Marie Barbe. Claudette was assigned to a room at the far end of the hall.

The rooms were barely large enough to hold four cots with a small table next to each on which to put a candle. Our travel chests had been deposited at the foot of our beds. On each of our cots were a wool coat, two new linen coifs, woolen stockings, a winter bonnet, sheepskin gloves, and a stoppered jar of a foul-smelling ointment.

"Bear grease," Sœur Gabrielle told us, laughing at our expressions as we sniffed it.

"What's it for?" I asked, holding the jar as far away from me as I could and quickly fitting the stopper back onto it.

"The mosquitoes here can be ferocious. It takes a bit of getting used to, but it will help keep them from plaguing you."

"I'd rather get bitten," Mary Barbe said, pushing the stopper back onto her jar.

"Oh, I doubt that." Sœur Gabrielle smiled. "You'll be glad to have it. Don't throw it out."

Jeanne and Claudette rushed back down to the kitchen as soon as we were settled. The rest of us were granted time to ourselves while we waited our turn to bathe. I decided this was a good time to write to Maman to tell her I had arrived safely. With any luck, I could get my letter onto a ship setting out for its return trip in the next day or two.

But first, I opened my trunk to look for some clean underthings and a clean dress for later. A flash of blue silk caught my eye. I pulled out the blue dress King Louis had sent to me along with my invitation to court on my sixteenth birthday. My stomach fluttered at the sight of it, remembering the dizzy innocence of the first time I wore it, the day I was first presented to the King and Queen of France.

But what was it doing in my travel trunk? I had not packed it. Lisette, my maid at Versailles, must have. Or Fleurance. Despite their good intentions, the dress held too many memories of my time at court, when it seemed the world was at my feet, before everything began to sour. For a fleeting moment, I thought to burn it with the clothes I'd worn on the ship, all too filthy to salvage. But Maman's "Waste not" admonition was too firmly planted in my head. With a grimace, I rolled the delicately embroidered skirt and bodice into a ball. As I shoved it to the bottom of the trunk, my hand rubbed against something unfamiliar wrapped in muslin.

Pulling out the bundle, I loosened the ribbons tied around it. Inside were three bars of lavender soap. I nearly swooned as I held the fragrant bars up to my nose. Another gift from Lisette or Fleurance. How I missed those two. They had been more than just servants to me; they were my friends. I decided I would use one of the precious soaps in the bath today to wash away the stench of the trip. The other two I would hang on to as a remembrance of home. But which home? My home at court, before it turned on me in my time of need? Or my home in Amiens with Maman and Tatie and Blondeau? Two bars of lavender soap. Two homes I missed in this moment more than ever.

Setting my writing things on the tiny side table, I opened my stoppered pot of ink, dipped my quill, and began to write.

8 August 1672

Dearest Maman,

You will be relieved to know I have arrived safely in this verdant if virgin world. The trip across the ocean was —

I closed my eyes against the memory of Hannibal's slender, linen-clad body sliding into the placid sea, the smell of vomit sloshing across the floor as the ship pitched to and fro during storms, the sense of nausea always coloring even the calmest of days.

— manageable. We made it to the new continent in a little over eight weeks. You will never guess who was on the ship with me. Claudette! Yes, that Claudette, from the convent school. Our meeting was awkward at first, but we have made a sort of peace with each other. I can't imagine what prompted her to come to this place. I suppose like everyone else, she is in search of a husband. The last I heard, she had been betrothed in Amiens, but she won't speak of it.

Should I tell her about the baby growing within me? I decided against it, at least for now. It would only be one more thing for her to fret over. And in her condition, she didn't need more worry. If the baby and I both survived the birth, that would be soon enough to give her the news. Instead, I wrote about the journey up the Saint-Laurent.

"Sylvienne! It's your turn. Everyone else is done."

Startled, I looked up to see Madeleine in the doorway. She wore a simple white tunic, and her hair hung loose and wet.

The light in the room had changed. How long had I been writing? There were three pages.

Picking up the bar of lavender soap, I headed down to the kitchen. I had determined I would wait and be the last to bathe. Not an easy decision as I was eager to scrub the dirt and grime off every inch of my body. But I hoped, if no one was in line behind me, I could linger a bit longer in the water to sooth both my body and my spirit.

My plan worked. I was the very last to approach the wooden tub in the large kitchen. But to my dismay, I hadn't accounted for the nuns' strategy to save water, time, and work by not refilling the tub between each bather. I gazed slump-shouldered at the tepid water, a film of scum floating across the top. Now I understood why Jeanne and Claudette were so eager to go first. A long sigh escaped my lips.

"Matthew 20:16 'So the last shall be first, and the first shall be last.'"

Startled, I turned to find Sœur Julienne standing behind me, flanked on either side by two girls. She wore a kindly smile on her weathered face. "You are quite brave to go last, no?"

As I shrugged forlornly, she chuckled and said, "Perhaps with Antoinette's and Marthe's help we can empty the tub and refill it for you. You can be both last and first, just as Matthew teaches us."

"Are you sure? Won't it be a lot of trouble?" I asked.

She indicated a row of water buckets already lined up on the kitchen hearth in front of the fire. "It won't take us any time at all." She turned and spoke to the girls in a language I had never heard before. To me she said, "When we have refilled your tub, while you bathe, we'll empty the one in the pantry."

They scurried to grab empty buckets, handing one to me. We scooped the scummy water out of the tub and carried it to the garden. In short order the tub was empty. We refilled it with fresh, hot water from the buckets on the hearth.

At long last I shed my clothes, keeping my back turned to Sœur Julienne in the hopes she wouldn't notice the slight swelling on my now sapling-thin body. I stepped into the water, my bar of lavender soap clutched in one hand. It felt like heaven. I slid down until my entire head was submerged. When I rose up again, the nun stood over me grinning. I shook my head at the lye soap she held out and held up my own. With a thrill of delight running through me, I lathered the soap and ran it over my arms, legs, and stomach. I scrubbed until my skin began to tingle and my hands ached.

After washing my hair, I lay back with my head against the side of the tub, my eyes closed, savoring the warmth of the water. My thoughts went to my first days at the palace. Was it only two years ago? I had been invited to bathe in a marble bathtub. What a heady time that was! And not a little hedonistic, if I were to be truly honest. In the end, I was glad to put that life behind me. Though, what kind of life was I trading it for?

Opening my eyes, I surveyed the crude kitchen, not unlike the one I'd grown up in back in Amiens—the kitchen where I had learned to cook alongside Tatie and Maman. I sighed. The water in the cedar tub was cooling, but it masked the tears falling unbidden. For the first time, I was overwhelmed by how far I was from home.

I mourned Tatie's lamb stew and blueberry pastries, and the garden I had weeded to the hum of Blondeau's bees. Most of all, I mourned the feel of Maman's arms comforting me and her wise words warning me against my own foolishness, the loving voice I would never hear again. I chastised myself. Don't think that. I'll find a way. I will not live here forever, separated from those I love. Including Etienne.

I stood up, the water raining off me in sheets. "May I have something to dry with, please?"

"Oui, mademoiselle," one of the girls said. She handed me a linen towel, then held out a hand to help me out of the tub. After drying off, I pulled on the simple, white tunic she offered.

I made a point to thank Sœur Julienne for the bath. "But I fear I have created a lot of unnecessary work for you and the others. So much water to go to waste."

"Nothing here goes to waste," Sœur Julienne said with a sly grin.

At that moment a troop of girls, all in red tunics, marched into the kitchen, each bearing a chamber pot. They marched out the kitchen door to empty their pots in a latrine I later learned was dug just outside the wooden fence at the far end of the garden beyond the chicken coop.

Upon their return, the olde nun rolled up her long wide sleeves and knelt beside the tub to scrub out the pots. I quickly picked up a towel to help dry. As each vessel was cleaned and dried, a girl grabbed it to return it to from wherever it had been fetched. The leftover bathwater was scooped out and distributed throughout the garden as we had done before. Lastly, the cedar tub itself was scrubbed before being hauled away to a storage shed near the garden.

Before going back upstairs, I sought out Sœur Sainte-Agnès. I found her in the small convent library.

"I want to thank you for the wonderful bath. And to let you know how much I appreciated the help of Sœur Julienne and the two sauvage girls."

"Please don't call them that," she said. "They are Montagnais and Huron. Though the Huron call themselves Wendat. And they are anything but savages."

"But I thought…"

"I know it's what most colonists call them. Even our dear late Mother Superior, lovingly so," Sœur de Sainte-Agnès said. "But as she taught us, they and we are all God's children. Even the Iroquois, who have thankfully settled down and agreed to a peace treaty this past year."

"You mean, there are more than one kind of…of…"

"We also have Ojibwe girls and Cree in our school."

"Are they not all the same, the Natives?" I asked.

"Are the French the same as the English? Or the Germans? Or the Italians?" Sœur de Sainte-Agnès arched her eyebrows like a teacher scolding a student for lack of knowledge.

"No, of course not," I answered sheepishly.

"Just as in Europe, these people have different customs, speak different languages, have different temperaments."

Chagrined, I realized my knowledge of the world was terribly inadequate. I had much to learn. Taking in the room with its one wall of shelving and a single table and chair, I said, "You have a library. I didn't expect that."

"I am sorry it is not larger. We've collected what books we can, but we don't have a budget to purchase more. These have all been donated."

Running my hand along the spines of the books, I was pleasantly surprised to find works by Descartes, Galileo, and, of course, Thomas Aquinas. On the shelf below those were several hand-bound books. I pulled one off the shelf. The title had been written in ink on the cover: *Dictionnaire de la langue Huron/Wendat vers la langue Française*. Flipping it open, I was surprised to find an entire hand-written dictionary. "Who made this?"

Sœur de Sainte-Agnès glanced over. "Marie de l'Incarnation. Our foundress. She spent quite a number of years working on dictionaries for the various Native languages."

I picked up another, this one for the Iroquois language. Under the title were the words *Haudenosaunee/People of the Longhouse*. And another: *The Language of the Montagnais*. And yet another: *The Algonquin Language of the Anishinaabe or Ojibwe People*.

"The Natives…you said they speak more than one language?"

Sœur de Sainte-Agnès laughed. "Does all of Europe speak French?"

"Certainly not. But are there so many of them they have developed different languages?"

"I think there are far more aborigines than we can imagine. This continent is quite vast."

"What language do the Native girls here in the convent speak?"

"Most of them are Hurons, or Wendats as they call themselves. They speak a variation of the Iroquois language."

"Could I learn to speak it?"

"I don't see why not. You said you were convent educated. You must already speak Latin."

"And Italian. I had some thoughts to try to learn English, but I never took the time." I held up the Huron/Wendat-French dictionary. "May I come in from time to time to study it?"

"Any time. No one has asked to look at it in years."

Later that afternoon, Sœur Seraphine urged us to gather the clothes we had worn on the ship and bring them down to the kitchen. In the back courtyard, we sorted the clothing. Those that were yet wearable were set aside to be washed later; the rest—those too filthy or torn to salvage or too filled with vermin—were put into a pile to be burned in a stone-lined pit not far from the latrine. The pile of clothes to burn from our group of recruits was considerable.

When our task was completed, Sœur Seraphine presented us with a basket of wooden lice combs. I had my own prized, sculpted whale-bone comb in my trunk. It had been a gift from a friend at court, but I thought it too ostentatious to brandish here in the convent. So, I left it. The wood combs would do just as well. We paired off to take turns combing through each other's hair. Jeanne and I did our best to rid each other of the awful little creatures that caused us to itch so, but it would take many more combings to complete the task, if ever we could.

At long last we were called to supper. We lined up in the kitchen where Sœur Lucrèce, the convent cook, handed us bowls of stew which she called *sagamité* and a thick chunk of coarse bread. We carried our bowls into a dining room large enough to hold a dozen tables. The diners all sat facing a podium. Behind it, on the wall, was a large cross upon which hung a gruesome sculpture of the crucified Christ. Our meal was a quiet affair, with Sœur Gabrielle standing at the podium reading from a book called *The Lives of the Saints.* Looking around, I noticed that only some of the little girls were in the dining room.

I dipped my spoon into the sagamité. It was comprised of corn, carrots, peas, onions, and chunks of smoked fish. There was also some sort of grain similar to oats, but black. A type of wild rice, I was told. I sniffed the concoction before taking a bite. The combination of herbs and wild rice gave the stew an earthy, yet surprisingly sweet taste. There was nothing to compare it to in all the delectable courses we were served at King Louis's table, but it was delicious, nevertheless. I ate ravenously.

"Where are the other girls?" I asked Sœur Lucrèce when I took my bowl back into the kitchen. "Only about half of them were in the dining room."

"The French girls? They go home at the end of the school day. Only the Native girls board with us overnight. Their villages are too far away. It's the same over at the Jesuit seminary. The local boys study by day. Only the Native boys board with the priests."

I supposed that made sense. When I was younger, I went to a convent day school. But Maman had boarded at her convent until she was old enough to marry.

Our supper over, we were excused to our rooms to prepare for bed. Before the sky even darkened, my eyes drifted shut and I fell into a slumber, swaying with the ship we'd left earlier that day.

The next morning, we were roused at dawn to dress and walk the short way to the grey sandstone church of Notre Dame for Sunday Mass. Following the convent students down the center aisle—the nuns close behind our group of recruits—I was surprised to see how full the church was, more than any church I had attended in France other than for Midnight Mass. And by far, the greatest number of attendees here today were men, their faces scrubbed, and their hair combed back or pulled into tails, their well-worn attire noticeably clean.

The pews reserved for us were directly behind a small group I assumed to be the affluent and influential members of the city. Their fashionable dresses and waistcoats looked expensive, though they more closely resembled styles I'd worn in Paris the year prior.

As the Mass proceeded, the men in the back pews sang lustily if off tune. And it seemed as if a number of them didn't actually know the words to the songs, rather they mumbled or hummed or made-up words as they went.

Sœur Gabrielle had whispered to Claudette, and afterward Claudette let it be known to the rest of us that the church was only ever this full the Sunday after a ship bearing recruits arrived. The priest, Father François Laval, apparently aware of the custom, had taken the opportunity to deliver a sermon based on a reading from Genesis that caused heat to rise into my cheeks and made the girls on either side of me squirm.

"And God so blessed them. And God said to them, 'Be fruitful and multiply and fill the earth and subdue it and have dominion over the fish of the sea and over the birds of the heavens and over every living thing on the earth.'"

He followed his sermon with a psalm which deepened my blush and caused me no little chagrin: "Behold, children are a heritage from the Lord, the fruit of the womb a reward. Like arrows in the hand of a warrior are the children of one's youth. Blessed is the man who fills his quiver with them!"

When the Mass ended, the men stood in their pews grinning broadly as we paraded past, the nuns urging us to hurry along. Michel Leblanc stood among them. He winked when I glanced his way.

I cast my eyes down quickly. At court, I had never gotten used to the crowds standing in the gallery to observe the royal dinners, or those lining the streets when the royal caravans paraded. And now, to have these men ogle us openly here in the church was most unsettling. Outside, in the sun, men lined our path back to the convent.

I let out a deep breath of relief when we passed through the large wooden cloister gate and it shut behind us.

CHAPTER FOUR

During our late breakfast of eggs and toasted bread, just as at dinner, we ate in silence while listening to one of the sisters read from the *Book of Saints*. Afterward, we set to work outside, washing our salvageable clothes. I had assigned all of my dresses from the ship to the burn pile and so had only some underthings to scrub.

When the laundry was finished, as it was Sunday, we were given the rest of the afternoon to spend as we liked within the cloister compound. Jeanne and I roamed the grounds together, inspecting the extensive vegetable and herb gardens, the chicken coop, and the well which we discovered had two buckets on separate pulleys, one for water and the other to hold food that needed to be kept chilled such as butter and milk. The dairy bucket remained down in the well, apparently hovering just above the waterline. There was also a system of rain barrels at the corners of the main building and even some of the outbuildings and a stone-lined cistern. A complex as busy as this convent apparently used a lot of water.

A small open-air barn housed two cows and several goats. The goats were released during the day to munch the grass and weeds, but great pains were taken, by means of wooden fencing, to keep them out of the vegetable garden. Two girls carried pails of water to the goats.

"Look at the little sauvages, pretending to be French." Claudette startled me, speaking from behind us. She sniffed as she watched them rush about the yard.

"They are girls, not savages," I said, remembering Sœur de Sainte-Agnès's words. "God made them no different from you or me. Or the French girls here."

"I highly doubt that. Or these sainted sisters wouldn't have had to come all this way to convert them."

Sucking in a breath, I suggested Jeanne ignore Claudette's rudeness. But the joy had been taken from our exploration. We turned on our heels and went back into the convent house, leaving Claudette to her own nasty self.

Jeanne went up to our room to rest, and I sought out Sœur Sainte-Agnès again. I wanted to ask about my good friend Perrette from Amiens, who had been recruited and sponsored to come to New France several years earlier. I had been devastated at the time, thinking I would never see her again. We exchanged a few letters, but over time I lost track of her.

The abbess was in the chapel, leading her young students in a choral practice. I waited until they were finished, enjoying the youthful singing, which was mixed with a good amount of giggling between songs.

"You have much patience," I said when we were alone.

She smiled. "Children always take patience. What can I do for you?"

"I am wondering about a girl who came over about two years ago," I said. "Her name is Perrette Raveau. Would you know what happened to her?"

"So many girls have come on the ships. I can't remember them all. But Perrette, hmm? I think perhaps there have been only two or three Perrettes over the years. Let me check my ledger."

She led me to her office where she hauled out a large registry book and began flipping through its many pages, running her finger down the list of names. She stopped at one. "There was a Perrette who married a soldier. They moved to Trois-Rivières, perhaps five or six years ago." Her finger moved again. "And another I vaguely remember, but I don't see her name."

Sœur Seraphine came into the office looking for a quill and some paper. Sœur de Sainte-Agnès said, "Sister, do you remember a girl named Perrette, who came through a couple of summers ago?"

"Yes," Sœur Seraphine said. "I believe she married a farmer. They moved to Beaupré, I think. Or maybe Île d'Orléans. I'm not sure. I'm sorry I can't be more helpful."

Dispirited, I thanked them both, wondering if I would ever locate my friend in such a vast land. To comfort myself, I grabbed one of the books I'd carried on the ship in my travel bag and went out to sit under a large maple tree. So engrossed in reading was I that it took me a moment to realize someone was watching me. Claudette. Again.

"Ever since we were little, you've always had your nose stuck in a book," she said looking down at me.

"You don't care to read?" I asked, shading my eyes against the bright sky above her.

"I had enough of books when we were in school. I would rather experience real love and intrigue." Her lips curved into a smirk. "The gazettes are fun, though."

The gazettes. I glared at her. I loved reading those gossip publications when I was younger, still living in Amiens, still dreaming of a life grander than the one I had. But once at court, I saw first-hand how vicious those scandal sheets actually were. For I had become the subject of one of their parody sketches, and later of a pen portrait hinting at all sorts of rumors.

"Fiction is more palatable than real life sometimes," I said. I dropped my gaze to my book again and pretended to read until she walked away, the sound of her snickering grating on my nerves.

After supper, Sœur de Sainte-Agnès presented us each with small wooden caskets. They were the trousseaus that had been promised to the girls at the time of recruitment. She suggested we spend a few minutes examining the contents in preparation for sewing lessons on the morrow.

The small chests held several dozen needles, a thimble, white and grey thread, a pair of scissors, a vast number of pins, two knives, and a length of linen cloth. What would Maman think of such a trousseau? Maman. What must she be thinking now, having lost her only daughter to the winds of fortune? I remembered the letter I had begun the day before, prior to being summoned for my bath. However, it would be several days before I could find the time to continue the missive to her, as we lost no time beginning our instruction on how to be capable wives to the men of New France.

The first lessons were sewing, which I counted among my few accomplishments, taught at the knee of my mother. Those of us who could already put together a garment and manage a decent stitch helped the others. We also learned to knit, making winter hats and mittens.

Cooking lessons were next. We learned to make the sagamité we'd eaten the first night, and to fillet fish, skin a rabbit, lay out a vegetable garden, and lay a kitchen fire, along with pointers on how to keep from burning down the house.

We made bread, working in groups to knead the batches of dough and bake it in the massive brick oven near the garden. In fact, we baked so much bread and made so much rabbit stew, Sœur de Sainte-Agnès suggested we pack food baskets, which we took to the Augustine sisters and their patients at the hospital not far away. Then we went to the Jesuit seminary where the priests educated the boys, and finally to the fort at the edge of the cliff overlooking the lower town. The eyes of the soldiers lit up when we dropped off the baskets, making the effort worthwhile.

When the subject of eligible young men came up—which of course it did often—Sœur de Sainte-Agnès lectured us on the qualities to look for in a potential spouse. The prime one being whether he owned a house, preferably one with a wood floor and glass windows.

"And you should say no to any man who earns his living as a *coureur des bois*," she added.

"A coureur des bois?" Marie Barbe asked. "What is that?"

"A fur trader. But one who is not registered with the Crown and refuses to obey the laws."

She also, during these weeks of tutelage, called each of us separately into her office for private counseling.

"I do not ask this to judge," she said when my turn came, "but in the spirit of education." She lowered her voice even though we were quite alone and the door shut. "Have you been with a man before?"

My surprise must have been evident for she hastened to repeat, "It is not for me to judge."

I looked her straight in the eye. "I have."

She nodded carefully. "Then I need not tell you, the best way to please your husband will be to submit whenever his need arises."

I had to bite my lips to keep from giggling at her innocent (I assumed) word play.

"I am quite well educated in that regard."

Her eyebrows rose imperceptibly.

"I am recently widowed."

"Ah!" She said this with much relief. "I am so sorry."

I did not tell her the kind of man my husband had been or how he had died, or of the man I truly loved, who was now on the run. I gave no hint of the seed which grew within my belly. As I rose and thanked her for her sympathy, I wondered what kind of counsel she gave to those who were still virgins, she who was presumed to be an avowed virgin herself.

As soon as I had a moment to myself, I gathered up my quill, the inkpot, a stick of wax and my seal and carried them to the library. At the lone table, I looked over the letter I'd begun some days before. I dipped my quill into the ink.

Maman, you will be astonished, perhaps even a bit chagrined, to know I am living in a convent. However, this place is unlike any convent in France. The sisters here are filled with joyful purpose. They hum as they work, and it is not unusual when two or three of them are weeding in the garden to hear them break into song. I even found the Abbess up on a ladder one morning, directing the workers where to place their shingles. These women have made it their mission to convert and educate the Native girls. These girls all are sweet and smart and have learned to speak French quite well. I wonder if I might learn their language one day.

I told her how the sisters offered shelter and advice to the girls from the ships seeking husbands. I even told her of the glorious bath in the kitchen my first day here. Then I added a few more lines.

But, Maman, I must tell you. I am not like the other girls here. I do not plan to marry again. You managed all those years without taking a new husband after Papa died, and you taught me well. I am determined to return home one day. No one at court needs to know. We can live quietly together in our little cottage away from the royal favor-seekers and the gossip. I promise I will make it happen.

I must end for now and get this letter down to the ship's captain before he sails away without it. I miss you dearly, and Tatie, and

Blondeau, and even his bees. But mostly I miss the warmth of your embrace. I will dream of it tonight.

Your loving daughter.

A tear dropped unbidden onto the page. I blotted it quickly with my sleeve lest it smear the ink, wiping my eyes with my other sleeve. I folded the pages and addressed them, then melted the wax and pressed my seal into it. The seal with the single letter S. I had left behind the ornate seal purchased for me by the King when I first moved to court, and another by my husband when I married. I had no wish to use either of them again.

My thoughts drifted to Etienne. This would be a good time to write to him as well. To let him know of my resolve to find a way home. I was reaching for my quill again, when the touch of a hand on my arm startled me.

Marie Barbe said, "Would you pen a letter for me? I would like to let my grandfather know I have arrived safely."

Hesitating for the briefest of moments, dismayed to have to put off my own letter, I smiled my encouragement. "Of course," I said "Letters home are important." After taking her halting dictation, I sealed her letter.

Marie Barbe and I walked together down to the dock and handed our letters to the purser of a ship preparing to head back to France. He took our money and promised to include our letters with others to be transported in a water-proof box kept in the captain's quarters.

"Monsieur," I said. "Can you tell me the price of passenger passage back to France?"

"You wish to return so soon?" He raised an eyebrow.

"No! Of course not. But since the King paid our expense to come over, I have no idea the size of my debt to him. I was just wondering." Did he detect my ruse?

"Most of the passengers pay anywhere from fifty to seventy-five livres, depending on the type of accommodation they wish."

I thanked him, making an effort not to show my dismay. The King's secretary had given me a pouch with fifty livres before I boarded the ship in France, with the promise of a pension to follow. But in my condition, I could not conceive of making another ocean voyage until after my baby was born, and that would double the price of passage. And realistically, I couldn't even consider returning until the furor over my indiscretions had died down. I vowed silently to do whatever it took to hold onto my coins, even if it took a year or two before I could arrange passage back to France and civilization.

After supper, while the other girls chatted and worked on their sewing, I pulled out my writing supplies and went back to the library. It had become my favorite room in the convent as it was seldom occupied, and it afforded me a bit of solitude. When I put my quill to paper, the words flowed.

My Dearest Etienne, My Love,

I am here in Québec in the part of New France they call Canada. The village is small and the mosquitoes ferocious, but the air is clear, and we can drink water straight from the river! You will laugh to know I am housed at the convent, the one place I most wished to avoid. Surprisingly, I don't mind. The nuns here are kind to all.

Oh, my love, my heart was torn asunder the night you were forced to flee for your life. And again, when my ship left the harbor at La Rochelle. Where are you? Are you safe? I dream about you every night. Your smile, your eyes, your warm lips, the way you touched me and filled me with a delight I had never known before. My passion for you is no less than before I left our beloved France. If I can't have you, I want no man. Please be safe. Perhaps one day I will find my way home. Please be there for me.

With boundless love, Your Sylvienne

Setting my quill down, I sat with my eyes closed, one hand on the slight swell of my belly. *If I can't have you…* I shook off the malaise that threatened. I blew on the paper, waving it back and forth to dry. Gently, I pressed my lips to the letter that held my fervent words. I folded it, lit the wax stick on the flame from a nearby candle and watched as it dripped onto the paper. Finally, I pressed my seal into the melted wax.

I wrote no name on the outside. No address. For I had none. Instead, I tucked the letter into the bottom of my travel chest under my winter clothes, next to the silk slippers he had surprised me with on New Years Day. Had that been only seven months ago? It seemed a lifetime.

CHAPTER FIVE

The next day, having finished my assigned chores, I snuck away to the library again, this time to read without distraction. I was startled when one of the little girls rushed in.

"Mademoiselle! You are needed in the grand parlor." She was out of breath, apparently having looked everywhere to find me. "The captain of the militia is here."

"Why? What is wrong?"

"Not wrong. He is here to take the census."

"Census?"

"We must each give an accounting of ourselves to be tallied for the intendent. I have already done so." She flashed a proud smile before disappearing back through the door.

Dismayed at having to put my book aside, I looked around for something to tuck into it to keep my place. There was nothing available, so I stuck my thumb in between the pages before heading to the parlor.

There was a line of girls waiting their turn to talk to the man sitting behind a table. He made notes in a great book of lined pages. I took my place in the queue and opened my book. So engrossed was I in the text, I didn't realize I had reached the front of the line.

"Name?" a voice asked.

I looked up, startled, to see the man waiting with quill in hand. He wore the brown coat with grey cuffs of the local militia. I judged him to be no more than thirty. His dark brown hair was pulled back into a tail, much the way Etienne used to wear his, perhaps still did.

Etienne. Where was he? I had hoped he would somehow find his way to the port at La Rochelle and onto my ship. I'd dreamed of sailing away together, starting our lives over. But of course, he hadn't come. And the reality of never seeing him again washed over me like a wave dragging me through the undercurrent. If I were to stay whole, to survive while I was here in Canada, I had to stop thinking of him.

"What is your name, mademoiselle?" the census taker asked again.

Flummoxed by his question, I almost dropped my book and certainly lost my page as it snapped shut. Apparently, he noticed my dismay.

"That must be an exceedingly good book to enthrall you so." He seemed amused by my clumsiness.

I glanced behind me. I was the last one at his table.

He cocked his head to catch a glimpse of the title. "*Fables* by La Fontaine. I can see why you can't put it down."

"You have read it, monsieur?"

"Several times." The corners of his hazel eyes crinkled in amusement, and he seemed to be making an effort not to smile overly much.

"Really?"

"No. Not really. I am afraid I am unfamiliar with Monsieur La Fontaine's work altogether." He grinned broadly now.

I frowned, discomfited. "What was your question?"

"Your name?"

"Oh! Sylvienne. Sylvienne d'Aubert." I hesitated and he stopped writing, looking up at me expectantly. "Yes. Sylvienne d'Aubert," I reaffirmed.

He nodded. "And your age?"

"Nineteen."

"Country of birth?"

"France, of course."

"Parents names?"

Again, I hesitated. And again, he glanced up, his brow furrowed this time. I blurted, "Isabelle de Bourbon and Guy d'Amiens." He nodded and wrote again in his book.

"Marital status."

"Widowed."

This time he didn't look up, but as he wrote his brows rose ever so slightly before he comported his face. "Merci, madame." He blew lightly on the inked words, then picked up a cloth to wipe his quill. He looked as if he intended to speak again, but at that moment a scream rent the air.

Alarmed, I swiveled toward the parlor door. "The kitchen!"

He rose and followed me as I ran down the hall. In the kitchen we found two of the older girls cowering in a corner holding towels over their heads, and Sœur Lucrèce, swinging a broom wildly at the ceiling. Something black swooped past her. The girls screamed again.

"A bat!" Sœur Lucrèce grunted, ducking. She swung mightily as the bat swooped again. But her efforts were futile.

"May I?" The census taker reached for the broom which Sœur Lucrèce gladly relinquished.

She stepped back into the pantry doorway, hands covering her veiled head.

The census taker observed the harried bat for a moment or two as it flew back and forth. Then he swung once, knocking it so hard it fell onto the carving table. The poor creature was obviously stunned, but by no means dispatched. One webbed wing fluttered listlessly. An ear twitched.

"It's still alive!" one of the girls shrieked.

"Do you have a blanket or a large towel?" the census taker asked Sœur Lucrèce.

While she scurried into the pantry in search of a towel, I reached behind me and grabbed a woven bushel basket from where it had been abandoned by one of the panicky girls. I thrust the basket onto the table, over the fluttering bat.

"Trapped!" the census taker said with a grin as Sœur Lucrèce came out of the pantry empty handed. "Now we just need to find a way to get our little friend out of here without escaping again. Perhaps that?" He pointed to a baking tray leaning against the wall.

I held the basket in place while he slid the tray under the rim, the bat hopping about and fluttering against the sides of the basket, squeaking and chirping its distress. Together we lifted the tray. I held one end with both hands while he grasped the other with a single hand, holding the basket firmly in place with his other. Sœur Lucrèce held the door open wide and we walked our captive to the far end of the garden. We set the tray down and I stood back as he lifted the basket. The bat didn't move.

"Is it dead?" I asked.

"I doubt it." He kicked the tray with one booted foot and with a start the bat flapped its wings and lifted off, soaring up toward the roof of the convent.

The census taker offered a broad smile. "Well, that proved a good day's work."

"Should we have killed it?" I asked, watching nervously as it flew back and forth over the building.

"Bats feast on mosquitoes. We should give thanks it lived." He watched the creature fly for a moment longer before saying, "I'd better go and collect my registry book."

"And my book!" I had no idea when or where I'd dropped it. He chuckled, and I grinned, suddenly embarrassed. I curtsied and thanked him. "You are a hero of the first order—for both the convent and our friend the bat."

"I believe you had an equal part in the rescue, Madame d'Aubert. A brave heroine." He bowed, then indicated I should precede him back into the convent.

Inside, Sœur Lucrèce and the two girls were madly scrubbing the table where the bat had landed. I found my book on the kitchen floor. The census taker and I went back to the parlor where he retrieved his register, quill, and ink pot. With a word of thanks to Sœur de Sainte-Agnès, who had come out from her office to see what all the fuss was about, he took his leave.

I stood near the open parlor window watching the census taker stride across the front lawn, his leather satchel slung over one shoulder. He stopped to talk with one of the other sisters in the yard. A moment later he bowed, turned, and whistled. A tan dog lounging under the maple tree jumped up and ran after the man as he strode through the gate.

"I wonder if he is married?" said one of the girls who had gathered behind me to watch him go.

"He would be a good catch," another said, giggling.

At church on Sunday, I walked down the aisle between Sœur de Sainte-Agnès and Sœur Gabrielle, their young charges leading the way. I couldn't help perusing the rows of congregants to see if the census taker might be among them. He wasn't. With an unsettling twinge of disappointment, I turned my attention to the prayers and the hymns led by Father Laval as he began the Mass.

After noon meal that day, I was assigned to help clean the kitchen. As I finished sweeping, I glanced out the back window to see bed sheets swaying in the breeze on clotheslines strung between rows of sturdy poles. A Native girl not much younger than I lifted a sheet off the line, struggling to fold it before setting it into a large woven basket. I put my broom away and hurried outside.

"May I help you?" I asked.

She looked up, surprised.

"It goes faster with two." I grabbed the end of the sheet she was desperate to keep from dragging in the dirt. I walked my end toward her. The linen was crisp and fine and smelled of the sun and wind. She grasped the edge of the sheet , her hand and arms a shade darker than my pale skin. Though our hair was the same deep brown, almost black, hers fell straight across her forehead under her coif, mine a riot of curls barely contained by my white linen cap.

I lifted the folded edge of the sheet and handed it to her. "My name is Sylvienne."

"I know. The other recruits speak of you often."

My eyebrows rose.

Her eyes widened in alarm. "Mostly good things!" she said quickly.

"Mostly?" I smiled.

"That was rude. I am sorry." She took the edge of the sheet from me, made one last fold and tucked it into the basket.

I reached for another sheet on the line. This time she grabbed the loose end. "I was given the name Marie-Catherine at my baptism several years ago." She took the sheet from me. "But everyone here calls me Catherine."

"Marie-Catherine! My very best friend in France is Marie-Catherine." Memories flooded in — exchanging forbidden books in the convent courtyard, scrubbing floors together, Marie-Catherine's visit to Paris after I had married René. How I missed the way we giggled together, shared our confidences. Her brother, Etienne. I shook my head to clear it.

"France is very far away. Will you never see her again?" Catherine asked.

A yearning I had forced aside crept back in. A sigh escaped my lips. "We can only write to each other now." I reached for the last sheet, held it out, refusing to give in to tears. Something occurred to me. "You said you were baptized just several years ago. Not at birth?"

She nodded.

"What were you called before then?"

"*D'hanate*. It is the Wendat word for rainbow."

"It is a pretty name. Do you mind being called Catherine?"

She shrugged. "Catherine is who I am here. Only when I am with my people, am I D'hanate."

D'hanate. I supposed it was not much different from being called Madame de Narbonne within the household of my husband, la Duchesse by his acquaintances, and simply Sylvienne by those who knew me intimately.

"It is nice to meet you, D'hanate. I hope we can be friends."

"Catherine. You must call me by my baptismal name here."

"My apologies, Catherine."

We each grabbed a handle of the basket and carried it between us into the kitchen.

Several days later, I was in the garden pulling weeds and chatting with Geneviève and Françoise, who shared the room next to mine. The morning was overcast and breezy, and the mosquitoes were at bay, for they did not fare well in the wind.

Sœur Julienne came out to say the abbess requested my presence in her office. I cleaned my hands in the water bucket left by the kitchen door for that purpose, then went to see her. In the office was a gentleman who stood when I entered, bowing politely. Someone of rank, I guessed by his dress: a fine doublet of brown velour he wore over a silk tunic with ruffled sleeves. His breeches matched the doublet, both with black piping to accentuate the cut.

"Sylvienne," Sœur de Sainte-Agnès said. "This is His Excellency, Monsieur de Rémy de Courcelle. He is the Gouverneur Général of New France."

I immediately dropped into a curtsy.

"It is good to meet you, Madame la Duchesse," he said.

I stiffened. My eyes shifted briefly to Sœur de Sainte-Agnès, whose own face did a poor job of masking her surprise at hearing him address me thus.

The governor looked to be a man in his forties, with long dark hair brushing his shoulders, thick eyebrows, and a firm chin.

"Please, do sit." He waited until I had seated myself in the chair next to Sœur de Sainte-Agnès before taking the chair opposite us. "I hope you are being well-attended here at the convent of the Ursulines."

"I am, thank you."

He cleared his throat. "The reason for my visit today is that I received a letter from the office of the private secretary to the King."

"Indeed?" I tried to hide my alarm, but my brow furrowed a bit regardless. My glance shifted briefly again to Sœur de Sainte-Agnès. Her expression was one of mild curiosity.

"It came in the mail packet delivered by the captain of the very ship which brought you and the other young ladies to Québec. I would have attended to this matter sooner, but I have been visiting the fortifications at Trois-Rivières, only returning yesterday." He looked at me imperiously. "According to the instructions sent by the King's secretary, I am to check on your welfare to make sure you are well-housed and in no way feeling destitute."

"I am very well-housed. The sisters here have gone to great lengths to make me and the other girls feel welcome."

Courcelle nodded. "I was further instructed to provide whatever protection you might require in the event of an attack on the population."

"An attack?"

"By the Iroquois," Sœur de Sainte-Agnès said.

"Oh! I hadn't thought…does that happen often?"

"Not since the peace treaty was negotiated, no," the governor said. "But we are always watchful. Peace is a fragile concept."

Sœur de Sainte-Agnès nodded in agreement.

"You can be assured your safety will be my highest priority."

"As it would for any of our girls," Sœur de Sainte-Agnès hastened to add.

"Yes. Of course," he said.

"Thank you, Your Excellency," I said. "I am grateful."

"That was the extent of the letter. There was no explanation as to why you are to be afforded these considerations." He paused as if waiting for me to offer the missing information. I sat without speaking, there being nothing I wished to say. After a moment, he cleared his throat. "But of course, as it is my responsibility, I will do everything within my power to ensure the orders of the King are carried out."

I did not know whether to be happy or disturbed to learn the King had ordered such a letter sent on my behalf. I supposed I should be appreciative but, for some reason I couldn't justify, it disturbed me to be singled out from the other recruits. I had hoped to blend in within this community, to start my life anew until I could find a way to get back to France; but now the Gouverneur Général was aware of my existence and my connection to the court. I had an unnerving feeling that I would need to be careful. Of what, I wasn't sure.

He stood abruptly. "I will leave you to your work with the good sisters. And I trust you will let me know if you are in need of my service. Good luck in selecting a husband." He bowed to me and to the abbess before striding out.

Sœur de Sainte-Agnès closed the door behind him, then turned back to me. "I did not know you are a duchesse."

"My late husband was the Duc de Narbonne. However, I gave up my title after he died. I…if you don't mind, I think it best not to say anything to the other girls."

"They don't know?"

"I've said nothing. I am here to forge a new life."

"Yet, the King thought to send a letter to the Gouverneur Général on your behalf."

I hesitated before saying, "I understand my mother came into the King's acquaintance sometime in the past. Before I was born. Perhaps she beseeched him on my behalf." I tried to hold Sœur de Sainte-Agnès's steadfast gaze but looked down at the last moment.

"I see. Perhaps that explains it." After a moment's consideration, she said, "I agree that it would be best to say nothing of your former status to the others."

Before I could thank her, a commotion of voices from the front yard drew us to the open window.

"Dear Lord! How did that get into the yard?" Sœur de Sainte-Agnès exclaimed.

CHAPTER SIX

Sœur de Sainte-Agnès ran to the front hallway with me close on her heels. A crowd of little girls hovered in the foyer craning their necks to look out the windows at the monstrous animal with thick flat antlers on either side of its head. It was chewing leaves from a mulberry tree. A moose.

"How did that thing get in the yard?" Sœur de Sainte-Agnès asked Sœur Julienne, who peered out through an inch of open door.

"One of the new girls left the gate open when Governor Courcelle left. It was an accident."

"Help! Please, someone!" The frantic voice came from the courtyard.

"Is that Sœur Seraphine?" Sœur de Sainte-Agnès pulled the door open wider and stepped out. "What is she doing up on that ladder?"

"She's been repainting sections marred by pigeon droppings," Sœur Julienne said.

I followed the abbess out into the yard, ignoring the cries from those inside to be careful. Up on a tall ladder leaning against the wooden-palisaded wall stood Sœur Seraphine, clutching the sides of the ladder and visibly quaking.

The moose left the mulberry bush and ambled across the yard. Sœur Seraphine screamed and climbed a rung higher as the moose began rubbing an antler against the ladder below her. "Get away! Get away!"

"Sœur Seraphine! Don't move," Sœur de Sainte-Agnès shouted. "Don't talk. He'll move on. He'll…Good heavens! What can we do?"

"What do moose eat?" I asked.

"I don't know. Leaves, twigs, fruit. Oh no!"

The enormous animal turned around and began rubbing its flank against the ladder. Sœur Seraphine screamed again.

"Apples." Catherine had followed us out.

"I saw apples in the kitchen," I said. "Will you fetch them? Bring me as many as you can carry."

"Those are for the pie," Sœur Lucrèce said from the doorway. But Catherine had already disappeared into the house.

"Shoo! Shoo!" Sœur Seraphine waved her hand at the moose below her.

A moment later Catherine reappeared with a bowl of apples and a knife. I took an apple in hand and walked slowly toward the moose.

"Sylvienne, no!" Sœur de Sainte-Agnès said. "If you agitate him, he will charge you."

Carefully, I rolled the apple toward the moose's feet. It bumped one hoof. Startled, the moose lifted its leg and snorted. Sœur Seraphine muffled another scream. Catherine cut a second apple in half.

"He'll be able to smell it better," she said as she handed me the pieces.

I tossed the apple half toward the moose. It landed near the first one. The moose huffed and bent down to sniff the apple. He sucked it up with his lips.

"Good boy," I muttered under my breath. I tossed the other half a little farther from the first. The moose sniffed and stepped away from the ladder, taking up the apple and chewing. I threw another a little farther away, toward the gate. The moose followed and ate that one. Three more apples and he was at the gate, happily munching the fruit. I lobbed one over his head and out the gate. He followed the apple. I followed him, keeping my distance. Two more apples and he was beyond the gate.

"He's leaving!" Sœur Seraphine shouted, peering over the palisade.

Sœur de Sainte-Agnès ran to the gate and shut it, pulling the bar down into its cradle to ensure it couldn't return. Sœur Seraphine, on shaky legs, made her way down the ladder and threw herself into the abbess's arms. Sisters, recruits, and girls poured out of the convent and surrounded us.

"That was a dangerous thing to do," Sœur de Sainte-Agnès said, her voice stern. Then she heaved a sigh of relief. "We shall call you Sylvienne the moose herder."

Sœur Lucrèce took the empty bowl from Catherine, her voice mournful as she said, "There shall be no pie tomorrow."

The next day, after our pie-less noon meal, Sœur de Sainte-Agnès gathered us in the grand parlor. "You will meet the first round of eligible men tomorrow."

"So soon?" I asked.

"The men here are under edict to marry as quickly as possible," she said.

Sœur Gabrielle added, "They risk losing their fishing and hunting privileges if they don't marry. They can even be prohibited from trading."

I understood the purpose of our coming here was to help grow the King's colony. And these young women, my traveling companions, stood to benefit from swift matches. But to coerce the men in such a way seemed exceedingly odd to me.

The other girls had lots of questions. When the meeting was over, Sœur Lucrèce announced there was to be a lesson in baking sweet treats for their intendeds.

In no mood for their giggling and gossip, I slipped away and hurried upstairs to fetch my quill, ink, and paper. As I was coming out of my room, Beatrix stopped me.

"Would you read the stones for me again?" she whispered, her voice hesitant.

"Oh, Beatrix, no. I don't think—"

"Please!" She grabbed my arm. "It would give me no end of comfort. Meeting the men tomorrow…well, I…I…" She looked so anxious, I couldn't bring myself to refuse her.

Lowering my voice, I said, "If I do, you must promise not to tell anyone. Not any of the other girls." I didn't want to be assailed with last minute requests. "And especially not the sisters." They likely wouldn't look kindly on the practice.

She nodded. "Of course."

I told her to meet me in the library. Fetching the pouch with the stones from my travel chest, I wondered if this was a mistake. If the abbess found out, I would be chastised for harboring sacrilegious talismans at best and branded a witch at worst.

In the library, I closed the door before pouring the stones into her hands. Beatrix's eyes lit up with relief.

"I'm a farm girl. I don't have much experience with men, but I do love children," she said. "But…what if I don't choose the right man?"

She closed her eyes and chose the stones. Pretending I could read their secrets, I told her she had nothing to worry about. That the man she chose for a husband would be a good match. And he would love children as much as she did. I prayed I was right. Heartened that her future held promise, she hurried off to join the others in the kitchen.

However, Beatrix's relief and contentment only served to underscore my own heartache and despair. I sat for a long while, staring out the library window. Tomorrow. A horde of men crowding into the convent looking for wives. I couldn't imagine anything more awful. And I couldn't think of any way to get out of it, short of pretending to be sick. And that would only postpone the inevitable.

With a sigh, I dipped my quill into the inkpot.

My Dearest Love,

How will I survive in this godforsaken colony? The people have been welcoming and generous of heart, but it is all I can do to not show my dismay at this forlorn, backwoods community filled with men who smell of feral living, Natives with their strange customs, and wild animals that wander about. How little I appreciated the life we had in Amiens. What irony that I found our small city to be provincial and unsophisticated. Now I desire nothing more than to return to the home of our youth. And to you.

How I wish I could rewrite our history. That day on the steps of the cathedral in Amiens, why did I not say yes when you asked me to marry you? What arrogance resided in my soul that encouraged me to accept the invitation to Court? Had I accepted your betrothal, I would not be here a world away, and you would not be...where? Did you even survive? Or were you hunted down like a fox by dogs and killed on the spot? I weep when I think of what you must have gone through. And I weep knowing my vanity caused our circumstance. Can you ever forgive me, mon amour? ~ S.

Back upstairs, I found a lace kerchief just big enough to wrap around the thin bundle of letters to Etienne I had been writing. I included this latest missive and tied it with a ribbon, blue, the color of his eyes. I buried the letters in the bottom of my trunk.

The furniture in the grand parlor had been pushed out of the way to make room in the center. I took my place in the circle of girls waiting nervously around the edge of the room. We wore a rainbow of colors. Mine was the same green satin skirt and bodice I wore when we stepped onto the shore of New France for the first time.

I had wrestled with my curly hair in an attempt to tame it into some semblance of order with two pretty pearl-laden barrettes, but I quickly lost the battle. I decided not to fight any further. I wasn't interested in impressing anyone anyway.

When the nuns weren't looking, Françoise pulled a small, tarnished reliquary from her pocket and dipped her finger into it. Quickly she rubbed something red onto her cheeks and lips, then passed the small box on to Geneviève who did the same, in turn passing it on to Claudette and thus around the circle. When it came to me, I thought of refusing to use it; but I didn't want to stand out, so I dabbed the smallest amount possible. Later, I scrubbed my face hard when I learned the rouge had been made of beet juice and pig fat and carried all the way across the Atlantic, smuggled in Françoise's traveling chest.

When Sœur de Sainte-Agnès surveyed our group, her forehead creased into lines of concern. She put the back of her hand up to Geneviève's forehead. Shaking her head, she went back into her office. Perhaps she worried we had all come down with fevers, our cheeks were so red.

Sœur Gabrielle handed us each a small stack of cards on which our names had been written in an elegant script. She instructed us that if a suitor requested an interview, we were to hand him our card and invite him back. "You will likely get more than one request," she said.

"What if we meet someone we would like to get to know, but he hasn't asked for an interview?" Claudette asked.

"You can certainly offer him a card and ask if he'd like to return," the nun said.

"What if no one asks for an interview?" Jeanne looked worried.

"That won't be a problem. You will get many requests."

"What if we don't like any of the suitors after the interviews?" Marie Barbe asked.

"There will be a ship going farther upriver to Trois-Rivières and to Ville-Marie. Some of our girls in the past have chosen to go on to those locations. You may not find the perfect husband anywhere, but I am very sure you will find an adequate one either here or in one of those settlements."

When Sœur Gabrielle finished with her instructions, Madeleine showed me her cards. "Is this my name?"

"It is. Mademoiselle Madeleine Desjardins," I told her.

She gazed at it, her eyes wide with wonder. "I've never seen my name written out before. It looks so pretty."

I smiled at her. "Your name is very pretty."

She glowed and squeezed my hand. Just then the door to the parlor opened and a line of rough-hewn men filed in, hats in hand. A subtle aura of sweat and bear grease pervaded the room despite the men looking freshly scrubbed. At the front of the line was Michel Leblanc wearing a waistcoat with no patches. He strode eagerly over to me as the other men fanned out to awkwardly introduce themselves to the women in the circle.

"Bonjour, mademoiselle! Do you remember me?" He ran a hand through his recently cropped hair which now hung just below his ears.

"I do." I smiled, but inwardly I groaned. He was a sweet man but not someone I would wish to marry.

"And do you remember…I am building a house?" He shifted from foot to foot.

"I remember that as well. A very nice house."

"Will you allow me to meet with you again? So you can get to know me?"

His eyes were so eager I could not turn him down in front of so many people. I handed him my card. He stared at it blankly.

"My name is Sylvienne," I said. "It says, 'Madame Sylvienne d'Aubert,' on the card.' I am from Amiens in the region of Picardy."

"Madame?"

"I am a widow."

"I am so sorry. You are very young to have such sorrow."

"I appreciate your kind words." Out of the corner of my eye I saw a man walking away from Jeanne with her card. "Do you see the girl over there?" I said to Michel. "Her name is Jeanne. She has a very sweet singing voice, and I hear she is an extraordinary cook."

"Is that so? Do you mind if I ask for her card as well?"

"Of course not. You must get to know several women, just as we must introduce ourselves to several of the men."

He bowed politely then strode over to Jeanne, cutting off a man who was heading her way. The man looked perturbed for a moment but saw I was free and hurried over to me. I steeled myself, as he had a fierce countenance. But when he spoke to me, his voice was soft and pleasant. "Je m'appelle Denis Lauzon. Et toi?"

"I am Sylvienne d'Aubert, " I said. "It is nice to meet you."

We spoke for a few minutes and when he asked for an interview, I handed him my card.

Despite my resolve not to remarry, I thought it prudent to at least do my part in this rather odd and awkward event. I worried lest the nuns think I should be banished from this safe haven for not taking my responsibility to the Crown seriously. I thought it always best to keep one's options open. However, after the sixth man in a row asked for my card, I took the opportunity of a brief distraction when Marie Barbe started to swoon and three men rushed to catch her before she fainted, to slip the rest of my name cards into a pocket in my skirt.

When yet another man asked for an interview, I told him I had run out of cards. His face sagged in disappointment, but he bowed politely and moved on.

At long last the reception came to a close. The prospective suitors all shuffled out holding their precious interview cards. The girls gathered, eager to count how many cards they had left and to figure out how many were given out. Sœur Gabielle said the formal interviews would begin the next day.

CHAPTER SEVEN

Sitting in one of the small classrooms, I girded myself for my first interview. It was to be with Monsieur Lauzon, the man with the fierce countenance. Sœur Julienne had been assigned to serve as my chaperone. She would also serve as my scribe, recording the names of my suitors, any identifying characteristics, and their occupations. Afterward she would also jot down anything I wanted to remember from my conversation with the suitor to help in my decision in the event he should offer a proposal of marriage.

And indeed, he did make an offer that very day. I did not need Sœur Gabrielle's exhortation to refrain from saying yes immediately. I had no intention of saying yes at all. Despite bragging about being an accomplished carpenter with an almost-completed house and proudly telling me he had helped build the altar in the convent chapel, I said I believed I would not make an adequate wife to meet his needs.

His nervous smile drooped, and his bright hazel eyes seemed to dim.

"Did you receive a card from Françoise?" I asked.

He shrugged. I realized he was unable to read the names.

"She has straight blond hair and a dimple when she smiles."

He nodded. "Yes. I believe so."

He fanned out his cards, and I pointed to her name. "I hear she is a very good cook. And the other day she mentioned how beautiful the chapel looked, especially the altar."

His eyes lit up. "Perhaps I will see if she is available for an interview today."

"I wish you success."

I had another interview that same day with a farmer who owned a plot of land on one of the seigneuries along the river — a widower with three young children. He, too, made an offer of marriage right away. I turned him down as gently as possible.

"Will you be meeting with a tall girl with a mole under her right eye?" I asked. "Her name is Beatrix." When he nodded, I said, "I understand she is an extraordinary cook, and she loves children. I've seen her teaching some of the younger girls here to sing lullabies from France." He brightened and hurried off.

That evening after supper, I joined Sœur de Sainte-Agnès, Sœur Gabrielle, and the other recruits in the private parlor and listened to their chatter about their prospects. Jeanne smiled in a secret way and said she had had a very good interview with Michel Leblanc.

"Does he have a house?" Françoise asked.

"He is building one."

"They are all building a house or planning to build one," Madeleine said, skepticism shading her voice. "I don't believe any of them have one ready to live in."

"I can wait for a nice house," Jeanne said, "if the man I marry is nice. Monsieur Leblanc is very nice."

"He didn't propose, did he?" Geneviève asked.

Jeanne grinned. "He did! But I told him he must come back and then I will decide."

"Good for you," I said.

Sœur de Sainte-Agnès nodded in agreement.

"I have already accepted a proposal," Claudette announced.

A gasp went up from the group. Sœur de Sainte-Agnès and Sœur Gabrielle both frowned.

"You did not tell him to wait for your decision?" Sœur Gabrielle asked.

"I did not. He is a merchant with a well-established business and an apartment above his shop already built and furnished. He has been married before, but his wife died of smallpox last year, leaving him with no children."

"Are you speaking of Monsieur Gravel? Robert Gravel?" Sœur Gabrielle asked. "I know his shop well."

"He has a seat on the Sovereign Council," Claudette said.

Sœur de Sainte-Agnès nodded. "Such a sad day when God took his wife, Marie-Josette. But I do wish you had waited to see if you would perhaps have received other offers."

"I don't need other offers," Claudette said, a note of defiance in her voice. "I am satisfied with Monsieur Gravel. He is well set financially. He has a pleasant demeanor. And his teeth have no bad spots, nor does his breath smell."

"Did you make him open his mouth for inspection?" Françoise asked, her eyebrows raised in incredulity."

"Of course not."

"So, how did you see his teeth?" Jeanne asked.

Claudette grinned. "I made him laugh."

To my dismay, all my suitors offered earnest proposals of marriage. All but one that is. Michel Leblanc came to me on the second day and sheepishly admitted that while he thought me the most beautiful of all the girls, his heart had been given over to Jeanne to whom he had already proposed.

Of course, I already knew of his proposal, but I refrained from saying so. I also knew Jeanne planned to accept his offer later the same day. I was so happy for Michel I wanted to embrace him. Instead, I smiled and said, "I sincerely hope she will accept your offer. She is my dear friend, and I believe you would make her happy and she you."

By the end of the week most of the girls had accepted proposals of marriage. Those who hadn't made plans to go on to Fort Ville-Marie.

The first wedding we celebrated was Claudette's. Several days earlier, she and Robet Gravel had signed the wedding contract at the convent in front of a notary. Madeleine and a brother of Monsieur Gravel served as witnesses.

On the day of the wedding Mass, a bright sunny morning in mid-September, we readied to gather at the church. Dismayed at how pronounced the rounding of my belly was becoming, I pulled out from my trunk the *robe battante* my maid Lisette had thought to pack for me in the rush of my leaving Versailles.

The loose, flowing dress had been designed for the King's mistress, Madame de Montespan, for her first pregnancy with his child. It had quickly become the fashion *du jour* of Paris, regardless of whether or not one was pregnant. I had owned several such dresses during my time serving as her maid of honor, but only one, a soft sage silk, was available to me now. I donned it with a silent prayer of thanks to Lisette.

We filed into the small church much the way we had our first Sunday in Québec, the Ursulines following on our heels. But now, instead of a gaggle of eager-faced men ogling us as potential wives, most of the women in our group were betrothed and sat next to their fiancés. I sat between Sœur Gabrielle and Catherine.

Fresh coneflowers, purple asters, and purple loose strife were set in vases around the altar. The wheezing hum of the small pipe organ, carried over on a ship some ten years earlier, was nothing like the proud notes of organs in the grand churches of Paris I had become accustomed to. But the familiar wedding hymn set a festive tone as we waited for Father Laval to begin the opening prayers. The Latin verses and the musty scent of the sanctuary transported me back to the chapel at Versailles—a structure easily twice as large as this rustic church—where my own wedding had been celebrated to great pomp and circumstance. It seemed eons ago. A different world, a different age, a different me.

Claudette stood at the altar, alongside Monsieur Gravel (that was what she called him, never Robert), looking radiant in a yellow skirt and bodice she had adorned with fresh embroidery. Her smile when she looked at her groom might have been interpreted as one of adoration. But I knew her better. She was triumphant in her conquest. This union was a business transaction. I hadn't figured out what she brought to the table, but she was gaining a husband who had the means to become quite wealthy through his merchant business, and who was already well-enough regarded in the community to hold a seat on the Sovereign Council. Claudette would settle for nothing less.

When the nuptial service was concluded, they strutted down the aisle and out the doors, taking up position in the churchyard to receive the congratulations of their guests.

Afterward, Claudette supervised the transporting of her trunk and her other personal belongings to her new residence above Monsieur Gravel's shop. He had commissioned a cart and dray horse to carry the load. Claudette, in her wedding dress, rode on the bench alongside the driver. Gravel walked behind. They took the longer winding road to the lower village as the usual path was too steep for horse and cart.

The newlyweds returned a short time later to host a luncheon at the convent to which all the local dignitaries and merchants had been invited. For once we did not have to eat in silence listening to stories of the lives of the saints. The students were put to work serving the guests.

I was on my way to join Jeanne and Michel, who had saved a seat for me, when someone touched my elbow. "Governor Courcelle would like you to join his table," Catherine whispered.

Across the room, the governor sat with the wedding couple, Father Laval, and a man I did not recognize. I looked back longingly at Jeanne and Michel, but then dutifully made my way to the governor's table. As I approached, the men all stood.

Claudette beamed graciously as I curtsied. "How lovely of you to join us," she said, though I detected a hint of chagrin in her voice.

"Monsieur," the governor said, addressing the unfamiliar man. "May I introduce Madame Sylvienne d'Aubert, the Duchesse de Narbonne. Madame, this is Intendant Jean Talon, the colony's fiscal administrator."

My stomach tightened at his words. No one but Sœur de Sainte-Agnès and the governor knew I was—had been—a duchesse. I glanced warily at Claudette who stared at me, her wine glass paused momentarily at her pursed lips.

Jean Talon bowed. A man in his forties, he wore a curly, shoulder-length black wig in a style that was just becoming the fashion in Paris. His thin moustache was overshadowed by his thick, arching eyebrows. And his bright red, tightly fitting justaucorps with gold trim seemed out of place in this frontier convent dining room.

"Bonjour, monsieur. It is a pleasure to meet you."

"The pleasure is mine, Duchesse." His gaze roamed over me as I sat down. He sat then, the others following suit.

"A duchesse?" Claudette's voice was pitched noticeably higher.

"Widowed, sadly," Governor Courcelle said. The men at the table all offered their condolences. Fortunately for me, no one asked how my husband had died.

"Did you know," Courcelle asked, "that our own Father Laval is soon to be made a bishop?"

"Is it true?" Gravel said. "Too bad we didn't know. We could have scheduled our nuptials for after your investiture."

"I'm afraid it would be much longer than you would care to wait. I must travel back to France for the ordination and installation."

"Good point. But Madame Gravel, wouldn't it have been wonderful to have been married by a bishop?" Robert Gravel said.

Claudette said nothing, still gaping at me.

Gravel pressed on. "We will have the pleasure of telling our children our wedding was presided over by a bishop-in-the-making." He made it sound as if he were saying, "A saint in the making."

The priest glowed.

"My congratulations again to you both," I said to new couple. "Such a lovely ceremony. And to you, Father Laval on your impending ordination."

"Madame is a personal acquaintance of the King," the governor said, reaching for his wine glass. "I have been charged with seeing to her comfort and safety here in Québec."

"Did you spend time at court?" The Intendant raised one of his bushy brows in question. When I nodded, he asked, "In what aspect?"

"I…I was in service to one of the ladies of court." I didn't mention that the "lady" in question was Athénaïs de Montespan, the King's favored mistress. "Have you been intendant long?" I asked to divert the conversation.

"For several years now," he said, his smile indicating he thought my question naïve.

Gravel spoke up. "Monsieur Talon is highly regarded throughout New France. He has been the moving force behind a number of initiatives to raise the economy of the colony, including the recruitment program which brought you and my dear Claudette here."

"I am here only to serve the King's interests," Talon said, his humble tone sounding just a bit disingenuous to my ear.

The conversation moved on to different topics, during which I took the opportunity to glance at Jeanne and Michel's table. Michel had a hand in the air, signaling someone near the door. A tall, broad-shouldered man in an officer's coat and sash. The census taker. The officer smiled and tapped his forehead in salute to Michel, but he strode over and approached our table.

"My congratulations, Monsieur Gravel, Madame Gravel." He bowed politely.

Claudette sat up straighter at the sound of "madame" directed toward her.

"Captain Gervais! I didn't think you would make it," Gravel said, beaming.

The officer turned and bowed toward the governor and the Intendant with a murmur of greeting, nodded at the priest. Then he noticed me and hurried into a bow, seeming embarrassed. "Madame d'Aubert."

"You've met?" Gravel asked.

"At the convent, when I was there for the census." He cleared his throat awkwardly. "Thank you for the invitation to lunch. I am sorry I could not witness your nuptials."

"I'll have another chair set." Gravel raised a hand to signal one of the serving girls, but Captain Gervais interrupted him.

"No. please. Don't go to any trouble. A friend has saved a seat for me several tables over. I only came to offer my good wishes."

Gravel lowered his hand. "Good. Good! Please enjoy your lunch. And you'll join us in the dancing afterward?"

Captain Gervais shook his head with a look of regret. "I cannot stay. I'm afraid I have drawn watch duty."

"Well, I suppose someone must guard the gate. Enjoy the luncheon."

The captain bowed again before striding over to Michel LeBlanc's table. He bowed to Jeanne and slapped Michel on the shoulder. Taking a seat, he greeted their tablemates with hearty pleasantries. I had an odd moment of jealousy watching them as they chatted and laughed.

Intendant Talon's voice startled me out of my pensiveness. "Monsieur Gravel has been a wonderful addition to the Sovereign Council." Gravel beamed. "In the five short months he has been in attendance, he has brought much business acumen and insight to our plans to grow the economic future of the colony. Monsieur, your advice to create a ship-building enterprise and to add logging to our export offerings was well received at the last meeting."

Gravel murmured his gratitude for the praise.

"And Madame Gravel," Talon said. "I understand you have brought to this marriage a financial package that will enable your husband to invest in some of our newer enterprises including the King's Brewery."

Now *my* eyebrows were raised. A financial package? She ignored my look.

"Monsieur Talon," she said, "I am happy to support my husband's endeavors and my new homeland in any way I can."

"Is it true the King is planning to end the sponsored recruitment program?" Father Laval asked. "Such a pity. You young women have added so much to the growth of our dear colony. I can't tell you how many baptisms I have performed in the past two years alone."

Talon nodded his head in obvious disappointment. "Unfortunately, I believe the last group is expected next July or August. I agree, it is a great disappointment to see the program end."

"But why is it ending?" Claudette asked.

"I would imagine His Majesty is running out of funds." Talon cleared his throat. "It is said he's spending it all on his new palace. Versailles. Have you been?" He directed his question at me.

My mouth full of food, I coughed, nearly choking. Wiping my lips with my linen napkin, I gulped the remnants down. "I have."

"Is it as extravagant as they say?" Father Laval asked. "Is it worth the money he spends on it?"

"It is quite a large complex," I said. "I suppose its worth will demonstrate itself over time."

Everyone seemed satisfied with my rather vague answer. The truth was I had lived in the quarters of the King's pet mistress, bathed in her marble bathtub, swam naked in the garden pool under the midnight stars after drinking too much wine. Certainly, Versailles was as extravagant—and as decadent—as one could imagine. As to its worth, how does one judge the worth of a King's obsession?

At the conclusion of the meal, Claudette and her new husband led the way from the convent down the steep path to the cobblestoned *Place Royale* where three men with violins stood in the town square tuning their instruments. The parade of guests snaked down the hill after them, all of us in bright-hued clothing; we must have looked like a rainbow of a river.

I had hoped to catch up with Jeanne and Michel, but Intendant Talon stayed close to my elbow, prattling the entire way about the many forms of commerce he'd had the pleasure to initiate within the colony.

As our group filled the square, shopkeepers shuttered their stores and emerged with their wives and children, filling the square with fellowship and jollity accented by their own colorful attire. What a wonderful change from the everyday dull-toned practical clothing they typically wore. Chairs, benches, and stools seemed to magically appear along the edges of the square, quickly filling with older women and a few who were obviously pregnant, their proud husbands standing behind them. To the chanting of the merchants, the newlyweds stepped into the center of the square and, as the violinists lifted their bows and took to their strings, Gravel held out his hand. Claudette put hers in his and together they danced a minuet.

At the end of the dance, the trio struck up a lively tune and women rushed to line up opposite their men, Jeanne and Michel among them, the wedding couple at the head of the two columns. The women curtsied and the men bowed. The musicians played a piece unfamiliar to me, and the townspeople engaged in a contradance like none I had ever seen before.

The partners skipped toward each other briefly holding hands before moving around each other and back to their place. Then the newlyweds skipped down the center and back as the others stomped their feet and clapped in rhythm. Claudette and Gravel traded places and weaved in and out of the opposing columns—Claudette weaving among the men and her husband among the women.

When they reached the end of the columns, the next couple in line clasped hands and skipped down and back, the dancers clapping the whole time before they, too, wove among the opposing dancers. This went on until all the couples had a turn. I couldn't help but smile and clap along, my feet tapping a rhythm of their own accord. How I missed dancing. Whether in a ballet production or a masked ball, dancing had been my favorite thing to do at court.

Finally, the dancers all clasped hands in one large circle skipping in one direction, then in the other, until the music ended and, exhausted, they fell into one another's arms. The throng in the courtyard erupted into applause, men hooting and whistling. Claudette glowed.

The music started up again and I glanced over to see the Ursulines bobbing their heads and clapping in time as the convent girls in their red smocks formed lines along one edge of the square and engaged in their own dances. Children ran and skipped around the square and among the dancers with no one objecting or corralling them.

Two men I did not know came over to shake Michel's hand. "I hear you've caught a sweet one from the last boat," the older one said. He winked at Jeanne, who blushed delightedly.

"What happened to you?' Michel said to the younger of the two, a man of about thirty who sported an obviously broken nose and a black eye.

"Denis's nose had a rendezvous with Jacques Farley's fist a couple of nights ago," the older one said before the younger could respond.

"Farley's back in town?" Michel asked. He said to Denis. "It's a good thing he let you keep your scalp."

Denis grunted before lifting his tankard of beer to his mouth.

"Who is Jacques Farley," I asked when the two men had moved on.

"A local coureur des bois," Michel said. "A fur trader."

"I thought they were called voyageurs," Jeanne said.

"The legal ones, yes. But Farley refuses to pay the registration fee and so trades on the sly."

"He doesn't sound like a very nice man," she said. "I hope you don't ever rendezvous with his fist."

Michel laughed. "I steer clear as much as possible. I'm not keen to have my nose take a turn to the side."

"He's not here today, is he?" I asked, peering around at the crowd for a coarse fur trader with a fist of iron. It would be a shame to have this lovely celebration brought to an end by a man who could not control his temper.

"I haven't seen him. He comes and goes. Doesn't spend a lot of time in the village here."

"Good!" Jeanne said.

Tavern owners wove in and out of the guests with great mugs of beer and glasses of locally made brandy, collecting marked playing cards as payment. For the first time since I'd arrived in New France, I found myself laughing and enjoying the gathering as I tasted brandy for the first time.

"May I have the honor of the next dance?"

I looked up, startled to see Intendant Talon towering over me.

"Yes, of course."

He extended a hand, and we joined the dancers. The steps were simple, easy to follow, but the joy of dancing again filled me with an exhilaration I had not felt since dancing in the King's production in what seemed ages ago. Could it have been only a year since we had performed for the court? Talon was a confident dancer, keeping time with the music, his steps fluid and assured. Of course, this was only a country dance, a *bourrée*, nothing like the ballet movements I had learned at the hand of Pierre Savard, the King's dance master. Quite fun, nevertheless.

Afterward, Michel Leblanc and I took a turn together, giving me an opportunity to congratulate him on winning Jeanne's hand.

The dancing and drinking, the chatter and laughter went on until well after the sun had set. With a most pleasant feeling of exhaustion, I made my way back up the steep path with the other girls and into the convent and my bed. If every day could be like today, perhaps I wouldn't be quite so determined to find my way back to France.

CHAPTER EIGHT

My Dearest Heart,

Today is Sunday. I'm afraid I blasphemed during Mass, because my mind wandered to our days swimming in the pond in Amiens and riding through the woods near Versailles. I miss riding. There are very few horses here in New France. I think it is not in my future to ever ride again, but I hold in my heart the pleasure of feeling a lithe mare under my legs, or of racing down a country lane, or meeting my lover in a secluded glen. Alas, it does no good to dwell on dreams. That life is forever gone.

My love, I must tell you, a new life has begun. One that grows within me. For the longest time I did not want to believe it. But it is true and becoming more and more evident each day. Sadly, I must confess I know not whether the babe's eyes will carry the hue of the sky on an autumn morning like yours or be brown like those of the duke. Or perhaps green like mine, in which case I will never know who to credit for her being. Life can be so complicated.

I will love you forever. ~ S

Jeanne and Michel were due to marry in a few days with just a small luncheon afterward.

The day before the wedding, Jeanne pulled two dresses from her travel trunk and held them up for Madeleine and me to inspect. "I don't know which one to wear. They are fine for everyday use. But for my wedding day?" She set her lips in a grimace. "I suppose I could add some ribbon to this one." She held up a tattered lavender dress. "And I could cover this tear with a patch, perhaps a heart or a flower. But see this stain here? I tried so hard to get it out last wash day." Her eyes filled with tears, and she sank onto the bed, the dress crumpled in her lap.

An idea came to me. "Jeanne. I have the perfect wedding gift for you. You go out to the garden." I took the tattered dress from her. "See if the girls there need any help. I'll call you in an hour or so."

A look of confusion and skepticism washed over her, but she acquiesced and headed downstairs.

As soon as her footfalls faded on the steps, I rushed to my own travel trunk. From the bottom I pulled out the now badly wrinkled blue skirt and bodice. Enlisting several of the other girls to help, I hurried down to the kitchen. Françoise filled the kettle with water and placed it on a hook over the fire. Madeleine helped me hang the skirt and the bodice from a line in the kitchen. Together we steamed and brushed the fabric until it shone smooth again.

"Such a beautiful dress!" she exclaimed. "I can't believe you brought it all this way."

"I can make whatever alterations are needed," Madeleine said. "It won't take much. You and Jeanne are fairly close in size."

When we were ready, we sent one of the little girls to fetch Jeanne from the garden. Françoise met her at the door and bade her close her eyes. For good measure, she tied a strip of cloth over Jeanne's eyes, then led her into the kitchen. When she had positioned our friend in front of the dress, I nodded, and she took away the blindfold.

At first, Jeanne looked at the dress with confusion.

"Your wedding dress," I said. Now her eyes grew wide. "How? Where did it come from?"

"Paris, silly," I said, laughing. "I brought it all the way just for you."

Jeanne brought her hands up to cover her mouth. Then she reached out, hesitant at first, to touch the silk of the skirt. Her eyes filled with tears for the second time that day, this time tears of joy. She threw herself into my arms. "*Merci, mon ami*! I can't thank you enough."

The next day, looking radiant in the blue silk dress, Jeanne stood proudly at the altar as she and Michel said their vows.

When Françoise and Denis Lauzon had their day in the church, Jeanne altered the blue dress for the new bride. After her wedding, Françoise gave the dress to the next girl to get married.

With each wedding, the size of the gathering in the church grew smaller. Many of the girls had moved away with their new spouses to smaller settlements along the river. But each of them wore the lovely blue dress that had travelled all the way from Paris and the court of King Louis.

When all the marriage contracts were signed and the wedding celebrations over, Sœur de Sainte-Agnès called me into her office. "I am interested to know…what are your intentions, Sylvienne?"

"My intentions?"

"You've said no to every man who has proposed."

"I did not find any who were suitable."

She steepled her fingers in front of her as she studied my face. "I think perhaps you hold too high a bar in comparison to your late husband."

I lowered my eyes. She couldn't have been more wrong. "Perhaps," was all I said.

"May I be blunt? If you did not come here to marry, why did you come?"

I hesitated. "After my husband died, I had a falling out with my father. He sent me here."

"I see." Obviously, she was hoping for more information, but when I supplied none, she said, "You do not have to marry. But you do need a means of support."

"May I stay here at the convent until I decide what to do with my future?"

Her face brightened. "Are you thinking perhaps you have a calling? Might you study to take holy vows?"

"No!" I grasped the sides of the chair and forced myself to steady my voice. "I mean, no, I do not think I am meant for the veil. Despite our differences, my father has supplied me with a small pension. I thought perhaps I might rent a room here in the convent for a short while."

She seemed deflated but did not let my words discourage her. "Of course. We are always available to women who need a temporary refuge. A small remittance and participation in daily chores would enable us to offer you a private room."

"That would be quite acceptable. Thank you."

I rose to leave, but she laid her hand on my arm. "Sylvienne, you seem...I don't know how to say this. Perhaps...lost."

"How do you mean?"

"I don't know why you chose to come here, but...well, New France is not for everyone. Are you sure of your decision?"

"It's a bit late for that question, isn't it?" I forced a smile. "I'll be all right. You have all been quite kind. My stay in this house will only be temporary."

"Please, I don't mean to suggest you shouldn't stay as long as you like. But if you ever feel the need of spiritual counsel, please, don't hesitate to seek me out."

"I appreciate your offer, Sister." I hurried out before she could see the tears filling my eyes. It wasn't spiritual advice I needed as much as a good friend. And all my travel companions had moved away.

After lunch, I was helping Catherine clean up when one of the little girls rushed in.

"Mademoiselle Sylvienne, you are wanted in the grand parlor. Sœur Julienne says you must come immediately."

"Go," Catherine said. "Marthe can stay and help me finish."

The girl nodded and reached for my towel.

When I entered the parlor, Sœur Julienne sat off to one side, pushing and pulling her needle with its strand of bright red floss through a square of cloth stretched taut within an embroidery hoop. As I looked at her with some confusion, her eyes shifted toward the window. There stood a man, hands clasped behind his back, gazing out over the convent grounds. He wore the coat of a brigade officer. A slight flutter teased my stomach. The census taker.

He turned at the sound of Sœur Julienne clearing her throat. "Madame d'Aubert. Bonjour." He bowed from the waist, his arms hanging awkwardly at his side. In one hand he held a book I assumed to be his ledger.

"Bonjour, monsieur." We stood in awkward silence until I said, "Do you have a question for me?"

"A question?"

"For your census ledger. Isn't that why you have come?"

"Actually, no. I…uh…rather, I…"

Sœur Julienne spoke up. "Captain Gervais has come for a social visit."

"A social visit?" It was then I noticed he wasn't carrying his ledger, nor did he have his leather satchel.

"You might invite him to sit down." The amusement in Sœur Julienne's voice was evident.

"Yes, of course! Would you like to sit?" I indicated a nearby chair.

"Thank you." He crossed the space in two steps and sat. Jumping back up, he waited for me to take my seat before sitting down again, blushing. He smelled vaguely of lye soap and lemon balm.

Neither of us spoke at first, both looking at our hands. Then we both tried to speak at the same time, and we ended up chuckling awkwardly. After another moment, he held out the book.

"You like to read." An observation, not a question.

I nodded, taking the book from him. *L'école des femmes.*

"Do you know this fellow? Moliere?" Captain Gervais said. "He is a playwright,"

"I do, actually." And not just his work. I knew the man himself. I had danced in two courts ballets created for the King and for which Moliere had written the stories. I did not say this, but said instead, "He is a very good playwright."

I leafed through several dog-eared pages. It had obviously been read many times.

"I found it in the bookseller's shop." He shuffled from foot to foot. "I thought you might enjoy it."

I knew the play well. What did Captain Gervais mean by offering me the text of *The School for Wives*? Did he recognize the irony of his gift as I sat in the parlor of this convent which was committed to educating young recruits to be good wives to the local men? When I glanced up, his eyes were studying mine, and his lips were pursed as if to keep from grinning. I began to laugh, and he laughed, too.

"I hope you enjoy it," he said, standing. "I must take my leave now. Perhaps we will meet again?"

"I would like that." The words came out before I had given them any thought.

He bowed toward me, then toward Sœur Julienne. Did I just see him give her a wink before striding out?

"Well?" Sœur Julienne asked, craning her neck to be sure we were alone.

"Well, what?"

"Did he offer a proposal of marriage?"

"He did not."

"Oh dear. Most disappointing."

"If he had, I would have refused."

"Why ever so?"

Giving her the sternest look I could manage, I said, "Sœur Gabrielle has warned us more than once not to accept a proposal on the first meeting."

"But this would not be the first meeting. He was here to take the census not so many weeks ago."

"I hardly think that counts."

Sœur Julienne nodded, looking a bit chagrined, as if caught in a conceit. "But if he does ask?"

"Then I will have to think about it." I ran my hand over the cover of the book, unable to hide my smile. "Perhaps he will think I am not educated enough for his taste."

"But you are highly educated, especially for a young woman."

"Perhaps he will think I am too educated. Or perhaps he has no interest in marriage."

"All the men here are interested in marrying. The King says they must do so."

The teasing left my voice. "If such is the case, it is a poor reason to offer a proposal." I glanced down at the book again; disgust replaced my delight. If Captain Gervais courted me only because he was required to by the King, that was enough reason for me to refuse.

CHAPTER NINE

I was beginning to feel at home in the convent, humming as I swept the kitchen floor. Sœur Seraphine and Sœur Julienne conversed as they finished drying the pots and pans.

Catherine appeared at the kitchen door. "You have a missive." She handed me a letter with a seal I didn't recognize. "The courier said it is from the Intendant."

"Monsieur Talon?"

Sœur Seraphine and Sœur Julienne edged closer.

Breaking the seal, I perused the elegant handwriting. "I have been invited to dine at his residence." I couldn't hide the surprise in my voice. "Tomorrow night."

"I think perhaps he enjoyed dancing with you at Monsieur Gravel's wedding celebration," Catherine said.

He had looked exceedingly handsome in his bright red coat, black leggings and black boots. I had enjoyed dancing with him as well, but I had not expected an invitation to dinner.

"He is respected throughout the colony as an exceptionally able administrator," Sœur Julienne said.

"So I understand." I refolded the invitation.

"And he is unmarried," Sœur Seraphine said, a note of hopefulness in her voice.

"I've heard the same," I said. "I wonder why that is?"

The nun looked askance. "Perhaps he, too, holds a very high bar when considering marriage prospects. If he proposes, I advise you not to be too quick to give your answer."

Birds sang and a breeze rattled leaves as we followed the path to the Intendant's residence in the late afternoon sun. Catherine and Sœur Seraphine chatted animatedly. I worried over whether it was a mistake to have accepted his invitation. After one dance in the public square, had he decided I met his standard for marriage? Even though I had vowed never to marry again, the tightening around my middle reminded me I would soon have more than just myself to look out for. Perhaps a husband who was well-appointed in the community would not be a bad thing.

I decided to reserve judgement until after I had seen his abode, conversed with him about his plans in life. Did he intend to stay in Québec? Or would he one day go back to France. Even as his wife, I couldn't just waltz into the country from which I'd been banished. But was there a way to return unnoticed? Could he install me in his country manor, never showing my face at court or in Paris? A silly notion. Would he perhaps intercede with the King on my behalf?

More importantly, would he accept that it wouldn't be just me he was marrying? There was a baby to be had in the bargain. Perhaps he didn't need to know I was already pregnant. Even at four months I had been able to hide the thickening around my stomach with my clothing. Many babies came well before they were due. If we signed the contract immediately, likely I could convince him I had only newly become pregnant. Men were easily fooled when it came to the spread of their seed.

"We are here!" Catherine announced.

I squinted and looked up at the blocky stone building with its rows of mullioned windows. It struck me as odd that the intendent's "palace" was nothing more than a residence within the commercial brewery he had built near the bank of the Saint-Charles River. *La Brasserie du Roy*, he called it.

Girding myself as I stood before the double entry doors with their sculpted panels and heavy brass knocker in the shape of a bear's head, I willed my best smile to overshadow my doubt. After all, I told myself, anyone who might be able to aid my return to France and allow my child to grow up there was worth considering.

Before I could reach for the knocker, the door opened. An uncommonly handsome young man greeted me. "Madame." He gave a nod of dismissal to my escorts, who looked at me with alarm.

"I'll be fine," I said. "You may go back to the convent." I stepped through the door.

Inside, the handsome manservant took my cloak before ushering me into a receiving room with a large fireplace. Jean Talon immediately stood when I entered. "Madame de Narbonne. Or should I call you Duchesse? I'm delighted you accepted my invitation."

"I am no longer a duchesse," I said, irritated to have to explain again. "I relinquished the title after the death of my husband."

"Ah, yes. My condolences to you. Would you care for a glass of wine?"

The manservant was already at my elbow with a crystal goblet.

Talon gestured to an upholstered armchair next to his. I sat down, and he followed suit. The oak logs burning on the grate crackled, giving off a sweet, earthy scent that mingled with the subtle tang of hops and brewer's yeast. On the mantel above ticked a gold-framed clock mounted on a brass pedestal with the figure of a woman lounging against it. I had seen similar timepieces at Versailles.

Talon leaned back casually in his chair. He brushed a finger across his moustache. "I understand all the recruits in your group have successfully married."

"They have."

"But not you?"

My chin jutted out instinctively. "There has been no one I wished to contract with...as of yet."

He tapped the stem of his wine glass with one finger. "You haven't found it to be a problem then, not being eligible to receive the promised dowry? Are you in need of a loan to pay your expenses?"

"A loan? No." Why was he asking such a thing?

"Good. That's good. I must tell you, I have been charged with ensuring you do not suffer hardship while here in Québec."

"Charged by whom?" Now the muscles in my neck tightened. I suspected I knew by whom.

"The Crown."

Of course. He must have received the same letter that was sent to the governor. I brought my goblet to my lips to hide my unease—I did not know whether to be concerned or relieved by the news.

"It seems your marriage to the Duc de Narbonne put you in good stead with King Louis. D'Aubert. Is that...?"

"Very minor nobility. From Amiens." Apparently, the letter sent by the King's secretary had not revealed any information about me other than that my person and my purse were to be safeguarded.

The manservant, now standing in the doorway to another room, cleared his throat.

"Ah! Dinner is served. Merci, Laurent." Talon took my wine glass, and we followed Laurent into an elegant dining room where the rosewood table was set for two at one end, lit by a cluster of candles. Laurent held my chair while I sat.

"I hope you will find our fare to be acceptable," Talon said, taking his own seat. "I brought a wonderful chef over from Paris, but of course he must make do with local ingredients."

A second servant, a middle-aged man, placed bowls of squash soup in front of us, sprinkles of cinnamon dotting its surface.

"It smells delicious," I said. The aroma rising with the steam caused my stomach to gurgle.

While we spooned our soup, I learned he had been educated by the Jesuits in Paris. He was curious about my convent school in Amiens, my widowed mother, what had brought me to Versailles. I found myself getting more evasive in my answers the closer he came to questioning my relationship with the King.

Once our bowls had been taken away, plates of roasted salmon drizzled with maple syrup and dried cranberries were placed before us, along with warm bread and stewed carrots, parsnips, cauliflower, and peas. Nothing as elegant as the meals at Versailles, but tantalizingly luscious, nevertheless. If this was how Intendant Talon ate on a regular basis, it was a mark in his favor. I smiled inwardly, picturing Sœur Julienne's hopeful face.

"Why does New France have both a governor and an Intendant?" I asked.

"Governor Courcelle is in charge of the security of the colony," Talon said, offering me the last piece of bread. "He commands the militia, deals with the Natives, and ensures forts are built where they are most needed. I, on the other hand, am commissioned to administer to the financial, commercial, and judicial needs of the colonists."

"I understand the Sovereign Council was your idea."

He seemed pleased that I mentioned it. "It is important to have a body of advisors who understand the complexities of the colony. Robert Gravel is a wonderful example of someone who knows the challenges the local merchants and craftsmen face. The council members also serve as judicial advisors."

"You are fortunate to have such a Council member," I said. Claudette knew of Gravel's position on the Council before she accepted his marriage proposal. That was exactly the kind of standing in a community she would require in a husband.

"He is a good man," Talon said. "Highly thought of."

The elderly servant interrupted us to clear the dinner plates. He offered us berry tarts for dessert.

Talon ran a finger in idle circles on the tabletop until the server left the room. His gaze drifted briefly to Laurent, standing off to the side, before returning to me. "Tell me, is it your intention to take holy vows?"

My hand with the tart stopped halfway to my mouth. "What? No." I set the tart down. "I am at the convent only temporarily."

"I see." He held out his wine glass for Laurent to refill.

I left the tart on my plate, distracted for a moment by how much Laurent reminded me of the young rakes who inhabited the circle of Philippe, the King's brother, all pretty and obsequious, ready to do his every bidding. After Laurent topped off my glass, he stepped back again.

"Monsieur Talon, may I ask…why you have yet to marry?"

"You may not." He wiped his lips with his linen napkin. "However, now that you mention it, I have a proposition for you to consider."

"A proposition?"

"I believe we are each in a position to help the other."

"In what way?"

"You have set a high standard in regard to marriage prospects. I think perhaps I could meet that standard. I wonder if you would consider a…shall we say, a pragmatic marriage arrangement."

"Pragmatic?"

"Something more along the lines of a business contract."

Finally, the point of my invitation to dinner. But why had he couched it in terms of a business contract? My glance fell on his manservant standing quietly off to the side, a studied look of indifference on his face. A very practiced look.

Now I understood. I thought of Philippe's marriage to Princess Henriette. The sole purpose of which was to produce heirs. He with his male lovers, she allowing her brother-in-law the King to seduce her. I could never live that way. While I knew most marriages here in Québec were contracted for pragmatic reasons, if I were to marry again, it would be a relationship bound in love. I had no wish to serve as a front for my spouse's true romantic inclinations, especially if the subject of his ardor was another man, or more likely a revolving door of men.

I made my face a mask. "It is kind of you to offer, but I—"

He leaned toward me. "You would do well to take my proposal seriously." His gaze held mine for an uncomfortable moment. "There have been questions raised about your...reputation."

"My reputation? What questions? By whom?"

"You do understand, the purpose of the King's sponsorship is to provide colonial growth for the Crown."

"Of course."

"Yet you choose not to marry. And you say you are not interested in joining the convent."

I held his gaze, hoping to mask my discomfort with the arched tenor of his voice.

"When you were at court," Talon said, "you served in the household of Madame de Montespan, his Majesty's..." He cleared his throat. "*Maîtresse-en-titre*."

My jaw tightened. How did he know? "King Louis's favorite mistress, yes." There was no point in hiding it. "I was her maid of honor." He appeared not to know the details of why I left France. That it hadn't been by choice like the other recruits. I knew it was only a matter of time before he would find out. After all, my transgression was no secret in Paris. And word would eventually travel here. But I had no intention of revealing that part of my past now. "My position was never called into question."

"I apologize for having to say this, madame. However, I must tell you, there has been some concern on the part of the Council that your role at court was more expansive than simply maid of honor."

"I don't know what you mean."

"It has been suggested that when Madame de Montespan was, shall we say, indisposed, that you were called upon to...fill in for her? In regard to her duties to the King?"

I inhaled sharply, my back suddenly rigid. "You mistake my relationship with the Crown, monsieur."

"That is my sincere hope. You must understand, here in the colony there are only two paths for unmarried women."

"And they are...?"

"Well, the convent, of course. Or..." He coughed politely.

I waited, barely breathing.

His smile of apology was aggravatingly insincere. His voice lowered. "Entertaining men for profit."

I laughed, then looked at him, my unwarranted amusement quickly turning to shock. "I assure you, Monsieur l'Intendant, I have no desire to entertain men for a living, here in Québec or anywhere else." I stood, pushing the chair back before Laurent could rush to hold it for me. "I think it's time I return to the convent."

Talon remained seated. "You do not wish to discuss the possible advantages of a marriage contract to salvage your reputation? Provide you with status?"

"My reputation is not in need of salvaging. And I have no concerns about my status." Which, of course, wasn't true, but I would not give him the satisfaction of knowing that. I started for the door.

The pretty manservant rushed toward me with my cloak. I grabbed it from him, swirled it around my shoulders. Talon had not followed me from the dining room.

"I shall summon an escort to accompany you back to the convent," Laurent said.

"There is no need. I know my way." I stepped out into the hazy light of dusk.

Breathing heavily, my hands shaking with anger, I strode down the path back toward the convent. How had I not anticipated that something like this might happen? I knew exactly who had whispered that awful rumor to her husband, a member of the Sovereign Council. I wanted to strangle Claudette.

I hadn't gone but a dozen paces when a man stepped out of the shadows. I screamed.

CHAPTER TEN

"My apologies. I didn't mean to frighten you," Captain Gervais, the census taker, said. The dog I'd seen with him at the convent followed him now.

"What are you doing here?" I wasn't sure if I should be worried or relieved to see him.

"I saw you go by earlier, accompanied by your escorts from the convent. But then they left when you went into Intendent Talon's residence."

"I had dinner with Monsieur Talon."

"I see." He looked confused. It was rather untoward for a single woman to dine with a man alone. "He did not assign someone to accompany you home afterward?"

"I told him there was no need. But…you waited here all this time?"

"I, uh, had a book with me." With a shy grin, he showed me the book tucked under one arm. "And that tree over there looked like a nice place to sit under and read."

I put my hands on my hips. "Captain Gervais, were you spying on me?"

"No! No. Of course not. I simply happened to be in the area, so…" His face turned red. He wasn't an overly handsome man, but he had two dimples which emerged when he smiled. I found those dimples to be oddly endearing.

"Uh huh." I crossed my arms and stared at him, taking delight as his blush deepened.

"May I…" He took a deep breath. "May I escort you home?"

I couldn't help but smile. "Yes, I would appreciate an escort home. The sky seems to be darkening quickly."

He offered his own smile of relief and held out his arm. "The path is rough, especially in the dark."

Taking his arm, I could feel the firmness of his muscles under his military coat. His scent was surprisingly pleasant. So many of the men here smelled of bear grease.

I slapped at a mosquito with my other hand. "Don't these tiny creatures torment you?"

"They have never particularly bothered me." He grinned. "I think perhaps they find my natural scent too odious to consider me a worthy meal."

"Lucky man."

I wondered how I smelled to him. I found the mosquitos to be relentless in their pursuit of me, and I had taken to using all the local remedies to keep them at bay.

"And who is this?" I asked when the dog I had seen before jumped up from where it had been sitting and, tail wagging, approached as if having received an invitation. He had the tawny coloring and the height of a young mastiff, but the dark face of a spaniel. And his downward pointed ears and thin tail seemed to be of an entirely different breed altogether. I scratched behind one of its ears. "What is his name?"

In all seriousness the captain said, "Madame, meet Monsieur LeDuc."

My head jerked back as if struck, but then I began to laugh. I put a hand to my mouth to stop my rudeness, but my giggles burst through anyway.

The captain's cheeks turned red, and he looked as if he were about to take his dog and flee.

"I'm sorry," I said, the insane giggles refusing to abate. "That was…is…rude of me. But I…you see…my…my late husband." I made a poor attempt at sobering up. "That's how people used to address him." I took a deep breath, forcing myself to be serious. "Monsieur le Duc." I swallowed to keep from laughing again.

His face drained of all color now. "Madame. I am so sorry. I didn't mean to offend." His horror dissolved into utter confusion as I wiped tears from my eyes. Tears produced by my laughing fit, not sorrow.

I held up my hand to signal no offense. After another deep, settling breath, I said, "I am quite sure your Monsieur LeDuc is much more deserving of the respect due his title than mine was." I scratched behind the dog's other ear now, and LeDuc leaned against my leg as if in agreement.

"Did you enjoy your dinner with the Intendant?" Captain Gervais asked.

"The food was quite delicious." I was surprised he would ask such a question. In France, a soldier accompanying a noble woman for safety would never be so bold as to engage in conversation of this nature. But we weren't in France. "I haven't seen you at Mass."

"You've looked for me?" There was a note of surprise in his voice.

"No! I…I mean, of course not, but I…"

He rescued my awkward moment by saying he was generally on guard duty at the city gate on Sunday mornings.

"Every Sunday?" I asked.

"It affords my men the opportunity to attend the service."

"It would seem many do not choose to do so. Attend Mass."

"It is not one of my duties to direct their free time."

"There were quite a few men in the church the first Sunday after I arrived."

He nodded. "So I understand. It is always that way after a ship arrives with recruits."

"But not so many since then," I observed.

"No, I imagine not."

We walked in awkward silence for a moment, until I asked, "It doesn't bother you to miss Mass so often?"

He cleared his throat with a cough. "I...was not raised Catholic. My father was of the Huguenot persuasion."

"So, when did you convert?"

"When I signed the contract to join the regiment. The King will have none but Catholics fight his wars."

"Ah. I thought perhaps you had converted to be eligible for marriage. I am told there are severe consequences for men who do not marry here."

Captain Gervais said, "I have been given a dispensation, as I am required to travel frequently. Often as not, when I arrive back in town after a ship has arrived, all the young women have been spoken for. All but one this time, apparently,"

I stumbled on the path, and he took my arm to steady me. He placed my hand back on his arm.

Heat rose in my cheeks despite the cool evening breeze. "The Intendant is not married either." I knew I was being bold, perhaps too bold, but I cared not.

Captain Gervais took a moment before speaking, apparently weighing his words. "Yes, well, he who creates the rules is allowed to break the rules, I suppose."

He said nothing more.

Finally, I asked, "Have you been in the King's army long?"

"Just over seven years now. I joined the Carignan-Salières Regiment just before we were shipped over here."

I realized his accent was from somewhere in the southern regions of France. "And what drew you to the army?"

"My father was a soldier. He said the only proper way to die was at the point of a saber."

Shocked at this idea, I asked, "Did he die that way?" We passed the hospital now.

"Both he and my mother, and my younger sister, too, died of the pox when I was but seventeen. I was left without a family."

"I am so sorry."

He nodded. "It made the most sense to join Father's regiment. But I hadn't anticipated being assigned to the colony. I thought this to be the most dismal place when we first arrived in Sixty-Five." He smiled shyly, his dimples showing. "I guess I've gotten used to it here."

"I thought I'd heard the regiment was withdrawn after the Iroquois were quelled."

"For the most part it was." He steered me down a path toward the convent gate. "I took advantage of the offer of land along the Charles River and an extra year's salary to stay. I've been commanding a retainer company of soldiers since then."

We stood before the gate to the convent grounds. A thought occurred to me. "Captain Gervais, would you happen to have come across a girl…a woman…named Perrette Raveau during the taking of the census? I believe she married a farmer."

"I do remember Perrette Raveau. She is married to Jean Bordeleau. He is a wheelwright. They own a small plot of land over on Île d'Orléans."

"You've found her!" I clapped my hands in delight.

"I didn't know she was lost," he said, his smile sidewise in a tease, the dimples in his cheek evident.

"Lost no longer. Thank you, Captain, for the information about my friend, and for escorting me home. And you as well, Monsieur LeDuc!" The dog barked in response.

Captain Gervais laughed, his dimples deepening. "I think Monsieur LeDuc believes he has a new best friend." He stood at the gate, LeDuc at his side, until I was safely inside.

In my head I'd already begun composing a letter to Perrette, but as soon as I stepped through the convent door, *Sœur* Julienne, *Sœur* Seraphine, and Catherine accosted me.

"Well?" *Sœur* Julienne said.

"Well…what?' I pulled off my cloak.

"How did the dinner go?" *Sœur* Seraphine asked. "Tell us."

"There is nothing to tell. We had a pleasant meal." I folded my cloak over my arm.

"That is all?" *Sœur* Julienne looked crestfallen.

"I'm sorry, but I am very tired. If you don't mind. I think I shall retire."

Their whispers followed as I climbed the steps. What had they expected? What had I been expecting from this evening? Surely not a warning about rumors that I was a prostitute. Intendant Talon seemed mostly concerned that I not besmirch his colony by engaging in an unsavory occupation. There was mention of marriage, but only in terms of a contract for the purpose of benefitting the Intendant.

And then there was Captain Gervais who had waited to walk me home. Something about him intrigued me. I threw myself on the bed without undressing. The mound in my stomach pressed urgently against the fabric. I would have to find something more comfortable to wear—the letter to Perrette forgotten in the moment.

CHAPTER ELEVEN

It was several days before I got around to actually writing to Perrette. Afterward I had to find someone who would be rowing over to the island. A carpenter who had been commissioned to work on the altarpiece for the new church being built there promised to deliver my letter for me. He said he knew where the wheelwright lived.

That task complete, I was feeling restless, especially now that the other girls had all wed and were gone from the convent. On a rainy afternoon, my chores completed, I wandered into the small convent library. Picking up the Wendat dictionary, I paged through it, parsing the words, trying them on my tongue, but with no idea how to pronounce them. A thought came to me. I hurried out in search of Catherine. I found her in the kitchen, sweeping.

"Catherine," I said. "Will you teach me to speak Wendat?"

"You wish to learn my language?"

"Very much so. And some of the other Native languages as well. Perhaps even Iroquois."

"There are many Iroquoian languages. I could teach you Mohawk."

"You speak Mohawk?"

"I spent time among them after…" She shook her head as if dismissing a thought. "The languages aren't so greatly different from one another."

"I would love to learn both."

"Let's start with Wendat. Once you learn that, it will be easy to learn others. *Kwe*. That is hello."

"Kwe," I repeated.

"Or you can say, *ndio*."

"Ndio."

We quickly settled into what would become an evening ritual. My studies in Latin and Italian put me in good stead for learning this new language. My mind seemed well suited to sorting out speech conventions and learning vocabulary quickly. Often, we would meet in the library, but just as often we wandered around the convent or out in the yard where she could teach me vocabulary having to do with the garden or the animals or things in the sky.

One morning, as I was finishing my chore of dusting and mopping the chapel, Catherine approached me. She was dressed to go out. "Sœur Lucrèce wishes me to go to Monsieur Gravel's shop for some items for the kitchen pantry. Will you go with me?"

"Can we use the walk down to the village square for me to learn some new words? Like river and ships and—"

Catherine laughed. "Yes. Of course. *Yahndawa'*."

"What is that?"

"It is the word for river."

"Yahndawa'!" I ran to get my cloak.

The wind was gentle as we walked out of the convent compound, and the sky clear with only an occasional cloud scudding along. Soon the weather would turn, and the Atlantic would be too wild for ships to cross. The Saint-Laurent River— the yahndawa'—would freeze for a good four months, or so I'd been told. I wasn't looking forward to winter in New France. I pulled my cloak tighter across my chest at the thought of it, even though the weather this day was mild.

Nearing the path to the lower village, I could feel the tension in my shoulders as my body girded itself for the fetid smell of the river. But that was the Seine in Paris. The Saint-Laurent was unspoiled. My shoulders relaxed as the fresh breeze bathed my face. The air carried a hint of pine and wood smoke, teasing my nose. A half-dozen ships sat at anchor mid-river, bobbing and dipping in the current, their mast chains clinking musically. The noisy *gabble* and *herronks* of geese congregated along the shore competed with the shouts of the shoremen helping to unload the last of the ships from France. It took only minutes to wend our way down the steep, well-trodden path to the Place Royale.

"Bonjour, demoiselles." A voice startled me.

I shaded my eyes to peer up into a familiar face. "Bonjour, Captain Gervais. It is nice to see you again."

He nodded and smiled at Catherine who bobbed in curtsy.

"Whoa, young man!" He reached out and grabbed a boy of about seven or eight who was running so fast he almost ran into Catherine. "Watch where you are going."

"Sorry," said the boy. He backed away, turned, and sprinted off, nearly running down a man carrying a bundle of firewood. The man swore at the boy, who jogged around him and kept going.

Captain Gervais shook his head with a smile. "It's been a long while since I've had that kind of spunk. How are you doing, demoiselles?"

"We are well," I said. "Enjoying the fresh breeze off the yahndawa'."

His brow rose in confusion. "The what?"

Catherine hid her smile behind her hand.

"That is Wendat for river. Catherine is teaching me to speak her language."

"I'm impressed. I'm sure she's a good teacher."

"An excellent teacher. I'm afraid we are on an errand, though. So, we must keep going."

He bowed. "Have a good day, both of you."

Gravel's shop was located near the bottom of the path and was busy with customers. Claudette greeted me with exuberance, bussing me on both cheeks, ignoring Catherine. Apparently married life had made her magnanimous, at least toward me.

"Let me give you a tour of our shop, Madame la *Duchesse*." She emphasized the honorific.

"Claudette, no. That was in the past. Here, I am just Sylvienne, the same girl you grew up with."

"Well, here, I am the wife of a successful merchant."

I sighed. "So you are."

"Come, I'll show you around."

Behind the main counter were shelves filled with sacks of flour, rice, and sugar, and containers of spices, tea, coffee, and even chocolate. Barrels of dried and salted beef, pork, and fish, as well as oil, lined the floor. Tables displayed pots and pans, knives, ladles, wooden stirring spoons, and other kitchen goods. A separate room was dedicated to brightly colored bolts of fabrics, ready-made breeches, skirts, and bodices, and personal items such as combs and hairbrushes. There was even a table with books for sale. Most were used and worn, but several looked to be in good shape.

"This is quite impressive," I said, perusing the titles. "You must be very happy."

"Monsieur Gravel is a good husband. He allows me to help in the shop, and he is teaching me how to reconcile the accounts. Soon they will be my responsibility."

Catherine busied herself inspecting her list and picking out the items requested by Sœur Lucrèce with the help of a young man, an employee of the shop.

Claudette took the opportunity to pull me aside. "Sylvienne, you know my husband sits on the Sovereign Council."

"He has made quite a name for himself throughout the colony, I hear."

"He is well regarded. And because of that, he hears things." She glanced about as if to make sure no one was near enough to overhear us. "People are wondering why a young woman as beautiful as yourself is not yet married."

I shrugged. "I am hardly beautiful."

She looked at me oddly. "Do you never look in a mirror? But that is beside the point. What are your intentions?"

Exasperated at hearing the question yet again, I said, "Whether I am married or not is no one's business but mine."

"I agree. But…" She hesitated dramatically. "It is no secret you once resided at Versailles. And you were a close associate of Madame de Montespan, the King's mistress."

At my look of chagrin at her boldness, she said, "The Paris gazettes make their way here. They may be months old, but even here people are eager for news about the goings-on of court."

I forced myself not to react as I listened to Claudette's whispered gossip.

"Some have suggested you yourself was once a mistress of the King, but you were discarded, and that is why you reside now at the convent."

I burst into laughter. "You are not serious!"

Claudette grabbed my arm. "Sylvienne! This is serious. It is said Governor Courcelle paid you a visit at the convent not long after we arrived."

"He did. It is no secret."

"They say that despite being married, he asked you for special favors and you refused him because of your attachment to the King."

Now I was shocked, but only for a moment. "Do you honestly think the governor propositioned me with Sœur de Sainte-Agnès right there in the room?" I couldn't hide my amusement.

Claudette stepped back, consternation furrowing her brow. "Perhaps not. But you have also been to dinner at the residence of Intendent Talon. And he is not married."

"People can think what they wish. The reason I am not married is because I do not wish to be. You very well know I am widowed."

Claudette looked disappointed. She put her hands on her hips. "Well, you'd best be careful of your reputation. This is a small village. Nothing like Paris, or even Amiens. What people say can have consequences."

"Village or city, idle talk has consequences everywhere," I replied. "I advise you not to be party to gossip and make-believe." I chose some coffee and a few spices to contribute to the convent's larder. "What do I owe you for these items?"

Our purchases made, Catherine and I stepped out into the lane between the rows of shops.

Catherine said, "Monsieur Gravel's engagé told me his master has signed a contract to build a second ship."

"His business does seem to be doing quite well," I said.

"Pierre says Monsieur Gravel has a new source of revenue. Assets he has attained only since his wedding."

"Did he say what this new source of revenue might be?"

Catherine shook her head. "It is all very mysterious, but he delighted in spreading the rumor."

"Seems everyone is delighted to spread rumors today. Please don't let it go any further." The smell of fried fish from a street vendor across the lane caused my stomach to rumble. "Let's get something to eat. I'm famished."

Catherine looked over at the woman frying fish on a grate over a half-barrel filled with hot coals. "I'm not hungry. You can go."

"Come with me. We haven't eaten since breakfast. I'll pay." I linked my arm through hers and walked her across the street. She pulled her arm away as I called out to the fish fryer, "Bonjour, madame!"

The woman looked up at me and offered a smile that was missing two teeth. "Bonjour, mademoiselle!" Her voice was cloying in the manner of all vendors hoping to entice customers. "My fish was caught from the river this very morning. Would you care to try some?" Suddenly her face darkened. I realized she was looking over my shoulder at something behind me. She sneered. "What is *she* doing here?"

"Who?" I turned to see Catherine shrink back a step.

"*Sauvage!*" the fish fryer yelled. A snarl contorted her face. "Heathen! Spawn of murderous defilers! My husband burned alive at the stake because of your kind!"

Catherine turned to flee, but the woman was faster. Before I could intercede, she had scooped up a tin cup of some liquid and a ladle full of the hot coals and rushed after Catherine. She threw the liquid onto Catherine's cloak and flung the hot coals after her. Immediately, the hem of Catherine's cloak caught fire. I realized with horror that what the woman had thrown was oil.

Catherine screamed as the fire crawled up the back of her cloak. She swirled, trying to bat at it, but the motion seemed only to make the fabric burn brighter, faster. I ran toward her, but already her skirt and sleeve were on fire, and then the hood of her cloak caught the flame. People came running out of the shops, but no one seemed to know what to do. One man threw a bucket of water at her, but Catherine was moving so fast, trying to dodge flames that would not be dodged, he missed entirely. In a panic, I pulled off my own cloak, threw it around her and pushed her to the ground, rolling the screaming girl as best I could to douse the flames. Finally, the fire was out, but the odor of singed wool and burnt flesh and hair assailed my nostrils. As I pushed to my knees, Catherine had stopped screaming but instead whimpered piteously.

"Someone, help! Please!" I cried.

As the crowd stood staring, one man pushed through and swept her up into his arms. "Follow me," he said. "We must take her to the Hôtel-Dieu." Captain Gervais.

He strode off with Catherine in his arms without looking back to see if I was following. My cloak wrapped around the hurt girl, I ignored the rising wind as I ran to keep up. By the time we reached the top of the hill path, I was gasping for breath. But Captain Gervais never broke his stride. Catherine's whimpers had reduced to only an occasional moan. Minutes later we rushed through the hospital doors.

"She has been burned," he shouted to the surprised sisters. "Badly, I fear."

We were directed to a room with a single bed. Two hospital sisters rushed in. One pushed us out of the room with kind words of thanks and sympathy, closing the door behind her. A scream, followed by moaning, told me they were removing Catherine's burnt clothing. I stood in the foyer trembling.

"She's in good hands," Captain Gervais said. "The best care possible." He gritted his teeth. "I will personally see to it that deranged woman is arrested and punished."

Another nun and a man approached us.

"This is Sœur Hélène, the hospital director," Captain Gervais said to me. "And Docteur Suret."

"What happened?" the doctor asked.

"Someone set fire to her. Her cloak went up in flames." I shivered violently.

The doctor nodded and went into the room where Catherine was being tended. In the moment before he shut the door behind him, I could hear her fearful, pitiful cries. I closed my eyes for a moment as the foyer began to swim.

"What is her name," Sœur Hélène asked.

"Catherine. Marie-Catherine. But her family knows her as D'hanate." I looked up at the captain. "We must send for her family."

"What do you know about her?" Sœur Hélène asked.

"She is a student at the convent," I said. "One of their best."

"She is Metis," Captain Gervais said.

I shook my head. "I don't know what that means."

"Her father is French," Sœur Hélène said.

"Louis Charbonneau," Captain Gervais added. "But he was killed during an Iroquois raid several years ago."

"Her mother?" the nun asked.

"Yenhta' was her name. Wendat. She and Catherine were taken captive in the Iroquois raid. Her mother died trying to protect her."

"Mon Dieu!" I cried. "The evil woman with the fish blamed Catherine for the killing of her husband before she threw the oil and hot coals at her. She yelled that he had been burned at the stake."

"Catherine's people had nothing to do with his death," Captain Gervais said. "You can credit the Iroquois, the same ones who killed Catherine's parents."

"Does the woman not know that?" I felt my legs begin to give way. Captain Gervais put an arm around me to steady me. I sagged against him, giving no care for etiquette or propriety.

"I suspect she did not care," he said grimly, guiding me to a nearby bench. "Sometimes anger and grief can be all consuming."

We waited for what seemed like hours, Captain Gervais never leaving my side, even when I questioned whether he needed to be on duty somewhere.

"My duty is here now," he said.

When Catherine's burns had been cleaned and salved and dressed, she was moved to the women's ward where two of the half dozen beds were already occupied. She had been given a draught to dull her pain, but she moaned in her sleep and her breathing became labored. I sat in a straight-backed wooden chair next to her bed, wringing my hands. Captain Gervais stood next to me, stoic.

I glanced up, startled, to see the sisters from the Ursuline convent file into the ward—all except for Sœur Julienne who, I later learned, had stayed back to comfort Catherine's grieving classmates.

Captain Gervais took his leave then, stopping first to speak quietly with Sœur de Sainte-Agnès. I heard her gasp and glance over at Catherine, but she quickly comported herself. She nodded her thanks before coming over to me.

"Would you like to go back to the convent?" she asked. "You must be exhausted."

I shook my head. "I'll stay with Catherine.

The sisters formed a semi-circle around her bed. They knelt and recited the Rosary. When they finished, each stopped for a moment by Catherine's side to make the Sign of the Cross over her. As they left, they stopped by the beds of the other patients, speaking words of comfort and praying over them. Sœur Seraphine stayed behind to sit with me and keep vigil.

I must have dozed off, my chin on my chest, for the sound of a woman's voice jerked me awake.

"How do you spell that?"

In one corner of the ward an older nun sat at a small table writing laboriously into a large ledger. Docteur Suret hovered impatiently over her. The nun's hand shook as she held the quill just above the page.

"Sœur Marie-Louise, do be careful," the doctor said. "The ink from your pen is dripping onto the page."

"Oh, dear." She attempted to dab at the ink with a small bit of linen, but I sensed from the way the doctor cringed that she was only making the situation worse.

"Catarrh," the doctor said. "C-a-t-a-r-r-h-e. T not d." He sighed. "*Catarrhe bronchique*. Bronchique is spelled with a c-h."

Sœur Hélène, the hospital director, walked into the ward just then.

"How long do you think Sœur Bernadine will be out?" the doctor asked her. "Sœur Marie-Louise is trying her best, but…"

"I'm afraid my talents lie in the herb garden," Sœur Marie-Louise said with a grimace. "Writing was never something at which I was accomplished. What did you say the new girl's name is?"

"Marie-Catherine Charbonneau," Sœur Hélène said.

I stood up. "D'hanate is her birth name."

"And how do you spell that?" the old nun asked.

"I have no idea," the hospital director said.

"I can write it for you, if you like," I offered, approaching them.

"Would you?" Sœur Marie-Louise said.

I took the quill from her, dipped it carefully into the ink pot and, as she turned the ledger toward me, I leaned over to write D'hanate's name next to the nun's shaky rendering of Catherine which came out looking more like catarrh.

"And make a note that we gave her laudanum as an analgesic and dressed her burns with salve of honey, camphor, and rose oil," the doctor said. "We bound the burned areas with wet compresses of linen soaked in water and vinegar. I performed a bloodletting to avert flux, putrefactions of humours, and fever. Am I going too fast? Do you need me to spell analgesic for you? Or putrefaction?"

"No. Thank you. I believe I can spell them." I wrote the words swiftly, yet taking great care with my letters.

The doctor and the nursing sisters finished their rounds, and the ward settled into a wheezy quiet. I went back to check on Catherine, rubbing my eyes. Sœur Seraphine, who had taken the chair on the opposite side of Catherine's bed, suggested I lie down on the nearby unoccupied bed. She assured me she would alert me if I was needed in any way. Grateful, I collapsed onto the unmade mattress.

In the morning, after offering me a breakfast of bread and honey, Sœur Helene asked if I would consider helping record the doctor's notes for another of the patients. "I'd very much like to release Sœur Marie-Louise to her garden." She glanced over to where the older nun sat laboring over the register. "The patient I speak of is in the men's ward."

I hesitated, looking back at Catherine. Sœur Seraphine caught my eye and nodded her encouragement.

I turned to Sœur Hélène. "Yes, of course. I would be happy to help."

"Merci, my dear!" Sœur Marie-Louise pushed herself up from the writing table and limped away.

Sœur Hélène gathered up the ledger, quill, and inkpot and led me into the men's ward where Docteur Suret was examining a new patient, a man who had shot himself in the foot. I sat at the small writing table in the corner of the room and wrote out the details of his wound and the treatment prescribed as dictated by the doctor. "I will need to remove the bullet and cleanse the wound," he said.

With the assistance of one of the nursing sisters, he removed the offending bullet, dictating the details of his surgery to me all the while. When he finished suturing the leg and wrapping it in linen gauze, he said to me, "I am indebted to you. The notes we keep are important, not only because they are required by the Crown, but I often refer back to them when diagnosing patients."

When I finished, I handed the register to Sœur Hélène.

"Sœur Bernadine serves as our scribe," she said. "But she broke her wrist a week ago, and it is not setting well. You seem well accomplished at writing. Would you consider taking over the position of scribe until Sœur Bernadine is healed?"

"Me? I suppose I could." I hadn't realized such a position even existed, but the thought of it suited me.

"I can't offer you more than a pittance each month in payment," she said.

I almost told her there was no need to pay, but I remembered the rumors circulating about me. If it became known I already had a source of income—my pension from the King—it might add fuel to the gossip embers. "Whatever you can afford is fine," I said. "If I can be of help, I'm happy to accept the position."

CHAPTER TWELVE

My work as a temporary scribe with the hospital sisters proved to be more rewarding than I had anticipated. I was near Catherine on a daily basis and could keep an eye on her progress. And using my writing skills to help maintain the hospital's records gave me an unexpected sense of purpose.

I had no real interest in learning medical skills, but I did find being with the doctor and the Augustinian nuns, all of whom were accomplished nurses, to be invigorating. Sœur Helene took pride in the completeness of their day-to-day records. Indeed, as the doctor said, the patient register was often referred to when there were questions about care, repeat visitors, or new patients with symptoms similar to others who had been treated before. Also, I found I was able to offer comfort to patients who were in pain or frightened by their circumstance, just as Catherine was.

The first time Sœur Helene presented the coins to me for my salary, I accepted them with an awkwardness I'm sure the good sister interpreted as humility. But the truth was, I planned to save my earnings to purchase passage back to France. I couldn't tell her that. I couldn't tell anyone. My deep desire to return to my homeland was my secret to keep.

Several days after Catherine's admittance, the prayers of the Ursulines seemed not enough. She moaned and writhed in delirium. The burns on the outside of her body caused a fever within that would not abate. I spent as much time as I could at her bedside, but prior patients were being dismissed and new patients admitted, and Sœur Helene wished to have a record of all. Exhaustion began to overtake me.

A tap on my shoulder and a gentle voice in my ear told me I had fallen asleep again in the wooden chair next to Catherine's bed in the women's ward.

"Mademoiselle d'Aubert," Sœur Helene said. "You need sleep. In your own bed."

"No...I..." I rubbed my eyes. "I can't leave her."

"Sœur Gabrielle is here from the Ursaline convent. She will sit with Catherine through the night. Captain Gervais will see you home safely."

A shuffling of feet drew my attention to the doorway. Captain Gervais stood waiting.

Sœur Gabrielle offered an encouraging smile. "I am well rested. I will stay and pray for her until you return in the morning."

Sœur Helene took my arm to help me up. I swayed dizzily. "I suppose a few hours' sleep would be good."

"I won't leave her side. I promise," Sœur Gabrielle said.

At the door, Captain Gervais offered his arm. There was only a sliver of moonlight, and the path was rocky.

"Merci." I gripped his strong, solid arm, grateful for the support as my legs were surprisingly wobbly. LeDuc met us just outside the hospital door, his tail wagging in welcome.

Captain Gervais said very little during the short walk to the Ursaline convent, except to let me know the woman who had done this to Catherine had been arrested and tried before a judge. For her punishment, she was whipped, branded, and banished from Québec.

"Where will she go?" I asked.

"Trois-Rivières, perhaps. Or Ville-Marie. She will have a rough time of it with the brand on her cheek."

"Deservedly so." But I shivered at the thought of it. Why did people have to be so cruel?

The next morning, I arose with the sun and made my way back to the hospital with the intention of relieving Sœur Gabrielle. But as I approached the women's wing, I heard an odd sound coming from the ward. Moaning? No. Chanting. A male voice, humming, singing words I did not recognize. A flat tune unlike anything I had heard before. Sœur Gabrielle stood in the hallway, like a sentinel. A faint whiff of something burning wafted through the doorway. Cedar, perhaps? Sœur Gabrielle put out a hand to stop me from entering.

"What is going on?" I asked.

Catherine was the only patient in the ward now. Two men stood near her bed. One was dressed in some sort of Native regalia—a long beaded vest, a braided band around his head with several feathers tucked into it. He wore deerskin leggings. Beaded bands with small metal disks attached surrounded his ankles. They jangled as he moved his feet. With one hand, he held a burning stick, with the other he waved a feather, wafting the sweet aromatic smoke from the burning stick over Catherine's body, all the while chanting and humming, his feet constantly stepping in rhythm.

Off to the side, watching, was another man, broad shouldered, dressed in deerskin, but somehow seeming not Native to my eyes.

"The man who is chanting, he is an *arendiwane*," Sœur Gabrielle said. "A diviner or shaman. He is here to add prayers from Catherine's people to aid in her healing process."

"And it is allowed?" This was a Catholic hospital after all, run by Catholic nuns.

"Sœur Helene says God works in many ways, through many different people. While she prefers us to recite the Rosary for our sick and injured, she will not refuse prayers of any sort as long as the intent is to heal and not to harm. Would you like to sit and wait with me?" She pointed to a bench on the opposite side of the hall. I followed her and we sat down together.

"And the other man?" I asked. "Is he French?"

"Yes. That is Monsieur Farley."

"Farley?'

"Jacques Farley."

"The one who broke—?"

Before I could say more, the jangling and the chanting stopped. We looked toward the door expectantly. After a few more moments, the two men emerged from the ward and strode past us. The Frenchman—Jacques Farley—had such a scowl on his face, I found it frightening. At the front door, he stopped and slammed his hand against the wall.

"I'll kill the hag myself," he said, his voice full of menace. "Do you see how D'hanate suffers because of her?"

The Native man put a hand on Farley's shoulder, spoke to him quietly. Farley ran a hand through his hair in a manner as if struggling to compose himself.

Sœur Helene stepped out from her small office. "Merci, messieurs," she said. "Your prayers, added to ours, can only help."

Farley nodded. "I'm grateful to you, Sister. And the other sisters. Tell the doctor if he needs anything, I will get it for him." He handed her a small pouch which she tucked into her apron pocket, murmuring her gratitude.

She made the Sign of the Cross at the men's backs as they pushed through the door and out of the hospital. Then she turned to Sœur Gabrielle and me. "We should check on our patient."

I bobbed my head in assent and hurried into the ward, Sœur Gabrielle on my heels. Catherine slept, but her breathing was easier and the restlessness in her body seemed to be gone. I pressed my hand to her forehead. It felt cool.

"She is improving?" I directed my question at Sœur Helene.

"It would seem so. We have no new patients this morning for you to register. If you would like to sit with her, you may. But please let me know when she wakes up."

When. She had said when, not *if.* I grasped Sœur Gabrielle's hand in relief. I thanked her for her vigil through the night. She patted my shoulder, made the Sign of the Cross over Catherine, then took her leave.

The still burning cedar stick lay on a metal plate on the night table. Its sweet, earthy scent was comforting in an odd way. I offered my own private thanks to God and settled in to wait for Catherine to awaken, making a mental note to ask Sœur Helene about the fierce man, Jacques Farley.

CHAPTER THIRTEEN

Catherine's health improved, albeit slowly. I suspected the scars on her face and body would forever be a marker of her ordeal and of the hatred of that ignorant, now banished woman.

Despite her red, puckered skin, Catherine's eyes shone with delight when, at the end of the fourth week, Sœur Helene declared her ready to return to the Ursaline convent school. Beds were needed for new patients, and Sœur de Sainte-Agnès had assured the hospital nun the teaching sisters could take care of the girl as she continued her recuperation. Sœur Helene agreed, saying Catherine would progress faster in a familiar environment, surrounded by people who cared deeply about her. Captain Gervais came to help me transfer her. We laid her on a mattress-buffered wheeled cart he had harnessed to LeDuc. We walked slowly to avoid bumps and bruises.

At the convent, the little girls had been forewarned about their friend's disfigurement, but a few had trouble hiding their gasps. The nuns all wore stoic smiles, pretending nothing was amiss with the girl. But the pain in their eyes reflected her own.

Sœur Bernadine's wrist was taking longer than expected to heal, and so I continued my work as scribe at the hospital. I also lent a hand serving the noon meal and hanging washed sheets in the courtyard to dry, as well as other small tasks.

There was much work to do, and the sisters were often exhausted from tending to patients and keeping up with the day-to-day cleaning, gardening, and cooking. It didn't take long for me to feel the same exhaustion.

Gusts of early October wind whirled in fits and starts as Sœur Angeline and I struggled to get all the bed linen hung before the noon call to help serve the midday meal. A sodden sheet slapped me in the face for what must have been the fifth time causing me to groan. Just one basketful left. I reached for another sheet, my chapped hands shivering. Out of nowhere it seemed, a dog's eager snout nosed my hand. LeDuc! I rubbed his ears, pushing him away from the clean wet sheets lest he dirty them again.

"Someone in this place must love doing laundry," a familiar voice said.

I pushed aside the wet fabric, to discover Captain Gervais hovering between the rows of white soppy sails.

"They've no choice," I said. "It's what happens when they change the sheets between every patient."

"Between *every* patient? Seems like a lot of extra work."

Indeed, the hospitals in Paris only changed their sheets when they were too bloodied or covered in excrement to be used again, and then they generally burned them. But the sisters here had a different view on the practice.

"They're a funny lot, these nuns," he said, lifting my basket and following me to an empty spot on the line. He lifted out a wet bed sheet. "That and their custom of blessing their hands before helping a patient."

"Blessing their hands?"

"In holy water. I've noticed they have a basin in every room. And a pitcher. They pour the holy water over their hands, then dry them before making the Sign of the Cross."

With a laugh I said, "They are not blessing their hands. They are washing them. But, yes, the Sign of the Cross is for the benefit of the patient."

It occurred to me I'd seen the nuns also wash the doctor's medical instruments after each use. Perhaps their attention to cleanliness had something to do with their success rate of dismissing patients alive. In Paris, when someone went to the hospital, their loved ones assumed they would be carried out on a plank and straight to the burial ground.

"Perhaps we would all do well to adopt some of the practices of the nuns here." I put two of the clefted wooden pegs between my lips to free my hands as I reached for the next sheet.

He took the sheet from me and tossed it over the line. "Madame d'Aubert, I was thinking...well, I was wondering, actually...they, um, say you have received numerous offers of marriage since you arrived."

"Hmm..." I pulled the pegs from my mouth to clamp onto the sheet.

"And you turned them all down."

I grabbed up another sheet and struggled to get it over the line in the wind.

He lifted this one for me as well. "Have you no interest in marrying again?"

"It seems a bit soon."

"I suppose so. And I'm very sorry for your loss if I haven't said so before."

"You have."

"Yes, well, the thing is, winter is coming. And I...well I have a house some would say is a bit big for just one person." He coughed and cleared his throat. "And I wondered, are you truly committed to living in the convent?"

Holding the next wooden peg in mid-air, I stopped and looked at him. "What are you asking?"

"Would you consider moving out of the convent? Before the winter sets in, that is."

"You want me to live with you?"

"Well, not in sin, of course. And I understand if you are committed to taking the vows, but..."

"Captain Gervais, are you saying you wish to marry me?" I looked up at him, stunned.

Sœur Angeline materialized from between two sheets. "My basket is empty. Yours?" She looked up startled to see the Captain, then looked down at my half-empty basket. "I can finish those."

"It's not necessary," I said.

Ignoring my protest, she hefted the basket and carried it farther down the line.

"Thank you!" I shouted to her before a sheet slapped me again. "Let's go inside." I said to the captain. "Someplace private." I led him into the hospital chapel and shut the door behind us. "Come, sit."

He pulled two wooden chairs from the last row and positioned them to face each other.

As we sat, he said, "So, you *are* committed to taking vows?" The disappointment in his eyes made him even more dear to me.

"No. I have no interest in living in the convent any longer than I have to."

Now he looked confused.

"Before you say anything more, I have to..." I took a deep breath. It hadn't taken me long to weigh his offer, the reasons for and against accepting it. For the longest time I had believed I never wanted to marry again, never wanted to love again. But if I could never have Etienne, this man standing before me, eyes so hopeful, was someone I had already grown quite fond of. I enjoyed his company. He was kind and good-hearted. And no longer could I think only of my own sparse needs. However, he deserved the truth about me. "Captain Gervais, I...I have to be honest with you. You see, there wasn't a lot of honesty in my prior marriage, and well, it ended badly."

"I'm…I'm sorry."

Touching his hands, I said, "I don't want to relive any of my past life. And I would gladly marry you, but…" My mouth suddenly dry. "The truth is…I am…I'm already with child."

"Oh." His glance shifted briefly to my midriff, and he seemed at a loss for words. "I…I suppose it's to be expected. After all, it was not so long ago you were widowed."

"There is more."

He waited, his eyes searching mine.

I let go his hands. "The father might not be my late husband."

He blinked as confusion washed over his face.

"As I said, our marriage was rather a difficult one. My husband had a mistress. And I… I took a lover as well. A man I truly did love. And who I would have married if I'd had a choice."

He stood abruptly and strode toward the door. My heart dropped even though I expected this would happen; that once he knew the truth, he would be done with me. I hadn't realized until this moment how much I cared for this man, his thoughtful, gentle ways. True, I didn't love him. Not in the way I had loved Etienne. But Maman hadn't loved Papa when they married, hadn't even met him until the day of their wedding. Yet she had grown to love him in the short time they had together. I could grow to love this man. But it was too late; I had driven him away.

To my surprise, he stopped, ran a hand through his hair, then walked back to where I sat. "So…you are saying you don't know who the father is."

Nodding my assent, I fought the urge to look away, to lower my gaze in shame.

"And this other man, the one you loved…?"

"He is no longer in my life."

"He is dead as well?"

"There was a price on his head when we parted. I don't know how he could have survived the manhunt."

"Dare I ask what law he broke?"

"He broke no law. That is the terrible part of it. What happened was my fault. And please don't ask any more."

He pressed his fist against his leg, his jaw tight. He sat heavily, clasped his hands between his knees and stared at the floor as if to find answers etched in the stone tiles. After several moments, he looked up at me. "Are you committed to never marrying then? As a result of whatever happened back in France?"

"Well, no. I suppose not. But how could anyone…how could you want me under such circumstance? And I understand. I truly do. You are a sweet, dear man, and you deserve someone better."

He put his hands on his knees, a new resolve in his voice.

"But you *are* with child. And winter is approaching. Winter here is not like it is in France. And the nuns—I suppose they will let you stay even after you give birth. They never turn anyone away, bless them. But to raise your child within the convent walls…" He looked into my eyes, his own suddenly determined. "Is that what you want?'

My voice barely a whisper. "No."

He took my hands in his. "Then marry me."

"You would still have me?" Tears, unbidden, splashed onto our clasped hands.

"I want you more than anything. And I believe I could be a good father to your child."

My heart swelled. This man, this soldier of fortune, as rough as he might be, was willing to care for my baby by another man. To care for me without reservation. "I…I don't know what to say."

He put a gentle finger to my lips. Then he pulled me to my feet and kissed me. There in the chapel. A sweet, tentative, tender kiss. So unlike Etienne's passionate ones but so loving.

When we pulled apart, he said, "Say yes. That's all you have to say."

"Yes." I laughed with relief. "Yes! I will marry you."

CHAPTER FOURTEEN

Dearest Heart,

I know now I will never see you again, touch you again, love you again. It burdens me to write these words, but they are as true as the leaves that drop from the trees. I deceive myself otherwise. If you are alive, the ocean that separates us might as well be the sky between the Earth and the moon.

I have had to make a very difficult decision. A kind, gentle man has asked to marry me. He has offered to make a home for me and the baby I carry. He loves and respects me. And I have deep feelings for him. Not the passionate love you and I had. But a caring and a respect sincere enough to allow us to build a life together.

Please do not be angry with me. Do not hate me. If you can find it in your heart, please try to understand what it means to be a woman in this rough and infant country of Canada. I am on the verge of giving birth. I need a man to shelter my child. Possibly our child. And please know I would not choose just any man, but one whom I believe with all my heart will be the kind of father you would have been.

My heart weeps to say these words, to admit the truth. But so I must. Forgive me. Do not stop loving me. For I will never stop loving you. ~ S.

Captain Gervais and I met with Monsieur Becquet, the local notary, who drew up our wedding contract listing what each of us were bringing to the marriage. I had the dowry promised by the Crown for being a "recruit," and the items in my trousseau, my dresses and winter coat, my gold wedding band from my marriage to Rene, the silver memorial ring from Princess Henriette's funeral, and the braided gold ring, which I claimed was a family heirloom.

In turn, the Captain listed his house, two stories tall, a hundred and twenty arpents of land bordering on the Saint-Charles River, four chickens, two muskets, a field pistol, and two changes of clothes. Along with his land, he also had a year's extra salary for staying in country when his regiment was called home.

We would by no means be wealthy, but we would have more than enough to live comfortably. As I watched the notary write out our list of possessions, I couldn't help but think about how much this contract differed from the one the King had negotiated on my behalf with Rene Lorgeleux, Duc de Narbonne before our wedding. The duke had pledged to the King hundreds of soldiers recruited from within his duchy and an immense tract of huntable forest land near Versailles. For my dowry, the King had promised seven hundred thousand livres in coin and another several hundred thousand worth of jewelry. What a different life I'd led then.

"Anything else?" The notary looked at each of us, and we shook our heads. "Sign here."

I took the quill, dipped it into the ink pot, and wrote my name. Sylvienne d'Aubert d'Amiens, widow of René Lorgeleux de Narbonne. I handed the quill to my husband-to-be and watched as he signed his name in the same neat script he used to enter the names in the census register. Jeanne and Michel LeBlanc were delighted when we asked them to serve as our witnesses. The Captain could have chosen from any number of men in the community who held him in high regard; but he said Michel was a good man and would do just fine. He was especially impressed that Michel had signed up for the volunteer militia the year before. They each marked an X next to where the notary pointed out their names.

Two days later we stood at the altar in the Church of Notre Dame. Earlier that morning we had gone to Father Laval to make our confessions. The Captain went first while I knelt in the nave agonizing over what to confess as I stared up at the body of the crucified Christ hanging on the cross. Should I confess to killing my husband? Was I even sorry I had? Was saving Etienne's life by forfeiting that of my enraged, drunken husband truly a sin?

Armand emerged, smiling, from the small private space set aside for penitents to meet with the priest. My turn.

Inside the confessional, I spoke quietly. "Bless me, Father, for I have sinned." I hesitated only a moment before going on. "I am sorry for having disappointed my father by not being a more faithful wife to the husband chosen for me before becoming a widow."

Father Laval coughed once before he spoke. "Will you be faithful to this husband? To the good man, Armand Gervais?"

"Yes, Father. For I have learned the error of my ways and have suffered the harshest of punishments."

"But not as harsh, my child, as what will be rendered by God should you stray again." The priest's tone was conciliatory more than judgmental.

"Of course." I did not wish to get into a discourse as to whether any punishment God would see fit to render could be worse than what had been meted out by the King.

I could sense the priest nodding in satisfaction behind the woven screen. "You must say a rosary every night just prior to meeting your wifely obligation with your new husband. Do this for two weeks."

I nodded. I would have to borrow a rosary from one of the sisters to fulfill my penance. A small price to pay for absolution.

I had asked the Captain if he minded an intimate wedding—just the two of us, Jeanne and Michel, and the priest. My wedding in France to the Duc de Narbonne had been a large, public affair. A high Mass in the enormous chapel at Versailles with more than two hundred people in attendance, and even more at the banquet and ball afterward. That marriage had not turned out well. I saw no advantage to a large wedding.

Captain Gervais said he cared not whether we had a Mass at all. All he desired was the commitment to spend our lives together, turning his house into a home, and starting our family.

The priest's voice in the near empty church reverberated as he pronounced us man and wife. Captain Gervais put Princess Henriette's silver memorial band on my finger, as he did not have a ring of his own to give me. That suited me just fine. I had no wish to wear the gold band from my previous marriage, and I felt the "heirloom" ring to be too ostentatious to wear among the hard-working people of Quebec. Afterward, Father Laval consecrated the Host, served it to us, and gave a short sermon extolling the benefits of remaining faithful to one another and fulfilling our responsibility to God and King to create a large family with many babies. On that last point, I already had a head start.

When the service was over, my new husband squeezed my hand and gave me a quick kiss on the lips. We thanked Father Laval and Jeanne and Michel before walking down the aisle and out the front door of the church—where we were met by a raucous crowd of well-wishers. How had they found out? We hadn't told anyone except Jeanne and Michel who, of course, had guilty grins on their faces.

A group of men from the Captain's regiment lifted him onto their shoulders. Several others picked me up. The crowd cheered as they trotted us to the path leading down to the lower town. I shrieked with laughter all the way. When we entered the square, the musicians were already playing. More people had gathered there and were awaiting us.

When, finally, the men set me down, I staggered into my husband's arms, and he embraced me. Townspeople lined up to congratulate us and wish us good cheer. Shopkeepers, soldiers from the garrison, even the sisters from the convent and some from the hospital. Sweet Catherine, with a scarf hiding the ugly burn scar on one side of her face, hugged both of us.

Just as the reception line was dwindling, Claudette and her husband approached. Gravel gave the Captain a hearty handshake.

Claudette offered me the customary buss on each cheek. "It seems you have gotten over your aversion to men," she said in a sly voice. "Congratulations. Though I wonder how someone who has lived at Versailles will settle into a village like Québec." She glanced around at the villagers drinking, laughing, dancing.

"Much like you will," I said. "We both come from the same humble beginnings."

"Mm...yes. But I don't plan to live humbly here or anywhere else." She cocked her head as she looked at me. "Again, my congratulations. I've no doubt the women of Québec will sleep better at night knowing you are no longer available."

"What do you mean?" I asked.

"Just that I am happy for you and the captain. He must be pleased to know he married someone who was held in such high regard by the King. Someone who knows how to please a man."

Had I heard her correctly? What was she insinuating? I was about to reproach her for spreading rumors about me when someone shoved a mug of beer into my hand. My new husband put his arm around me, his own mug sloshing over the rim. When I turned toward Claudette again, she and Gravel had melted into the crowd.

The people in the square raised their drinks and cheered, "Santé!"

To my surprise, the Captain kissed me right there in front of everybody. We drank again to more cheers. Wiping the beer foam from my lips and still disconcerted, I turned and encountered another familiar face. It took a moment to place her. Then I cried out, "Perrette!"

Thrusting my ale mug at my husband, I threw myself into Perrette's arms. We embraced as if we would never let go--my dear friend Perrette from Amiens who had sailed out of my life several years ago. I had wondered how we could ever connect in this vast wilderness. But here she stood, with a toddler grasping her skirt and a man standing awkwardly next to her holding a baby.

"I received your letter," she said when we pulled apart. "I'm sorry I wasn't able to write back. I didn't have any paper or ink."

"How did you know to come today?" I asked.

"We heard the census taker, Captain Gervais, was getting married. Someone mentioned your name, and that his betrothed was a green-eyed woman from Amiens. It couldn't be anyone but you."

We hugged again, tears flowing freely, until my husband put an arm around me. He greeted Perrette and her husband, Jean Bordeleau, saying he remembered them from his visit to Île d'Orléans when he took the census there.

Jeanne and Michel rushed up and, grabbing Captain Gervais and me by the hands, dragged us off to begin the first dance. "We'll talk later," I called over my shoulder to Perrette.

The unexpected wedding celebration was joyous. We danced until we were exhausted. Perrette and her husband joined in when her cousin Annette took their children in tow along with her own and waved the couple off to have a good time.

In the middle of one of the dances, however, I noticed Intendent Talon leaning against a nearby storefront, his arms crossed over his chest. The expression on his face as he watched us dance a local variation of a bourrée was inscrutable. His manservant walked up to him and whispered something into his ear. The next time I had the opportunity to glance in his direction, Talon and the man servant were both gone.

I didn't know what to make of his dour presence, and I had no time to dwell on it. The moment the music stopped, Michel LeBlanc held his mug of wine high and shouted, "Off to bed with you two! Off to bed!"

The crowd joined in the chant. When they threatened to hoist us on their shoulders again, the Captain picked me up in his arms and strode up the hill, the revelers following, cheering and singing all the way to our house.

Carrying me inside, to the delight of LeDuc barking his welcome home, the Captain set me on my feet. He quickly shut and bolted the door. While we waited for the revelers to disperse, he lit a fire in the fireplace. Eventually, the noise outside subsided, and the quiet inside deepened.

"It's getting dark." He seemed hesitant to touch me.

"Mmm…perhaps we should light some candles."

Before long a warm glow filled the room. He stood before me again, awkward, hesitant. "What do you think?" he said.

A banging on the door startled us both. LeDuc ran toward it, barking sharply.

"I thought they were all gone," I said, the mood broken.

With a look of consternation, the Captain unbolted the door.

"Delivery!" a man called out.

"Now?" the Captain said. "Bring it in then. Though I must say, your timing leaves something to be desired."

"Thought maybe you could use it tonight." Arnauld Ducharme, the barrel maker, chuckled and winked at me. He backed his way into the house holding the straps to something large. Another man followed holding straps at the other end. Was that a bathing tub?

I put my hand to my mouth to hide my surprise and delight.

"Set it down over there." Armand pointed to a spot in front of the fireplace.

The men set the wooden tub down. "A wedding gift from your husband," Ducharme said. He reached down into the tub and pulled out a burlap sack. "A wedding gift from my wife."

Inside the sack were several crude chunks of lye soap. "Merci, monsieur," I said.

The men tipped their hats, grinning, and walked out into the night.

"A wedding gift?" I asked, running my hands over the smooth wood edges. The tub was easily the size of the one in the convent, perhaps even a bit larger. "How did you know?"

"I asked Sœur Julienne if she had a suggestion of something you would like."

"This is incredible. Thank you." I kissed him. "But I don't have a gift for you."

"You are the only gift I need." He kissed me and I gave into him, his lips rough but warm.

He cleared his throat and said again, "So…what do you think?"

"I think you need a bath."

"A bath?" His eyebrows rose, incredulous.

"You did not take one before the ceremony," I said, my voice teasing but only just.

"Do I smell that bad?"

"You stink of sweat and spilled beer. I think a bath would make you more…palatable." I twisted my lips into a seductive smirk. "And now that we have a bathtub, we might as well make good use of it."

"You are the lady of the house," he said. "Whatever you command, I will do."

Together we heated water and filled the tub. When it came time for him to take off his clothes, he asked if I would turn around.

"Seriously?" I couldn't hide my smile.

"No. I suppose not. We are married after all." Instead, he turned *his* back to me, pulled his shirt over his head, and slipped out of his shoes and breeches.

As LeDuc settled down in front of the fire, his head on his paws watching, my husband climbed into the tub, allowing me to see only his backside. He quickly sank into the water almost to his chest.

An image of Etienne swimming in a pond flashed into my head, his clothes lying on the shore, me throwing blueberries at him to get his attention. I closed my eyes, willing the memory away. Etienne was part of my old life, an ocean away. Even if he were alive, this man was my husband now.

"How does the water feel?" I asked.

"I can't remember the last time I bathed in a tub. Do we have soap?"

"We do." Leaving the bag of lye soap on the table, I went to my travel chest and pulled out one of the precious bars of lavender-scented soap Lisette had packed for me. Now there would be one bar left. It felt as if my old life in France was fading away just as a bar of soap fades into nothingness with use. I lifted my chin. This was my new life. I had committed to spending it with this man.

When I handed him the soap, he seemed taken aback. "It smells like some sort of flowers."

Laughing, I said, "And well you would do to smell more like flowers than a bear."

He started to scrub. I slipped off my shoes and pulled off my stockings. Then I untied the lacing on the front of my bodice.

"What are you doing?" he asked.

I shrugged off the bodice and stepped out of my skirts.

"Sylvienne?"

"I could use a bath, too." I pulled my chemise over my head and stood in front of him naked.

His eyes widened. This was the first time he had seen me unclothed. A deep sigh escaped his lips. He let out a startled cough and pulled his legs up to make room as I stepped over the rim of the tub. "Both of us?"

"No point in wasting water."

"I suppose not."

"Give me the soap."

He held out the bar, but it slipped from his fingers, plopping into the water between his legs. We both reached for it at the same time, the water splashing, my hand bumping into his manhood, which had stiffened and risen.

"I'll wash you," I said, my voice husky.

He watched me for a moment unblinking as I rubbed the soap to lather. When I ran the lather along his leg, he closed his eyes with a groan. After washing his legs, I ran the soap along his chest and washed his hair. When I finished, he took the soap and signaled for me to turn around. He washed my back, then my arms. Reaching around me, he washed my stomach. His hands lingered there. I could hear his breathing, feel his breath on my back.

"Have you never been with a woman, Captain Gervais?" I asked, wondering at his shyness. I moved his hands to my breasts.

"Never one I have loved." His voice was a husky whisper. "And certainly, never in a bath. Will you call me Armand?"

I turned back toward him and kissed him on the lips. Then I settled myself onto his manhood. His tongue pushed eagerly into my mouth, and in due course we consummated our marriage.

Later that night, in bed with Armand's arm slung affectionately over me, I listened contentedly to his soft snoring. As I drifted off to sleep, I realized I had neglected to say a rosary — the penance given to me by the village priest — before submitting to my wifely obligation. Which had been no obligation at all.

CHAPTER FIFTEEN

The first morning of our married life, I prepared a breakfast of eggs and pork hocks for Armand. The eggs were from his own chickens, the pork hocks from the many gifts of food provided by delighted neighbors and friends. My duties at the hospital had ended just before the wedding, and I was excited to start putting Armand's bachelor abode in order and make it our home.

"Would you like a tour of the seigneurie?" Armand asked as he wiped the last bits of egg from his plate with bread.

I readily agreed. I had already acquainted myself with the house, pleased with the size of the great room where the hearth and kitchen area were located, and happy to have a separate room for our bed. A set of steep stairs led to a loft that stretched the entire length of the house. For now, it served as a storage space but could easily be made into sleeping rooms as our family grew.

Once I had cleaned up our breakfast dishes, Armand grabbed his musket and we stepped outside, LeDuc happily trotting along. The mid-October weather was surprisingly warm. I needed only a light wrap. Though it served as the "manor" of the seigneurie, our house was not much larger than the gardener's cottage Maman and I had shared with Tatie and Blondeau back in Amiens. Sturdily built of stone, with a roof steeply slanted to keep the winter snow from building up, it had plenty of windows to let in light and fresh air. From the front of the house was a lovely view of the Saint-Charles River meandering along in the distance on its way to meet the larger Saint-Laurent.

As an officer, Armand explained, he had been granted a rectangular plot of land outside the village wall. Unlike farms in France, seigneuries here tended to be long and narrow, with the short edge of the property fronting the river. Armand, in turn, was allowed to subdivide the property and rent it out to *habitants*, families who would farm the land and provide him with a portion of their crops. Currently there were two families sharing his land, each having built small houses of their own some distance back.

Behind the house he had built a gristmill and a stone bread oven, both for the use of his tenants. Closer to the house, he had dug and installed a water well. There was a ramshackle-looking chicken coop, the hens wandering about looking for bugs and seeds to eat. It would need some tending if we were to have eggs on a regular basis.

He had made a half-hearted attempt at a small vegetable garden, but it fared no better than the chicken coop. I planned to rectify that, cleaning it up while the weather was amenable and planting in the spring. It needn't be more than a potage garden, but I was determined to have as many kinds of fresh vegetables and fruits at hand as the soil and weather would allow.

Off to one side was a timber-plank barn with a thatched roof and a small, fenced paddock. Grazing on the grass within the paddock was a beautiful chestnut mare. I had only seen a few horses since my arrival, and those were assigned to pulling dray wagons. I was immediately smitten with this one. We walked over so I could pet her nose. Armand offered a bit of carrot he had carried out of the house in his pocket.

"You didn't mention a horse in our marriage contract," I said, stroking her neck.

"Her name is Shadow. She doesn't belong to me. I'm simply her caretaker. She belongs to the King."

My head jerked up. "The King?"

"As captain of the militia, I am permitted to house the King's horse and to ride her at my discretion."

"I had begun to think nobody rides horses in New France. I've not seen anyone do so."

"There aren't many for that purpose. The first were brought over seven or eight years ago. Most have gone to farmers to help with their fieldwork. I had to beg for the regiment to be allowed to own one for riding."

"But how can an army not have horses?"

"Horses aren't as useful in the dense woodlands here. With the number of rivers and tributaries, most people, French and Native alike, rely on canoes to get around."

"Well, I'm glad you have her." I stroked Shadow's neck and her soft nose. "Do you think I might ever ride her?"

"You ride?" Armand asked, sounding impressed.

"When I was at court, I had my own mare. Phoebe."

"This one could certainly use more exercise than I have time to give her. But I don't have a woman's saddle."

"I can ride with any style saddle. I would love to exercise her." I grasped his hand. "Armand, this is almost as good a gift as the bathtub."

He broke out in hearty laughter, his dimples forming in earnest. "I don't know which I'll like better, bathing with you or riding Shadow with you."

He quickly saddled her and hoisted me up to ride behind him. With LeDuc racing crazily back and forth, eager to be off, Armand reached for the musket he had propped against the barn. He slipped it into a leather scabbard attached to the saddle.

I wrapped my arms around his waist. The heady scent of horse and the ripple of muscles in Armand's thighs took me immediately back to the forests of Versailles, riding Phoebe alongside Etienne. Chastising myself for my moment of unfaithfulness to my new husband, I pushed thoughts of my old life out of my mind and focused on the here and now.

The property we traversed was lush, if a bit wild, only a portion of it cleared for cultivation. We rode toward the back end where Armand introduced me to our tenants, Andre Delaporte and his wife Marie, and Pierre Lemaire and his wife Noelle. I'd seen them in town on occasion but had never really got to know them. Both couples congratulated us on our nuptials and expressed delight at having me as a neighbor.

Reaching the far end of the seigneurie, we circled around and headed back toward the river and home. After I slid off Shadow, Armand handed me the musket to hold until he could dismount.

"Do you carry this with you everywhere?" I asked. He hadn't always carried his weapon in town.

"Here, outside the village walls, it's best to keep it close." He looked thoughtful a moment before asking. "Have you ever fired a musket?"

I snorted. "I've never even held a musket before today."

"Then that will be this afternoon's lesson."

The *boom* when I pulled the trigger and the recoil of the musket stock against my shoulder caused me to jump and miss the target. The air filled with the acrid odor of sulfur. I couldn't say I enjoyed the experience of shooting, but I was determined to learn to hit the target Armand had set up on a bale of hay, an iron silhouette of a wolf made by the local blacksmith.

Armand told me every man, woman, and able child in New France who lived outside the town walls knew how to shoot a musket. "Even with the Peace Treaty of '67, you can't be too careful. And it's not just the Iroquois. One drunken Frenchman wandering where he doesn't belong can be just as dangerous. Or a bear or wolf."

He had first demonstrated how to shoot, knocking the wolf clear off the hay bale. Then he reloaded the musket for me. But after my first shot, which ended up somewhere in the trees on the edge of our property, he insisted I load the weapon myself. It would do no good to know how to shoot, he said, if I couldn't load the weapon when he wasn't around. I shot several more rounds, each time getting closer to hitting my target.

The next day I practiced again and managed to nick the target once. Armand declared it a good session and said we would continue to practice when we had time.

That afternoon we saddled Shadow, and this time rode the length of the fortification wall that ran along the western edge of the upper portion of the village. Primitive, like the one surrounding the Ursulines' convent, the city wall was nothing more than a timber palisade. I wondered how much longer before they felt the need to build a stone wall. And how much longer I could ride before it became too uncomfortable.

Armand had only been granted two days' leave before he had to be back at work at the fort. After breakfast, he fed and watered Shadow and let her out of the barn. He kissed me goodbye and headed out for the day. I took scraps out to feed the chickens, then went to work in the tiny garden. I was amazed at how black the soil was. Holding a handful to my nose, I inhaled the rich, fertile scent. With a little care, this garden would yield a bountiful harvest.

As I pulled weeds, my mind drifted to our wedding celebration. Smiling just thinking about the villagers waiting outside the church to carry us down to the village square, the music, dancing with Armand, my delight at discovering my old friend Perrette. And of course, the bathtub.

But the memory of Intendent Jean Talon, arms crossed, leaning against the wall and watching as I danced, marred my thoughts. We hadn't spoken since the dinner he had hosted and from which I had so abruptly stormed out. Indeed, even within the confines of this small village, I had managed to avoid him. Now I wondered what he had been thinking, watching me dance with the captain of his militia at our wedding celebration. Did he resent my refusal of his marriage offer? Did he still think me someone with a reputation that might lead to scandal? Was he satisfied that I posed no moral threat to his community now that I was married, even if not to him?

And there was Claudette. And the ugly insinuation she had made in the midst of our celebration. As I dug out weeds and an occasional rogue rutabaga and carrot, I bristled at the memory of her suggestion that I was wanton. I had harbored a notion on the voyage across the Atlantic that perhaps she and I could at last be friends, especially now that we were no longer competing for grades or the attention of the school nuns. I was sorely mistaken. However, since there were so few options for purchasing goods from France, there was no way I could avoid the store she owned with her new husband.

Back in the house, I sliced an apple and ate some bread, both purchased in town. I wondered what it would take to fire up the bread oven out back. I had never made bread on my own before. Even in Amiens, we had purchased our bread from Perrette's family bakery. She must know how to bake bread. Perhaps I could ask her to teach me.

As I gazed about my new living space, I wondered if there was anything in my travel chest I could use to make the house feel a bit homier, perhaps something to set out on the table or the fireplace mantel. I was sure I had some lace or a scarf that would serve the purpose. Rummaging through the chest, I came across my etchings of Maman and Papa. And a small, ornamental wood box I had picked up in the lower village marketplace to hold my small collection of stones. What would Armand think of my proclivity for reading peoples "fortunes"? Perhaps telling him they were pretty keepsakes would be explanation enough. I found a blue shawl I could lay over the table when not in use. At the bottom of the chest were the handful of letters I had written to Etienne, wrapped in a lace kerchief and tied with a ribbon.

Taking the bundle to the chair in front of the fireplace, I untied the ribbon. Seven letters. All sealed, no addresses. There was no point in rereading them; I knew every word by heart. It grieved me to think Etienne would never read them. That he could have survived the King's men was an impossibility, I was sure now. Guilt settled over me like a mantle of sod over a grave. If I hadn't gone to him that morning. If I had simply mounted Phoebe and ridden away from Versailles, perhaps he would be alive today.

My heart ached, but I needed to break away from my old life if my marriage to Armand was to survive. With a new-found resolve, I fed the letters, one after the other, to the fire. I watched as the edges browned, curled, then caught the flame, burning until my past had disintegrated along with the paper and ink. When the last of the pages had crumbled into ash, I went out to the paddock to saddle Shadow. Together we rode for almost an hour, first around the property, then down along the river. I'd forgotten how much riding always soothed my soul.

Several days later, I was in the garden again, setting out rocks I'd gathered to expand the outline of the area I wished to plant come spring. A movement caught my eye. I looked up, surprised to see a Native woman standing several paces away.

I hadn't heard her approach. She said nothing, but her doe-shaped eyes beheld me with a sort of bold curiosity.

"Bonjour," I said, stopping to wipe the sweat from my forehead with my sleeve. She didn't respond so I tried my limited Wendat. "Kwe." When she still didn't respond, I said, "Ndio." Perhaps I was pronouncing it wrong.

She put her hand to her mouth in a gesture I took to mean she was looking for food. I realized her stomach protruded. She was with child. Without thinking, I put a hand to my own stomach. She offered a knowing smile. She recognized I was with child as well, though not nearly as far along as she.

"I have some eggs. O'nhonhchia' Would you like them?" I didn't wait for an answer, because of course she didn't understand me. I set my stone in line with the others, then hurried into the house, coming back out with a small basket of eggs and several thick slices of bread.

She accepted my offerings, putting a hand to her heart in a gesture I took to mean gratitude. Then she turned and silently padded down the path, her moccasins barely raising any dust, her food treasures in hand. It felt good to help a fellow mother-to-be. I hummed as I returned to my work in the garden.

Two days later, she appeared at our door while Armand was having his breakfast, this time with my empty basket in one hand and a beaver pelt in the other. I jerked back at the sight of the pelt and shook my head.

"Thank you, but no." I waved my hand to indicate I didn't want it. The look in her eyes was one of curious disapproval.

"Sylvienne," Armand said as he placed his breakfast dishes into the wash bucket. "You should take it."

"But what will I do with a beaver pelt?"

"That's not the point. She comes in good will."

I sighed, gave her a smile, and took the pelt and my basket. Nodding her approval, she touched her hair, then pointed to a clasp I was using to hold my hair away from my face.

"My barrette? You want my barrette?" I asked, touching the bauble. She nodded again. "Doesn't seem like much of a trade. Wait a minute." I held up a finger to indicate that I would be right back. I dug in the chest at the foot of my bed and pulled out a square of tatted lace. Back at the door, I pulled the barrette from my hair and held it out along with the lace. "Will this do?"

Smiling broadly, the woman accepted my gifts. She touched her heart with her hand before turning to go. I did the same. Armand took the pelt from me and brought it out to hang in the lean-to where we kept the logs for our fire.

"I'm going down to the lower village," he said, when he came back into the house. "Would you like to go with me? Do you need anything from any of the merchants?"

"I can't think of anything at the moment," I said. "I'll stay here, if you don't mind. I have some mending I want to attend to while the light is good."

He kissed me on the forehead. "I'll see you this evening." Then he was gone, LeDuc happily chasing after him.

I found my sewing notions and picked up a shirt of Armand's with a torn sleeve. I was just tying the final knot in the thread when someone rapped on the door.

A boy of about twelve or thirteen said, "I have a letter for you, madame. It came on last night's ship."

I reached into the clay jar filled with coins Armand kept on a shelf near the door and gave him one in exchange for the letter. He thanked me profusely before bowing and skittering off.

Taking the letter to the window where the light was better, I perused the folded sheet of fine linen addressed simply "To Mademoiselle Sylvienne d'Amiens in Québec, New France." I flipped it over and immediately recognized the seal, my heart suddenly beating faster. Opening the letter, I read the first line —

Ma Très Cherè, you will never believe who paid me a visit this morning!

The handwriting was elegant but hastily wrought. My eyes dropped to the bottom of the letter to confirm the signature. Philippe!

Simply called *Monsieur*, Philippe, the Duc d'Orléans, brother of King Louis, had been my first champion at court. How I missed him. More than anyone in the royal family, he had been my favorite. Holding the letter close, I breathed in the faint scent of his musky, citrusy perfume. He'd had a special lemon and orange blend made for him with hints of clove and amaryllis. I smiled. Many times, I had watched him dab it onto the letters he penned.

Reading further, I stifled a wry chuckle of disgust at his mention of lying naked in bed with that ungodly Chevalier de Lorraine. That was a man I did not miss.

Then my breath caught as I read of a man breaking into his bedroom, pointing a pistol at him, and asking about me, saying I had saved his life. He never mentioned Etienne by name, but I knew. Only Etienne would ask which choice I had made when the King told me I could go into a convent or come here to the New World as punishment for my wickedness.

My legs wobbled, and I sagged onto the chair. Was it possible Etienne was alive? That he hadn't been caught? And hung because of me? In the eyes of God, I was sure, my misdeed wasn't the crime I had committed to save Etienne's life. My sin was having married the Duc de Narbonne in the first place. Or perhaps having gone to court, to Versailles, at all.

The date on the letter indicated it had been written five months prior. That was a long time for a man to remain free with a price on his head and the King's soldiers scouring the land looking for him. And there had been no letters from Etienne. Even with this glimmer of hope, I deemed it unlikely he had remained free much longer.

It didn't matter anyway, I told myself. Etienne lived in the past. I lived in the present. There was no looking back. But did I really believe that?

The note from Philippe ended with news of Louis having chosen a new wife for him, flooding me with memories of poor Henriette, her tragic death, and her royal funeral in the Basilica of Saint-Denis in Paris. I could still hear the requiem Mass sung in Latin, smell the incense and the burning candles, taste the salt upon my lips after so many tears.

I reread the letter, committing it to memory, inhaling the prince's perfume one last time, running my fingers over the words "your beloved shoemaker." Then I ripped it in two and ripped it once more before feeding it to the flames in the fireplace. As I watched to be sure every bit of it blackened to ash and went up the chimney in smoke, I hoped beyond hope that its message was true. That my beloved shoemaker was alive, even though he could no longer be a part of my life.

Wiping my hands on my apron, I picked up Armand's mended shirt and folded it to put away. Armand was my future now. And I would not risk our marriage in the hope an impossible dream could ever come true.

A week later, the Native woman was back with another pelt.

"I don't know what I could possibly give you." I held up my hands and shrugged my shoulders hoping to indicate I didn't know what to do. She pointed to the blue shawl folded over the back of a chair. "My shawl?"

She nodded.

I supposed I could knit another. I fetched the shawl, but when I handed it to her, I muttered. "This has to stop. I have nothing left to trade."

The woman smiled and put her hand to her heart. "Merci, madame, you have traded honorably." Her French was perfectly accented. My jaw dropped as I watched her pad down the path in her moccasin-clad feet, my blue shawl around her shoulders.

At supper that evening, Armand laughed when I told him the story.

"But Armand, she spoke French. She understood everything I was saying all along."

"Of course she did. Many of the Natives in these parts speak French, especially the women. They do most of the commerce. She was likely Wendat."

"But why did she not speak at all from the very beginning?"

"She wanted to take your measure first. To see what kind of tradeswoman you are."

"I am hardly a tradeswoman."

"Regardless, you seemed to have passed muster."

"And what am I to do with the beaver pelts hanging in the woodshed?"

He laughed again. "I know a fellow who would be happy to take them off your hands. I'll let him know the next time he comes by."

Despite the lessons I'd already had, I decided I needed to improve my limited grasp of the Wendat language. As soon as I could, I stopped by the convent to get another lesson from Catherine, and to set up regular times to meet. I also borrowed the handwritten French/Wendat dictionary from the convent library, taking it home with me. And thus, I restarted my language lessons in earnest. I found it a bit like being in school in Amiens again, going to the convent each day and taking lessons. But this time it wasn't the nuns who were my teachers, but a disfigured, Wendat girl younger than myself. Regardless, I relished the lessons and improved my grasp of the language quickly. And Catherine and I enjoyed each other's company.

Some weeks later, when the Wendat woman came to our door again, her stomach had shrunk, and she carried her new baby swathed and strapped to a board on her back. I congratulated her in French and asked her name in her own language. At first, she seemed surprised. Then she broke into a huge grin. In Wendat she said. "I am Cécile, daughter of *A'taentsik*, known in your language as Sky Woman, grandmother of our people, the Wendat."

CHAPTER SIXTEEN

After a cold, rainy spell, mid-October breathed the gift of unseasonably warm air across the river and into the settlement. Sunday morning Armand was on guard duty at the gate, giving his men respite to attend church — or not, as they saw fit. Even though I no longer experienced nausea in the morning, I used my growing girth and discomfort as an excuse to stay home from Mass. I hummed as I chopped vegetables for our evening stew. A loud rapping on the door startled me so much I nearly chopped off a finger.

It must be Cécile, I thought. But why so early in the morning? And why so noisome? Opening the door, I took a step back, alarmed to find a strange man standing before me. I had to work to keep my face from showing my revulsion. He was filthy with the grime of having not washed in God knows how long, and reeking of bear grease, sweat, and God knows what else. His beard showed several weeks' growth. Yet he seemed familiar.

"Excuse me," he said, craning his neck to look past me. "But I thought Captain Gervais lived here." His French had just the tinge of an accent. Irish? His eyes shone through the dirt on his sun-darkened face.

"He does. I am his wife."

"His wife?" His eyes shifted from my face to my bulging stomach and back to my face again. "Well, I'll be damned." He ran his hand through his unkempt hair. "Would you have a bit of leftover soap you'd oblige me with?"

"Soap?" Where had I seen him before? He wasn't one of the villagers.

"*S'il vous plaît*. The river is calling me to wash."

I left him standing in the doorway while I fetched a bar of lye soap. He wasn't going to get rid of that dirt with anything less.

"Merci, madame"

As he trotted back down the path toward the river where a birchbark canoe had been pulled up onto the rocky shore, I remembered where I had seen him before. He was the man who had accompanied the shaman when Catherine was at death's door in the hospital. Jacques Farley. The man who broke other men's noses when he got angry.

Armand was home and changing out of his uniform when the sharp rap sounded on the door again. LeDuc barked only once, running to the door with his tail wagging. When I opened it, Jacques Farley stood before me once more. LeDuc rushed out and barked happily, pushing his nose into the man's hand until he reached down and ruffled the dog's head and ears.

The visitor was scrubbed clean, his wet hair hanging to his shoulders. Bare-chested and bare-legged, he wore only a deerskin breechclout, the kind I'd seen some of the Native men wear. Over his shoulder he'd thrown his sopping tunic and breeches. On his forearm a black marking. A tattoo? When he raised his hand to push his wet hair out of his eyes, a long-legged bird danced along his muscles, a crane or heron.

"I hope you don't mind," he said, his gaze locking onto mine a moment too long. "I had planned to return your soap, but there wasn't much left after my scrubbing in the river. I brought you a pheasant instead." He held up the freshly slaughtered bird by its legs, its neck limp, its wings fluttering loosely in the breeze.

I sucked in a breath. What was I going to do with a pheasant? And what was that glimmer of amusement in his grey eyes? Did he guess I had no clue what to do with a freshly killed pheasant? It was one of my favorite dishes, but I'd only ever had it at Court dinners where the palace chefs performed all the culinary miracles. Curiously unsettled by his broadening grin, I accepted the bird just as Armand came out of our bedroom.

"Jacques!" Armand exclaimed. He strode over and grabbed the man by his shoulders and drew him into a hug. When they separated, Armand said, "Sylvienne, this is my good friend, Jacques Farley."

My eyes widened. My husband was friends with the infamous *coureur des bois*, the outlawed fur trader who other men feared?

Offering an impertinent half curtsy, I said, "We met earlier. Though we didn't exchange names."

Farley laughed. "Indeed. I came begging for soap, never imagining you had a wife, much less one so beautiful. Madame." He bowed from the waist now. He was not quite as tall as Armand, but just as broad-shouldered with powerful-looking arms.

"Did he bring us supper?" Armand said, pointing at the bird dangling from my hand.

Farley must have noticed the look of consternation on my face because he quicky said, "I am more than happy to pluck and dress it for you. Assuming I'm invited to dine, that is." Was he hiding a smirk behind his beard and moustache?

"We'll work at it together," Armand said. "We've a lot to catch up on. You've been gone this time, what? Five, six months?"

"I came back briefly, a month or so ago, but I didn't have time to stop by. Can I hang my clothes in front of your fire to dry? I gave them a good scrub when I was bathing in the river."

"You'd be best to hang them on the line out back," I said. "The sun and wind will dry them more quickly." I wasn't sure I wanted him in my house in such a state of undress.

Armand led him out to the backyard to hang his clothes and then to the cleaning table under the back eaves. LeDuc trotted happily after the men.

Reaching for two mugs and a carafe of wine, I headed outside. I poured the wine and set the bottle and mugs where they could reach them.

"Are you staying in town?' Armand asked as they set to plucking the bird.

"I'm renting a room above the Gray Goose tavern for a couple of days. I had a good haul this last trip. Sold a good number of pelts. Prices are up this year."

Grabbing my broom, I swept near the doorway to listen as they conversed about various traders and their travails. When Armand brought the naked, gutted bird in, I slathered it with butter and rubbed it with sage and thyme before skewering it.

Setting the prepared bird on the spit over the fire, Armand pulled up chairs for Farley and himself. By now Farley's clothes were dry, and he'd pulled his tunic on over his head and replaced the breechclout with deerskin leggings. As they continued to talk, Armand turned the spit handle to ensure the bird roasted evenly. "Must have been a good season for you then?"

"Possibly the best in a couple of years. I've enough to repay all my debts with some left over. Madame Sylvienne, would you like help carrying that pot?" Farley jumped up and took the pot of carrots, rutabagas, peas, and onions from me to set onto a hook over the fire.

"Thank you," I said, wiping my hands on my apron. Was he really as notorious as everyone made him out to be?

When we sat down to enjoy the roasted pheasant, Farley poured the wine, making sure my glass was filled first. As the two men talked, his gaze occasionally drifted to me. Despite my initial unease, I quickly became enthralled with his stories, laughing as he described mishaps when he and his crew encountered bears and moose as they paddled their canoes on the Saint-Laurent and Ottawa rivers in search of Natives with whom they could trade for beaver pelts.

They apparently had a good haul, not just beaver furs but fox, mink, and other animals for which he had traded European-made goods such as axes, knives, some jewelry, brightly colored ribbons and even some fabrics. They'd had to portage many times to get to the grouping of great inland seas that had become legend throughout New France—Huron, Mishigami, and Supérieur. He spoke of a Jesuit missionary and explorer he met, Père Jacques Marquette, on an island in a narrow waterway connecting two of the great lakes, a place he called Michilimackinac.

The moon was setting when our guest finally left. I had said, "Bonne nuit" and gone to bed, barely stirring when Armand crawled in next to me. But his touch on my shoulder, his fingers tracing down my arm, and his breath on my neck aroused me. I knew what he wanted, and I turned toward him, happy to oblige, although the image of Jacques Farley standing wet-haired and bare-chested in our doorway tantalized me.

In the morning, as I cooked eggs in a large flat pan over a freshly stoked fire, I asked, "How do you know that man?"

"Jacques? He's been a friend ever since I've lived here." Armand settled himself at the table.

"I've seen him before. At the hospital. When Catherine was there." I spooned the eggs onto a plate and set it in front of him. "He was with a Native man, a shaman of some sort."

"The *arendiwane*?" He lifted a spoonful of eggs to his mouth and ate with relish.

"Farley gave money to Sœur Helene. I meant to ask her about it. Do you have any idea why he was there?"

"I suppose to pay for Catherine's hospital stay." He spread butter and honey on a slab of bread. When I looked confused, he said, "Jacques is Catherine's sponsor. He pays her fees at the convent."

"Jacques Farley does that?" I couldn't have been more astounded. "The man who broke Denis Boutard's nose in a tavern brawl?"

"True, he is not a man you want to cross." He bit into the bread, wiped his sleeve across his mouth before continuing. "But when Catherine's parents were killed by the Iroquois and she was held captive, Jacques found her and bartered for her freedom. He brought her to the Ursulines and has paid her upkeep ever since."

I handed Armand a linen cloth in the hopes of salvaging his honeyed sleeve. He used it to swipe at the sleeve in earnest.

Just as I couldn't understand the hatred of someone like that hag of a fish seller who harbored such hatred toward Catherine, I was baffled by this man who caused fear in others with his fists, but took a young, orphaned Metis girl under his wing and made sure she had a place to live and an education. Did he have designs on her? Did he wish to take her as his wife when she was a few years older? But what of her scars? Will they change the way he thinks of her? What would this Jacques Farley do, now that she was too scarred for most men to look at? So many questions peppered my mind, but they weren't the kind I felt comfortable asking my husband about his good friend.

Instead, I said, "People say he's an outlaw. A coureur des bois."

"People say a lot of things. I wouldn't listen to them." He set the napkin down and reached for the mug of apple cider I had set in front of him.

Sinking into the chair across from him, I said, "I guess I don't deserve to throw stones." I couldn't shake the memory of King Louis giving me a choice between going into the convent or coming here to Québec in order to save my head.

"I think none of us do," Armand said. "According to the King's law, he's not exactly official. He trades on the sly. But here in New France, if you can man a canoe, and you're brave enough to go out into the wilderness to make your living, and you manage to come back alive, who's to stop you? Jacques is a good man at heart."

He spooned the last of his eggs into his mouth. "A good breakfast." He stood and bussed me on the cheek before heading to the door where his musket stood at the ready. "I hope to be back before dark."

I watched as LeDuc followed him out the door, thinking about what I needed to do with my day.

That afternoon I went into town to the Gravel's store to see what fabric they had in stock. While Armand had built wooden shutters to close off our windows in cold, drafty weather, I wanted something to hang inside. Claudette's words about me being a threat to the wives in town still rankled, but hers was the only store selling the embroidered wool panels I would need to keep the winter winds out.

Claudette was alone in the shop when I walked in, the chimes over the door tinkling as it opened and closed. "Sylvienne? What can I do for you?" Her glance drifted to my stomach, which had recently become obvious, and which I no longer took pains to hide. "It seems you and Captain Gervais are soon to become parents. That will please the Intendant. But you are big so soon."

Ignoring her comment lest I lunge at her and choke her to death, I strode over to the table with folded panels of woven wool fabric imported from the Languedoc region of France. While some of the farmers here in the colony raised sheep, the process of converting the raw wool to a usable fabric was so time intensive, the resulting fabric was seldom offered for sale but used directly in the home of the sheep owner.

"This one is pretty." I held up a cream-colored woolen curtain panel woven with green vines and leaves.

"Did you hear?" Claudette said in an undertone, looking around to make sure no one else was in the shop. "That outlaw is back in town."

"Which outlaw?" I kept my expression neutral, but I suspected we were thinking of the same person.

"His name is Jacques Farley. He grew up in France, but they say he is half Irish and has a temper and the fists to match."

"I didn't know the Irish were temperamental," I said as we walked to the checkout counter with the panels I had chosen.

"This one is. I hear he broke Denis Boutard's nose the day before my wedding just for talking about one of those sauvage women when they were drinking in the Grey Goose."

I felt my hackles rise at her use of the word. "Please stop calling them that. The man must have said something wholly inappropriate to deserve such treatment."

"Apparently a man doesn't have to say much around this brute Farley to get his face bloodied." She wrapped my purchase in burlap. "He fancies himself half-Indian, they say. Living out in the woods."

"A lot of people have houses in the woods. Not everyone lives within the village walls."

"He doesn't live in a house. He lives *in* the woods. With the sau—" At my look of warning, she finished with, "the Natives."

"People say a lot of things. It's best not to listen to them," I said, repeating Armand's words.

I left after handing over my coins, the door chimes tinkling again upon my exit. In truth, I was glad Claudette had listened to the gossip this time. So, Jacques Farley lived among the Natives. That was interesting. Maybe the Native people had more influence on his demeanor than his French and Irish forebears.

Pushing open the door to the house, I was immediately assailed by the stench of damp fur and skinned animal hides. A row of pelts hung from a rafter near the fireplace. Armand sat at the table cleaning his field pistol, the parts spread out on the table.

"What are those?" I said, holding a finger under my nose.

"Beaver pelts." He polished the barrel with a cloth.

"I know they are beaver pelts. But why are they hanging in our house?"

"Jacques brought them. Repayment for some money he owed me."

"Beaver pelts? And what do you intend to do with them?"

"I'll take them down to the wharf." He started reassembling the weapon. "And sell them to one of the ship owners getting ready to set off for France. They'll fetch a good price."

"And why doesn't Monsieur Farley take them to the wharf and sell them himself? And then give you the money?"

Armand shrugged. "It's just the way we've always done it."

"And what if the price of beaver pelts goes down before you get to the river?"

Armand gave me a quizzical look. "What's gotten into you, Sylvienne? What's done is done."

I glanced at the beaver skins. "They smell awful."

He stood up, hefting his cleaned pistol, "I'll take them out to the shed."

Jacques Farley stopped by again a day later. Armand pulled out a jug of locally made beer and two mugs. He poured a glass of wine for me, and we sat around the kitchen table. The men talked and joked for a while, Farley telling more stories of his time on the river.

I studied the face of this man, this coureur des bois who sponsored a young Wendat girl at the convent. His eyes were lively, his skin darkened from the sun and weathered from wind. His smile was broad and genuine. When there was a break in the men's conversation, I couldn't resist quizzing him to learn more.

"Are you not married, Monsieur Farley?" I asked.

"At the moment, no."

"Why not?" I asked as I poured more beer into his mug.

"What do you mean?" He seemed surprised by my question.

I poured another glass of wine for myself. "I understand you are half French."

"I am."

"And so, under the jurisdiction of the King." My voice took on the tone of an inquisitor.

"Supposedly." He narrowed his eyes, likely wondering where I was going with this line of inquiry.

Glancing over at Armand, I lifted an eyebrow, but I directed my question to our guest. "Are you not bound by the rule of the Crown?" I'm not sure why I felt the need to nettle him so, but I couldn't stop.

Armand remained impassive, watching me with guarded eyes as I pushed on. "There is an edict requiring men to marry or lose their hunting and fishing privileges."

Farley leaned back in his chair. "That there is." He glanced at Armand, bemusement crinkling his eyes.

I pressed on. "Armand was exempt from seeking a wife while he conducted the census. But now, even he has married."

"That is because he found a beautiful woman willing to marry a man with no manners." He winked at Armand.

"That's beside the point," I said. "Do you not see the problem here?" This last directed at Armand.

"Honestly, no," my husband said.

"This man flouts the law. In this respect and many others." I turned back to face his friend. "Do you disdain women? Or just the King's rule?"

Farley stiffened. "Neither." Flattening his hands on the table, he stood abruptly. "If you will excuse me, madame, I think I have overstayed my welcome." Without another word, and only a nod to Armand, he strode out the door.

LeDuc followed part way, his tail sagging as if he sensed the mood in the room had changed.

I turned to Armand who had yet to speak. "Did I say something wrong?"

Armand put a hand on my arm. "Sylvienne, this is not like you. Don't be so quick to judge."

His words hit me like a hammer. Of course. What had I done? Jacques Farley was a guest and I'd been rude to him. With a grimace of remorse, I started clearing the table. "I wonder, Armand. Will I ever be like you?"

Now Armand sounded confused. "What do you mean?"

I stood with the mugs in my hand. "I *am* being quick to judge. Finding fault where there is none with someone I just met. I think I do it too often."

"You didn't judge me when we first met." He offered a conciliatory smile.

"Don't be so sure." I gave him a sassy look, before taking the mugs to the wash bucket.

CHAPTER SEVENTEEN

It was getting harder to get out of bed in the mornings. My stomach was rounder, and it seemed I was tired all the time. But I was looking forward to this day. Armand had the day off, and he had promised to row me over to the island they called Orléans to visit with Perrette. Probably the last chance we would have before the weather turned and the river became unnavigable to small craft.

The sun rose, a ball of melted butter in the haze. There was little wind, and I was hopeful the river would be calm so we could make the trip without me getting nauseous. I stoked the fire, then prepared our breakfast.

Armand was just coming in through the back door from having fed and watered Shadow when someone called out his name from the front yard. I glanced up with curiosity as he answered the door to a young soldier who looked as if he'd been running.

"Captain Gervais, there's been an accident." He bent over a moment to catch his breath. "Lauzon's weapon misfired during shooting practice. He is severely wounded."

That was Françoise's husband. I set down my cooking pan and moved closer to hear what had happened.

"Where is he now?" Armand asked.

"The men carried him up to the Hôtel-Dieu."

"I'll come." Armand turned toward me apologetically.

"Go. Go!" I urged. "We'll plan the trip for another day." Even though another day with weather this perfect was unlikely to occur again until next spring, I didn't want him tarrying if Françoise's husband was in danger.

He bussed me on the cheek and hurried out.

With a sigh, I ate my breakfast alone, musing about how to rearrange my plans for the day. My first thought was to go to Françoise. But by now she would be at the hospital, her sister Geneviève at her side to give her support. What they didn't need was another body crowding the premises. She would need my support later if the worst happened, and her husband didn't survive.

There was always laundry to do. The rugs needed beating. It wouldn't hurt to write a note to Perrette apologizing for not coming. I could send it with one of the ferry boats down at the landing.

A knock on the door and Jacques Farley's head peering in startled me out of my planning. "Bonjour!" he said.

"Oh! Monsieur Farley. I...I didn't expect to see you. I want to apologize for being rude to you the other day," I said.

"Apology accepted." He smiled as he stepped inside, and I knew instantly his words were sincere.

"Armand has already left for work."

"I know. I passed him on my way over. He said you were planning a trip to d'Orléans, and he has spoiled the day for you."

"One of his men was injured. It couldn't be helped."

"So I understand. It would be unfortunate to waste one of the best days for traveling before the weather changes. I could ferry you over."

"That would be too much trouble."

"It's no trouble. I have business acquaintances there. It would be good for me stop in and see them."

Still, I hesitated. Did I want to be beholden to this man? On the other hand, I didn't want to wait until next spring to see Perrette again. "I would have to get word to Armand."

"He was the one who suggested I take you. But only if you wish it. And only if you call me Jacques."

"He said that?"

"No. I am requesting it." His grin was almost shy as he ran a hand through his hair. "Call me whatever you like, I am happy to ferry you."

I bit my lip. Armand thought highly of his friend. He wouldn't have asked him to take me if he didn't trust the man. "I only plan to visit for a couple of hours."

"That is exactly how many hours I have available today."

Accepting his offer, I packed a few things in a cloth bag, and we walked down to the river where Jacques's birchbark canoe was tucked up under a tree about a dozen paces from the water. He gave me the paddle to carry, then picked up the canoe and hefted it over his head, marching it down to the water's edge. He helped me across the sandy embankment and into the canoe. I had never been in a craft such as this and was nervous lest I tip it over.

"Hang on to the edges for balance. You'll be fine," he said.

Once I was settled, he pulled off his deerskin moccasins and threw them into the canoe before pushing it farther out into the river. When he was about knee-deep in the water, he deftly grabbed the edge of the craft and heaved himself over and into it. To my surprise, even though I clutched the edges fearfully, the canoe barely rocked as he settled himself in the back. He picked up the paddle and shoved it against the water, the canoe quickly finding the current.

"Are you comfortable?" he asked.

I nodded, barely registering his words, so enthralled was I by the landscape. On one side of the river was the village of Québec, on the other the lush greenery of virgin forests. Of course, I'd been on the Saint-Laurent in the ship, but this was different. We were on the narrower Saint-Charles, sitting close to the water. Everything felt more intimate, our craft more vulnerable.

After a while I glanced back at my helmsmen. Despite his deerskin leggings and the fringed sleeves of his tunic, I could sense the strength in his lean body. We sliced through the water at a fast pace, even though it seemed he put barely any effort into paddling. Before long, we reached the mouth of the Saint-Charles and merged onto the larger Saint-Laurent River.

After a long period of awkward silence, awkward on my part at least, I asked, "How do you manage when you are out collecting beaver hides? I mean in talking with the Natives?"

"Some speak French. I have learned enough of the local tongues to get by."

"How many languages do you know?"

"I haven't counted."

"French. Wendat, I assume," I said, holding up my fingers.

"Wendat, yes. I've managed to learn enough to trade with the Mohawk, the Oneida, and the Seneca. I've spent time among the Ojibwe. And I get along with the Cree. So a few, I guess."

"And English? Your father was from Ireland, wasn't he?"

"He spoke Gaeilge, as he called it. Irish Gaelic. So, yes, I speak that. And a bit of English"

"So that's…I've lost count.

He laughed. "And what about you? You must have studied Latin at the convent school growing up."

"I did. And some Italian and Greek. But I've forgotten most of both. I am learning Wendat."

"Good for you! It will be most helpful here in New France. Who is your teacher?"

"A girl at the convent school. I think you know her. She goes by Catherine."

"D'hanate," Jacques said. "She is a sweet girl. And very smart. You have a good teacher."

"Armand says you pay her tuition fees."

"Ah! We are here."

The canoe shuddered as it scraped the rocks in the shallow waters near the island. Jacques jumped out. I reached out a hand to take his, but before I knew it, he had grasped my waist and lifted me out as easily as he might a toddler and set me on the dry shore. After he pulled the canoe up out of the water, we found the path to Perrette's house.

Perrette hugged me warmly, the older of her two little ones peeking from the doorway of the modest stone farmhouse. Eying Jacques warily, Perrette's eyebrows rose when I introduced him. He bowed gallantly, then took his leave, saying he would come to fetch me in two hours' time.

As he strode off, Perrette said, her eyes wide now, "Jacques Farley ferried you over here?"

"Do you know of him?" I asked.

"Everyone on the island knows of Jacques Farley. Everyone in Québec, too, I would venture."

"Why? Is he so infamous?"

"Depends on which side of him you encounter. Some say he's the kindest, most generous rogue they've ever met. Others say to keep your distance if you want to keep your limbs intact. His temper is fierce and his counsel swift."

Watching his back disappear down the path, I shrugged. "He is an enigma."

Perrette apologized that her husband, Jean, was not home. He was a wheelwright and was at a neighbor's outfitting a wagon. Her gaze fell to my stomach. Her eyes lit up. "You're with child!"

Instinctively, I put a hand on the mound. It had grown considerably since my wedding.

"A legacy from your husband in France?"

Of course, she would know there was no way I could be this large from being so recently wed. I tried to tell her she was correct, but my voice caught in my throat and my eyes welled with tears. Before I could stop myself, I was sobbing. She led me inside and to a chair near the fireplace and pulled up another to sit next to me. She took my hand. It occurred to me the last time we were together in Amiens, our positions were reversed, Perrette sobbing in despair and me comforting her.

"Oh, my dear friend, you must miss your Monsieur le Duc terribly," she said.

I wanted to agree, to make her think my life in France had been perfect, but she was too good a friend to fool. "Perrette, the truth is, I do not know if it is his."

Her eyes widened in surprise for the briefest of moments. "Your marriage to the duke, it was not…?"

"He was a terrible man. A womanizer from the beginning. But I must confess, I was not a faithful wife either."

"And now he is dead. How did it happen?"

"It is a long story."

"I have all the time in the world."

I told her everything. She already knew I had married a duke, but she did not know the circumstances under which it had happened, the unexpected announcement of a betrothal without my consent. The wedding. Discovering Rene had a lover, the wife of his banker.

"And the other man in your story?"

My cheeks reddened and my gaze would not rise to meet hers. "I think you know."

"Etienne?" She was shocked and delighted at the same time. "I always knew you were meant to be together."

I told her, then, about my life at Court, my wedding to René, his abusiveness, especially when he was drunk. About my trysts with Etienne, with the help of Philippe, the King's brother, my ally at court.

"I heard about the sad death of his wife, Madame Henriette," she said.

"Henriette was a good friend to me. I missed her terribly, I still do."

When finally I came to the end of my story, how my husband had tried so viciously to kill Etienne, and how I had stopped him, forever, and the King's anger and my ultimate decision to come here to New France rather than hide away in a convent, she hugged me again. "And this baby you carry? Is it the duke's? Or could it be…?"

"I won't know until she is born. Until I can look into her eyes."

"You think it will be a girl?" She smiled.

"I know it will be a girl. It just seems right."

"And if her eyes are like yours rather than her father's…?"

I shrugged. "Maybe it would be for the best—that I should never know."

She squeezed my hand. "Perhaps you are right. Let her begin her life as the daughter of Captain Armand Gervais. Though I wish your mother was here to read her stones for you."

"Perrette, you are not going to believe this." I told her about my own collection of stones that I'd brought with me from France, and how the girls on the ship all wanted me to read for them. And about Beatrix, the night before we were to meet the eligible men at the convent.

"And did you? Could you? You always said you didn't have the gift like your mother."

"I don't know if I have the gift, but I seem to know what they want to hear. So that's what I tell them."

"Have you been wrong with any of them?"

I shrugged. "Not so far as I know."

She smiled. "I'm not surprised." Rising, she said, "We must have some lunch, and you will tell me about your new life here. And why the infamous scoundrel, Jacques Farley, ferried you to my island."

We had a glorious time together, and when it was time to go, Perrette walked with me down the path to where the canoe had been left. "Thank you for bringing my friend safely across the water," she said to Jacques.

"My pleasure, madame."

Perrette and I hugged while Jacques slid the canoe back into the water. As we set out across the river, he had to paddle against the current, but it seemed as if it took not much more effort than when the current was with us. Sitting facing him, this time, I prattled like a bird about Perrette and our lives in France, and how delighted I was to be in her company again. Jacques listened with a curious smile, speaking little. After a while I ran out of words and sat quietly, watching the other craft on the Saint-Laurent. Before long we merged onto the smaller Saint-Charles.

Without thinking, I asked him, "Why do you do it?"

"Do what?"

"Ply the rivers. Spend your life trading for beaver pelts."

He shrugged.

"For *la gloire*?" I asked.

At this he laughed. But when he saw my earnest look, he shook his head. "The life of fur trader is hardly one of glory."

"What then?"

He pondered for a moment. "It's sort of like an itch. A thirst for knowing, I guess."

"I understand the desire to learn. But didn't you go to school? Don't you read books?"

"I read. But this…it's more akin to an insatiable curiosity. A need to know what is around the next bend in the river." He pointed his paddle toward a mound on the far shore. "Or on the other side of that hillock. Those vast lakes to the west I spoke of at dinner that night…they are only just being charted. You won't find them in books."

Ahead was the bend in the Saint-Charles beyond which we would see my house.

"What is going on there?" I asked as he maneuvered the curve. A group of men stood on the shore at the edge of Armand's property. Two of them wore soldier's uniforms and held muskets aimed toward us.

"*Merde!*" Jacques cursed under his breath.

"Why are they there? What do they want?"

He grunted. "We'll find out soon enough." He paddled to the shore, jumped out of the canoe, then lifted me out. Two of the men sloshed through the water and grabbed the canoe.

As Jacques set me onto the dry shore, a man I recognized from Talon's office stepped forward. "Jacques Farley, you are under arrest."

CHAPTER EIGHTEEN

I met Armand at the door. After preparing a quick meal for his return, I had begun to pace, watching the sun sink toward the trees as I waited for him. Why had Talon's men taken Jacques away? What had he done? What would happen to him? Did Armand know of this?

My head jerked up at the sound of LeDuc's bark, the happy one he always gave when he was within sight of the house. I pulled open the door and LeDuc sprinted toward me, anxious to get his ears rubbed and nosing for a treat.

Armand immediately noticed my distress. "What's the matter?" he asked. "What's happened?"

"Jacques has been arrested."

"What? Why? What did he do now?" Armand followed me inside, slung his musket from his shoulder and set it against the wall.

"I don't know. Nothing. You didn't know? He took me over to see Perrette. We had just gotten back, and Talon's men were waiting on the shore. They took him away." My voice must have manifested my anxiety, for he put his hands on my shoulders to calm me.

"It's all right. I'll go to the administration building and find out what's going on. LeDuc should stay here with you."

"What about your dinner?"

"I'll eat when I get back. You go ahead, don't wait for me." Reaching for his musket again, he headed back out.

LeDuc whined when he realized the door had closed, and Armand was leaving without him.

"It's okay," I said. "Come over here. I have a treat for you."

The dog barked once at the door before trotting over to claim some scraps of meat and a bone I had saved for him. I covered Armand's dinner with a towel to keep the flies off. And mine. I had no appetite for eating alone.

It was dark by the time Armand returned, looking weary and frustrated.

"What did you find out?" I asked as I pulled the towel from our now cold dinners.

He dipped his hands in the wash bucket. "They're threatening to charge him with collaborating and trading with the British."

"Threatening?" I poured beer into a mug for him as he dried his hands and sat down at the table.

"Courcelle needs his help with some negotiating." He tore off a hunk of bread, smeared it with butter, and stuffed a portion into his mouth.

"The governor? He couldn't just ask?" I set plates of sliced beef and stewed carrots and peas on the table, then sat down across from him.

Armand snorted. "You'd think that would be the easy way, wouldn't you? But with Jacques, the easy way never seems to work."

"What kind of negotiating? With whom? Where?"

Armand washed his bread down with a swallow of beer. "At a settlement called Kahnawake. It's a Jesuit mission. The Mohawk have taken a group of priests there hostage."

"Mohawk? Aren't they part of the Iroquois confederacy?"

"Mm." He started in on the cold beef. "This is good."

"Armand, you've spoken often about how dangerous the Mohawk are despite the treaty."

"Unfortunately, Jacques is one of the few who speak their language with any level of fluency and the only one they respect enough to negotiate with."

"So...he can go and face down a dangerous group of Iroquois or sit in the garrison prison for God knows how long?" I set my knife down. "Is he going to do it?"

"Doesn't have much choice. But he...um...made one condition." He glanced up at me.

I waited as he reached for his beer.

"He will only do it if I go along with him." He took a long drink to avoid my eyes.

In the morning, I watched with sullen worry as Armand packed a leather haversack with pemmican, hardtack, ammunition, gunpowder, and a few other supplies. He had assured me they would be gone no more than two weeks.

"But why must you go alone? Can't you take some of your men with you?"

"A large group of soldiers would only raise tensions," he said. "I promise you we will be careful." He took my face in his hands and kissed me. "I want *you* to be careful here. See if Catherine will come and stay with you. And I'm leaving LeDuc with you also."

"Why? So he can lick an intruder to death?" LeDuc had proven to be one of the friendliest and most amenable dogs I had ever known.

"Don't let his gallant nature fool you. He will protect you. And don't go outside without the musket."

Jacques appeared at the door. "Are you ready?" he asked Armand. "Sorry to leave you alone this way," he said to me, a grim look on his face.

"Just come back safely. Both of you."

Armand kissed me again. I watched as he hefted his pack and his musket. The two men headed down to the river where Jacques's canoe waited, already laden with items to barter or to offer as gifts, as well as his musket and the hatchet I knew he always carried with him. A shiver of dread traveled down my spine.

LeDuc trotted part way down with them, but when Armand ordered him to go back to me, he stood watching, his tail sagging.

Once they had pushed off, I called out, "LeDuc! Come."

He barked in the direction of the river, then turned and ran back to me, his demeanor suddenly protective. He nosed me for a treat, and I gave him a bit of the pemmican he loved so much.

I put on a clean coif and my cloak, as the weather was beginning to turn. "Shall we go find Catherine?"

LeDuc wagged his tail and trotted to the door.

We made the trek into town. I stopped at the hospital first to say hello to the sisters and to visit with the patients—two men, one with a head wound from a tavern fight, the other with a gunshot wound to the leg, a hunting accident apparently, and one woman with fever and an abscess in her tooth. I had learned from my time there as a temporary scribe that regardless of why the patients were there, they took great cheer whenever a visitor stopped to say a few words to them.

Afterward, we made our way to the Ursuline convent. Catherine was more than happy to spend two weeks with me at the house when I asked. She packed a few personal items and some spare clothing while I walked down to the lower village to buy bread, fish, and some late season vegetables. When I had first arrived in this rustic place, I thought I would have to learn to hunt and fish and make my own bread. I was ever thankful that this small village was not unlike villages and cities in France, with a boulangerie that sells bread and a meat and fish market with fresh offerings on a daily basis. I was even more grateful that with Armand's income and the money from my dowry we could afford to do so.

When Catherine was ready, with LeDuc tagging happily along, we walked back out through the town gate and along the river to Armand's property. Catherine had not been to the house yet, and she delighted in exploring it, declaring it to be grand. We settled in to cook our first dinner together.

I had a list in my head of projects she could help me with, things that needed doing around the house before winter set in: adding bindings to the wool window coverings, making berry pies to store in the well for winter, mending the dresses I'd brought from France which were already starting to fray. I had it in mind to make some wool dresses that would be more practical and keep me warm in the winter. And there were baby swaddles, gowns, and caps to be stitched. With Catherine's help and no distraction from the menfolk, I thought we could get much done.

The second day she was with me, an early frost caused the pair of black walnut trees out front to drop their nuts. Catherine and I went out to scoop them up.

"So many!" I said.

"You will have enough to last through the winter."

We quickly filled the first couple of baskets, and I went into the shed to get two more. When I stepped back outside, I heard a huffing sound from behind the bushes edging the front side of our property.

"Did you hear that?" I asked.

Catherine straightened up to listen. She stiffened as a large black animal, not as tall as a horse but heftier, emerged from the brush. It sniffed the air. Catherine drew in a deep frightened breath.

"What is it?" I asked.

"Have you never seen a bear?" she said, her voice quiet as she edged slowly back toward me and the house.

"We don't have them in France, except in the mountains near Spain. Is it dangerous?"

As if in answer to my question, LeDuc, who had been lying in the shade of the tree, rose to his feet and growled. At that moment, a baby bear ambled out from behind a bush on the other side of Catherine.

The mother bear huffed again, swaying her head back and forth. Catherine stood frozen, but she was caught between the mother and baby and was too far from the house to get back to it safely.

Moving quietly but quickly, I stepped inside and grabbed the musket from against the wall. It was already loaded. Armand insisted we keep at least one at the ready at all times.

Catherine edged toward the house, but the mother bear loped toward her. I hefted the musket against my shoulder, aimed, and...*BOOM!*

The shot missed the bear, instead hitting the dirt around its feet. The startled bear paused and swirled around once in confusion. Then it headed toward Catherine again. She screamed and ran. That's when LeDuc went into action. He charged the bear, barking and snarling, nipping its hind quarters, dodging its clawed paw slashing out at him. He ran toward the cub and harried it until it took off, running back through the brush, the mother following. LeDuc chased them to the woods.

Catherine ran into my arms, and we stood clutching each other, shaking. I called out for LeDuc who had disappeared after the bears. I called him again. We waited a few anxious moments until finally he emerged from the brush, his tail wagging in triumph,

I hugged him tightly.

"I think we have enough walnuts," I said to Catherine. "And you, Monsieur LeDuc, have earned a royal treat today."

We grabbed our baskets and lugged them around back where we would remove the outer hulls. I went inside to prepare a bowl of left-over roasted rabbit for LeDuc to glory over.

Catherine set the green walnut globes we'd collected on a section of hard-packed earth and began stomping the hulls to loosen them while I reloaded the musket. From then on, I always made sure the gun was close at hand when I was working in the yard.

It turned out to be nearly three weeks before Armand returned. LeDuc barked loudly to announce the homecoming. I threw my arms around my husband in relief. Once he had put his gear away, I asked "Jacques did not come back with you?"

"He went on to the Ojibwe village on the other side of the Saint-Laurent. The one where he spends his winters."

"I didn't know he did that." I felt a discomfiting disappointment that he hadn't returned with Armand. I shrugged it off. "The negotiations? Were they successful?"

"It seems so. The priests were let go. Unharmed for the most part. The Mohawk want certain concessions from the governor. But we expected that going in, so we were able to make the necessary deals. Hopefully this peace will last for a while."

"That's good. I was worried." I touched his hand, and he responded by squeezing mine. We would celebrate his return in bed that evening.

After giving him a quick meal of smoked fish, bread, and stewed apples, I proudly showed Armand the baskets of black walnuts Catherine and I had harvested, now reduced to the rough, dark inner shells needing a few more weeks of drying before we could start hammering them open to use. And I told him of the bear, and how I tried to shoot it but missed.

"You were not wrong about LeDuc," I said. "It was he who saved us." The dog's ears perked up and his tail swung wildly at the mention of his name.

Armand nodded approvingly and ruffled LeDuc's ears, then the dog's tummy when he rolled over for more attention. "Too bad you didn't hit the bear, though," he said looking up at me with a teasing smile. "We could've had enough pemmican and bear jerky to last a year."

CHAPTER NINETEEN

Catherine went back to the convent. I missed her during the day while Armand was at the garrison. Fortunately, LeDuc had become content to stay with me. Armand said he preferred it that way.

Snow started falling the last week in October, huge, elegant flakes settling on the bare tree limbs like lacy sleeves. We'd had snow in France, of course, but it never lasted more than a day or two before soaking into the ground, turning the usually hard-packed roads and paths into muddy lanes. Here it fell whiter, brighter, deeper, first covering the fields like a thin sheet, then a thick blanket. Eventually the flakes thinned out and began blowing sideways, the bare trees and the pines swaying in a restless dance.

Watching out the window, wrapped in the bed quilt, I worried about Armand at the fort. Was his capot, his coat, heavy enough? Did the toque I had knitted to keep his head warm cover his ears? Had he remembered to take the woolen mittens I'd set out for him to wear inside his deerskin hand coverings? I glanced back at the bench next to the door. The mittens were gone. My shoulders eased, though only a bit. Earlier in the day the snow had been beautiful, mesmerizing as it floated lazily down; but now it looked angry, desultory. I already had a pot of pea, cabbage, and ham hock soup hanging over the fire, something hot for Armand's return.

When he finally trudged up to the house, the snow reached nearly to his knees, clinging to his deerskin boots and wool leggings as he walked through the door.

"Time to get the *raquettes* out, I think." He shook the flakes off his shoulders and cap.

"Raquettes?" At Versailles, King Louis and his brother Philippe had played tennis with raquettes. Why would Armand want to take them out now, in the middle of a snowstorm?

"You'll want a pair as well. I can commission Joseph Medard down in the lower village to make some sized to fit you." He hung his coat on the peg nearest the fire. When he saw the confused look on my face, he said, "They are for walking on the snow."

"Shoes for the snow?" I served up two bowls of hot soup and set them on the table along with some sliced bread. Armand sat down eagerly, barely waiting for me to sit before he dug in.

"Exactly. They are webbed and fit under your boots so you can walk on top of the snow."

"Why do we want to walk on top of the snow?" The image of it seemed funny to me, walking on the snow with shoes shaped like King Louis's tennis raquettes.

"Have you seen it out there?" He motioned toward the window. "You don't want to sink in."

"It won't last. Will it?"

"It will last until spring. This is just the beginning. A couple more storms and we'll have to dig out to get the front door open."

My soup spoon halfway to my mouth, I stared at him. "You're joking."

"Wait and see." He tore off a chunk of bread and dipped it into his soup, savoring the flavor as he bit into it.

After supper I glanced out the window again. It was too dark to see much, so I opened the front door. A gust of wind and snow blew in, and I shut it quickly. But it had been open just long enough for me to glimpse a mound of snow about a stride's length from the door. I shivered.

"Will it snow like this all night?" I asked.

"Hard to say. Most likely. Come sit by the fire with me. You're shaking."

He wrapped the quilt around me, and we snuggled together, drinking brandy in front of the blazing fire. Fortunately, he had laid in a large enough stock of firewood to last for several days.

When the snow finally stopped, Armand fetched his raquettes from the shed behind the house. They were odd looking contraptions with netting stretched across oval-shaped wood rims. He worked flax oil into the wood frame and the moosehide webbing to keep it supple. When he finished, he took a length of twine and measured my height and my feet. Afterward, he slipped his boot-clad feet into the leather bindings of his snowshoes and trod off toward the lower village to commission a pair for me.

A week or so later, Armand brought home my new snowshoes. I put on my woolen cloak and my deerskin boots and went outside to try them on. Giggling the whole time, I wobbled, struggling to find my balance with my protruding stomach. But eventually I got the hang of it. I quickly understood the advantage of wearing raquettes in deep snow.

Christmas Eve was upon us before long. Armand asked if I wanted to attend Midnight Mass. Neither of us had been to Mass in many weeks, he not since our wedding, and me, only sporadically due to my growing fatigue and the clumsiness of getting around, especially on snowshoes. Mostly, I had become ambivalent about regular attendance. I still sought solace in the religion I had been brought up in, but I didn't feel as dependent upon the rituals as I had when I was a child. I suspected some of that had to do with the irony of being required by King Louis to attend daily Mass at Versailles despite his own daily breech of the Ten Commandments.

However, this was our first Christmas together, and I was glad Armand had asked. Fresh snow fell in the morning, adding to what was already on the ground. By the late evening, the sky had cleared, and a multitude of stars crowded the inky heavens. A crescent moon hung low on the western horizon. We bundled in woolen layers and stepped onto our snowshoes. Armand lit a pine knot torch to light our way, the oily, sooty smoke rising gently into the calm, frigid air. Because there was no wind, I found the cold to be tolerable, and the night walk surprisingly pleasant, despite the fact I felt like I was waddling the entire way. The snow crunched under our snowshoes, and in the distance the church bell clanged, inviting us to Midnight Mass.

As we approached the church, I could see that a path leading up to the front door had been tamped down by early arrivals, their upright snowshoes lining both sides of the walkway. Behind each pair of snowshoes were the lit pine knot torches stuck into the snow, ready to be retrieved when Mass ended. What a magical scene for Christmas Eve! Nothing like the faerie lights that twinkled throughout the gardens of Versailles all year long, but still it took my breath away.

Armand stuck our raquettes into the snow along with the others and our torch behind it. We headed into the church and found our seats. Armand admitted to being a Catholic of convenience, having converted in order to join the King's army in France. He once confessed to me he didn't understand all the arguing and competition over religion. He said he suspected

God didn't really care what prayers were said or where they were said. It saddened him to see people persecuted for how they chose to worship. He didn't believe people were inherently evil just because they belonged to a different religion. He said he had never held the enemies he fought against to be evil either. And he took no joy in killing them in battle, whether it be the Dutch, the British, or the Iroquois. He believed in the tenet of "live and let live," unless of course, his life or those he cared about were threatened.

When he spoke such thoughts, he sometimes reminded me of Maman. Despite having been raised in a convent from the age of seven until she was given in marriage to Papa at fifteen, already with child, she did not believe she had to attend Mass every week in order to be a good person. She believed God would judge us all on how we behaved toward others. She told me once that the reason she sent me to the convent school in Amiens was because it was the only place a girl could get an education. Maman held education to be the most important way to nurture God's gift of an intellect. I was equally ambivalent about religion. Perhaps that was Maman's intention, for she never required me to go to Mass.

Lost in such thoughts, I was startled when the first notes of the small pipe organ sounded, and the congregation began singing the first carol. I quickly joined in, the words to "*Entre le bœuf et l'âne gris,*" forever etched in my mind, and the tune so lovely I often hummed it this time of year. One man's voice, rich and almost lilting, caught my ear as it rose above the rest of the congregation. I couldn't resist taking a quick look over my shoulder. To my surprise, the voice belonged to Jacques Farley, who stood at the far end of the last row. When he caught me looking, he winked. Turning away quickly, I felt heat in my cheeks as we finished the last verse.

After Mass, we stopped outside the church to chat with our many friends. I was glad to see Denis Lauzon, who had survived his wound from earlier in the fall when his weapon misfired. He walked with the use of a cane but was otherwise healthy. Françoise was pregnant and glowing.

Jacques slapped Armand on the back, his tone good-natured as he said, "So you decided you could put up with the priest's lecturing one night out of the year." Then to me, "The cold air suits you. You look radiant."

Despite the cold, heat reddened my cheeks again. "I was surprised to see *you* in church."

"I enjoy the carols," he said. "There's no point in coming any other time, as the good Father refuses me communion."

"Why is that?" I asked, realizing I hadn't seen him go up to the altar at communion time.

Armand answered for him, smirking. "Because he refuses to go to confession."

"And why is *that*?" I repeated, though I suspected I already knew the answer.

Jacques made his voice sound serious. "I fear Father Laval would die of apoplexy if he heard my tales of sinning."

Armand laughed and slapped his friend on the back. "Truer words were never said. Will you come to the house and join us in our *petite réveillon?* Sylvienne has tried her hand at her first *tourtière* for tonight."

"Pork pie? How could I say no?"

We invited Jeanne and Michel Leblanc to join us in the *réveillon* as well. The five us trudged along on top of the snow, the men lighting our way with their pine knot torches, our snowshoes *shush-crunching* as we walked along. The moon had set, and the stars seemed even closer. The scent of pine filled the air. Suddenly Jeanne stopped and grabbed my arm, nearly toppling me over.

"Something is wrong with the sky!" She pointed toward the north.

Following her gaze, I gasped at the sight of curtains of green and purple shimmering and pulsing across the sky. A whorl of magenta rose up forming angel wings before dissipating. All the while the stars shone through the mass of colored dancing light. A shiver ran through me. Was the world coming to an end?

"Armand!" I pointed upward, my hand trembling. "What's happening? Something terrible is going on."

"Mon Dieu!" Armand said, gazing upward. "I've heard of it but never thought I would see it with my own eyes."

"What is it?" I asked.

Jacques said, "The Ojibwe call it *waawaate*. In French, *les aurore boréale*."

"C'est magnifique!" The words came out in a whisper of awe.

"But why is it happening?" Jeanne asked. "It's as if the sky will explode."

"The Ojibwe say it means someone died. Their spirit is dancing through a portal to the other side. Those lights are their ancestors dancing to welcome them home."

"It's happened before?" Without thinking, I put my hands protectively over my bulging stomach.

"Many times," Jacques said.

The mesmerizing ribbons of color danced through and around the stars our entire walk home. Just as we reached the house, the lights faded, leaving me with an empty feeling. A longing. As much as it frightened me, I wanted to watch it all night.

In the house, we shed our outerwear and pulled up chairs around the table. LeDuc made the rounds of our guests for ear rubs and petting. Armand stoked the fire until it burned bright.

The tourtière, which I had baked earlier in the evening, was still warm. Its husky fragrance filled the house. I cut the pie into six pieces, one for each of us and one for baby Jesus, which Armand would eat in his honor Christmas day. He poured rounds of brandy for the men, Jeanne and I preferring red wine.

Armand, laughing, told of my attempt to chase off the bear while he was gone with Jacques to Kahnawake.

"You can fire a musket now?" Jacques said, his smile teasing.

"Yes, but I cannot yet hit a moving target, even one as big as a bear."

Jacques laughed. "The next time I come, I'll teach you to shoot a bow and arrow. Or maybe throw a hatchet."

Armand poured more brandy and wine, and we sang the songs of Christmas from our youth.

"Monsieur Farley," Jeanne said, "I heard you singing *'Entre le bœuf et l'âne gris'* at Mass. Would you sing it again for us?"

It was the first time I had ever seen the man blush, but in a soft, lilting voice he sang the familiar story of the ox and the grey ass keeping watch over the infant Jesus as he slept in his mother Mary's arms, while thousands of angels fill the sky overhead. This was a song I'd grown up with, one Maman had sung to me when I had trouble falling asleep as a child. By the time he sang the last refrain, and as we clapped for him, my eyes were moist.

"That was beautiful," I said.

He smiled and brought his brandy cup to his lips.

Jeanne broke the awkward silence, asking, "Monsieur Farley, how did you and Captain Gervais meet?"

A good question. Why had I never asked it? They seemed like such an odd pairing, my clean-shaven, uniformed, law-abiding Armand, and the unruly, unshaven, coureur des bois.

Armand laughed. "My first winter here, I had gone out on patrol when I stepped into a gully where the snow was waist deep. I was mired and couldn't get out. I thought I would freeze to death. I heard someone call out to me and looked over to see this man standing on top of the snow I was stuck in. 'How are you doing that?' I asked. And he said — "

"Haven't you ever heard of raquettes?" Jacques finished for him.

We all laughed.

"He packed the snow down with his snowshoes, and eventually I was able to walk out of the gully behind him. I invited him to join me for a drink as my way of thanking him. A week later he shows up at the barracks with a pair of raquettes for me, and we sealed our friendship."

"I couldn't believe someone as worldly as the captain of the King's militia had never heard of snowshoes!" Jacques said, setting everyone to laughing.

Armand said, "Truth be told, I had never been to a place in this world as cold or as snowy as Québec."

We all toasted to the idea of Québec winters and snowshoes.

When the toast ended, Michel stood. "I'm afraid we must go." He patted Jeanne on the arm. "A couple of hours sleep would be helpful before I go on duty."

We bid our friends, "Bonne nuit." Jacques started to rise as well, but Armand quickly stopped him with the offer of more brandy. As the two men dragged their chairs in front of the fire, I said good night and headed off to bed.

When I awoke in the dim light of dawn, Armand lay snoring softly beside me. As I watched his chest rise and fall, I couldn't help but think of the good fortune that had come my way since I stepped off the ship last summer. I had many good friends, Jeanne and Perrette being the foremost among them. I had a solid stone house with a sturdy roof over my head. And I had a husband who was kind and loving, and who I was sure would make a good father to my child.

When I left France, I thought my life was over. More than once, I had contemplated climbing over the side of the ship and letting the ocean waves devour me. I missed Maman greatly. And Tatie and Blondeau. They were the family I had enjoyed many *réveillons with, the family* I would never see again. And Etienne. It occurred to me I hadn't thought about him in a long while, not since my visit with Perrette before the snow set in and life took on a different measure of existence.

Forcing myself out of our warm bed, I dressed quickly and threw a shawl around my shoulders. I needed to stoke the fire before preparing breakfast. Walking out of the bedroom, I stopped short at the sight of a figure sprawled under a rough woolen blanket in front of the almost dead fire. Jacques, snoring not nearly as quietly as my husband. LeDuc lay snuggled alongside him.

I shouldn't have been surprised. I suspected he'd spent many a night sleeping off generous rounds of brandy in front of this very fire before I moved in. I didn't mind his being here, but unfortunately, neither he nor Armand had thought to bank the fire before crawling drunkenly into their respective bedding. The fireplace was nearly as cold as our front stoop.

With a grunt of frustration, I knelt before the hearth to arrange several split logs and add kindling. I used the flint fire-striker to create a spark. Once I had the kindling lit, I blew gently until the flames caught. The fire took hold and heated up so quickly, I thrust off my shawl.

As I watched the flames, I had an odd sensation of eyes upon me. I peered over my shoulder, surprised to see Jacques lying with his head propped up on his arm, gazing at me.

I grabbed up my shawl. "Did I wake you?"

"I thought maybe I was still dreaming."

"Dreaming of what?" Immediately, I regretted my impulsive question. Heat filled my cheeks for the third time that night.

He sat up, the blanket loose around his shoulders. "I find it quite pleasant to wake up to a roaring fire on Christmas morning."

I turned away to hide my embarrassment. What was I thinking? Feeling foolish, I picked up another log to add it to the already blazing flames, but I groaned inadvertently when a muscle in my back twinged.

"Let me help you with that." Jacques moved out from under the blanket and squatted next to me. I realized he was shirtless. The crane tattooed on his arm danced with his muscles as he ran his hand through his hair.

I blinked, realizing I had been staring at him. He reached for the log I held, and for a moment our hands touched. I breathed in sharply, quelling the unexpected heat stirring inside me now. He flashed a quick, almost embarrassed smile in my direction before adding the log to the fire.

"Bonjour! It's nice and warm out here."

We both jumped at the sound of Armand's voice.

CHAPTER TWENTY

Armand emerged from the bedroom, rubbing his eyes and looking as if he weren't quite over the effects of the wine, beer, and brandy he had consumed the night before. "Sylvienne, do you have anything in those herb jars of yours for my aching head?"

"Good morning, husband," I said, jumping up, while Jacques slid his shirt over his head.

I delivered a kiss to Armand's scratchy cheek before going to the kitchen area to fix him a draught of gingerroot, dried hyssop, and dried chamomile blended into boiled coffee. He sat at the table, head in hand, sipping at the concoction while I cooked eggs served with the leftover tourtière.

Jacques ate quickly, speaking only briefly to Armand, who grunted his replies. It was obvious my husband's head hurt too much for conversation. When he finished, Jacques handed me his plate and cup, then went to the hearth to pack his gear into a leather haversack.

While washing the dishes, I happened to glance over to find Jacques watching me. He quickly looked away and began dressing in layers of leggings, tunics, and his winter moccasin-style boots. He pulled his wool capote on last. The greatcoat hung to his knees. He thanked us for our hospitality, tucked his hatchet into his belt, and hefted his musket. Then he headed out the door, the frigid air wafting in behind him.

I moved to the window and watched as he stepped onto his snowshoes, tied the thin leather straps, and trudged off following the river trail, the snow glistening like diamonds around him. We likely wouldn't see him again until spring. Unbidden, a knot tugged in my chest.

Shrugging the tension from my shoulders, I turned back to Armand who was snoring, his head on the table cushioned by his arms. I shook his shoulder gently. "Go back to bed."

He sat up and squinted at me through bleary eyes. "Maybe just for another hour or so." But he didn't rise. "I've been thinking."

"Be careful," I said in a tease. "Thinking will make your head hurt more."

"I doubt it could hurt more." He rubbed his temple. "But…it looks to me like it is getting harder for you to manage around the house."

He wasn't wrong. I had grown so large with the babe my back often hurt. Simple tasks like pulling the quilt up over the bed exhausted me. As did cooking and cleaning, not to mention bringing in wood for the fire. Armand did what he could to help, but he was out of the house much of the day, working with his men or meeting with the governor and intendant regarding security issues in the colony.

Sitting now, with a cup of chamomile tea and a slice of bread with honey, I said, "My time is not far off." I tried not to let the worry of childbirth creep into my voice, but Armand's glance told me he was concerned as well.

"I don't like leaving you alone here so much. Do you think Catherine would be willing to come and stay with us? At least through the birth of the baby?"

"That's a wonderful idea. We should ask her."

"I'll go to the convent today and see what she says. Though not right this minute. I am going to take your suggestion and go back to bed for a while."

Reaching out to touch his hand, I was reminded how blessed I was to have this man. "I'll make some currant tarts for you to take to the sisters."

"You won't come to bed with me?" His eyes looked hopeful.

"If I do, neither of us will sleep, and I'll get no work done. You go."

He kissed me and headed back to the bedroom, while I puttered slowly about the kitchen preparing the treats for him to take to the convent.

When they arrived late in the afternoon, both their cheeks red from the cold, Armand swaggered like a man who'd accomplished a precarious mission. Catherine's eyes shone with delight. She threw herself awkwardly into my arms and thanked me profusely for allowing her to come and wait on me.

"Catherine," I said with a laugh. "I don't want you to wait on me. We will work side by side. I want your companionship."

"I'll take her things up to the loft," Armand said after he'd shed his outer cloak. "Then I need to head out to the barn."

Catherine and I clasped hands, hers still cold despite her deerskin mittens. We had lots to talk about, lots to do.

We celebrated the new year, just the three of us, with a blizzard fierce enough to keep us indoors the entire day. However, Armand needed to check on Shadow and the chickens. He pulled on his heavy capot, toque, and mittens.

"I won't be long," he said. "Warm some wine for my return."

He ordered LeDuc to stay inside with me.

Catherine filled a small cauldron with wine and hung it near the fire, while I watched nervously as he disappeared into the blinding snow. The wind blew so ferociously I could only keep the door open for a moment, and I had to put my shoulder against it to get it to close. I shivered with the cold, and Catherine ran to get my quilt and wrap it around me. LeDuc paced at the door, waiting for his master's return.

I instructed Catherine to add cinnamon sticks, cloves, anise seeds, and a splash of brandy to the heated wine, while I sliced a loaf of bread and set out some plum preserves.

"He's been gone a long time," I said, looking out the back window. All I could see was a flurry of white.

"He's likely still in the barn," Catherine tried to reassure me.

I waited a while longer, busying myself with everyday chores, but Armand still didn't return. LeDuc whined at the door, then began barking frantically.

"Something must have happened. I should go look for him," I said.

"Madame, you can't. It's too dangerous out there. You'll get lost between the house and the barn."

"Lost? Could Armand be—?" Mon Dieu! What if he was out there in the snow? As I reached for my heavy cloak and mittens, I glanced around the room. "Catherine, the rope over there. Fetch it for me. Tie it around my wrist."

Once we had secured the rope, I pulled the door open. LeDuc immediately dashed out. I tied the rope to the outside handle of the door and turned to follow him. The path to the barn was almost completely snowed over. I called out Armand's name. LeDuc appeared from out of nowhere and barked at me. Trying to follow him, I left the path and stumbled through deep drifts. I tripped over something and landed on my knees.

"Armand!"

He was lying in the snow. He groaned. "I can't feel my feet." His teeth chattered.

"Can you stand? Lean on me." I managed to help him to his knees, then to his feet. Slowly we made our way back to the house using the rope as our guide.

Catherine shoved the door closed behind us. We pulled off Armand's coat and he collapsed onto a chair in front of the fire, shivering. I pulled off his mittens, horrified at how white his fingers were. After pulling off his boots and wet leggings, I wrapped him in the quilt I'd used earlier.

Catherine filled a mug with warm, spiced wine and offered it to him, but he was shaking so much I had to hold it for him while he sipped it. LeDuc nestled at his feet.

"I made it to the barn, but when I came out the path had disappeared," he said. "I thought I was going in the right direction. But then I tripped over something and fell. How did you think to use the rope? You saved my life."

"Drink your wine," I said. "You are safe now. That's all that's important." As I turned to fetch the bread and jam, a cramp in my stomach nearly doubled me over.

"Sylvienne! What is it?" Catherine asked.

"Nothing. I am fine." The pain subsided. I took a breath. I was fine, but the unexpected cramp unnerved me.

The days following the blizzard were filled with brilliant sunshine that belied the frigid air outside. Armand recovered with no loss of fingers or toes. His nose developed a blister which turned black, but it eventually healed. He was careful to wrap his face with a scarf when he trekked to work.

Catherine and I spent our time laying out baby clothing we had made last time she was here, and we made a list of what was yet needed. Diapers, lots of them. I had set aside swaths of linen and flannel for this purpose. They simply needed to be cut to size. Or rather, to a variety of sizes, to accommodate a growing baby. Friends had given me blankets and quilts for the cradle Armand constructed, and linen coverings for the tiny mattress I had already assembled.

We stitched several nightgowns that would allow me to easily put the baby to breast to nurse. I hadn't had a menses flow since before I left Versailles. I would need some padded cloths for when my bleeding started up again.

Catherine had learned lacemaking at the convent and was eager to get to work on the baby's baptismal gown. It wasn't long before we were humming as we measured, cut, and sewed, storing our finished items in the new cedar chest, another of Armand's projects.

A banging on the front door startled me. I opened it to find Michel LeBlanc breathing heavily. Even on snowshoes, he had practically run all the way from the village.

"I need to talk to Captain Gervais," he said. When I invited him in, he shook his head. He didn't want to take off his snowshoes. I directed him around back to the barn where Armand was working, and he took off at a clumsy run.

Moments later, Armand came in looking grim. "There's been a fire over in Beaupré. Joseph Mansart's place. It started in his barn. Took out his entire house. The family is staying with relatives, but there are too many of them, and they need a new shelter built before the next storm. I need to collect some men to go and help."

"Beaupré is more than a day's journey." My hand went to my stomach without thinking. My time was drawing near.

"Yes. We need to collect tools and gear first. I will spend the night at the fort, and we'll leave at first light." Suddenly he looked distressed. "I can't say how long I'll be gone. What if…?"

"Catherine is here. She will fetch the midwife if need be. If you aren't back in time."

He grasped me and kissed me, then barked a few orders at Catherine about what to do with the chickens if another blizzard blew in, how to keep the snow from the doors, and to be sure and bring in enough wood each morning from the cord out back and set it near the hearth. She bobbed her head, until he finally went to the barn to dig out the sled he kept stored there. He loaded it with what tools he had and harnessed it to Shadow.

In the meantime, I filled several baskets with food supplies. He loaded those onto the sled as well as a cask of beer. When they finished, he and Michel headed into town, plodding alongside the horse in their snowshoes. The late afternoon sun was already nearing the horizon.

Standing at the window, rubbing LeDuc's ears, I watched them disappear up the path. LeDuc whined for a moment, before nuzzling my hand. He knew the benefit of staying with me. I gave him special treats he didn't get from Armand. Our secret.

The first pains were mild and so short-lived I thought perhaps they were stomach vapors. Armand had been gone just over a week. Catherine finished laying in the day's supply of firewood. She fed the chickens and brought in the eggs. Now she was preparing an eel stew, enough to last for several days. I had been trying to keep up with my share of the housework, but more and more my back ached, and I found myself short of breath.

Later that same day, while I was standing over the chamber pot in the bedroom after having relieved myself, I felt a dribble run down my legs. My first reaction was disgust and frustration—I was so large and bloated I couldn't hold my water anymore. But a moment later, when another, larger gush let loose, I realized this was different. The baby was ready to come.

"Catherine!" I called, holding my skirt away from my legs. "Catherine, I need you!"

CHAPTER TWENTY-ONE

Catherine appeared in my doorway just as I felt the onset of another pain. This one fiercer than the first. I gasped and clutched my stomach.

Her eyes widened. "Madame Sylvienne! Are you…?"

"It's too early. I'm sure it's too early." But the pain came again. Sucking in a breath, I said, "You must fetch the midwife."

Without another word, she grabbed her wool cloak and a pair of snowshoes and pushed open the door. A waft of frigid air carrying the scent of winter washed over me before she closed it behind her.

After wiping the water from my legs, I began to pace. I didn't know what else to do. Several days earlier, the baby had dropped, its position noticeably lower over my hips. I prayed it was in the correct position to emerge head-first. I'd heard horror stories of women being ripped apart by babies who presented with their bottoms or their elbows first, then bleeding to death. That was a danger every woman who ever gave birth faced.

When the next pain came, I stumbled to the bed and collapsed. I'd never felt anything like it before. Fortunately, it passed quickly. How I wished Armand were home. Of course, he wouldn't be of much use, not once the midwife arrived, for she would send him away, tell him to go to the tavern. Leduc stayed close to the bed, but he seemed bewildered as to how to comfort me. Occasionally, he pushed his nose into my hand.

Chilly and afraid, I pulled the quilt up over my shoulders. As I waited for the next onset of pain, my mind drifted to the house on *rue de l'Echelle*, just blocks from the Louvre and Tuileries palaces in Paris. Athénaïs, King Louis's mistress, had given birth there in an overly warm, dark bedroom under the care of a midwife and a surgeon. They'd pulled the curtains tight and stoked the fireplace. Louis had ordered all the candles but one to be snuffed out so he could be near his love without being recognized. I remembered her screams of agony. And her apathy afterward. The indifference with which she allowed the sweet baby girl to whom she'd just given birth to be handed over to a governess and wet nurse and taken off into the night. Because, of course, Louis couldn't allow his bastard daughter to be raised at court.

Gasping, I clutched my stomach again and curled my legs up tight against me, but that only seemed to make the pain worse. Straightening my legs, I lay on my side waiting. I had felt sorry for Athénaïs because she'd had to give birth in that house, away from the comforts of her own rooms in the palace. However, she had reminded me she was lucky she wasn't the queen. For queens were required to give birth in public, under the gaze of a roomful of courtiers and nobles, in order to ensure there was nothing amiss with the line of succession. I closed my eyes and groaned in the clutches of another wave of pain, glad I was not a queen.

By the time Catherine returned, the pain was coming with insistent frequency. The midwife was not with her.

"I am sorry. Both midwives were already called away. I brought my aunties instead. They will know how to help you."

Two Wendat women, one with a cradleboard on her back, took off their snowshoes and tromped into the house behind

Catherine. To my relief, I recognized Cécile, the woman I had met shortly after my wedding when she tested my bartering skills. The baby she carried in the cradleboard was now about four months old. I didn't recognize the other woman whom Catherine introduced as Marie. She helped lift the cradleboard off Cécile's back, and with the wrapped baby still strapped to it—apparently contentedly so—she leaned it upright against the wall where the baby could watch us until it fell asleep again. Leduc positioned himself next to Cécile's baby and, head on paws, watched as the women went to work.

Marie reached for a sack she had brought with her and set some fabric squares, soap, a knife, and a hank of wool cording on the table.

"It's too early," I said to Cécile. "It shouldn't be happening yet."

Cécile took my hands and with a warm smile said, "Babies come when they will." She stroked my forehead and immediately I felt comforted.

Marie then pulled something that looked like dried moss from another sack and spread it on the floor in front of the fireplace. She took a blanket from my bed and laid it on the mound of moss.

"What is she doing?" I asked between groans.

"Preparing a soft place for the baby to land," Cécile said. "Come. Stand. It is time for you to be washed."

"What do you mean? I need to be here, in bed."

Cécile chided gently. "The bed is not an appropriate place to give birth. We will help you do it the right way. The way I gave birth to my healthy baby boy."

At Cécile's direction, Catherine stoked the fire, then moved about the house pushing the curtains open as wide as they would go.

"But I can't...I have to...aaaghh!" Gritting my teeth, I tried to edge away.

"The baby will come faster if you are on your feet." Cécile's voice was patient. "But you can sit or lie down on the moss bedding until it is time. First, we will wash you so your baby will know you are ready for it."

She and Catherine helped me to the moss bedding in front of the fire. They took off my bodice, skirts, and underthings, then used soap and water warmed on the hearth to cleanse my entire body. Once I was dry again, they dressed me in my night shift. I sank gratefully onto the moss mattress.

When the next pain came, it was so intense it frightened me. I began to scream.

Cécile knelt next to me and stroked my head. "Hush. I know it is the fashion among white women to scream during this time before birth, but screaming will only frighten Baby and make it want to stay inside longer. Try to make as little noise as possible." She reached up and began untying the fabric holding my hair in a knot. "You must redirect your strength to help your body push baby out."

The pain came again, more intense. I gritted my teeth.

"Good. That is good. Now, when the next one comes, take a deep breath, and slowly let it out." She demonstrated.

A moment later, I thought my insides would twist until my body tore apart. I couldn't help myself and screamed anyway.

"Breathe in," Cécile said, her voice quiet but firm. She demonstrated.

I sucked in air, clutching her hand and inhaling the earthy, woody scent of the moss.

"Now let it out, slowly. Yes. Again." When my hand tightened on hers, she said, "Now breathe like this, like a dog panting." She took short little breaths and encouraged me to do the same. As I panted, she said, "Look at the fire. Take its energy as your own." When my body started to relax, she told me to breathe in again then out.

"How long does this go on?" I asked, my eyes filled with tears.

She put her hand on my stomach, then felt between my legs. "It shouldn't be long now. This baby is ready. Can you stand up?" She and Catherine helped me to my feet. Marie pulled the blanket away.

The pain came and I squeezed Cécile's hand again, hard, but focused on the fire and on my breathing the way she showed me. But just as I started to pant, she said, "Grit your teeth and bear down now. Put all your strength into pushing."

Marie knelt before me on the blanket, her hands under me between my legs. "It comes," she said. "Push more!" I gritted my teeth and bore down. Suddenly there was a release.

"A girl!" Marie said, holding the wet, bloody infant up for me to see.

"Praise God!" I started to cry, tears of joy and wonderment. I sank onto the moss and lay down on my back, exhausted.

"She is small but listen to how strong her voice is," Cécile said as the baby squalled. She chanted a welcoming song as she laid the tiny infant on my stomach.

"I will cut and tie the cord. Then Marie and Catherine will clean the baby. You must pass the afterbirth before you can take her to your breast." Cécile handed the baby back to Marie. She helped me stand again so the bloody afterbirth would fall upon the moss. She pressed gently on my stomach to help my body move the mass out.

I felt another, manageable pain and then the expulsion of the afterbirth. Afterward, I watched Marie and Catherine wash and dry my baby girl. They swaddled her in rabbit fur. Cécile gathered up the afterbirth and wrapped it in what looked like birch bark.

"It is sacred," she said. "I will hang it in the tree out front. When the snows are gone, we will bury it so Mother Earth can take it back." She put the cord from the baby into a small moosehide sack. "This we will hang from her cradle so she will not cry for its loss. But first, you must feed your baby, and I will feed mine."

Armand arrived home to happy barking from LeDuc, who led him back to the bedroom where I sat up in our bed, nursing the new baby. Later, he made a point to thank Cécile and Marie, as they had stayed several days preparing meals and cleaning the house.

"I know your husband, Haro'nu," he said to Cécile.

"He has spoken of you. He says you are an honest man."

Armand smiled. "I appreciate that. I have much respect for him as well."

"I will tell him."

Cécile nursed her baby before strapping him back onto the cradle board. With the baby on her back, she and Marie headed back out into the snow.

Armand returned to our room and sat down on the bed next to me while Catherine prepared our evening meal. "Have you thought of a name for her?"

"I would like to name her Marie Anne Henriette, in honor of the Princess Henriette who died while I was at court."

"Henriette is a pretty name," he said.

"That will be her baptismal name. But I would like us to call her Minette."

"Kitten?"

"Yes. That was the princess's nickname."

Our Minette had fallen asleep, so I pulled her away from my breast and held her out to him.

"I like the name Minette," he said, taking the tiny infant in his big hands. "She's soft like a kitten." He held her up close to look at her face. For a moment she opened her eyes and stared at him, before falling back asleep. "Her eyes are so blue!"

"Yes, they are." I pulled the quilt up over me contentedly and closed my eyes. Armand nestled the baby in my arms just as I was drifting off, the press of his lips on my forehead soft as a dream.

CHAPTER TWENTY-TWO

We took Minette to the church to be baptized in early March, as soon as the weather was warm enough to safely take her outdoors. Michel and Jeanne were delighted to serve as her Godparents. They threw a feast in her honor at their newly renovated house two seigneuries over from ours, inviting many of our friends.

But I soon regretted allowing the celebration, for within a week, Minette began to cough.

She was only a month old. What was I thinking, taking her out of the house before the snow had all disappeared? Her little body was too fragile to endure air still holding the chill of snow that refused to melt despite Easter having come and gone. The humours that governed her health were so easily put out of balance.

Her cough and stuffy nose quickly turned into raspy breathing. Catherine and I took turns walking with her at night. She fussed when I tried to nurse her and stopped feeding. Panic grew inside me. Infants in France generally did not survive something as simple as a cold.

"Let's take her to the hospital," Armand said. "Perhaps the sisters can help."

"I don't know," I said. The nuns there worked miracles with Catherine and other adults who came to them with injuries and sickness. But in my time there, I hadn't seen any children cared for. And certainly not babies.

"What then?" he asked.

"I'll fetch my aunt," Catherine said. "Cécile will know what to do."

"Sylvienne?" Armand asked.

I nodded. "Yes. Go. Fetch her." I cradled my baby girl. She was so weak she had stopped crying. Dread settled over me.

Cécile arrived a short while later. Tears poured down my face as I said, "Her fever will not abate, and she won't eat."

She felt the baby's forehead with her hand, unwrapped her swaddling and checked her limbs and stomach, put her ear close to the baby's mouth and chest. "We will make fish broth. You can feed it to her by dipping a cloth into it and wringing it into her mouth."

"Fish broth?"

"It will give her the nourishment she needs, strengthen her until she can nurse again."

To my relief, Cécile's remedy worked. By the next day, Minette had regained enough strength to put her lips to my now swollen breast. Slowly, her fever ebbed, and she regained strength, crying heartily when hungry.

I had never known such fear in my life as when I thought my baby might die. I didn't know how to thank Cécile, but she said she required no thanks. She only hoped I would provide a home for Catherine for as long as was needed. To that, I readily agreed. Catherine had become like a sister to me. I couldn't imagine ever turning her out.

A week later, Cécile came by the house again to check on Minette. She brought with her a beautifully beaded cradleboard.

"Would you stay and have something to drink? Wine? Or tea?"

"Tea would be good."

Cécile, Catherine, and I sat around the table, and I poured tea for all three of us.

"You've always been near when I've needed you," I said as we savored our tea. "But Catherine says you don't live in Québec."

"No," Cécile said. "I live in a Wendat village north of here called Wendake. My sister Marie lives here. She has adopted the French ways. She converted to Catholicism when we entered the convent school and later married a Frenchman."

"You went to the convent school? The one here in Québec?"

"A long time ago now. The sisters provided a good education. I can speak and read and write French. I am grateful for that. But I cannot worship our Creator the way the good sisters wish me to."

"What do you mean?" My curiosity was piqued.

"My people are taught, as you were, that we each have a soul, and our souls live on forever. I believe this. But I also believe everything around us has a spirit. The animals, the trees, the river."

"Like a soul of their own?"

"Yes, though not exactly the same as ours. Some spirits are more powerful than others. And the creation story of my people is different from the story in the Bible."

"In what way?"

"We believe, in the beginning, the Wendat people lived in the sky. The daughter of the great sky chief, A'taentsik, fell through a hole near the roots of a sky tree."

"A'taentsik," I repeated the name. "You once told me she was your grandmother."

"A'taentsik is the grandmother of all Wendat," Cécile said. "When she fell from the sky, she landed on the back of a great turtle."

"The great turtle that broke her fall is the land we live on now," Catherine said, happy to tell the story. "A'taentsik had twin sons, Tsesta, who created order or good. And Tawiskaron who created evil and chaos."

"Not so different from Cain and Abel," I observed.

"Just as with the Bible, there is more to our creation story," Cécile explained. "But this story is the basis of our belief."

"Catherine, which do you believe?" I asked. "The story of A'taentsik falling to Earth? Or the story of Genesis in the Bible?"

Catherine frowned. "Why do I have to choose?"

I had no answer for her. So, I said to Cécile, "I do believe God brought you to me in my time of need."

"Perhaps you are right. I dreamed I was needed in Québec. And I believe in heeding dreams when they are sent to me."

"Thank you," I said. "*Tiawenhk.*"

Cécile smiled. "I must go. My own little one is at my sister's house, and I don't want to leave him too long. Let's try out the cradleboard before I leave."

She taught me and Catherine how to swaddle Minette tightly, strap her onto the board, and hoist her onto my back. I was surprised at how little the baby fussed when she was in the cradleboard. And, in the weeks to come by how much work I could get done around the house and in the barn with Minette on my back or propped against a nearby wall where she could watch me or doze off.

The spring equinox arrived with the snow still knee deep. It seemed as if winter would never end, the trees never bud, and flowers never emerge from the frozen soil.

Apparently, however, the frigid landscape didn't bother the locals as much as it did me. They turned out *en masse* one sunny afternoon for the annual spring canoe race across the ice-floe-filled Saint-Laurent. And Jacques Farley's return turned out to be one of the anticipated highlights of the event, though as hero or foe, I wasn't certain.

Jacques's birchbark canoe was among the two dozen teams competing. With anywhere from four to ten paddlers in each canoe, the teams braved the swiftly flowing river, paddling around boulder-sized chunks of ice to get to the opposite side and back. Villagers lined the shore and the cliff above placing bets and cheering the racers on as the canoes crashed into each other, the paddlers kicking at rival canoes in an effort to upend them, and sometimes even standing up to beat an opponent with a paddle, sending him overboard.

The winning team was treated to free drinks in taverns throughout the lower town for the rest of the day. Jacques's team came in second, but he declared it a victory that none of his men ended up in the river. And for that he was happy to contribute to the celebration of the winning team. He invited Armand to join them as they made the rounds of the drinking establishments.

"Go." I said. "Have fun. "I need to head back to the house. I don't wish to leave Catherine and the baby alone too long."

He bussed me on the cheek, and with a bounce in his step, hurried off to join Jacques and the other men.

As I approached the steep path to the upper village, a woman's voice called out, "Sylvienne, wait!" Claudette, wrapped in a heavy wool cloak, hurried toward me. "Will you have a drink with me? The new little café across the road sells steamed chocolate with cream."

I didn't really want to spend time in Claudette's company, but the memory of hot chocolate—which I hadn't tasted since I left Versailles—was too tempting. I followed her into the shop.

We sat at a table near the front window. Claudette placed the order, then turned to me. "How is the baby? I heard she was ill."

"She's fine now. Growing every day."

"Good, good. And the Native girl you took in. Charlotte?"

"Catherine. She is Wendat."

The shop owner put the cups of frothy chocolate in front of us. Claudette gave her a coin.

"Is she working out well? But how horrible to have to look at that disfigured face every day. Doesn't she frighten the baby?"

"Claudette, what do you want?"

She took a sip and sighed. "Mon Dieu, this is good."

I pushed my cup aside; I'd lost my taste for the chocolate.

"I wish to ask a favor," she said.

I stared at her. "Of me?"

"Yes. You see, Monsieur Gravel and I have petitioned the Crown for a charter to supply the new forts being built along the Saint-Laurent." When I said nothing, she added, "Exclusive rights."

"And what does this have to do with me?"

"We have yet to obtain a reply. I hoped you might have a word on our behalf with Intendant Talon and perhaps offer him a letter of reference he could provide to the King."

I sat back in my chair, my chocolate growing cold. "What makes you think the King would care about anything I have to say?"

She took another sip, licking the foam from her lips afterward and dabbing at them with a linen handkerchief. "Perhaps because you bore his most recent child?"

"What?"

"Certainly you were with child before you got on that ship. It was obvious to me then."

She had never given any indication that she knew. I doubted her now. Regardless, she pressed ahead with her assertion.

"You were in his service, were you not?"

"I was in the service of Madame de Montespan. I was married to the Duc de Narbonne when I became with child."

"Hmm, yes. Madame de Montespan. I'm not a fool. It is well known, when his mistress is, shall we say *indisposed*, the King still insists on having his needs met. Of course, no one but me needs to know the outcome of your…service."

I leaned toward her and lowered my voice. "If you think Minette is anything other than the legitimate daughter of my late husband, you are indeed a fool. And I would appreciate it if you would stop spreading rumors about me."

I stood and walked out of the café, leaving the cold chocolate on the table, and leaving Claudette sitting in the window alone.

Catherine looked at me with alarm when I slammed the front door behind me, breathing heavily after my hasty walk home, my face flushed with anger. "Madame, what is wrong?"

"Nothing. Damn that woman!" I scooped up Minette from the floor where she was lying on a blanket.

"Who?"

"Claudette." At the look of confusion on her kind, scarred face, I said, "Madame Gravel. She is a hateful woman. You need have nothing to do with her."

I took Minette to my room to nurse her, but I stopped in the doorway and turned toward Catherine. "I'm sorry to be so cross. And please, no more 'madame.' You are family and I am Sylvienne."

Catherine nodded, her eyes wide. "Sylvienne."

She hurried off to start her chores, and I sank onto the bed. As I put Minette to my breast, my mind ran over Claudette's words. And my response. Both were lies. Claudette's ridiculous lie was meant to hurt me and sway public opinion about me. Mine was meant to protect Minette, whose blue eyes offered testament as to who her real father was.

And the notion I had been a mistress of any sort to the King was laughable. But to counter the rumor, I would have to reveal my true relationship with him. And that I was not prepared to do. What would Jean Talon think if this new lie were whispered to him? Which it likely would be. The Gravels were part of his inner circle after all.

And what about Armand? What if this new rumor came to his attention? He'd already discounted the earlier one about me being a mistress, thankfully. But what if people repeated the new lie about Minette? Would he discount it so easily? Would it make him doubt his trust in my word? Gossip and truth formed such a tangled web. And I was beginning to feel ensnared in it.

A resolve formed within me. I would not let Claudette take advantage of me. I would tell Armand about the ugly new rumor. If he heard it from me first, he would know it wasn't true. And if it spread any further, he would quickly tamp it out.

Thankfully, Armand came home from the tavern festivities while he could still walk, if just barely. Happily drunk, he kissed me and Minette goodnight and stumbled off to bed. This obviously was not the time to engage him in a discussion of gossip. Catherine had already gone up to her room. After a short while, I put the baby in her cradle and crawled into bed myself.

Sometime later, a loud banging on our front door roused me out of a sleepy stupor. I tried shaking Armand, but he slept on.

Grudgingly, I slipped out of bed, the wood floor cold on my bare feet. Wrapping a wool shawl around me, I padded to the door, the ever-faithful LeDuc at my side. He barked once, his tail wagging.

When I opened the door, Jacques Farley stood in the frosty winter moonlight, a soused grin on his face.

"What are you doing here?" I asked. "It's past midnight."

He held up an immense fish. "Speared you a *poisson*. A walleye."

Behind him stood a young man, shivering fiercely, his skin darker than any man's I had ever seen before. His black hair, wild with tight curls, peeked out from under a wool hat.

LeDuc greeted Jacques, nosing his hand, then turned and investigated the newcomer. He took no issue with the man, so neither did I.

"This is Titus." Jacques belched, the stink of his brandy-laden breath assailing me. "He needs a place to sleep. Me, too. And you can cook this fish for us. Not tonight of course, but tomorrow."

"Shh! You'll wake the baby. Come in. But quietly."

I took the fish from him. While the two men shook off their snowshoes, I laid the fish outside the kitchen door in the snow. If the night creatures made a meal of it, so be it. Once inside, the men headed immediately for the fireplace, sinking to the floor in front of it.

"You're drunk," I said, hands on hips, staring down at them.

"Yes. Soused we are. And cold. Cold and hungry." Jacques's voice slurred. "If you have a bit of bread, maybe some left-over chicken or…or venison, we'd be most a-a-appreciative. And beer. We need beer."

"I think you've had enough beer. I'll get you blankets." I dug two wool blankets out of the cedar storage chest, but by the time I got back to the hearth, both men were asleep in their coats and boots. Shaking my head in disgust, I threw a blanket over each of them and went back to bed.

Minette's fussing woke me just as the sun was coming up. Sleepily, I brought her into bed and nursed her, Armand never stirring.

An odd noise from another part of the house caught my attention. Snoring? Then I remembered the two men in front of the now cold fireplace. I groaned, determined to let Armand feed them when they woke up, which was unlikely to be anytime soon. When Minette was finished, I put a protective arm around her and fell back to sleep.

Later, I awoke to the sound of men's hoarse voices in the kitchen. Armand's side of the bed was empty. A soft curse escaped my lips. Minette's eyes fluttered open. I nursed her for a few minutes, then changed her diaper. I dressed myself while she lay happy and kicking. Finally, I picked her up, and we went out to greet our guests.

"Bonjour, mes belles!" Jacques said, his voice surprisingly hearty considering the state he'd been in the night before. He and Titus sat at the table, each with a steaming mug in front of them.

Armand welcomed the baby and me to the table, kissing each of our cheeks. He handed me a mug. Sniffing it, I gave him a chastising look. He'd used some of our precious and expensive coffee beans for these roustabouts. Armand, in turn, raised his eyebrows in challenge. He needed the strong, invigorating drink as much as our guests did. Relenting, I sipped the wonderful brew while cradling Minette with one arm.

Before I could say any more, Catherine came down the stairs from the loft, hesitant to show herself. Jacques spied her and stood up, a huge grin on his face. "D'hanate!"

Catherine's face lit up. "Papa Jacques!" She ran into his arms. He lifted her off her feet, twirling her around.

"How is Miigwan? And his okomisan?" she asked when she could catch her breath.

"They are well. They send greetings to you."

Realizing there was another man sitting at the table, she quickly ducked her head and pulled her shawl to cover the scarred side of her face. Armand offered her coffee and a seat to join us. I wanted to ask who Miigwan was, but the conversation moved on too quickly.

"I was pleased when I heard you had become part of Captain Gervais's household," Jacques said to her as he sat down again. "This is my new friend, Titus."

Catherine nodded shyly at the dark-skinned man.

"Bonjour, Titus." I said, being careful not to stare. I'd only ever seen a few people of his coloring, and those were in Paris.

"Bonjour, madame," he said, then he said something in English.

"He apologizes for not speaking French," Jacques said, mirth in his eyes. "He's only been in New France a short time."

"And how does he come to know you?" I asked, setting my mug down.

"I won him in a game of dice. That and beating the poor fool who didn't want to give him up into a bloody pulp."

"You won him? Is he a slave?" I frowned at Jacques. "You own a slave now?"

Jacques scoffed. "Can one man really own another? I told him he's free to come or go as he likes." He turned to Titus and said in English, "Free, yes?"

Titus nodded vigorously. "Liberté!" he said proudly.

Armand chuckled. "He was part of Jacques's race team yesterday."

"I told him if he could survive the race without drowning, I'd offer him employment in the spring," Jacques's said, slapping Titus on the back.

"Employment? With wages?" I asked.

"Oui, of course." Jacques smirked. "But he turned me down."

"Oui, pas d'emploi," Titus said, his accent not quite English. African, perhaps?

I said to the former slave, "You don't wish to engage in fur trading?"

Jacques interpreted my question. The young man looked suddenly contrite, as if he feared he had offended his benefactor. He responded in English. Jacques laughed, put a hand on the man's shoulder. "He says fur trading is a good career. But he has ambition. He wants to learn to build ships."

"A ship builder?" Armand was impressed.

"I thought perhaps he could apprentice with Arnauld Ducharme."

"The barrel maker?" I asked.

"To learn to use tools and work with wood. After a couple of years, he can get a job helping to make boats. Small ones at first—canoes, row boats, small sailing barges. He would like to go to France and do a real apprenticeship with a ship builder." He turned and slapped Titus on the shoulder again. "Vous allez en France, eh?"

"Oui! France!" Titus smiled broadly. "*Navires*." He looked at Jacques to see if he had said the word correctly as he made a motion with his hand indicating ships on the water.

"Oui. Grands navires."

Titus nodded his head happily.

"Ship building is a worthwhile ambition," Armand said.

"Have you ever sailed on a ship?" I asked.

When Jacques translated, Titus nodded gravely, spoke sadly. "Yes. But only in chains," Jacques said for him.

I realized how stupid my question had been. He had come from the continent of Africa. How else could he have gotten to this side of the world? "I'm sorry. That was foolish of me."

When Jacques told him what I had said, he waved his hand, dismissing my faux pas. He spoke with pride, Jacques translating his words. "The ships I build will never have chains or carry captives."

"I applaud you," I said. "But now let's see if there will be dinner tonight."

The men all looked at me quizzically. I went to the back door. To my relief, the enormous fish from the night before lay untouched in the snow. Bringing it in, I laid the near-frozen carcass out on the carving table. Hands on hips, I said to Jacques, "You'll have to clean this if you want it for dinner." His grin told me he was happy to do my bidding.

CHAPTER TWENTY-THREE

Late April arrived along with the first of the season's ships from France. I hadn't found an opportunity to mention to Armand my conversation with Claudette and the rumor that Minette had been fathered by King Louis. It seemed at this point not to have gone any farther than her own laughable musing, so I decided it was better to ignore it.

I asked Catherine to go down to the dock to see if anything had come for me in the mail pouch on the ship anchored in the river. I gave her my bundle of winter letters to give to the ship's purser for its return trip to France. She returned with a single letter.

As she took Minette from my arms, she said, "Monsieur Talon's secretary hailed me as I was leaving the dock area."

"Talon's man?" I turned the letter over to study the seal. Maman! At long last. The first missive from her.

"He said to tell you the intendent requests that you come to his office at your earliest convenience."

"Did he say why?"

"No."

I couldn't imagine what Talon wanted with me, and in this moment I had no desire to find out. "Perhaps I'll go later," I said, breaking the seal and sinking onto the chair at the kitchen table.

Closing my eyes, I held the folded paper close to my nose as if I could detect Maman's scent even after its long journey across the ocean. All I could smell was a musty saltiness. I unfolded the paper and read and reread the words, savoring each one.

Maman apologized profusely for not writing sooner. She assured me her condition had not worsened, though her handwriting looked shaky. She was grateful to receive the letters I sent before ice closed off the riverway. She was surprised but delighted to learn I had remarried, and even more delighted to learn I was with child. She sent her blessings and those of Tatie and Blondeau, who, she said, missed me as much as she did. She thanked me for sending Lisette, my maid from my time at court. Lisette was proving to be a great help to all of them, but especially to Maman. By the end of her short letter, tears rolled down my cheeks. How I missed her, more so now that I had a daughter of my own whom I longed for her to meet, to cradle, to kiss her sweet toes and fingers the way I did.

I glanced over at Minette lying contentedly in Catherine's lap, gazing up at the girl's sweet, disfigured face as Catherine sang to her in Wendat. A moment later, the baby's sleepy eyes closed. With a conspiratorial smile, Catherine rose and took her to the cradle in the bedroom to nap. *Oh, Maman, how I wish Minette could hear your voice singing.*

While Minette slept, Catherine and I enjoyed a mid-day meal of left-over pea soup and day-old bread with maple butter.

"Sylvienne, if you wish to go see the intendent today, I can watch over Minette," Catherine said.

I groaned. "Ach! Talon." I had managed to avoid him since before my wedding. "I suppose I must go and be done with it."

Laurant, the pretty manservant, ushered me into the intendent's office. The pervasive scent of brewer's yeast brought back the unpleasantness of the dinner I had walked out on.

"Madame Gervais." Talon rose and offered a chair in front of his desk for me. "I must apologize. I never congratulated you on your marriage to the captain."

His voice held no rancor, nevertheless I clasped my hands awkwardly in my lap. "Merci."

"And you have a baby now?"

"A little girl. We call her Minette."

"After our poor late princess? The King's sister-in-law?" At my nod, he said, "I'm sure she will wear the name well. And Captain Gervais, he accepts the child as if she were his own?"

There it was. The implication. Claudette's words rang in my head. *Because you bore the King's most recent child.* Had she whispered her rumor to Talon after I refused her request to provide a recommendation for her husband's business? Did Talon now believe the lie?

"He does," I said. "As would any man who marries a widow."

"Ah, yes. A widow." He clasped his hands in front of him on the desk. "A former duchesse."

Exasperated, I blurted out, "Why did you ask to see me?"

He nodded as if reminded of his mission. "A delivery came for you on the ship."

"A letter from my mother. I have it already."

"This one did not arrive in the mail pouch." He picked something up from his desk. "It was hand-delivered by the ship's captain." He placed a small leather pouch on the desk near enough for me to take it. "I understand it is a remittance from the royal treasury. The accompanying letter said it was by order of the office of the Crown. Were you expecting a pension?"

"No, I...well, yes. I suppose." There had been mention of annual payments, but my leaving France was so sudden and fraught with distress, I didn't hear most of what was being said. I untied the leather cord that held the purse closed. Inside were coins. Livres in varying denominations. Resisting the temptation to pour them out and count them, I retied the cord.

"I will need you to sign the register. Record of receipt."

"Of course."

He opened a ledger and dipped a quill into the inkpot on his desk. I took the quill and signed my name where he pointed. The amount, fifty livres, had been entered in careful script. He had counted the coins. When I finished, I handed the quill back.

He cleared his throat. "The King is quite generous."

I met his gaze. "He has been generous with *all* the women he sponsors in the recruitment program."

"The other women received their dowries on the day of their weddings." He closed the ledger and tapped the cover with his finger. "Did you not receive a payment on your wedding day as well?"

"I...yes, of course."

"So why—?"

"Thank you for delivering the pension." Ducking my head in a quick curtsy, I hurried out before he could question me further.

When I arrived home, Minette was awake and fussing. Catherine sang as she changed the baby's diaper, but I could tell Minette was hungry.

The purse full of coins weighed heavily on my mind. What did this unexpected pension payment mean? That I'd been banished but not forsaken by the King? Grateful for the gesture, I slid the coins into the chest in the bedroom, combining them with my earnings from the hospital. We didn't have need of the money; Armand's salary was more than sufficient. However, this new contribution to my fund, added to my previous savings, would be nearly enough to enable me to bring my entire family to France one day. Perhaps even take Catherine with us. We would have to wait until Minette was hearty enough for sea travel, of course. Heartened by my plan, I picked up Minette and put her to my breast.

To celebrate the opening of the river and the arrival of a new shipment of wine and brandy from France, Governor Courcelle and his wife, Marie-Anne, sent out invitations to a spring ball at the governor's residence, the Château Saint-Louis. Armand and I were invited, but I cringed at the thought of encountering Intendant Talon again. And he was sure to be there.

I had come down with a chill and a headache and used that as an excuse to beg off. "Do you mind terribly if we don't go?" I asked Armand.

"Given a choice, I'd rather party at the Grey Goose than at the governor's château. I'll happily send our regrets. We'll stay home and nurse your headache with warm brandy and a comfortable fire."

A week later, Armand was called away yet again on a scouting trip with the governor. It seemed these trips were becoming more frequent and each of longer duration.

I left the dishes for Catherine to clean up and sat down to write to Maman. Before I had even set ink to paper, Minette's cry brought me back to the bedroom. LeDuc was already there, nose in cradle, surveying the situation. Minette wanted my breast, demanded it. My healthy baby making demands on me again. My heart soared.

After the feeding, Catherine took Minette and LeDuc outdoors for a bit of fresh air. I went back to my letter.

Dearest Maman,

I finally had the opportunity to visit a Native village. In my last letter I mentioned a woman named Cécile who helped me when I gave birth to Minette. She also helped when Minette became sick. I wanted to find a way to thank her, and a friend of Armand offered to take me and Catherine to her village so I could give her gifts I had prepared…

What I didn't say in my letter was that it was Jacques who had taken us to see Cécile. He had shown up on our doorstep a few days earlier, this time with a freshly killed turkey in hand.

"Don't worry. I'll pluck and clean it. All you have to do is cook it," he said with a teasing smile.

"Armand is not here," I said.

"Gone with Courcelle on his latest excursion?" When I nodded, he said, "If you prefer, I can just leave it." He held the bird out toward me.

"No!" I took a step back. I had no idea how to prepare such a bird. However, the thought of roasted turkey made my mouth water. And I knew Catherine would be disappointed if Jacques left without seeing her. "We can't let it go to waste. You'll have to pluck and clean it."

He nodded, grinning, and took the bird around back to the cleaning table. When Catherine returned from her jaunt down to the river with Minette, she happily went out to help Jacques with the turkey. LeDuc had already discovered he was here, and had dashed to the backyard, barking, to greet his friend.

Once the bird was cut into manageable pieces, Jacques soaked the breast, thighs, and legs in brine to which he added a bit of maple syrup and some herbs from my kitchen. By noon the turkey was ready for the fire, and together we skewered the pieces for roasting.

"Armand doesn't know what he's missing," I said, as the aroma began to fill the house.

Supper that night was glorious. Catherine prepared a soup of carrots, onions, and turnips from the root cellar, and we ate fresh bread with honey butter along with roasted turkey. As we sat around the table, I mentioned how grateful I was that Cécile had come both for Minette's birth and again when she was ill. I wanted to find a way to thank her, but didn't know how.

"We could go visit her, if you like," Jacques said. "Her village is a couple hours north of here."

"You would go with us?" I asked.

Catherine's face lit up as well at the prospect of a visit to her aunt's village.

"We could leave first thing in the morning," he said. "If you don't mind my staying overnight. I can sleep in the barn." He hesitated. "I mean, since Armand isn't here."

"Catherine can sleep with me. You can have her bed."

Jacques protested. "A blanket in front of the fireplace is all I've ever needed."

Jacques saddled Shadow for Catherine and me to ride. He lifted the cradleboard with Minette onto his own back, and we set out for Cécile's village, Jacques walking alongside the horse. LeDuc happily blazed the trail ahead. The path through the forest smelled of damp earth, musty leaves, and the faint tang of balsam and pine. The tapping of woodpeckers was interrupted by the occasional call of a nuthatch and the distant jeering of blue jays. The sun was high overhead by the time we arrived. Catherine and I slid off Shadow, and Jacques transferred Minette onto my back before walking through the front gate.

The Wendat village was larger than I expected, perhaps thirty or so lodgings surrounded by a high wooden palisade not much different from the one that protected Québec. The village bordered a river on one side. On the opposite side were community gardens.

"We are here to visit Cécile. " Catherine said to the man on watch as we passed through the main gate.

"Do you mean Ora'wan?" the watchman responded. "Over beyond those houses on the river side. You will find her there."

We found the house, and Catherine spoke to a boy of about ten playing in front of the structure. The child nodded and ran inside. Moments later Cécile came out to greet us, her plump baby boy secure in his cradleboard on her back.

"Bienvenue," she said, bussing us on our cheeks. She spoke to the older boy in Wendat, and he scurried off. "I've sent for Haro'nu. He is out in the field, planting corn." Lifting the moosehide covering the entryway, she invited us in.

The longhouse was large, framed with wooden posts and horizontal poles covered by cedar sheathing. Inside, the scent of cedar mingled with smoke and tantalizing cooking aromas. Sleeping platforms lined the sides of the longhouse. There appeared to be plenty of room for multiple families. Cécile said that she and Haro'nu, shared the longhouse with the families of her two sisters.

Delighted that I was using the cradleboard she had given us, she took the baby from my back and held her up for all to see. She carried Minette in her cradleboard as she guided us to the farthest of three stone-lined fire pits, introducing us to her two sisters and their families, each seated around their own hearths. I counted eighteen people who lived in the longhouse, though I was never sure of the exact number, so many adults and children of all ages came and went.

Cécile propped both babies in their cradleboards against a large log near her family's hearth. Sinking onto a mat in front of the fire, I explained the reason for our visit and presented her with my gifts—a small brass cooking pot, an ivory comb I'd brought from France, and a pair of brass embroidery scissors I thought she might like. She took delight in each one, setting them on a nearby platform to be admired by all.

"You look healthy," she said, as her eyes took in the whole of me. Then to Catherine, "You are taking good care of her."

Catherine smiled proudly.

Cécile turned to Jacques. "How is the boy? Miigwan?"

That name again. The expression on Jacques's face softened. "He is growing fast."

Haro'nu entered at that moment, keeping me from asking who they were talking about.

*"Yiheh!"*he said, welcoming us. Then he greeted us in broken French before turning to Cécile and speaking to her in Wendat.

"He apologizes because his French is so poor," she said.

"Ndio. Kwe." I said, using my new language skills to say hello.

Haro'nu broke into a wide grin. He shook Jacques's hand, the two men speaking in Wendat.

After proudly showing her husband the gifts I had presented, Cécile dished out food which had been warming by the fire—smoked sturgeon and sagamité, the wonderful stew made of corn, beans, and squash I had tasted when I'd first arrived in the colony. While we ate, she nursed her baby. Soon Minette began fussing to be fed. I unstrapped her but felt awkward baring my breast in front of Jacques and the men in Cécile's family. She must have sensed my discomfort, for she took a blanket and draped it over me. Tucking Minette inside the folds of the blanket, I nursed her white we chatted.

The conversation flowed surprisingly well with Cécile, Catherine, and Jacques switching between French and Wendat as needed.

"Your Wendat name," I said to Cécile. "Ora'wan?"

She smiled. "It means sunflower. You know the tall flowers with heads that face the sun?"

"Yes! We have sunflowers in France. Maman grows them in her garden. Ora'wan is a lovely name."

The conversation grew somber as Haro'nu told Jacques there were rumors of British traders in the area.

"I have heard the same." Jacques gritted his teeth. "Will you send word if you encounter them?"

"I will," Haro'nu said. "Friends of the Iroquois are no friends of the Wendat."

By now I knew how horribly the Wendat had been treated by Iroquois in the past, with tensions continuing even today. The Wendat had already suffered great losses due to illnesses introduced to them by the early French explorers and settlers; then the Iroquois started attacking their villages. Many were killed, some were captured and assimilated into the Iroquois nation to grow their numbers. The Wendat were so decimated, only a few villages remained near Québec. And the hostilities continued, as evidenced by Catherine's tragic loss of her parents. It wasn't good news that British traders were trekking into French territory and making alliances with the Iroquois.

Jacques summed it up. "Where British fur traders go, British soldiers and the Iroquois won't be far behind."

A steady parade of villagers came to pay their respects, as word of the French visitors had swiftly made its way through the village. Children and adults alike danced around the fire pits, singing, while the elders kept beat on their drums.

When we readied to leave, Cécile loaded us up with food for the trip home. Jacques and Haro'nu greeted another man from the tribe who had rushed in at the last minute. Though he spoke in Wendat, I heard the man use the word for muskets.

Jacques replied, "I'll see what I can do." He clapped the man on the shoulder, then nodded to me and Catherine to let us know he was ready to go.

The sun sank low in the sky as we made our way back along the path through the woods. Catherine rode a few paces ahead on Shadow with Minette strapped to the cradleboard on her back. The horse seemed to know the way instinctively. I chose to walk with Jacques. I had much to think about. I worried about the conversation about guns, as selling them to the Native people was forbidden. But I decided that was none of my business.

"Jacques, did you know Cécile went to the convent school?" I asked.

"I did."

"But she never converted."

"No."

"Armand told me you insisted Catherine not be forced to the veil, or even to convert if she chooses not to."

"That is true."

"I don't understand. Cécile says she appreciates the education she was given, but I sense she resents it at the same time."

"She does not wish to become French."

"Is that what she thinks the sisters are doing? Turning the girls from Wendat into French?"

"Aren't they?"

I had no answer for him. It seemed more and more I had questions but no answers. The Ursulines in Québec were kind-hearted, they treated the girls well, respected them, even to the point of learning their language. But in truth, everything they did was for the purpose of converting them to Catholicism and making Frenchwomen of them. It dawned on me that to become French for the Wendat meant leaving behind the character and ways of their families, their own culture. When Sœur de Sainte-Agnès spoke of Cécile, it was always with a hint of regret. Regret for what? That she refused to be French? Something else was on my mind.

"Who is Miigwan?" I asked.

"A boy I know." He stopped suddenly. "Listen!"

At first, I heard nothing. Then…*whoo-whoo-whoo, whooo, whooo.* An owl!

"Where?" I whispered.

Jacques pointed to a tree in the distance. But there was nothing there. No, wait. On the second branch. Its eyes blinked. The owl blended in so well, I could barely make it out. Jacques put his hands up to his mouth and made the exact same sound. *"Whoo-whoo-whoo, whooo, whooo."*

The owl in the tree swiveled its head one way, then the other. Then it replied. *Whoo-whoo-whoo, whooo, whooo.*

"She thinks I am courting her," Jacques said, his voice low.

"Are you?" I asked.

He shrugged. "I think she is committed to someone else." He curled his fingers through Shadow's halter, and clicked his tongue, urging the horse forward.

The first *thunk* didn't register. Nor did the second. But the third caused my eyes to spring open. What was that sound? The early summer sun poured through the bedroom window as I lay in bed with Minette, half asleep, comforted in knowing Armand was home again, though his side of the bed was empty at the moment. He had arrived the day after our visit to Cécile, delighted to see Jacques, and grateful his friend had taken me and Catherine to the Wendat village.

Thunk.

I laid Minette in her cradle then wrapped a light shawl around my shoulders and went outside. Armand and Jacques stood about twenty paces from a makeshift target, a board they had nailed to a tree. The target consisted of several roughly drawn concentric circles with a thick dot in the center. I watched as Jacques raised his arm and threw the hatchet he often kept in his belt. It stuck in the target, near the dot.

Both men had their shirts off and were glistening with sweat in the morning sun. Armand was taller, solid. Jacques was more broad-shouldered, his chest and abdomen more muscular. The crane tattoo danced on his arm when he threw the weapon.

"Sylvienne!" Armand greeted me with his usual morning cheer.

Heat rose into my cheeks. I'd been staring at Jacques's tattoo.

"Bonjour, madame." Jacques's smile teased.

A butterfly flitted in my stomach. Murmuring a quick "Bonjour," I hurried back into the house. Why did I react so when he was around?

After supper, while Catherine cleaned up and Armand did his evening chores, I took Minette out to watch Jacques throw the hatchet again, hitting the tree target with a thud each time.

"Would you like to give it a try?" he asked.

"Me?"

"You've learned how to shoot a musket. After a fashion." He grinned and I knew he was referring to the incident with the bear last fall. "I don't have my bow and arrow with me, but I can teach you to throw a hatchet."

"Like a real woman of New France?" I said, thinking of how the women here learned to use tools and weapons that I never thought about in France.

"Exactly. Let me take Minette."

He cradled the baby in his arms and handed me the hatchet. I hefted the weapon. It felt odd in my hand, shorter than the ax I used to split wood. Trying to imitate his stance, I put one foot in front of the other, hefted the hatchet over my shoulder, and in a single swing brought it forward and let it loose. The hatchet somersaulted through the air and thudded into the dirt in front of the tree.

Jacques walked over to retrieve the hatchet, Minette in one arm as if carrying her was the most natural thing in the world. He handed it back to me. "Try again. But this time put a little muscle into it."

Determined to do better, I swung the hatchet back over my shoulder and let loose with as much force as I could. The hatchet sailed through the air to my delight, and…somersaulted right past the tree, landing on the ground beyond it.

"Not bad!" Jacques said.

"But I missed the target entirely."

"You did. But look how far it went. Now go fetch it."

"Me?"

"Yes, you," he said with a laugh. "You will learn faster if you have to retrieve it yourself each time. And I'm busy with this little beauty." He nuzzled Minette and made her squirm and giggle.

When I came back to the throwing spot and pulled the hatchet over my shoulder, he called out, "Wait."

He set Minette down in the grass for a moment and adjusted my leg stance and my hips. My cheeks grew hot at his touch, but I said nothing. He moved my arm into the correct position. "So...like this, yes?" He stood alongside me and demonstrated the throw. I mimicked him, first without letting go.

He demonstrated again, and I went through the motion again.

"Now," he said. "Put your back into it." He quickly scooped up Minette and jiggled her in his arms while he watched.

I pulled the hatchet back, then drew my arm forward, putting all my muscles into the throw and at the last moment opening my hand to let it go. The hatchet somersaulted through the air, hitting the target. And falling to the ground.

"I hit it!" I yelled. "I hit it!"

"Did you see your maman?" Jacques said to Minette. "With a bit more practice, she'll get it to stick."

I retrieved and threw the hatchet three more times; each time it bounced off the thick board. On the fourth try it stuck into the wood, just outside the circle.

I whooped and danced in a circle. "I did it! I did it!"

Armand had come out to watch. He took Minette from Jacques, and the two men clapped and stomped their feet on my behalf.

"Sylvienne, the hatchet thrower!" Armand said. He kissed my cheek. "You are the perfect wife."

He handed Minette to me, then picked me up by the waist and twirled me around with the baby in my arms.

Embarrassed, I glanced over at Jacques, who grinned as he strode over to retrieve his hatchet. He thumbed the blade. "I'll need your whetstone tonight," he said to Armand. Tossing the weapon into the air, he caught it by the handle as it came down.

Jacques was due to leave on a trading excursion at the end of the week. The day before, he stopped by the house again. He found me out back hanging wet clothes on the line.

"Armand left for the armory a few minutes ago," I said. "You just missed him."

"I'll stop there on my way out to say goodbye. I brought you something." He held out a brand new hatchet. His eyes crinkled with delight when I took it.

"A hatchet?" I hefted it.

"A friend of mine made it."

"One of the Wendat?"

"Ojibwe. He crafted it with a fit and balance that should work well for you."

Indeed, the handle was slimmer than his. It fit my hand perfectly. I took a couple of swings, amazed at how well-balanced it felt. Turning toward the tree, I sighted the target, drew back, and let go. The hatchet hit the wood with a satisfying *thunk* and stuck.

I threw my arms around Jacques. "Thank you!"

Realizing I was being inappropriate, I backed away quickly. Embarrassed, I ducked my head and walked over to retrieve the hatchet. He followed.

"You will need to use the whetstone to keep it sharp," he said. "And store it out of reach of the little one when she begins to crawl."

As I reached for the hatchet, Jacques's fingers drifted lazily down my arm, sending a guilty thrill through me that caused my heart to thump erratically.

"I wish I had met you first." His voice was low, barely a whisper.

Had I heard him correctly?

Tugging on the hatchet, freeing it from the wood, I couldn't, wouldn't tell him I sometimes wished the same. I resisted turning to look at him.

He leaned closer, his lips brushing against my neck.

A soft moan escaped my lips.

"Merde." He ran his hand through his hair, then turned abruptly and strode off.

Biting my lip, refusing to allow myself to watch him go, I clutched the hatchet until my hand hurt.

In bed that night, I lay next to my softly snoring husband. Moonlight played with the branches of the black walnut trees, causing shadows to dance on the wall.

The thrill of Jacques's lips on my neck kept me awake. I likely wouldn't see him again until late fall, after all the black walnuts had dropped from the trees and his beaver pelts had been collected. I counted that a good thing.

I thought about how freely I'd given myself to Etienne even while I was married to René. But René had never asked for my love. He only wanted my body in order to produce an heir and to gain favor with the King. When I hesitated in bed, he grew abusive. When I complained about his mistress, he struck me. Etienne had been the salve for my bruised soul.

I didn't need a salve with Armand. He loved me without condition, and I had come to love him for the gentle soul he was. I would never, could never be unfaithful to Armand or hurt him in any way. And the strange thing was, I knew Jacques felt the same. He loved Armand as a man loves a brother. His devotion to Armand, his willingness to walk away from temptation, was one of the things that drew me even more strongly to this rough riverman.

How was it possible to love more than one man? Why was love so complicated?

Damn the entanglements our hearts created!

CHAPTER TWENTY-FOUR

Despite the brick oven Armand had built for the use of our neighbors, I still bought our bread from the baker's shop in the lower village. One of the indulgences I refused to give up. As I walked through the village gate and stepped onto the path that would take me to our house, the basket of warm bread on my arm, I heard an oddly familiar huffing sound I couldn't quite place. A half-moment later, a large, black bear lumbered out of the bushes.

I froze.

The bear sniffed the air, then turned to take its measure of me.

Glancing around to see if there was a cub—none in sight—I said, "Good bear." Though I was quite sure my attempt at a soothing tone was useless.

I took a nervous step back. The bear took two steps forward. It sniffed the air again. I realized it had detected my basket of bread. Why I didn't just give it to him, I'll never know. I eyed a nearby tree, its lowest branch within reach. The bear started to lope toward me. My basket slung over my arm, I ran. I'd had plenty of experience as a child climbing trees, so it didn't take much to grab the branch and hoist myself up and onto the next branch. The bear, however, was undaunted. It stood on its hind legs and wrapped its front paws around the tree. Before I knew it, it had begun to climb after me.

With a scream, I threw my basket at it, hitting the beast on its head. The bear growled, annoyed. Looking over its shoulder to where the basket had landed, it shimmied back down and immediately went for the bread, pawing at the basket and pulling out the warm loaves I had planned to serve at dinner.

As I clung to the tree, my heart beating wildly, I wondered what to do. The bear was enjoying its meal and looked like it had no intention of moving on.

"Hiyaah!" a voice shouted. And out of nowhere, a rock flew past the tree and hit the bear on the hind end. The beast backed away. Another rock hit it on the shoulder. The bear huffed, grabbed what remained of the loaf in its mouth and scampered off.

I looked down to see who my rescuer was. A man with two months' worth of beard stubble on his chin, his fair hair hanging about his shoulders, and eyes bluer than the sky. My breath caught in my throat, and I grabbed the branch to keep from falling.

"Still climbing trees?" he said. "I would have thought you'd outgrown that."

"Etienne?" I could scarcely believe my eyes. But there he was, standing below me, his eyes dancing with delight as he raised his arms to help me down.

Once my feet were on the ground, I fell into his arms. He held me tightly, the thumping of his heart as fierce as mine. When I lifted my head, he smothered my mouth with his, fervent longing evident in the fierceness of his kisses. Finally, we stood apart, both breathing heavily. He was even more muscular than I'd remembered, his skin tanned and wind-worn, his hands rough. And something new. A scar running down the side of his face, just missing his left eye.

"How did you get here? When did you get here? Mon Dieu, I thought you were dead. Why did you never write to me?"

He put a finger to my lips to quiet me. "The story is a long one. But I signed on to work on one of the cargo ships coming from Calais. "

"A sailor?" My fingers traced the scar, the length of his jaw.

"More like a swabber of the deck. But yes." He laughed. "I've become a sailor of sorts. Once we unloaded the ship here, I resigned my commission and took a room in a boarding house. A Madame Robidoux."

"I know her. Oh, Etienne, I'd heard there was a bounty on your head. I didn't believe you could survive. And it was all my fault. I should never have involved you." Tears rolled down my cheeks unbidden.

"Shh…" Etienne wiped my tears. "None of what happened was your fault. You have no reason to blame yourself."

"But I—"

"You saved my life." He held me close while I wept more.

Finally, I was able to ask, "How did you escape the King's men? And the bounty hunters?"

"I've been on the run a long time. But I'm here now." He took me in his arms again, kissed me tenderly. I breathed in the essence of him, not the familiar scent of leather and lanolin that I had always loved, but a raw manly odor mingled with sea brine.

When we pulled apart again, he said, "I've saved some money. Enough to build a house. Not a big one, but over time we can add to it."

My heart seeming to stop, I gazed into those eyes that exactly matched my daughter's. "Etienne, I…I'm married again."

He blinked, uncomprehending. "Again? Did the King…?"

"No." I took his hand and held it between my two. "He...he is a man of my own choosing. And we...we are a family. With a baby."

His face froze. Became unreadable. "Of course. It's been a year and a half. Stupid of me to think you'd wait."

"Oh, Etienne. I truly thought you were dead."

His eyes, despite their sudden steeliness, couldn't hide his hurt. "Are you in love with him?"

"He...my husband...he's kind, and...and sincere. I—"

"Do you love him?" His voice hardened.

My own came out in barely a whisper. "Yes."

Etienne stepped back now. "I see." Looking up at the sky, he closed his hand into a fist, then forced it open again. "And a child, you say. A baby?" After a moment he gave me a reluctant smile. "I'll not bother you any further then." He leaned down and gave me a quick peck on the cheek. "I hope your new husband realizes how lucky he is."

He turned to leave, but I caught his sleeve. "Don't be angry. Don't go. Please. I want you to come home with me. There is someone I want you to meet."

"You want me to meet your husband?" His voice dripped with sarcasm.

"What? Of course not. Someone else. Come with me." I ran my finger down the scar on his face again, then I took him by the hand. We walked the short distance to the stone house near the river.

When we arrived, I greeted Catherine, her eyes full of unasked questions at the sight of a strange man with me. I took Minette from her cradle, her sleepy eyes just opening. She smiled when she saw me.

"Is this...?" Resignation saddened Etienne's voice.

"Minette. My daughter. Our daughter."

"Our? What do mean?" A look of confusion crossed his face.

"I was with child when I left France."

"But…how can you be sure she is…mine?"

"Look at her eyes. And the birthmark on her left shoulder." The half-moon birthmark matched the one on his right shoulder almost exactly.

He took her from me and cradled her in his arms, his eyes softening, growing moist. "I never imagined…" He sniffed her hair. "Does *he* know?"

"Armand knows she is not his child. I was already carrying her when we married. Beyond that, he hasn't asked."

"Is he a good father?"

It warmed my heart to hear his concern. "Yes. Kind and loving toward her. Much as my papa was to me."

"That's all I ask." He kissed her softly on the cheek. "Will you ever tell her? Who her real father is? Who I am?"

"If you want me to."

"What would you have done if you'd known about Guy d'Aubert? Known as a child he wasn't your real father?"

"I think I would have gone on loving him. But perhaps my life would have turned out differently if I'd known from the beginning who my real father was."

Etienne, cradling Minette in his arms, looked up suddenly when the door opened and Armand walked in.

CHAPTER TWENTY-FIVE

Armand regarded the stranger in our house with cautious amiability. "Bonjour," he said to Etienne.

"You're home early," I said, taking Minette from Etienne.

"We completed the addition to the fort, and the governor gave me the rest of the day off."

"Armand, this is a friend of mine," I said, keeping my voice as natural sounding as I could, despite the nervousness in my stomach. "Newly arrived from France."

Etienne stuck out his hand to shake Armand's. "Damise," he said. "Etienne Damise dit le Rouge."

Damise. His mother's family name. Of course, he would have changed his name from Gerard to avoid being recognized by anyone seeking him for the price on his head.

"Armand Gervais." He shook Etienne's hand. "Monsieur Damise, welcome to Québec." I could see a subtle wariness in his eyes, but he kept his smile. "Le Rouge, did you say?"

The moniker was usually awarded to red heads. Etienne's hair was fair, but had no hint of red. He grinned. "I worked my way over as a sailor. A poor one, I'm afraid, never having sailed before. The men on board nicknamed me Red because I burned so easily out on deck."

Armand chuckled. "And what skill do you bring to the colony if not a sailor?" Armand's gaze shifted from Etienne's blue eyes to Minette's, but he said nothing, nor did his demeaner give any hint as to what he was thinking.

"I'm a shoemaker by trade. I'm hoping to start a business."

"We certainly need good shoemakers. Would you like something to drink? We make a pretty good beer here in the colony."

"Tempting," Etienne said, "but I'm afraid I must go. It was good to see you again, Sylvienne…uh…Madame Gervais. Nice to meet you, monsieur. The baby is quite a beauty."

Before I could respond, he nodded at each of us, then strode out the door.

Armand took Minette from me and tossed her up and down a few times, enjoying her delighted giggles. "Seems a nice fellow," he said to me, his voice unnaturally even. "How do you know him?"

"He…lived in Amiens. His father made shoes for my mother and me."

He handed Minette back to me. "If he decides to settle in Québec, I think I should like to get to know him. It's always handy to know someone who can make a good pair of boots." Something in his tone, however, caused me to wonder at the motive behind his comment.

The next morning, after Armand left for the armory, a dull pit formed in my stomach as I washed the morning dishes. Catherine offered to take Minette outside to enjoy the sunshine. LeDuc, as ever, followed them out.

Closing the door behind them, I sagged against it. Was it possible to love two men at the same time? Or three? Could I really let Etienne go again? And why did my heart thump so erratically when Jacques was near?

At supper the night before, I had picked at my food while Armand told me about his day. That night, lying beside him, I barely slept. Now, with a new determination growing, I put on a fresh dress and walked with purpose to Madame Robidoux's boarding house. When I knocked at the door, Madame Robidoux gave me an odd look.

"Monsieur Girard, please. I mean Damise. Monsieur Damise dit le Rouge?"

"He's gone."

"Gone?"

"At first light. Said he'd booked passage with a voyageur going up to Ville-Marie."

"I see." My heart sank. "Merci, madame." I turned and walked away.

My gaze drifted to the river, busy with sailing vessels of all sizes. Was he in one of those canoes? Chances were, if he left at dawn, he was well on his way to Trois-Rivières, the half-way point between Québec and Ville-Marie. Had I sent him away for good, this time? Perhaps it was for the best. He was alive. That was all that mattered. My heart rejoiced to know it. To have seen him, touched him, kissed his lips.

At the same time, I mourned for what could not be. He had crossed an ocean to find me. And again, I had turned him away when my heart, my body, desperately wanted him; when I had a child who belonged to him. My soul felt heavy. Was God still punishing me for the avarice I committed before coming to this land? How could I look Armand in the eye, sleep in his arms, when my heart still longed for Etienne?

I would find a way. I would overcome my confusion and make myself into the best wife possible for Armand. For we had sworn to be faithful and honor each other unto death. I was determined this was an oath I would keep.

Word spread that the Gravels had bolts of cotton fabric in their store. I had promised myself I wouldn't go in there again, but there was nowhere else to buy such fabric. And I wanted to make some baby gowns for Minette.

As I perused the fabric table, Claudette waited on another customer, Mathieu Pecquet, the gunsmith. I decided on two fabrics and took them over to her to cut the size I needed.

"Have you heard the news from France?" Claudette asked, pointing her shears toward a small stack of gazettes sitting on the far end of the counter. Her voice took on a conspiratorial tone. "According to the Gazette de Paris, the King has legitimized his brats by Mademoiselle de la Valliere. Marie-Anne and little Louis."

Typically, I would ignore such gossip, but today curiosity got the better of me. I picked up one of the gazettes.

"He has given them titles and property. A chateau in the north of Touraine for the girl, according to the story," Claudette said as she bundled my fabric and tied it with a ribbon, pretending nonchalance. All the while her voice held insinuation. "You'll have to read it yourself to see what the boy got."

"Good for them, I guess. It increases their marriage prospects. But honestly, it is of no concern to me."

"So you say. Did you never meet Mademoiselle de la Valliere while you were at court?"

"She had gone into the convent before I arrived." I handed over my coins.

"That's too bad. They say when she was the premier mistress and was indisposed, her maid-of-honor, Madame de Montespan, serviced the King."

"Mmm." I knew all about those stories. I couldn't get enough of them when I was a girl in school pouring over the gazettes—before I tasted life at court. "I paid scant attention to that sort of thing. And I have no interest in it now."

I picked up my fabric and turned to go. Despite my words to the contrary, the news of La Valliere's children being legitimized *was* of personal interest to me—but not for the reason Claudette thought. I turned back. "You might as well give me one of those gazettes. I'd like to see what they have been wearing in Paris as of late."

I handed her another coin. Her grin as she held out the gazette told me she thought she knew me. I tucked the pamphlet carelessly between the folds of my fabric and strode out of the store, blinking in the bright sunlight.

The King had legitimized La Valliere's children. The news caught me by surprise. I wondered about the children of Athénaïs de Montespan. Had he —

"Madame Gervais! Wait!" The boy who delivered mail from the ships trotted toward me. The mail pouch over his shoulder bounced as he waved a letter in the air. "The captain offers his apologies that he did not get this to you sooner, but they've been busy unloading cargo."

I fished a coin from my pocket and gave it to him. He thanked me and ran off. I immediately recognized the handwriting on the letter. It was from my dear friend from Amiens, Marie-Catherine. I tucked the letter into my pocket and kept going.

Once home, I checked on Minette sleeping contentedly in her cradle. Catherine was pulling laundry from the line out back, and LeDuc was having fun harassing the chickens.

I had a few precious moments to myself. So, after setting my new fabric on top of one of the chests to deal with later, I sat on my bed and examined the series of addresses scrawled across Marie-Catherine's letter. She had sent it to my late husband's house in Paris. But by then I was gone, so it was sent on to Versailles, where some kind soul took the time to forward the letter to me here in Québec. Marie-Catherine must have written the letter just before I left France, and it had taken a full year and then some to find me.

Breaking the seal on the letter, I scanned the contents. I could scarcely believe what I was reading. I read it a second time, making sure I understood each word.

Dearest Sylvienne,

I have astounding news. The most incredible scandal has happened here in Amiens. It involves the family of Claudette Grandin, our former classmate, and the poor girl herself. If you remember, her father was co-owner of a highly profitable textile manufacturing company. He was also the major contributor to the Ursuline convent and the very school we attended. Well! It came to light several weeks ago that he was stealing profits from his own company. His business partner, M. Fleury, enraged to discover the misappropriations, confronted M. Grandin with the accusation which M. Grandin is said to have taken umbrage with.

M. Grandin, in his own fit of rage, set upon M. Fleury, and beat him to death. However, just before the poor man expired, his son, Claudette's betrothed, came upon the two. With his last dying breath, the young man's father told his shocking story. Whereupon, the son chased down M. Grandin and ran him through with his sword. Said son now resides in our local prison awaiting trial. Claudette's mother, in the meantime, keeled over in a fit of apoplexy from which she never recovered.

Claudette was their only child and has disappeared along with the money her father stole from the business coffers. No one knows if ruffians have set upon her, or whether she has gone south to live amongst her Protestant relatives in the Cévennes. I can't say I blame her if the latter is the case. But what a mystery! And how awful to have such a stain upon our community perpetrated by her family. I don't know what will become of the Grandin & Fleury Textile Company. My father says it is a significant economic loss to Amiens.

I have only received one letter from you so far. I pray you are well.
Marie-Catherine

So that was why Claudette boarded the ship to New France at the same time I did. The timing was coincidental, but the circumstances of her decision to flee France were quite dire.

And the travel chest she hovered over so. Could it have contained the money from her father's business? Was that how Gravel was able to afford to build a new ship and invest in Intendant Talon's brewery?

What was I to do with this information? Certainly, the authorities in Amiens would want a reckoning if it were true Claudette absconded with money her father had stolen, money which had been the catalyst for the death of both business partners. Claudette was just as much a fugitive as I was. More so, as she was eluding the law with stolen money. I had no doubt what Marie-Catherine reported was true, as she was not one who traded in rumors.

I knew I should show the letter to Armand. No doubt he would want to take it to the Sovereign Council. Let them deal with it. But something caused me to hesitate. A nagging feeling that I did not wish to be the purveyor of someone else's scandal, perhaps?

Catherine came in with a bundle of folded diapers. She set them on the shelf near Minette's crib. I tucked the letter from my friend into the box where I stored my stationery. I would show it to Armand later, when we had a few minutes alone, and I'd had time to think about the repercussions of making it public.

He was spending long days at the armory lately. A new supply of gunpowder had arrived on the same ship as my letter, and he was charged with supervising the unloading of it, transporting it up to the armory, and storing it. When he came home that evening, he told me over a late supper that a number of barrels were missing, causing an investigation to ensue.

"One of the sailors claims the ship's captain sold the barrels to traders at Tadoussac," he said. "The captain is denying it. We're holding him and the entire crew in the garrison prison until I can ferret out the truth." Exhausted, he apologized and went to bed right after he finished eating.

It took several days, but finally he determined that two members of the crew had hidden the barrels until all the unloading in Québec was completed. "The thieves snuck the barrels onto a flat-bottomed boat and took them across the river," he told me. "They sold them to a couple of coureur des bois who planned to use the gunpowder in trade to the Natives."

"Did they really think they could get away with something like that?" I asked.

Armand shrugged. "The ship's captain was none too pleased with me, despite my apology on behalf of the garrison when we let him and the rest of his crew go."

"What will happen to the two men?"

"It's a capital offense to steal from the Crown. And to sell guns or ammunition to the Natives. They'll be tried and sentenced to hang."

The trial was swift, a guilty verdict returned the same day. But then, Armand told me afterward, one of the men was spared because he agreed to be executioner to the other.

"He agreed to hang his accomplice?" My jaw dropped in astonishment.

"And now he's got a new job."

"As executioner?"

"They are hard to come by. Talon was happy to grant him the position."

The investigation, the arrest, trial, and the execution all wore on Armand. He'd been coming home late most nights, gobbling down his supper and going straight to bed.

The letter from Marie-Catherine lay forgotten in my stationery box.

CHAPTER TWENTY-SIX

Armand finally took a day off. Usually, he was up at first light to feed Shadow, but when he groaned at getting up, I laid a hand on his back and said I would take care of it. He grunted his appreciation and a moment later was snoring again.

Minette stirred in her cradle, so I picked her up and brought her into our bed and nursed her. When she was finished, I put her back into her crib to sleep a while longer before dressing to begin my day. I could already hear Catherine in the kitchen, preparing breakfast.

"I'm going out to feed Shadow," I said to her. "I'll bring in the eggs when I'm done." LeDuc jumped up to follow me out. He loved nosing around the barn while I mucked out the stall and set out fresh hay. I led Shadow out to the paddock, then set to work. When I finished, I stopped at the chicken coop, which Armand had repaired and given a fresh coat of paint early in the spring.

I returned to the kitchen with nearly a dozen eggs nestled in my apron. Catherine edged past me, hauling laundry out to the backyard tub. She seemed in a hurry to get out of the kitchen.

By now Armand was awake and sitting at the table eating bread Catherine had toasted for him over the fire and smeared with butter and honey. A ledger book lay open in front of him. He kept careful accounts on the management of the seigneury — rents due and paid, cost of repairs to the house and outbuildings, sales of crops, and so on.

In the middle of the table lay the gazette I had purchased from Claudette's store and a familiar leather pouch. The pension from the King. Gold livres I had never told him about.

"What is this doing here?" I asked.

"I was digging through one of the chests looking for something, and I came across it. It's quite a lot of money." He pushed his plate aside. "Were you hiding it from me?"

"Not hiding. No. I…just never mentioned it, I guess."

"Not when I talked about wanting to put a new roof on the house? Or find a way to add on a room? It is your money, but I don't understand why you are averse to sharing it with me. I thought our marriage was a partnership."

"It is! We are. Partners. It's just…" I sat down heavily. "I've been saving…for passage back to France."

His eyes flicked toward the gazette. "You wish to return to France? I thought there were circumstances making that impossible?"

"There were. Still are. But I've always held a dream of returning to Amiens. Living quietly. Near Maman. Without anyone from…court knowing."

"You're not happy here? You wish to leave me?" The look in his eyes tore at my heart.

"No! I am happy here. It's just…I thought…perhaps if we went, we'd go as a family. Have you never thought about going back, Armand?"

He shrugged. "There was a time I did. But my life is here now. What would we do in Amiens?"

"My mother has a cottage. Not far outside the town walls. And there's…there's a house, a manor house, next door, that should belong to her. But my uncle bribed a judge into assigning it to him when Papa died, claiming the inheritance laws wouldn't allow us to keep it. I thought if you were with me, as my husband, we could petition to get it back. I couldn't inherit it as a woman, but you could, as my husband."

When he didn't say anything, just gazed at me with confusion in his eyes, I said, "It's a silly dream. I don't think I ever really planned on it. But would you…ever consider going back?"

He sighed. "I've never been wedded to any one spot on this earth. But Sylvienne, we've made this our home. We have standing in the community. Why did you never speak of this before?"

"I don't know. I guess I always knew it was nothing more than wishful thinking. I thought of bringing it up a number of times, but it never seemed like the right moment. And now…you're right. This is our home." I pushed the pouch toward him. "We have need of this money. Things you want to do for the house. Use it."

He shook his head. "You earned it. At the hospital. Put it away."

I winced inwardly. The pouch held the pension the King had awarded me. Why did I not speak up and tell him that?

He stood up. "If the need becomes great enough, we'll have it as a backup. But Sylvienne, please promise you'll tell me if you are unhappy."

"I will. I promise. But I don't expect to ever be."

He nodded and strode to the door before I could jump up to hug him, reassure him. I closed my eyes momentarily against the disappointment I knew I had caused. Heaving a sigh, I reached for the gazette. It must have fallen out of the fabric when Armand was lifting the chest lid. The lead article was about Philippe's new marriage. I had no desire to read it now.

My gaze fell upon the article Claudette had mentioned. The legitimization of the King's young children by his former mistress, Louise de la Vallière. I read just enough to learn that Athénaïs de Montespan's children were also to be legitimized.

She had delivered a second baby by the King. I was happy for them. No one deserved to live with the banner of "bastard" hanging over their heads, whether royal or no. Perhaps if I were to go back to France one day, I would feel differently. But that was a moot point. I wouldn't be going back. At least not any time soon.

I picked up Armand's plate and set it in the wash bucket, knowing I had so many blessings to count. I had a decent house. I had a baby who knew this place only as one of happiness. She was healthy in a way many children in France would never be. She wanted for nothing, despite not living in a palace. I had friends. Friends who cared for me not because of any political or financial advantage I could afford them. They cared for me because that's what friends did. And I had a husband who loved me, treasured me, would do anything for me. And who now felt betrayed by the simple act of my squirreling away a bit of money for a silly dream.

But I knew it wasn't the money that mattered to him. It was the betrayal of confidence. The lack of openness and honesty on my part. If he only knew, I thought with dread. I had promised ours would be a marriage where honesty was valued. But there was one secret I could never share with him. And it had nothing to do with money.

The crack of a log in the fireplace brought me up short. Leaving the money pouch on the table, I went to stir the fire. When it was blazing again, I dropped the gazette into it, watching as the pages singed, curled, and eventually caught the flame.

That night, after the house was quiet, I lay in bed next to Armand. "I'm sorry," I said.

"No need to be." He touched my cheek, then ran his fingers down my arm. I pulled him onto me, and we made sweet, quiet love with the moon shining through the window the way I remember it shining into my bedroom in Amiens.

With mid-June came the summer solstice and *la Fête de la Saint-Jean-Baptiste*, when all of Québec gathered to celebrate. There was to be a bonfire in the lower village, down near the river. At dusk, cannons would be fired from the fort to honor the saint. And, of course, there would be dancing and singing and drinking late into the night.

Perrette and her husband and their two children had made plans to ferry across from the island and stay overnight with Armand and me. I was excited for Perrette to meet Minette for the first time.

I was so a-jitter waiting for their arrival, I changed Minette into a different dress three times over. Finally, tired of my ministrations, she set up a squall. Armand took her from me and bounced her up and down until she laughed.

"Let's walk down to the river and watch for them," he said, passing Minette to Catherine.

Leaving the girls at the house, Armand and I went down to the water. It wasn't long before we spotted the flat-bottomed barge Perrette's husband Jean had hired to ferry them from the island.

Jean lifted the children and handed them one by one to Armand, who set them on the grass near me. Then he helped Perrette, who climbed clumsily off the barge. No wonder she was hesitant and awkward—she was pregnant again! We hugged, then walked arm in arm back up to the house, the little ones running in circles around us, the men ambling as they conversed.

When Perrette laid eyes on Minette, she gasped in delight and immediately took her from Catherine. "Oh, my! What beautiful big eyes." Her gaze shifted to me momentarily. "So blue."

She kissed Catherine on both cheeks, her eyes never lingering on the girl's burn scars. I had told her the story of the attack on Catherine the last time we met. She had expressed sympathy then, but she showed no apprehension concerning the girl's disfigurement when speaking to her.

After a quick lunch of fava bean soup, we packed dinner foods in a basket—eel crepinettes and strawberry tarts—and headed into town. Jeanne and Michel LeBlanc had saved room for us on picnic blankets near enough to the growing mound of bonfire wood to be able to enjoy the sight, but far enough away to keep the children from getting hurt. Jeanne was huge with their first child due in less than a month. She and Perrette immediately began talking about the needs of babies.

Arnauld Ducharme, the barrel maker and his family, with Titus in tow, set up a blanket near ours. Gazing around at the happy crowd, I couldn't believe I once thought my life was over. As I watched Armand playing with Minette and LeDuc, Catherine whispering with Titus, friends dancing in the town square, I realized Québec was a place of new beginnings. New families with young children. New opportunities to learn a trade. A new village rising out of the forest along the river. Each day filled with the promise of a new dawn. The thought of it made me giddy. Or perhaps I was feeling tipsy from the beer Armand had purchased from a nearby vendor.

BOOM! The thunder of cannon fire made me jump and set Minette to wailing. *BOOM! BOOM!* I covered Minette's ears. The salvo of cannons reminded me that despite the joy I was experiencing, this was a raw land filled with danger and requiring the constant presence of a militia.

That night, Perrette's two exhausted children curled up on makeshift mattresses near the fire, Armand and Jean nearby, allowing my friend and I to have the bed. While I nursed Minette to sleep, Perrette and I whispered in low tones.

"I'm so glad you could come," I said.

"It was a glorious day. My little ones will never forget it." Her eyes crinkled with mischief. "Can we try out your stones?"

"My stones?"

"I want to see if you truly do have your mother's gift."

"Oh, Perrette, no." But she gave me a look I couldn't resist.

I laid the now sleeping Minette into her crib then fetched the ornamental wood box in which I kept the stones. I poured them out on the bed. She knew the routine and chose several. Looking over the remaining stones with a dramatic expression, I said as quietly as possible, "You are going to be abducted by pirates and held for ransom. But you will fall in love with the peg-legged captain of the pirate ship and refuse to go back. You will become the most infamous woman pirate of them all."

She giggled. "You do have the gift. Now let me tell yours." For a change, I was the one picking up stones. Perrette waved her hand dramatically over the others. "You will grow feathers and wings and fly off to live among the swans in the great lake of Michigame!"

We giggled and made up more wild fortunes for each other. Finally, she pushed the stones aside and reached for my hand. "That was fun. Silly, but fun. But something is on your mind. I can tell." Perrette had always known when something was bothering me, even when we were children back in Amiens.

Hesitating, I tried to find a way to say what had been consuming my thoughts the past month. "Perrette, Etienne is alive."

"Alive? How do you know?"

"He's here. Not in Québec. Well, he was, briefly. I believe he's gone to Ville-Marie."

"Here, in New France? Sylvienne, what a relief!" She watched as I scooped the stones into the box and set them on the night table. "But what does that mean? For you?"

I shrugged. "It means nothing. I am married."

"It can't mean nothing. I very well remember those blue eyes of his. It's obvious he's Minette's father. Does he know?"

"He does. He's met her. I had to grant him that."

"Does Armand know?"

"I suspect so. Though he doesn't say. He's never asked. But he...he, too, noticed how well their eyes match."

"Armand met Etienne? That must have been awkward."

"For me, yes! Armand was a gentleman, as always. Etienne seemed a bit surprised and put off. But what was I to do?"

"Will you see him again?"

"Etienne? I don't know. I mean, if he ever comes to Québec again, it will be hard to avoid him. But I was unfaithful to one husband. I won't do that to Armand. Ever."

She nodded in understanding, then scoffed. "I was so sure you two were destined to marry."

"And now I'm married for the second time." I blew out the candle.

"And neither time to him. Poor Etienne." She pulled the blanket over us. "To have come all this way."

Fortunately, it was too dark for her to see the tears welling in my eyes.

CHAPTER TWENTY-SEVEN

The ship carrying the last of the King's recruits arrived in late July. Leaving Minette with Catherine, I walked down to the lower village to greet them along with the Ursulines. Those poor girls. I shivered remembering how it felt. It had been not more than a year ago when I arrived on *La Nativité,* dirty, flea-bitten, my hair dry and brittle.

The sisters hustled the two dozen young women off to the convent to clean them up, introduce them to their new life here in New France, and teach them what they needed to know in order to be good wives to the rough and ready men awaiting them. By August the weddings would begin, and there would be more music and dancing in the lower village square.

During one of our shopping excursions in town late in the summer, Armand said he wanted to stop by the gunsmith's shop. He needed some repairs done on one of our muskets, and he wished to pick up a flintlock pistol he had ordered some months before. Mathieu Pecquet, the gunsmith, was conversing with another customer when we arrived, saying he had recently returned from Fort Ville-Marie.

My ears perked up when he mentioned the tiny village, built on an island called Montreal, for that was where Etienne supposedly had gone. Pecquet told us the young community was growing quickly, and he predicted it would one day overtake Québec in size and commerce. I found the idea hard to believe but held my tongue.

He had brought back a Kalthoff repeater, a Danish gun, purchased from a merchant there. Armand was especially interested in the Kalthoff weapon, asking whether Pecquet could make something similar for his soldiers.

"That's why I bought it. I can use it as a model and make them here. For a price, of course."

"Of course," Armand said. "If you allow me to show this one to Governor Courcelle, I will put in a procurement request for three to start with. And what are those boots you are wearing? Something new from Fort Ville-Marie as well?"

"A new shoemaker from France has set up shop there."

My eyes shifted to the leather boots the gunsmith wore. They were knee-high, like most French boots, but made of the soft deerskin I had seen the local Natives wearing, with fringe at the top.

"I wonder if he's the same one I met on the ship coming over this spring?" another customer said.

"A new shoemaker?" Armand glanced at me. I tried to act nonchalant, but the gunsmith had grabbed my attention.

"This man knows his business, I can tell you that," Pecquet said. "He's familiar with many of the latest styles from Paris and Rouen and is developing a few of his own that make more sense in the coarse conditions here."

"If this is the same fellow I knew, he's had a rough go of it," the customer said. "Had a nasty scar on his face. When I asked him about it, he said a man in an ale house mistook him for someone with a price on his head. He proved them wrong with his fists. But later, they came back with knives and said they would get their money one way or the other. They beat him up and took the money he'd been saving for passage. He ended up working on the ship, mopping decks and dumping slop buckets to pay his way."

"It must be one and the same," Pecquet said. "This shoemaker has a pretty mean scar. He's combined his business with that of a glove-maker. I swear, this man will go places. Not that there are many places here in Canada to go except on the river." He laughed at his own attempt at a joke. Then he declared, "We can use more entrepreneurs like this one, with or without a scar."

When we left the gunsmith's shop, Armand said, "I think your friend has found his calling here."

"How do you know it's him?" I asked.

"Do you doubt it?"

I shook my head. "Does it concern you that he is wanted? Has a price on his head?"

"What happened in France is of no concern to me here." Armand looped my arm through his as we walked. "People with his business acumen are needed in the colony. As long as he doesn't cause problems, I see no reason to get involved."

I, on the other hand, was both relieved and distraught to learn of Etienne's new-found success and the harrowing time he'd had trying to get here. He was a man who knew how to chase his dream. It saddened me, though, knowing I could no longer be part of that dream.

Armand said he wanted to check in on Titus, to see how he was doing with the barrel maker. A new shop had opened in the lower village, and I wanted to see if they had cotton fabric I could use to make dresses for Minette, so we went separate ways. As I walked past Claudette's shop, she rushed to the door to call me in. I hesitated. Every time I encountered that woman, it turned out badly.

"I think you will want to see the gazette that came in with the latest shipment from France," she said. "There is an article about you. At least, I believe it to be you."

Frowning, I followed her inside. She led me to a back storage room which held a desk for keeping their accounts. A gazette from Paris lay on the desk.

"Only one copy. It was tucked into a box, used to cushion some plateware we had ordered. I almost threw it out. But goodness, it's a good thing I thought to look through it. There is a column devoted entirely to the sad death of the Duc de Narbonne. Your husband, no?"

I stiffened. My stomach churned.

"Let's see." She thumbed through the pages, making a show of looking for the article. "Here it is. 'Word from Versailles has it that the sudden death of the Duc de Narbonne happened under suspicious circumstances. While the Office of the Crown denies it, and his nephew remains mum on the topic — due to a large payout, it has been suggested — whispers along the corridors of Versailles hint that the duke did not die of apoplexy in his palace apartment, but rather in the workshop of the King's favorite shoemaker, from a knife lodged unceremoniously in his back.'"

I could feel the blood drain from my face. I grasped the edge of the desk to keep my legs from buckling.

"Oh, and listen to this…'The shoemaker in question evaded interrogation and has not been seen since. *Coincidentally,*'" Claudette emphasized the word, "'the sudden disappearance of the Duchesse de Narbonne, which had been previously explained by the noble woman's need to return home to her ill mother, has been called into question. Those who whisper now tell a different story. Could it be true the King offered said duchesse a choice between joining the cloister in Compiègne or boarding the first ship to sail for the New World? Why would he require such a choice? And which did she accept? The devout sisters at Compiègne have taken a vow of silence, so perhaps we'll never know.'"

With a dramatic flourish, she held the gazette out to me. "One copy. It is yours in exchange for the letter of recommendation I requested last spring."

As if in a dream, a nightmare, I reached out to take the gazette, but she pulled it away. Not quickly. Teasingly. "I have paper and pen at the ready if you care to use it." She pointed the gazette at a stack of linen stationery and an inkpot and quill.

I gulped.

"I take it the good Captain Gervais knows nothing of how the Duc de Narbonne died."

Unable to respond, my entire body frozen, I simply stared at her.

"It need go no further than this room," she prodded. She held up the gazette as if examining it intently. "Tell me, Sylvienne…was the 'favorite shoemaker' of the King by any chance the brother of our convent school classmate in Amiens? Marie-Catherine?" She let the gazette drop onto the desk next to the stationery. Her voice hardened. "The recommendation?"

Marie-Catherine. Her letter. I blinked as if coming up out of deep water. I could breathe again. "No. You will give me the gazette."

"What?" She asked as if she hadn't heard me.

In a firm voice, I repeated my words. "You will give me the gazette and drop your request for a recommendation."

"Why ever would I do that?"

"Because…" My voice became steely. "Because you are wanted as well."

Now she stiffened. "What do you mean?"

"In Amiens. Your father's business funds." I reached over and plucked the gazette from the desk. "He stole that money and beat his business partner to death. Then his son, your fiancé, killed your father. And now *he* is in prison awaiting the hangman. And you...you ran away with the money they fought to the death over."

"No...I...I...How did you...?"

"I assume Monsieur Gravel knows nothing of how you came to be in possession of enough gold to fund his new ship?"

Claudette's face went white. "You can't tell him." When I said nothing, her voice turned to pleading. "Sylvienne, you can't tell anyone. I...we...his business is so successful. I used that money for good." She sank onto the desk chair.

"Then we are in agreement. You will say nothing to anyone about the death of my first husband. And I will not speak of your family's sad misfortunes, and how you came to be in possession of so much money."

I folded the gazette and tucked it under my arm as I strode out of the stuffy, candlelit air of Gravel's store and into the fresh, sunlit breeze blowing off the river.

CHAPTER TWENTY-EIGHT

I didn't tell Armand about my confrontation with Claudette.

The truth was, the last time my husband, the Duc de Narbonne, had forced himself upon me in an ugly manner, I went to Etienne for protection. The Duc found us, intent on killing Etienne. He came within inches with his sword. If I hadn't stopped him, Etienne would be dead. My punishment was banishment from France.

What would Armand do if he learned of my crime? I didn't want to know. Even though he never said anything after walking in to find Etienne in our house, I knew it nettled him that Etienne and I had once been lovers. He could live with fathering Minette. Could he live with knowing I had killed my previous husband? I was not willing to find out.

And I saw no reason to tell him of Claudette's crime concerning her father's business funds. As she said, Gravel had built a profitable business and had standing in the community. Her past was behind her, as was mine.

Armand and I found less and less time to be intimate. He was exhausted from long days at work. And for me, summer passed in a whorl of diapers, gardening, and mosquitoes.

I'd finally learned to ignore the stench of bear grease, applying it not only to my exposed face, neck, and arms but to

Minette's as well, washing it off both of us every night before bed. While I didn't require Armand to bathe regularly—the tub was too large to fill more than once every week or so—I did insist he wash away the bear grease before climbing between the sheets. I applied dabs of honey to the inevitable itchy welts that rose up in the mornings. I swear, the nasty little beasts bit us while we slept at night.

Minette was on the move and curious about everything. She perfected crawling, most often chasing after LeDuc, with whom she snuggled when both napped. I set aside her cradleboard, determined to let her follow her curiosity, just as Maman had let me follow mine.

On the days Armand allowed LeDuc to accompany him on his rounds of the village and the military compound, Minette sat near the window, whining and waiting for their return. When the door opened, she shrieked and lifted her chubby arms for Armand to pick her up and hug her. Once he set her back down, she sought out LeDuc who happily played tug of war with rags and fetch with hemp dolls.

The new round of wedding celebrations began, with dancing in the village square almost weekly. Titus, timid at first, joined our family group whenever he could, usually choosing to sit near Catherine. When she struggled with the food basket, he was quick to help her carry it, and they lean their heads together in conversation more and more.

One day, when he was reaching to keep Minette from toddling off and hurting herself, I noticed his wrists. Both bore scars I could only assume were from his time in bondage. Were they the only scars he bore? I doubted it. Perhaps that was why he was able to look beyond Catherine's scarred face and see her for who she was. The thought of it endeared him to me even more.

Late one August night, while Armand, Minette, and Catherine slept, I found myself tossing and turning in bed. For some reason, my eyes would not shut. I worried I would wake Armand with my restlessness. It was warm in the house, so I grabbed a shawl and stepped outside hoping for a breeze, LeDuc padding along with me.

A ribbon of moonlight danced on the river in the distance. A warm wind kept the ever-present mosquitos at bay. I looked up seeking the Big Dipper. To my surprise, overhead danced the green and purple ribbons of the northern lights, the *waawaate* Jacques had called them. Tingles coursed down my arms. Had someone died? Was this the dance of their ancestors welcoming them into heaven? I watched for a long time as LeDuc sniffed the grass and the bushes nearby. After a while, he settled at my feet.

When my neck began to ache from looking up, I said, "Let's go inside."

LeDuc immediately jumped to his feet and headed to the door. Climbing into bed next to Armand, I fell into dreamless slumber.

The letter I had been dreading came from Marie-Catherine, writing to me from Amiens.

> *My Dearest Sylvienne,*
> *I have news of both joy and heartbreak. Your dear mother, Isabelle, is with God in His Heavenly Home at last.*

Maman was sick before I left Amiens, nearly four years ago. I'd always hoped it was nothing more than a persistent cold, but in my heart, I knew she was seriously ill. Her letters to me had grown fewer and farther between, and shorter in length. Sometimes she wrote only a few lines to let me know she was thinking of me, and how much she missed me.

My guilt over not being able to be with her at the end deepened my sadness over her death. I had always hoped one day Minette would know the joy of being in the arms of her grandmother, hearing her sing the lullabies she sang to me as a baby, knowing her smile. Maman died never seeing the delight and curiosity in Minette's eyes. Never feeling the joy of her sweet laughter. That their paths would never cross on this earth was of my doing, and it broke my heart knowing if I'd only followed a different path when Etienne first asked me to marry him, my daughter and my mother could have known each other. That was to be my burden for the rest of my life.

Unable to fall asleep again that night, I stepped outside to see if the colors were once more dancing across the sky. Would they whisper to me of Maman being welcomed into heaven by our ancestors? To my dismay the sky was shrouded in thick clouds threatening rain.

In the morning, taking a break from my chores, I pulled out the small box with my stones. Holding them comforted me now. What had Maman thought about my life in New France? Could she ever have imagined that I would remarry, have a child, live a kind of life that was closer to the one we had lived in Amiens than at Versailles? I know she would have approved of Armand. But what would she have counseled me concerning my confusion over Etienne? And Jacques. Would she have chastised me for letting my heart wander when I was already happily married? Certainly, she would have understood my need to provide for my child the way she had provided for me when she married Papa. I loved Armand in my own way, and I vowed always to be faithful to him, but ours wasn't the kind of love that filled my soul.

With a sigh, I tipped the box of stones and let them tumble onto the table. Why could I never see my own future in them? Maman had predicted the storm that would cause me to flee Versailles, though she hadn't foreseen any of the details. She wasn't able to see what was on the other side of the storm cloud. Perhaps just as well. She might have been horrified to know where I would end up.

"What are those?" Catherine's voice startled me as she peered over my shoulder.

"Nothing. Just some stones I've collected over the years."

She sat down and began fingering them, turning them over one by one. "They're pretty." An aura seemed to surround her. A sense of her future awaiting. Despite the scarring on her face, her beauty shone through when she smiled. She hummed a bit as she played with the stones. And in that moment, I knew for certain she was on the verge of a life filled with love, a home shared with a man who adored her.

Around the time of the harvest moon, Minette began pulling herself up with the aid of chairs or the bed. She took her first tentative steps, eager to catch LeDuc, who taunted her into motion.

An invitation to the governor's harvest luncheon and ball arrived in mid October. I tried to beg off, but Armand shook his head. "We can't keep avoiding these invitations, Sylvienne. The governor is my superior after all."

Indeed, there had been other invitations during the summer, but I had managed to come up with excuses for sending our regrets each time, and Armand hadn't pushed me on it. But this time we couldn't refuse.

Catherine helped me adjust one of the silk dresses I'd brought from France, a honey-colored skirt with a matching bodice trimmed with green and brown embroidered leaves and vines. We added some lace to the decolletage and wrists, and bows at the waist. I put my hair up in a chignon with loose tendrils on either side of my face. Armand's eyes lit up when he saw me. Since our wedding, I had taken to wearing the simple brown, gray, and muted blue wool skirts and bodices common to the women in the colony. And I always wore an apron in the house, and a coif to keep dust from my hair.

Despite our formal attire smelling vaguely of camphor from being stored in our clothes chest for so long, Armand looked quite handsome in his maroon justaucorps with black trim and black leggings.

The Château Saint-Louis, the governor's residence, was a single-story stone building situated next to the fort on a terraced bit of land between the lower and upper villages. Its garden overlooked the river. When we arrived, we were greeted by a reception line that began with Governor Courcelle and his pretty wife, Marie-Anne. His adjutant, a Lieutenant Baribeau, and his wife, Marguerite, stood next to them. Next was Intendant Jean Talon, dressed in a scarlet justaucorps. Standing at attention behind Talon was his liveried manservant, Laurant.

Talon bowed when we greeted him. "Madame Gervais. Captain. How delightful that you are finally able to make an appearance at one of our little gatherings." His voice was pleasant if stiff. "Madame will you allow me the honor of a dance after the banquet?"

My cheeks burned, though I had no reason to be embarrassed. "Of course," I said.

We were served glasses of wine and made small talk with several members of the Sovereign Council and their wives and some of the more prominent merchants. The sound of Claudette's voice caused me to turn suddenly and nearly spill my wine. Of course, she and Gravel would be in attendance. Not only was he a member of the Sovereign Council, but their store had become the most profitable in all of New France.

Claudette and I nodded politely to each other, then looked away while our husbands engaged in conversation about shipping. To my relief, when it was time for lunch, Armand and I were seated next to Lieutenant Baribeau and Marguerite.

"Nasty business about those soldiers up in Montreal who killed that Mohawk chief," Baribeau said.

Armand replied in an even voice. "He was Seneca, not Mohawk. They will hang for it."

"Doesn't seem fair, executing our own because of a brawl with one of the Natives."

"Murder is murder," Armand said. "And we have to prove to the Iroquois Confederacy that we believe in equal justice. It's the only way we'll keep the peace with them."

Baribeau grunted a reluctant acquiescence. He lifted his wine glass and turned to his wife, ignoring us for the rest of the meal.

"Do you think it will work?" I asked Armand.

"Will what work?" he said.

"Hanging those soldiers. I agree in principle, but will it make a difference?"

"Governor Courcelle is using it as an example and insisting the Iroquois leave the Algonquian tribes alone, especially the Wendat. We will have to see if it is effective."

When dessert was finished, servants cleared the dining room for dancing. A small orchestra settled into the corner of the room and was soon playing one of the minuets that was popular at wedding celebrations in the town square. Armand noticed my toe tapping and led me onto the dance floor to join the lineup. I quickly lost myself in the bliss of the music, dancing first with Armand, and then with the Lieutenant.

Governor Courcelle approached. "May I?"

"Of course." We took our positions on the dance floor.

The musicians struck up the first graceful notes of a courtly courante. As Courcelle and I performed the familiar steps, our fingertips barely touching, I found myself wistful for a time when I was *"la belle de jour"* at court.

Suddenly, inexplicably, I was back at Versailles—at the masked ball where I first danced with the duke, my then betrothed. A dizzying wave of nausea swept over me, and the momentary longing for court life turned sour with memories of betrayal and discord. I stumbled, nearly falling.

Courcelle grasped my arm. "Madame, are you unwell?"

"No, I...I..."

Armand hurried toward us, a worried expression on his face.

"Excuse me," I said to the governor. I grasped Armand's arm. "I need air. Can we go outside?"

"Of course." Armand walked with me out to the terrace. "Perhaps a glass of wine?"

Once assured that I would be all right, he went back inside to get the wine. I leaned against the marble balustrade, letting my gaze settle over the now familiar river crowded with ships and canoes. Breathing in the cool fresh air coming off the water, I listened to the creaking and clanking of the ships floating on the breeze against a backdrop of men shouting and hailing each other, punctuated by bursts of laughter or a foul word.

"You dance beautifully. Did you learn at court?" The voice behind me caused me to stiffen. Jean Talon stepped to the balustrade, standing next to me.

"I have had good instructors."

"Do you miss it? The balls. The dinners. The salons?"

"Not in the least. Well, maybe the salons."

He looked out over the river. "You enjoy reading?"

"I do."

"I understand Captain Gervais reads as well."

"We have that in common."

He turned and leaned casually against the balustrade, folding his arms and surveying the terrace. "Does he know about your position at court?"

"That I was maid of honor to Madame de Montespan. Of course. He knows all about my background." I wished that were true. But why was Talon bringing this up now?

He arched an eyebrow. "And how is your little girl?"

I glanced at him sharply. "She is well." Damn Claudette! Had she spread the crass rumor about Minette's paternity after all? "She adores her papa. And my husband adores her."

"I've no doubt." He brushed his fingers across his moustache. "Tell me, your husband, he hasn't been investing in the fur trade of late, has he?'

"The fur trade?"

"Perhaps with your pension money? It would be unfortunate to have to report to the King that you have been financing illegal trade with the British."

I turned to face him full on now. "What are you suggesting?"

"Your husband is known to associate with a certain…scoundrel, who has come to the attention of the governor."

"Scoundrel?"

"An unlicensed trader. Madame, I only say this as a service to you and the captain. Be careful with whom you associate. I would hate to see your husband caught up in something that would land him before the Sovereign Council."

"Monsieur Talon!" Armand strode across the terrace toward us, a stemmed glass of wine in each hand. "I didn't realize you were out here. Would you care for wine?" He held out a glass.

"No, thank you," Talon replied. "Your lovely wife and I were just discussing matters of finance."

"Finance?"

My stomach twitched as I took the wine glass from Armand. When I didn't say anything, Talon gave me a curious look. Did he sense I hadn't told Armand about the pension from the King?

"Investments advice would be a better word," he said. "I was just cautioning your lovely wife that there are scoundrels active in the fur trade who should be avoided when considering whom to subsidize."

Armand gave me a questioning look, then said to Talon, "I take it you are speaking of Jacques Farley." He offered a disarming smile. "The man does well enough on his own. He doesn't need my money. Why do you bring it up?"

"No reason. We just happened into the topic. I should get back to the other guests. If you will excuse me." He bowed and took his leave.

Armand watched him until he disappeared into the house. "What was that all about?"

"I have no idea. But he seems to think Jacques may be trading with the British."

"Let's hope not. That could be a hanging offense."

My chest tightened at the thought. "Even though he provided a service that time, when you and he negotiated for the release of the priests from the Mohawk?"

Armand grimaced. "You'd like to think so, wouldn't you? But for some reason the governor has taken a dislike to Jacques. He's looking for a reason to arrest him."

My head started to throb. "Armand, would it be too impolite to leave early? I'm not feeling well."

"Any time you wish."

The afternoon at the governor's chateau had unsettled me. But Armand, full of wine and humming one of the dance tunes on the way home, became amorous. That night in bed, he turned to me with a gentle confidence, and our lovemaking nearly approached the intensity we'd experienced the night of our wedding. He fell asleep a happy man. I, however, lay awake most of the night staring at the ceiling.

CHAPTER TWENTY-NINE

The first snowfall of the year was already coating the ground, when Jacques showed up on our doorstep in late October, flush with the success of a summer season trading for beaver pelts. This time, he had a cow in tow.

"What am I to do with a cow?" I asked, my consternation hiding the delight I felt at his return.

"Butter," he said. "Lots and lots of butter. The main ingredient in the recipes of our homeland, if I remember from my time there as a child. And cream. And perhaps cheese." His eyes twinkled, but his mirth did not hide the new scar on his forehead and the bruise under one eye.

"Did you win it in a card game?" I asked as we led the cow around back to the barn. "Or bludgeon someone to death for it?"

"You insult me, madame," he said in faux protest. "I came upon it honestly. Bartered a good many beaver pelts for it."

Before I could reply, Catherine came out of the house and discovered us. "Papa Jacques! You have returned!" They hugged.

"You brought us a cow? How wonderful!" she exclaimed, hugging him again.

"You must give her a proper name," Jacques said to us. "That way, I will be assured you will never eat her."

"Étoile," Catherine said, tracing the star-shaped marking on the cow's forehead. "She shall be the star that gives milk."

When we introduced Étoile to Shadow, the horse snorted in disgust at first, but it soon became evident she was glad for a companion. The chickens which ran wild in the yard didn't seem to have the right personalities to suit her.

That night, at dinner, I said to Jacques, "Is there a warrant out for your arrest again?"

He glanced over at Armand. Was he putting my husband in a compromising position? Governor Courcelle would expect Armand to arrest him. Jacques shrugged in answer to my question.

"Is what they say true? Have you been trading with the British?" I pressed.

The look on Jacques's face served as a gentle rebuke of my question. He resented the British intrusions into New France, and I knew that.

"But why does the governor think so?"

"He seems willing to listen to anyone who has a grudge against me." He spooned stew into his mouth.

"And that." I pointed to the bruise under his eye. "Is that from one of your grudge-making escapades?"

"Sylvienne, let it go," Armand said, frustration evident in his eyes.

"Fine." I stood and took their empty bowls. "So long as he doesn't bring the wrath of the governor down on this house."

Armand and Jacques set out to hunt together the next morning. LeDuc chased along eagerly. They returned midafternoon, dragging the sled with a beautiful buck tied to it. I was glad for the meat, but it broke my heart to see such a magnificent animal killed. The two men got to work right away dressing the carcass and preparing the meat to smoke and preserve. That night we had roasted venison for our evening meal. I silently thanked the beautiful buck for providing such delicious nourishment for our family.

Afterward, while Catherine and I cleaned up the kitchen, Armand and Jacques sat in front of the fire with mugs of beer. Armand bounced Minette on his lap as the two men chatted. When I glanced over, I realized Jacques was watching me with a pensive look. His eyes met mine for the briefest of moments before he quickly shifted his gaze to the fire.

When we finished cleaning, Catherine and I sat with the men for a while, Catherine cajoling Jacques into singing one of the ditties the fur traders sang while plying the river in their canoes.

"Alouette, gentille alouette, alouette je te plumerai." He sang lustily, teasing Minette as he did.

I'd heard the song before, often sung by children in the village square, but still I cringed at the words, telling a lark he will pluck its feathers. Then *"Je te plumerai la tête."* I will pluck your head off. And other parts of the bird: *le bec*, its beak, *l'aile*, its wing, and on and on. Poor bird. But Minette enjoyed it anyway, as did Catherine. And I have to admit, it was always fun when Jacques sang, and of course we all joined in on the chorus.

Eventually Jacques protested he had run out of songs. Catherine excused herself and went up to bed in the loft. I said my *bonne nuits* and took Minette to bed with me. The two men sat drinking in front of the fire, their voices low, unintelligible from the bedroom, occasional bursts of laughter punctuating their conversation. I feared I would find Armand asleep on the floor when the fire burned low and would have to help him stagger to our bed. But he came of his own accord while I was asleep. I barely stirred when he lifted Minette out from under my arm and tucked her into her own small bed.

Sometime later, I awoke needing the chamber pot. Afterward I wrapped myself in an extra quilt and padded out to see if Jacques needed a blanket. He typically fell asleep on the floor in front of the hearth seemingly impervious to the cold when the embers were low. To my surprise he was sitting up cross-legged in front of a blazing fire.

"Can't sleep?" I asked.

"I was hungry." He had a plate of left-over venison in front of him, alongside it a mug of beer.

Handing him the wool blanket I'd brought out, I settled down on the floor next to him. I pulled my own quilt tighter around me. We sat in silence for a while.

"Can I ask you a question?" I asked finally.

"I don't promise an answer."

"Why do you not apply for a permit to be an official voyageur? Register with the Sovereign Council. Trade legally?"

"What would be the fun in that?" He offered a crooked grin. Upon seeing my frustrated expression, he grew serious. "I think it's too late to ask for a license. The governor has made that clear to me. Truth is…I find the administration here and its politics to be…contemptible. Particularly in its dealings with the Native people."

I thought of the times he had shown up on our doorstep, the worst for wear after an altercation with a villager. Contrasting that with Armand's pride in upholding the law, I wondered what these two men had in common. Why were they so drawn to each other?

"So…you just take the law into your own hands?" I said.

"I mind my own business." He wiped his lips, greasy from the venison, on a rag he'd taken from the kitchen. "But when someone else decides to make my business theirs, or they abuse someone who can't defend themselves, I let them know where they stand. This is the frontier, Sylvienne. The King's law means nothing when a man is simply trying to survive."

"But that's why we're here, isn't it? At the frontier? To civilize it."

"Civilize?" He snorted in derision. "I see drunken villagers beating their wives. Are they civilized? Or when the Council orders a woman stripped naked and flogged in the public square for some minor offense? Is that what you call civilized? In France I once watched as a man was drawn and quartered. The crowd cheered. Men were laying bets on how long it would be before the first limb was torn out of its socket. If that is civilization, I want nothing to do with it." He folded the rag in half, then half again and set it on his now empty plate. "When I came here, I knew life wouldn't be easy. I knew I would have to find my own way. But I thought—foolishly, I suppose—I thought I would be left alone to do that. I suspect your life has been so sheltered, you can't fathom what that means."

"I admit I was sheltered. Until..." I shrugged. "Well, let's just say I learned first-hand what cruelty can be."

"And what did you do when you learned that?" he asked.

"I guess, like you, I did what I needed to survive." I shivered inside my warm quilt.

He reached out a hand and pushed a lock of hair behind my ear. "That's all anyone can do."

I let his finger linger on my cheek a moment too long. Pulling away awkwardly, I rose. "I'd better get back to bed."

"Yes," he said, his voice unusually husky. Then, "Sylvienne."

I stopped and turned back to him.

"I would never do anything that compromised Armand's position. Or hurt you or this family."

"I know that."

He nodded, picked up his mug, and brought it to his lips. I left him staring into the fire as I went back to Armand's bed.

The next morning, Jacques was gone before I was out of bed. I felt a void where I shouldn't have, a longing that befuddled me.

Catherine and I worked together preparing the deer hide for tanning. This was a new task for me, and to rid my thoughts of Jacques's tender singing, his finger on my cheek, I worked doubly hard, scraping and scraping, until Catherine finally warned me I would get cramps in my hands if I didn't slow down, stop for a rest.

After soaking, wringing, and stretching the hide, Armand smoked it over an outdoor fire using a hanging apparatus he had constructed from tree branches and hemp twine. Eventually, Catherine and I would use the hide to make mittens for the entire family. Perhaps there would be enough to make a pair for Jacques as a Christmas gift. Jacques, who never seemed to need thanks for his gifts.

CHAPTER THIRTY

We didn't see Jacques at Christmas or for the New Year celebrations. He didn't show up for the spring canoe race either. It seemed the entire village was disappointed with his absence, despite the inevitable brawls and tavern fights he usually managed to set in motion during the merrymaking afterward.

"Do you think something happened to him?" I asked Armand. The governor had posted a warrant for Jacques's arrest since his last visit. Charges of selling guns to Native tribes were pending. I hoped he was staying away because of the warrant, but I was worried, nevertheless.

"I'd hear about it if something had happened. He may not be back for a while."

Spring kept me busy planting the garden. Besides the turnips, carrots, onions, rutabagas, and peas, I decided to experiment with some strawberry and raspberry cuttings I had purchased from the Ursulines. I had also obtained a plum tree shoot. It would take years before it was big enough to produce fruit, but if I could keep the rabbits and other animals away from it, it would be worth the wait. The addition of Étoile to our small menagerie meant that I had to milk her daily. I generally took the morning shift. Catherine milked her in the late afternoons. And now we had even more manure to dispose of.

In June, we got word that Jacques had collected a rogue crew and set out to trade in the area around Lac Champlain, south of Ville Marie. Rumors connected him with British traders from the Hudson Valley area who supposedly had been spotted near Trois-Rivières.

Armand was called away again to accompany Governor Courcelle on a trip to establish a new fort and trading post where the Catarqui River flowed into one of the great lakes New France was becoming famous for. The Wendat called this lake *Ontarí'io*.

Armand expected to be gone for a month or more; his absence would be hard on all of us. I was grateful more than ever to have Catherine and LeDuc in the house. Michel LeBlanc stopped by occasionally to check on us and make repairs to the house and barn as needed, as did Titus.

Minette toddled everywhere now, and it was all Catherine and I could do to keep our eye on her and keep her out of trouble. LeDuc was now Minette's constant companion. He wouldn't let her go near the river, and he kept her from getting too close to the backsides of Shadow and Étoile.

During the day, I was generally too busy to dwell on Armand's absence. But in the evenings, I missed his smile when he walked into the house at the end of a long day at the garrison, his conversation over beer after dinner, the comfort of his arms in bed at night.

On the evening of the Fête de la Saint-Jean-Baptiste, Catherine and I took Minette down to the square in the lower village for the annual festivities. Jeanne and Michel had saved a spot for us on their blanket.

"Your baby has gotten so big!" I said to Jeanne. "How old is he now?"

"Ten months. He eats like a horse."

Minette plopped herself down next to the baby and grabbed his hands to show him how to clap.

I missed Perrette, who had sent word they would not be joining us this year. One of her children had come down with measles. Happily, we spotted Titus in the crowd and called him over. Minette's eyes lit up when she saw him, and her insistence on climbing onto his lap made Catherine and me laugh. While Catherine and Titus played with Minette, I chatted with Jeanne about their plans for a new house and visited with other friends who stopped by our blanket.

I had glanced over to check on Minette, when a shadow caused me to look up.

"Bonjour, Madame Gervais." Claudette stood over me; her voice was unusually pleasant.

Wary, I returned the greeting. "Bonjour to you, Madame Gravel."

"Your little girl is getting bigger every day."

"She is, yes."

"Your husband is gone, I hear?"

"He is on an expedition with the governor."

"It must be difficult for you with him gone so much." She tapped her toe until I took notice of her footwear.

"You have new shoes?" I said. "They are…beautiful." They were.

"Our buyer in Ville-Marie purchased them from a new shoemaker there. We are thinking of setting up a consignment with him to sell his shoes and boots in our shop."

My heart raced at the mention of the shoemaker. Because of course she was talking about Etienne.

"Oh, there is my Monsieur Gravel." She waved in his direction. "I must be off."

Watching her walk away, something niggled at the back of my mind. It was unlike her to trade pleasantries with me. But I shook it off. The mention of Etienne had unsettled me.

Several days later, as I was squeezing the last of the morning milk from Étoile, Minette toddled into the barn and grabbed my hand. "Maman! Maman! Come!"

She led me to the side of the barn where she had discovered an odd-looking clutch of kittens nestled in a depression in the ground. I reached out to pet one when Catherine shouted, "Sylvienne! Minette! No!"

Startled, I backed away from the three black kits with white stripes down their backs and tails. A movement by the walnut trees caught my attention. The mother was waddling toward us.

Catherine ran over and scooped up Minette. "We must go in the house. Quickly."

"What? Why?" A strange, sickly-sweet odor wafted in the air making my eyes sting. I hustled after Catherine and Minette. "What are they?"

"Moufettes. You must not go near them."

"Moufettes?"

"Don't you have them in France? If the mother moufette sprays you…" She held her nose and waved her other hand in front of her face. "You will be banished from the house until the river can clean it off." She made a disgusted face. "They are pretty animals. But…eww!"

I got the idea.

However, LeDuc didn't. He got it into his head to chase the moufettes away, barking loudly and charging them. He regretted it immediately. He came running to me, whining, but he reeked, and I wasn't about to let him in the house.

Not knowing what else to do, I grabbed the lye soap and marched the dog down to the river. I scrubbed and scrubbed, but the smell lingered.

Fortunately, the mother moufette did not like her encounter with LeDuc any more than he did. She took her kits and found a new place to call home—our neighbor's barn I deduced by the smell emanating from their property when we happened to pass by.

In the meantime, poor LeDuc had to sleep in the barn, and he got a river bath every morning for a week after I finished milking Étoile. I soon ran out of lye soap.

Catherine offered to go into town to purchase more, but I needed to get away from the lingering odor. I decided to go myself.

Hoping she wouldn't notice the scent on me, I went into Claudette's store to ask if she had any lye soap scented with lilac or rose oil. Some of the Gravel's merchandise were produced locally, but most was imported from France, including the scented soaps. To my surprise, her nose never twitched. Maybe the moufette odor was simply stuck in my nose.

As I paid for my goods, Claudette announced, "Monsieur Gravel and I have decided to sign a contract with that new shoemaker in Ville-Marie. He has partnered with a maker of gloves and another of hats."

"Is that so?" I kept my voice as nonchalant as possible.

"His name is Damise. Have you heard of him? Etienne Damise dit La Rose." She looked straight at me. Was she judging my reaction? When I shook my head and gathered up my soaps, she said nothing more. But I could feel her eyes on me as I hurried out the door.

One morning, a messenger came from Intendant Talon's office bearing a formal invitation. A surprise visitor from Paris had arrived on the latest ship — the Abbot of the monastery of Saint-Père-en-Vallée. Monsieur Talon requested the presence of Madame Gervais at a luncheon reception welcoming their distinguished visitor in two days' time.

"Do you know him?" Catherine asked.

"I've heard of the Abbey. It's near the city of Chartres. But I don't believe I've ever met the abbot. I hope my silk dress is still presentable."

On the day of the banquet, I donned the honey-colored dress I'd worn to the harvest ball. Unlike at Versailles where it was gauche to wear the same dress on two separate occasions, here in Québec it would be considered pretentious not to do so. Fortunately, I fit into it, though it seemed a bit tighter across my bosom than I cared for. Catherine helped me comb out my hair and added a ribbon on either side for effect — nothing like the hairstyles that had adorned my head at court, but it would have to do. This was an abbot, after all. What did he care how fancy I looked?

Catherine and Minette escorted me into the village and to the Château Saint-Louis where the reception was to take place. She planned to take Minette to the convent where the sisters and all the little girls would spoil her for the afternoon while they waited for me.

Entering the château, I waited while the majordomo announced my name. A small group of guests stood conversing at the far end of the room. Not surprisingly, Claudette and Gravel were among them. The man with whom they were speaking, a nobleman with very fine clothes and wearing a broad-brimmed hat over a wig of thick, blond curls, had his back toward me. When my name was announced, he turned, a broad smile on his face. I gasped.

Jean Talon stepped forward. "Madame Gervais. I am so pleased you have graced us with your presence. Do you already know our guest, the Chevalier de Lorraine?"

The chevalier swept his fashionable, wide-brimmed hat from his head with a flourish as he bent into an exaggerated bow. "Madame, I do believe we have met in passing at Versailles."

"I...I...yes..." Dropping into a curtsy, I was finally able to say, "I believe you are correct, monsieur."

Prince Philippe's notorious lover took my hand and brought it to his lips. "Now that we have met again, I bring you greetings from His Majesty King Louis."

What could de Lorraine possibly be doing here? The man had been banished from court on a number of occasions because of his infamously wanton relationship with the prince, most often ending up in one prison or another. Had he been banished to New France this time?

Struggling to maintain my composure, I said, "You have come a long way. But..." I looked around the small crowd. "Where is the abbot?" I saw no one except Father Laval in clerical attire.

De Lorraine laughed. "I am the abbot, my dear. I inherited the position from my brother, who inherited it from our father before him. It's a titular privilege only." He leaned over to buss me on the cheek, at the same time whispering into my ear, "And, yes, I have come a very long way at the behest of the King. He wants you to know that all is forgiven. And he has commissioned me to fetch you home."

CHAPTER THIRTY-ONE

Stewing over Chevalier de Lorraine's words, I was dismayed to find myself seated next to him at the luncheon table. Adding to my disgruntlement, the overwhelming pungency of his sandalwood, orange, and musk perfume caused my stomach to roil.

His brown velvet justaucorps with matching breeches fit him perfectly despite having just spent six weeks at sea. He made a point of telling me he'd had the privilege of inhabiting the cabin next to the ship's captain. Obviously, his diet during the journey was far better than what I had experienced. He spoke with the air of an emissary assigned to represent the King in a foreign land. But underneath, I sensed he was not at all pleased to have been tasked with coming to New France to bring me home.

Claudette, seated on the other side of him, engaged his attention, comparing our voyage with his and telling him exaggerated stories of life in Québec among the fur traders and the Native people.

Fortunately for me, she kept the conversation focused on herself. Neither of them said a word about me or my relationship to the King, though my stomach was in knots worrying that the chevalier, who knew my story full well, might say something. I likely needn't have worried, for if there was one thing I knew about the man, he was not one to show all his cards at the beginning of a game. He preferred to observe and get a sense of his opponent's situation and form. It would appear he considered me his opponent.

After the main course was served — roasted venison with creamed peas and early carrots I was too disconcerted to enjoy — we were offered a dessert of stewed apricots in a thick sweet cream that I barely tasted. Finally, we dispensed to the terrace, the men carrying out their glasses of spiced brandy. De Lorraine dodged Claudette and trailed me to a spot by the balustrade.

As we looked out over the river, I asked after my friend, Prince Philippe, "How is Monsieur?"

"Despondent. Surly. Remarried."

"I read about the wedding in the gazette. And his new wife? Liselotte, they call her?"

"Insufferable. Everyone loves her. Except Philippe, of course."

"And you."

"She has become formidable competition for his time." He sniffed. "And his bed. She's determined to provide him with heirs."

That caused me to chuckle. Good for her. I noticed de Lorraine's gaze had shifted away from the river and was following the intendent as he moved from guest to guest. Talon glanced over and smiled at us.

Raising his brandy glass in salute to him, de Lorraine asked me in a low voice, "Have you had enough of banishment, Madame la Duchesse? Are you ready to come home?"

"Why did he send you? Why now?" I said, keeping my voice equally low.

He shrugged. "Political winds shift. He's on to other conceits. Narbonne's family accepted the compensation offered and have backed off their desire for revenge. He sees new opportunities for financial and political alliances if he can broker a successful marriage to his oldest…"

"Bastard?"

He inclined his head to indicate they were my words, not his.

"This is my home now. I am married again."

"So I hear. It does complicate things, I suppose."

"And I have a child."

He turned back to the river and swirled his brandy glass. "You *would* make my life insufferably difficult, wouldn't you?"

"I have no interest in whether your life is difficult or not. But I won't be going back with you."

"And I cannot go back without you." He brought the brandy to his lips but said before taking a drink, "I'll be damned if I'll stay in this godforsaken place a moment longer than I have to."

Talon called on me at the house the next day. LeDuc announced his arrival with wild, protective barking. I had to send him outside while the Intendant visited inside.

"Can we speak in private?" Talon asked, looking pointedly in Catherine's direction.

At my nod, Catherine gathered up Minette and took her out to play with LeDuc.

Talon sat at my kitchen table, his hands cradling the cup of beer I had served him. "I haven't figured out what your relationship with King Louis is, but he wouldn't have sent someone as important as the Chevalier de Lorraine if he wasn't earnest about recalling you to France."

"It is just as likely he sent the chevalier here as punishment, knowing I have no intention of returning."

"Punishment? For what?" Talon asked.

"Certainly you know of his relationship with the King's brother. De Lorraine is constantly crossing the line and getting himself either thrown into prison or banished from court."

"I don't think that is the case this time."

"And what of Captain Gervais?" I asked. "We have made a family here. And there has been no mention of him returning with me."

"Indeed. The chevalier has brought with him papers of annulment for you to sign."

I leaned forward, pressing my hands against the table. "I will sign no such thing."

Talon sighed in disappointment and stood. "Captain Gervais is a very fortunate man. When he returns from his tour with the governor, I hope he appreciates what he has here." He bowed, but before turning to go he said, "However, I do believe every man has his price."

Furious, I picked up his unfinished cup of beer and was about to throw it at him. Before I could do so, he turned on his heel and took his leave.

Not two days later, Claudette knocked at my door. Despite my wariness and LeDuc's growling, I let her in. She eyed Catherine nervously and asked if we could speak alone. Sighing, I nodded to Catherine. She rolled her eyes behind Claudette's back but took Minette and LeDuc outside without complaint.

"I have come with some distressing news," Claudette said, taking a seat at the table where Talon had sat the day before. "Monsieur Gravel and I have been expecting a visit from that new shoemaker from Ville-Marie I told you about. Etienne Damise."

She had my attention now.

"I thought you said you didn't know him. But he offered you as a reference when my husband negotiated the consignment of some of his footwear for our shop."

"Me?" I couldn't imagine Etienne needing a reference from me. Did he have any reason to suspect Madame Gravel was Claudette, the same girl who had engineered my expulsion from the convent school back in Amiens? I doubted it.

"Since you do appear to be acquainted, I thought you might want to know. He was on his way here when his party was attacked by a band of Iroquois."

"Attacked?" Despite my attempts at a measured response, my hand went to my mouth. "Was he injured?"

"Quite seriously, I am told. He might not survive. That's why I thought to tell you, since you know him. I'm sorry to give you such bad news."

"I...I don't know what to say. Thank you for letting me know." Suddenly, I found it difficult to breathe. Grasping the fabric of my skirt under the table, I twisted it anxiously.

"Monsieur Gravel is concerned about the goods that were promised by Damise. If he survives, he will surely want the sale to go through, so we are planning to travel to Trois-Rivières to collect the merchandise he planned to consign to us."

"You are going there? You'll see him?"

"Yes, if he...survives his wounds." She cast her eyes down, looking as if she might cry.

"May I go with you?" I blurted. My response was unreasonably impulsive, I knew, but if Etienne were dying, I had to go to him.

"To Trois-Rivières? It's quite a distance. Several days by canoe. You wouldn't be able to take your little one along. What would you do with her?"

"No, of course not." Minette could barely sit still for ten minutes, let alone for a canoeing journey of several days. But if Etienne were mortally wounded... "If I could make arrangements for her to be cared for here, would you take me with you?"

"Monsieur Damise must be quite dear to you," she said, "for you to be willing to make such a journey."

"It's been some time since we have seen each other. But, yes, he is a dear friend," I said. She apparently hadn't connected him with the shoemaker from Amiens, the one who had been my lover at Versailles. "If he…if he were not to survive his wounds, I would be devastated not to have seen him one last time."

Claudette stood, her demeanor unusually sympathetic. "I will have to ask Monsieur Gravel if we would have room for you. We plan to leave in two days' time. I will send a message and let you know what he says. But I cannot promise he will agree."

"No, of course not. I understand. But if you could plead my case to him, I would be much obliged. And I would pay you."

Obliged to Claudette. The thought of it tied knots in my stomach, but I could not live with myself if I did not try to see Etienne one last time. Perhaps be with him if he were truly dying.

Fighting tears, I walked Claudette to the door. After she'd gone, I found Catherine and Minette near the barn. I picked up my little girl to keep Catherine from noticing my distress. The thought that Minette might well grow up never knowing her true father was painful. My darling girl wrapped her arms around my neck, but just for a moment. All too soon she was wriggling and pushing to get down to play with the chickens.

The Saint-Laurent was swift as always, but Gravel surprised me with his adeptness at maneuvering the canoe. Claudette and I paddled as well, though in the warm, muggy air we both tired quickly and alternated frequent rests.

Relieved that Gravel had agreed—reluctantly so, apparently—to allow me to accompany them to Trois-Rivières,

I had made arrangements for Catherine to take Minette and stay at the convent, where they would be safe and cared for.

Finding someone to take LeDuc was a different matter. Jeanne and Michel already had two dogs and with a baby in the house, I doubted they would want to house a third, even for just a week or so. Titus said he would have loved to take LeDuc, but he only had a small sleeping space in the tool shed of his new employer, Godfroy Brisson, the barge builder. When I suggested he could stay at our house, he was more than happy to take me up on the offer. A perfect solution as it meant he would also be there to let Armand know where I was if he should return before I did.

I wondered if I should say something to Jean Talon, to let him and de Lorraine know I would be away for a few days. But I decided my travels were none of their business. I was safe in the company of the Gravels, and that was all that mattered.

I had never been to Trois-Rivières, but I knew it was about half-way between Québec and the island of Montreal where the fast-growing Ville-Marie lay nestled. Several of the recruits from my ship had moved there with their new husbands.

We camped each night in clearings along the edge of the river, pulling our canoe up out of the water and tipping it onto its side to provide shelter. The mosquitoes, which were awful at best in Québec, were horrendous here, making me doubt the wisdom of my decision to accompany the Gravels on this trip. We made plenty use of the bear grease Gravel had thought to bring along.

Late in the afternoon of the third day—the high-pitched hum of cicadas filling the air as we paddled near the shore— Gravel pointed out a canvas lean-to nestled among a stand of birch trees. He said this was where we were to meet our party. A man who looked to be gathering firewood roamed among the distant trees, but there was no sign of Etienne. Was he in the lean-to? How hurt was he?

We climbed out of the canoe, Claudette and I pulling our skirts up to slosh through the shallow water to shore. Gravel tugged the canoe farther up onto the sandy bank. Once out of the water, I ran to the tent, my heart pounding.

"Etienne?" I called out, pushing the tent flap aside.

He stood with his back to me but turned quickly at the sound of my voice.

I gasped. It wasn't Etienne, but a man I didn't recognize.

"Who are you?" I demanded.

His eyes lit up. "The question is, who are you?" His French was heavily accented. English?

I turned to flee, but another man, the one who had been gathering downed branches, stepped into the tent at that very moment, blocking my exit.

"I don't suppose you are the Duchesse de Narbonne?" he asked, his French also heavily accented.

I tried to push past him, but he grabbed my arm. When I screamed, he covered my mouth with his sweaty hand and put a knife to my throat. He pulled me out of the tent where Claudette and Gravel stood waiting. The other man followed. I stared at my companions with panicked eyes, afraid to move for fear of the sharp blade pressing against my neck.

"Is this her?" the other man asked. "The duchesse?"

"Yes," Gravel said. "She's the one you are looking for. I take it you are Monsieur Moore?"

"You sure she's the right girl?" Moore peered at me closely, his hot breath in my face, his companion's hand still over my mouth. He pulled the linen coif from my hair, watching as my black curls fell loose around my shoulders.

"She is," Claudette said. "Sylvienne d'Aubert, Duchess de Narbonne. She's one of the King's mistresses, banished from court."

"No she isn't," the man said, his eyes greedy.

"She is. I swear. I've known her all my life," Claudette insisted.

"Well, you don't know her well enough. Look at those green eyes. This one ain't one of your damned king's mistresses. She's one of his bastards. The one that killed her husband."

"What?" Claudette rocked back with shock.

"Word is your king sent her away so she could keep her head. But now he wants her back. Grey here and I plan to help him out in that respect."

Claudette's eyes clouded with confusion. Mine burned with anger. How did this man know who I was?

"The King is her father?" Gravel asked, disbelieving.

Grey took his hand from my mouth but left the knife's blade at my throat.

"Aye," he said. "But like most lecherous monarchs, your Louis got himself more bastards than legitimate heirs. Ain't that right?" he said to me.

"And our good King Charles plans to give her back to good old Louis Quatorze," Moore said. "For a price, of course."

"You won't get a *sou* from him," I said, gritting my teeth.

Gravel spoke up now. "A daughter of the King? I believe our price just went up."

Claudette's confusion instantly vanished. "Doubled."

The first man snorted. "You're lucky to get what we agreed on to begin with."

Moore tossed a pouch of coins at Claudette's feet. It landed in the dirt. She scrambled to pick it up.

I hissed at her. "You lured me here to sell me?"

"We are simply sending you back to the King. Your...father." She poured the coins into her hand, frowning. "This isn't what we agreed on," she said to the British traders.

"I can't believe you would do this. Where is Etienne? You said he was wounded. You said you would take me to him."

"Who?" Grey said.

"Ah, yes. Your good friend. And lover?" Claudette's voice lifted a moment, as if delighted by her own news. "He's dead."

My breath caught. "No."

"You wouldn't have come if you'd known it was too late."

My eyes welled. "You're lying."

She shrugged, her attention on Moore again. "You promised us twice this."

He lifted his pistol. "You can go now with the money in that pouch." He pointed the weapon at Claudette's head. "Or don't go at all. Makes no difference to me either way."

Gravel grabbed Claudette by the arm and pulled her toward the river. "Let's go."

"What will you tell my husband?" I shouted. "He won't let you get away with this!"

"I'll tell him you begged us to take you to your lover, but you fell overboard and drowned in the river," Claudette said, clearly annoyed at their financial misfortune.

"Okay, princess," Grey, the man with the knife at my throat, said to me. "You are coming with—"

An arrow whizzed past my head and lodged itself in the other Englishman's throat. His eyes bulging, he grasped the shaft with both hands before opening his mouth.

Claudette screamed. Gravel grabbed her and pulled her behind a thick tree.

Blood gurgled out of the wounded man's mouth, and he dropped to his knees before keeling over. Stunned, my captor dropped his guard long enough for me to twist free and kick. I darted for a nearby tree just as an arrow hit Grey in the stomach. He grunted and fell to his knees. Another arrow hit him in the chest, and he fell over, dead.

Trembling, I watched as an Iroquois man—a Mohawk, judging by his shaved head with its long single lock of hair—stepped out of the brush, bow in hand. Another followed him. A third came out from behind the tent. They wore nothing but breechcloths, moccasins, and war paint, their bodies slick with bear grease.

Claudette screamed again, but Gravel put his hand over her mouth. The Iroquois man motioned for them to come out from behind their tree. The one who had been behind the tent strode over to me and grabbed me by the arm, dragging me out into the open, pushing me toward the Gravels.

"You saved us," I said, the Iroquois language clumsy in my mouth. "Thank you."

"You can thank your king when you are delivered to him," he responded in French.

My head jerked back, his words hitting me like a brick.

"No!" Gravel said. "We had a deal with these men. "And you just…just killed them?"

"We can sell her to the English king just as well as they can. We will take your payment as well." He held out his hand for the pouch.

Claudette, eyes wide, hands trembling, handed it over.

"Now look here," Gravel demanded, not noticing the Iroquois who strode up behind him, hunting knife in hand. "You can have the woman. We won't quarrel with you over her, but you can't take our money. We—"

The Iroquois grasped Gravel's hair from behind. Realizing what was about to happen, I pulled Claudette to me so she wouldn't see the warrior pull Gravel's head back and draw his knife across the man's throat. Gravel's eyes went wide with fright. He gurgled blood, then collapsed into a heap.

Claudette turned and, seeing him, screamed. The man with the knife started toward her. I clamped my hand over her mouth. "Be quiet, or we'll be next."

She trembled and moaned as her legs gave way. Crumpling to the ground, she pulled me down with her and buried her head in my lap so she couldn't see the Iroquois men dragging the body of her husband off toward the bushes.

CHAPTER THIRTY-TWO

Our wrists bound, Claudette and I walked single file along the densely wooded path, the Iroquois men in front and behind us. I had no idea where we were going, except I knew it was in the opposite direction from the river. As we walked deeper into the forest, the echoing whistles of cardinals and the chirps and warbles of other birds were overpowered by the ever-insistent buzzing of cicadas, setting my nerves on edge. Claudette's eyes were glazed, and she made no sound. Stumbling along in front of me, she didn't even swat at the mosquitoes plaguing us.

When we had started out from the area of the lean-to, where Robert Gravel's body lay, prey to the night animals, the sun was low on the horizon. Now the sky was darkening, making it harder to see what lay on the trail to trip us up. Every few minutes I swiped a sleeve across my face to ward off the mosquitos, the bear grease I had applied earlier in the day having worn off, or perhaps the combination of sweat and grime rendered it ineffective. Exhausted, I feared I would collapse right there on the trail. Would they leave my body to the night animals as well? I forced myself to keep moving.

Eventually, we came upon two more Iroquois who had set up a makeshift camp. A rough hand on my shoulder pushed me to the ground in front of the fire. One of the men tied my ankles. Someone else handed me a lump of overcooked meat. I was so hungry I tore at it like a wild dog. Claudette did not react when food was held out in front of her. The man offering it dropped it in her lap, where it lay untouched the entire night.

The men talked and laughed until they fell asleep. My mind was focused on survival, thinking only of Minette. What would happen to her if I died here in the woods? Why had I been so foolish as to come with the Gravels in the first place? Was the story about Etienne dying a ruse? I was not sure I believed Claudette that he was dead. I did not want to believe it. My jaw clenched. Damn Claudette and her husband for trying to sell me to the British fur traders! And now these Iroquois planned to ransom me. But what of Claudette? Would they see her as my companion and let her live, too? Or did they have other plans for her? I had heard horrible stories of what these people did to their captives, both French and Native. My thoughts spun and spun until finally, out of sheer exhaustion, my brain shut down altogether.

I must have slept. At daybreak the men put out the campfire. After a breakfast of pemmican, one of our captors cut our ankle bindings and prodded us to our feet. We left the camp surrounded by five men now. Another long day of marching through the woods.

When, finally, we made camp again, four of the men slept soundly around the new fire, their snores a chorus of nasally off-tune troubadours. The fifth man stayed up to keep watch during the night.

Claudette slept fitfully, her head on my stomach, but again, sleep would not come to me. I lay on the hard ground scratching fretfully at my mosquito bites, watching the half-moon edge its way across the sky as clouds caused the patchwork of stars to fade in and out. The same stars I had gazed upon while floating on my back in the palace pool at midnight alongside the Princess Henriette, my own little Minette's namesake. But these stars looked different. I had lost my bearing. I couldn't find Draco the dragon, or Ursa the great bear. Where were they taking us? And how far did we have yet to go?

I may have dozed, but at some point, one of the men awoke and traded places so the first watchman could sleep for a bit. My eyes refused to close again. It wasn't long before the new watchman nodded off sitting up, his chin against his chest.

And now with the moon sinking behind the trees, the sky was no longer black but a dull grey, awaiting the first birdsongs of the morning and the first rays of the sun.

A moan escaped my lips, my mind in a tumble. What would Armand think about my disappearance? Would he believe I had run off to meet a lover and drowned along the way? Of course not—that was a rumor Claudette had threatened to spread. And what about Jacques? That enigma of a man. My thoughts rambled unfettered. What would Etienne think when he learned I had been taken back to France? Would he find a way to claim Minette as his own? But no, he was dead. Thankfully, Armand loved Minette. He was Papa to her. What would happen if—

The soft sound of a pebble rolling past my head brought my muddled thoughts to a halt. A rolling pebble? With my bound hands, I pushed Claudette off me and sat up. She didn't react. The sleeping men didn't stir either. Had I imagined the pebble? Another flew low over the ground and hit the dirt near my feet. Where had it come from? I scanned the woods, ghostly in the predawn haze. There. By that stand of birch. A man edged out from behind the trees.

Jacques! He put a finger to his lips. I clamped my own tightly for fear I would squeal my relief and give him away. He tilted his head to the left before slipping back into the trees.

My heart thudding in my chest, I peered where he'd indicated. Nothing but trees. Then I saw a man crouched behind a mound of earth. The pale glint of steel on his musket caught my attention. He rose from his crouched position just long enough for me to recognize Armand. Another man stood behind him, his musket at the ready. Was that Theotiste, the gunsmith's son? I remembered he was among the militiamen who had accompanied Armand and the governor on their trip.

Now my eyes swept to the men sleeping around the fire. My stomach tensed as I realized there was no way out of this but bloodshed.

Whoo-whoo-whoo, whooo, whooo.

An owl. So close!

The man on watch woke up abruptly, his head cocked warily, listening. Another owl responded behind me. Not an owl. Jacques was signaling to someone in the trees beyond.

From behind the mound of earth came a blast and a flash of fire. The musket ball hit the dirt to the left of the Iroquois watchman, causing him to scramble away from it. Next to the mound stood Theotiste, his musket nestled at his shoulder, a cloud of smoke rising.

The sleeping men jumped from their slumber into crouching positions, one of them hurtling his hatchet in Theotiste's direction. Armand yanked the boy out of the way just before the hatchet embedded itself with an explosive *thwack* into a tree right behind where the reckless young soldier's head had been. Claudette screamed and threw herself on top of me again.

The Iroquois scrambled to gather their weapons—hatchets, knives, muskets. One of them kicked sand to douse the fire. They stood with their backs to the smoky embers, scanning the forest around them.

Desperate to crawl away from the line of fire, I tried to wiggle out from under Claudette, but she only whimpered and dug her head deeper into my lap. With my wrists and ankles bound, I was powerless to defend either of us. Just outside my reach lay a stone shard. I stretched as far as I could, but the shard was still a finger's length away.

Claudette's scream had devolved into a whimper, and I kicked her as hard as I could with my bound legs. To my relief, she rolled off my lap. I wormed along the ground until my fingers touched the shard. Grasping it, I rubbed the sharp edge against the cord binding my wrists.

Jacques stepped out from behind the birch tree, his musket at his shoulder. Armand moved away from the mound, his musket at the ready as well. Theotiste was madly reloading. The Iroquois raised their weapons, unwilling to give ground. A man in a buckskin tunic and leggings stepped out from the trees on the opposite side of the camp. Ojibwe, perhaps? He carried a musket.

"We want the women," Jacques said in Mohawk.

The last thread of my binding broke loose. My hands were free.

The lead Iroquois grunted. "You'll have to pay more than your king does."

Frantically, I sawed through the cord binding my ankles, kicking at Claudette when she tried to grasp me for comfort.

"They are not yours to sell," Jacques said. "You can hand them over, or we will take them from you."

Armand lifted his musket higher and aimed it at the Iroquois. Before I could shout a warning, one of my captors thrust a fistful of sand and ash directly at him. Taken by surprise, Armand fired, his shot going wild. The Iroquois men set up a howl and charged him.

The Ojibwe fired, bringing down one of them. With no time to reload, he dropped the musket and pulled out his hatchet.

Jacques fired at another, hitting him in the arm. Then, flipping his musket around to use as a bludgeon, he roared and rushed at our captors, knocking heads left and right.

Armand and the watchman grappled hand to hand, while Theotiste and the Ojibwe joined Jacques, fists, knives, and hatchets swinging wildly.

Instinctively, I crawled along the ground to where a hatchet lay abandoned, my heart thudding in my chest. Grasping the weapon, I struggled to stand, ready to ward off anyone coming for me, my legs shaking, my body swaying.

Watching in horror, I saw Armand take a blow that caused him to stagger and fall. As he rose to face his attacker, Armand dodged the jab of the Iroquois's knife. But the man thrust again, low, splitting open a wide gash on Armand's thigh. He buckled and fell again. The Iroquois raised his knife over my husband's head to finish him off.

In a panic, I threw my hatchet. The weapon hit its mark. The Iroquois man staggered. Theotiste ran at him and gored the man with the bayonet attached to his musket.

Falling to my knees, I vomited. When I looked up again, three Iroquois lay dead, the others lay unconscious. Sobbing, I crawled toward Armand.

Jacques reached him first and was already applying pressure with his hands to stanch the bleeding. Our eyes connected briefly before I tugged at my underskirt and ripped a piece from it. Pushing Jacques's bloodied hands aside, I applied a fold of linen and pressed it down on Armand's wound.

While Theotiste and the Ojibwe bound the surviving Iroquois and gathered their weapons, Jacques cut the strap from his munitions bag. He tied it around Armand's leg to hold the makeshift bandage in place.

"Sylvienne," Armand said, sweat breaking out on his forehead. "I thought I would never see you again."

Grasping Armand's face, I kissed him. "I can't believe you found me."

"I was in Trois-Rivières with the governor when we learned of the attack on the Gravels and the two British traders."

"Don't talk. Save your energy." I pushed his hair out of his eyes. "Lie back."

He laid his head on the ground but continued. "Theotiste and I went out to look for Madame Gravel. I didn't know you were with them until I ran into Jacques and his friend just before sundown yesterday."

My mind filled with questions. I searched Jacques's face as he wiped Armand's blood off his hands.

"A runner came to the village. He told Binesi," Jacques nodded toward the Ojibwe, "that a French merchant and two foreigners had been killed, and that the Iroquois had taken two women captive, one of them a green-eyed, wild-haired beauty who spoke to the men in their own language. I knew it had to be you."

Tears welled. Relief? Horror at what had just transpired? I turned back to Armand, grief overwhelming me. "Etienne is dead."

"Who?"

"Minette's father."

"The shoemaker." He shook his head. "When? No. I spoke to him just…" He winced in pain. "Just before Theotiste and I set out."

"You spoke to—?"

"He wanted to come with us." The words came out in short bursts. "To help search. For Madame Gravel. But there was a family. The new surgeon. For the Hôtel-Dieu. In Ville-Marie." He sucked in a breath. "I asked Damise. To escort them. Because of the attack. On Gravel. Travelers weren't safe. Damise is… very much…alive." He closed his eyes against the pain.

Sobs shook me unabated now. When I could speak again, I said. "I nearly lost you." Armand grasped my hand, but I told him, "This mission was no more than folly on my part. You risked your life for me."

"And I would do so again." His eyes closed again from weariness and pain.

After a few moments, letting go his hand, I stood up and walked over to Claudette, a wary look in her eyes at my approach. I slapped her. Hard.

When we were ready to go, Armand tried to walk on his wounded leg, arms around Jacques's and Theotiste's shoulders. But he collapsed after a few steps. With the help of Binesi and Theotiste, Jacques constructed a litter out of birch branches, lashing a blanket to it to carry him. They made a travois as well to carry the confiscated weapons, assuming the wounded Iroquois would eventually break free of their bonds.

Jacques and Binesi hefted the litter. Theotiste dragged the travois as we worked our way back to the river. It tore at my heart to see Armand gritting against the pain.

Claudette plodded along behind me saying nothing. At first, I was glad for her silence, but after a while I could no longer keep from questioning her.

"Why did you tell me Etienne was dying?" I asked.

"Who?" she said, her voice dull.

"The shoemaker. How did you know he was my Etienne from Amiens?"

She scoffed. "I'm not a dunce. Damise was his mother's family name. She and my mother served together on the cathedral altar guild. A shoemaker claiming that name was just too much of a coincidence to ignore. And I guessed right, didn't I?" She sneered. "You came running like an infatuated puppy as soon as you thought he was dying."

"But he wasn't. Yet you let me believe he—" My voice caught in my throat.

Claudette only shrugged. My fists clenched. I was bitter with rage at how she had lied to lure me out here. And not a little chagrined for believing those lies. I shuddered at the result of her scheming. Her husband dead. Mine wounded. Two British traders and three Iroquois dead. And for what? Greed? Jealousy?

As if reading my thoughts, Claudette spoke, her voice flat, "Three of those heathen dead is not enough to make up for the killing of my Robert. I wish they could all be slain. Every last one of them."

I could only shake my head in exasperation. She was unwilling to accept her role as the catalyst in her husband's death. Her blindness saddened me.

After two days walking, we reached the temporary encampment set up by the British traders. The lean-to was still intact. The Gravel's canoe sat on the rocky shore alongside Armand and Theotiste's larger craft. A rock-covered mound topped with a single cross made of twigs told us someone had come upon the site and buried the bodies of the three slain men. Claudette refused to look at her husband's grave.

Jacques pushed the larger canoe into the water. The men hoisted Armand into it. I could see him biting his lip to keep from crying out when they lifted his wounded leg over the side. I climbed in and sat with his head on my lap.

Theotiste knelt in front with Claudette directly behind him. Jacques took up his position at the back of the canoe where he could steer. Binesi pushed us off. Then, confiscating Robert Gravel's canoe, the Ojibwe headed upriver to warn the people of Trois-Rivières and then his own village of what had happened with the Iroquois.

We started downriver back to Québec, not stopping even at night. Thankfully, the moon was nearly full and the sky cloudless. Our urgency was driven by the fever which had taken hold of Armand's body. Ripping fabric from my skirt, I soaked it in the cold river, then wiped his hot face, neck, and chest with it; but his fever raged unabated. We needed to get him into the care of the hospital sisters as quickly as possible.

After a day and a half of paddling, it became evident the men were tiring. I offered to take a turn, but Jacques said that moving about in the canoe to position myself would be more trouble than my help was worth. It was just as well; I didn't want to disturb Armand, nestled in my lap.

We passed an encampment along the shore that hadn't been there days earlier when the Gravels and I were paddling upriver. Men waved and shouted greetings.

"Wendat," Jacques said.

He slowed the canoe and yelled back to them. I thought I made out the words, "help" and "wounded man." Moments later, two men from the shore pushed a canoe into the water and jumped in. They paddled swiftly, guiding their canoe alongside ours, then lashed a rope to connect us.

After a brief exchange, Jacques said to me, "They want to know if you are the white woman whose baby their cousin Cécile helped bring into the world."

Surprised by the question, I stammered. "That was me. And Minette. They are Cécile's cousins?"

"All Wendat are cousins," Jacques said. He told Theotiste he could sleep for a couple of hours. "We're in good hands. They'll keep us moving along with the current."

With the Wendat men guiding us, both Jacques and Theotiste slumped against the sides of our canoe and slept. After a time, I dozed off as well. Claudette, who hadn't spoken again after our short exchange on the trail, was so quiet I had no idea whether she slept or not. I didn't care.

About the time the sun's rays first began to glow through thick stands of trees, Jacques came fully awake. "Are you rested?" he asked Theotiste.

"I am," the younger man answered.

Jacques called out to the men in the other canoe, thanking them for their help.

As they unlashed the canoes, Jacques said to me, "They say to give that baby a kiss for them. They say the child is blessed to have such a courageous mother."

"Courageous?" I muttered. "Foolhardy is the better word."

Jacques didn't comment.

We waved and shouted our thanks again as the Wendat men turned their canoe and headed back upriver.

CHAPTER THIRTY-THREE

The sisters of the Hôtel-Dieu scrambled to prepare a bed in the men's ward, tucking in a clean sheet, the prior occupant having departed the hospital and our good Earth that same morning. Sœur Helene directed her staff much like a military commander preparing for battle, ordering one to fetch water from the well, another clean linen for bandages. Two others were dispatched to the herb garden for plants used to draw out infection.

Docteur Suret rushed in just as Jacques and Theotiste carried Armand through the door and laid him on the bed. He moaned, his voice weak, his breathing erratic.

To keep me from hovering over him, Sœur Angeline took me by the arm and guided me to the women's ward where she cleaned me up, washed my hair, and applied ointment to the mosquito bites I had scratched until they bled. Then she offered me a simple wool tunic to slip into in place of my torn and filthy dress.

When I was presentable again, she advised me the best place to wait was in the chapel, where I could pray for my husband while the doctor and the sisters tended to his festering wound.

Stepping into the familiar chapel, I was surprised to find Jacques there.

"They wanted me out of the way," he said. "I'd hoped to find you here."

"Theotiste?"

"He left to report to the watch commander."

"What about Claudette?" I realized neither of us had seen her since we ferried Armand up the hill in a horse-drawn cart, whose driver waived off the payment Jacques promised.

"No idea. Went home?" Jacques said.

I sank to my knees in front of the altar. This was where Armand and I had agreed to wed. Now I was here to beg for his life in the company of the man who, without trying, tempted me to sin. Jacques knelt down beside me. He made the sign of the cross. I suppose certain habits are with us forever. I did the same.

As I prayed for God to spare Armand for me, for Minette, for all the people in this colony whom he served so ardently, it occurred to me I should be praying to save my soul from being damned forever. But I suspected it was too late for that. Not just because of Jacques, or even Etienne, but for the entire life of indulgence I had lived. And now here we knelt, two people who had so little acquaintance with God of late, praying for the man we both loved. A lightning strike would have been most welcome at this point, though hardly punishment enough for my transgressions.

Governor Courcelle and Intendent Talon, with the Chevalier de Lorraine in tow, came to the hospital. Sœur Angeline had spotted the men striding up the path toward the building. She'd hurried to let us know. Jacques thanked her, then slipped out into the garden. He was not eager to confront either administrator under these circumstances.

"How fares Captain Gervais?" Talon asked when I rose from the bedside stool to greet them, feeling awkward in my borrowed tunic.

"His fever rages unabated," I said. "The sisters have applied every remedy they know."

Thankfully, the men did not tarry long at Armand's bedside. I walked with them out to the foyer where we met Sœur Helene. Courcelle questioned her about Armand's prognosis. She was not hopeful. The wound had been festering for far too long.

"If anyone can save him, the sisters can," he said to me. "He is getting the best care possible."

Talon said, "And you? How do you fare? Young Theotiste Pecquet gave us an accounting of what happened near Trois-Rivières and the Gravels' role in it. Shocking."

"An unbelievable ordeal," de Lorraine chimed in. He wore a suitably grave expression. "What would I have told the King had you not returned?"

Resisting the impulse to lash out at him, I said to Talon, "I'm bruised, but otherwise unharmed."

"I am glad to hear it," he said. "A horrific end to Gravel. I don't understand what motivated him and that woman of his. Quite out of character for the man."

I said nothing, judging it not entirely out of character for Claudette.

"I have ordered her arrest," Courcelle said. "She shall be tried and suffer the consequences."

Talon tapped his hand against his leg, as if in consternation. "Monsieur Gravel's death leaves the Sovereign Council with an empty seat."

"I suppose that will be an inconvenience," I said.

He grunted in agreement. Then as an afterthought he said, "There is a man who has been recommended to take his place. From Ville-Marie. A shoemaker and businessman. He has risen in the community's esteem quite quickly. I've sent a request that he come as soon as possible for an interview."

A flitter teased my stomach. "His name?"

"Damise, I think. He's only been in the colony a year or so, but he is educated. We need more educated men on the council."

The next time the nuns came to attend to Armand's wounds, I took the opportunity to visit the chapel again. Kneeling before the altar, I gazed up at the crucifix above. I had never been much for praying, but I prayed now. *Please don't take this good man away from me and from Minette who needs a father to protect her. I know I don't deserve him. I accept that his pain is part of my punishment, but it isn't fair to him nor to my daughter to have to bear the burden of my sins.*

A gentle hand on my shoulder brought me out of my reverie.

"Sylvienne."

I reached up and placed my hand on his. Jacques. Another of my sins.

"We need to talk," he said.

"Let's go outside. I need air."

We walked out to the herb garden and found a bench to sit on. The sun, low in the afternoon sky, sent shafts of golden rays through clotted clouds. Honeybees flitted from flower to flower. A gentle breeze carried the calming scents of basil, mint, and lemon balm.

"I don't think Armand can hold on much longer." Tears welled in my eyes.

"I know." The sadness in his voice matched my own.

"He loves you like a brother," I said.

"And I him."

We sat in silence for a moment. When he spoke again, his voice was low, cautious. "Sylvienne, I know what happened back in France. To the duke, your husband. What you were accused of."

Stunned, I looked up at him. "How? How could…?"

"Armand told me."

"He didn't know. I never told him the details."

Jacques studied my face, seeming to collect his thoughts.

"There was someone, a man back in France, who apparently wanted to do you harm. The man had written to Governor Courcelle. But the governor's adjutant, who had served under Armand when he first arrived, intercepted the letter and passed it on to him."

"He never told me he knew." I couldn't fathom Armand having been privy all along to what I had done and never saying anything to me.

"He didn't want to upset you. His only goal was to protect you."

"Who was this man who wrote the letter?"

Jacques shrugged. "Some chevalier or another. I don't know the man's name."

But I knew. De Lorraine. He had always had an aversion to me. From the very beginning he resented the way Philippe took me under his wing, championed me at court when others sought to humiliate me. But why go out of his way to add to my misery here? I was determined he and I would have a few words before he headed back to France—assuming he could go back at all.

"Sylvienne, I understand why you did what you did. Self-defense. But what I don't understand is...why did you marry the cur in the first place?"

"I didn't have a choice. My father arranged the marriage without my consent, or even my knowledge."

He looked at me intently, like he was trying to parse something out.

"Your father being...?"

I looked down at my hands, unwilling to meet his eyes.

"Someone of royal blood?" His tone challenged.

I nodded, but kept my eyes averted.

He went on. "Those British traders, the ones who were killed along with Gravel."

I looked up, dreading where this was going.

"They came after you because you are King Louis's daughter, didn't they?"

"They call all the girls who come here under his sponsorship the King's daughters." I glanced away again, unable to meet his eyes.

He took my chin in his fingers and turned my face to look at him. "But not all the girls who come here under his sponsorship have his blood."

After a long moment, my voice husky, unwilling to say the words, unwilling to look him in the eye, I admitted, "The truth is…my mother…she was seduced by him when they were both teenagers. Or perhaps it was she who seduced him. I don't think it matters. They were both very young."

He said nothing. I looked up at him. "It's a long story, but she, my mother, was a bâtarde herself. Her father was Louis's uncle. Gaston, Duc d'Orléans."

"And you…?"

"I am Louis's bâtarde." I scoffed. "One of many, as it turns out."

Jacques ran a hand through his hair. "Armand never breathed a word of that to me."

"He didn't know."

"How…? How could you not tell your husband a detail of such significance?"

I looked hard into his eyes now. "If you and I had only recently met, here in this backwoods village of Québec, and I said, 'Oh, by the way, my father is the king of France.' What would you have said?"

A sigh of understanding escaped his lips. "That you are an addled woman in need of locking away."

"Jacques, I've made a lot of mistakes in my life. Untruths have haunted me from the time I was born. But this truth, what good would it have done to have told him?"

"He would have been all the more protective of you, I suppose."

My voice was wry. "Protecting a crazy woman from her own delusions?" I sighed. "I don't know what I will do without him."

"I'll be here."

I touched his hand. "I know you will.

Sœur Angeline came into the garden. "There are soldiers at the front door. They demand to see Monsieur Farley."

Alarmed, I stood, ready to help him flee. But Jacques only nodded, resigned. "I won't put up a fight. It will only make things worse for Armand…and for you."

"I don't understand. What do they want now?"

"Courcelle believes I've been selling guns to the Iroquois."

"Have you?"

"To the Iroquois? No."

He rose and followed Sœur Angeline out of the garden.

Sinking back onto the bench, all I could do was pray. For Armand. For Jacques. All of this was my fault. Perhaps if I had told Armand the truth about me, about my father, he would have found a way to believe me. To protect me. Or maybe he would have thought me addled and kept me locked up so I wouldn't go wandering off to where malicious men wanted to harm me. So he wouldn't have to rescue me…at the cost of his own life. And now Jacques's as well. I hung my head, my face in my hands. I wept until my shoulders shook.

Sœur Angeline returned to fetch me a short while later. "You had better come."

Exhaustion overcame me. And fear of the inevitable. I wanted to curl up and pretend I hadn't seen her, but I rose and followed her to the men's infirmary where my husband lay dying.

Armand's breathing was shallow, his face pale. I sat on the stool next to his bed and took his hand. His squeeze was barely perceptible, but he opened his eyes.

"Sylvienne." His voice a whisper, raspy. "I want you to know…" He gasped. "*Je t'aime.*"

Gulping against the lump in my throat, I realized we'd never actually said we loved each other before. Squeezing his hand, I said, "*Je t'aime, mon mari.*"

He nodded, satisfied, closing his eyes for a moment. When he opened them again, he asked, "Where is Jacques?"

I hesitated. Armand didn't need bad news right now, but I knew he would want the truth. "He's been arrested. They've taken him to the garrison."

"Damn." He sucked in a ragged breath. "My fault."

"No." I covered his dry, mottled hand with both of mine now.

"If he hadn't…brought me here…" He coughed, wincing.

"Hush. He knew the danger. He wouldn't have it any other way."

His eyes closed. It seemed to take more effort to open them again. "Sylvienne…he's a good man."

My heart broke. That he would be thinking of someone other than himself at this moment. He didn't deserve such an end to his life.

His tongue ran over dry lips. "He will take care of you. And Minette."

"Hush. Please." I brushed his hair away from his forehead. "Save your strength."

"You…" His breath rattled. "Take care of him."

I reached for the water pitcher and poured a bit into a cup, holding his head up to aid him in drinking. He settled his head back onto the sweat-stained pillow. His breath came in short spurts now. "He…needs…someone. And you'll…need…."

"Armand, please. Don't talk like this." I stroked his cheek.

"No time… I need…to know." His eyes pleading.

"I have you," I said. We both knew he was dying, but I didn't want to admit it.

"Jacques…he's… in love…with you."

"You're talking nonsense." My voice was breathless now.

Barely able to keep his eyes open, he spoke as if dreaming. "He…would never…betray me…never…let you know. But…" His eyes drifted shut again. "It's true."

"Armand," I said through my tears. "I have always loved you."

A hand on my shoulder woke me. I'd been dozing leaning over the bed, my head on my arms. Blinking at the sunless sky outside the window, I sat up suddenly. Dusk. Armand's face was still, pain-free, peaceful.

"He's with our Lord now," Sœur Helene said in a quiet voice.

"No, I…we were just talking." I took his hand, dismayed at how cool it felt. My fingers immediately moved to his face. His cheek, also cool, the fever forever gone. A knot of grief pitted my stomach. Tears welled, unbidden. A low moan filled my ears, and I realized it was the sound of my own mourning. Closing my eyes, I forced myself to breathe. Finally, I leaned over and kissed his cold forehead. Straightening, I asked, "What am I to do now?"

"The sisters and I will wash him in preparation. You will need to speak to Father Laval about a requiem Mass and burial in the churchyard. You shouldn't wait too long."

I brushed the hair from Armand's forehead one last time before turning and walking out.

Before I realized where I was headed, I was at the garrison prison.

"I need to see Monsieur Farley," I said, my back rigid, my voice calm but resolute. "And then I will need to speak to Governor Courcelle."

The guard didn't seem to know what to make of my demand, but he knew me, knew my husband, knew his captain was dying, likely dead by now. He acquiesced. I followed him through the small prison building.

A woman sitting on a cot in a corner cell caught my eye. Claudette. She had apparently been given a change of clothes, a simple frock, but her hair was unkempt. Food sat untouched on a plate on the floor, flies buzzing around it. She glanced up at me with blank eyes.

My voice was low but bitter. "You sad, stupid woman. I hope you hang."

No response. Not even a flicker of an eye.

I moved on. At Jacques's cell, the guard bowed before heading back to his post, leaving us alone.

Jacques stood up from his cot as soon as he saw me. The look in his eyes told me he knew why I had come. "Armand?"

A lump wedged in my throat. My voice was barely a whisper. "He's at peace."

Jacques nodded, closing his eyes against his grief. When he opened them, he reached through the bars and touched my arm. "Are you…?"

"I have much to do."

He nodded. "Damn!" He banged his palms against the bars. "Why? He was a good man. The best. It should have been me." He looked at me with grief-stricken eyes. "It's my fault."

I reached for his hands. "It's not. He said the same thing about you being here in this cell. Neither of you bears any blame for the other."

He leaned his head against the bars, and I moved toward him, our foreheads touching.

"What will we do without him?" he asked, his shoulders heaving.

CHAPTER THIRTY-FOUR

The funeral Mass was an ordeal for me. Most of the village turned out. The church was hot and stuffy. I sat stoically through the prayers and incense, my eyes never leaving the crucifix hanging over the altar; but afterward, I broke into uncontrollable sobs as Armand was laid to rest in the churchyard, the dirt shoveled over his shrouded body.

After the funeral, Intendent Talon approached me to express his condolences. I had gone first to the governor immediately after my visit to Jacques to inform him of my husband's death. Then I went to Talon's office to ask about Armand's military pension. I had Minette to care for, after all.

Jacques was the other reason I went to see the intendent. I asked about the charges against him. Talon's answer shook me to my core. Jacques had been accused by the governor of colluding with the British and selling munitions to the Natives. Both were capital offenses. The room spun, and it was all I could do to keep a grip on my thoughts. Jacques had admitted to me that he'd been selling guns to the Ojibwe and the Wendat, saying they needed to protect themselves against the Iroquois. But colluding with the British? I refused to believe that. Why would he involve himself with people he despised?

A trial date had not yet been set. I suspected Courcelle was gathering as much evidence as he could to prove Jacques was a traitor to the Crown. If he was successful, the only outcome would be hanging. And without Armand to intercede there was little hope a trial would go any other way.

Walking home from the churchyard after the funeral with Catherine and Minette, a hollowness filled my heart. The house seemed oddly empty, even with LeDuc's welcoming barks. People stopped by throughout the day to drop off food, far more than we could eat. When Titus came to check on us, I asked Catherine to make sure he ate as much as he could before leaving.

Exhausted, I lifted Minette onto the bed with me and nuzzled her soft face. She would never know the man who unhesitatingly became her papa. How life seemed to be repeating itself. At least I'd had several years with my own papa. So many of the memories of him had long faded, but I had the sketch Maman had given to me when I left Amiens. Minette would have no memories of Armand. For her, he would be nothing more than a story told.

We had been napping barely an hour when a banging on the door interrupted my attempt at a nap. I groaned wondering which of the townspeople it was this time.

Catherine answered the door, then called to me, "Sylvienne, you must come!"

With a sigh, I pushed myself off the bed.

At the door stood a Native man I did not know. Behind him was a boy who looked to be about seven or eight years old. Also Native, he had straight black hair that hung to his shoulders. Both the man and the boy wore deerskin leggings and simple deerskin tunics. "Can I help you?" I said to the man.

"Where Jacques Farley?" he said.

"Monsieur Farley? He is not here."

"Where I find?" The man looked tired, hungry, worried.

"He's…" I hesitated. "He's being held at the fort."

Unfazed, the man grabbed the boy by the shoulder and pushed him toward me. "This Jacques boy."

"His boy?"

"Jacques is father. Boy name Miigwan."

Stunned, I stared at the child. "This is Miigwan? Jacques's…son?" Indeed, the child's eyes were grey instead of brown like those of the Natives I knew. He quickly shifted his gaze downward.

"Boy Ojibwe. He okomisan sick with white man pox. Many in village sick. Not safe for boy. I bring here. To he father."

"But he is—"

"You take." He pushed the boy forward again. "Keep safe." The man turned and strode away.

"Wait! You can't just leave him!"

But he didn't stop. Before I could utter another word, he was over the rise and gone.

The boy gazed up at me with fearful eyes. Jacques's son? How could this be? I turned to Catherine hovering in the doorway.

"Catherine, this is—"

"Miigwan, yes." She pulled him into a hug.

"You know him?

"Of course. He is Papa Jacques's boy." She ushered him into the house.

Following them in, I gave Catherine a look of consternation—no one had ever mentioned Jacques having a son—then I said to the boy, "I don't suppose you speak French?"

"Oui, madame, I do," he said, speaking for the first time. "Papa talks French to me when he is home."

"Where is your mother?"

A sadness filled his eyes. "She is dead. One year gone. My nookomis takes care of me when Papa not in village. But now she is sick."

So that was where Jacques went when he was not in Québec or off trading for furs. But why did he never mention he had a family? I simply could not understand that man. With a sigh, I said, "Catherine, will you give Miigwan something to eat?"

As I packed a meal for Jacques—the prison provided only hardtack and gruel—Catherine scooped a healthy serving of *fèves au lard* into a bowl for the boy. The beans and bacon dish sweetened with maple syrup had been dropped off by a sympathetic villager.

Once the boy was settled at the table under Catherine's care, I took up my basket. I was just passing through the village gate—the same one Armand used to guard on Sunday mornings—when a French boy from the lower village came running up the path, out of breath.

"Madame! A letter for you."

The handwriting was familiar. Etienne's. Breaking the seal, I read the words written in his careful script.

Dearest Sylvienne,

Word reached me of your horrific ordeal at the hands of the Iroquois, and of the death of Captain Gervais. I am stunned at what you have gone through. I pray you are recovering in body and spirit. And I am sorry for the loss of your husband. I know you cared deeply for him.

I will be in Québec in a day or two by the time you receive this. I would like to visit with you and Minette. Please do not turn me away. I have something very important I wish to discuss with you.

Etienne

Of course. He had been summoned by Talon to interview for Gravel's seat on the Sovereign Council. If the position was granted, he would be spending significant time in Québec, representing Ville-Marie.

As I walked to the garrison, I stewed over Etienne's letter, a quandary swirling in my head and in my heart. What did he wish to discuss? He had asked me to marry him back in Amiens when we were not much more than children. I hadn't given him an answer at the time. Was he seeking one now that my dear Armand was gone? Of course, he was. He had escaped France and the King's men, made his way across the vast, cold expanse of ocean looking for me. But what should I tell him? The truth was, I had never stopped loving him. I could easily picture a life with him. And Minette deserved to know her father. In a heartbeat, I could say yes.

Or could I? As much as I cared for Etienne, my heart was torn between two desires. And my greatest desire now was to free Jacques. Oh, Etienne. There had been such passion between us at one time. But so much distrust and anger had followed us from Amiens to Versailles. I had disappointed him when I left for court without giving him the answer he sought. And then again, when the King decreed I should marry the Duc de Narbonne. Our lives were never fated to be as one in France. But we were here. In a new world. What should I say if he asked for my answer now?

Grimacing at the dank stench of urine and mold in the garrison prison, I made my way to Jacques's cell. He was grateful for the bowl of *fèves au lard* and the biscuits I handed through the bars.

A guard offered me a stool so I could sit outside the cell and visit with Jacques. Being the widow of Captain Armand Gervais afforded me a level of consideration.

Jacques used a chunk of biscuit to scoop beans into his mouth. "Mmm…*c'est bon.*"

I watched him eat for several moments before speaking. "Jacques, there's a boy at my house."

He sopped another biscuit into the beans. "A boy?"

"His name is Miigwan."

His hand with the biscuit stopped midway to his mouth. "Miigwan? At your house?"

I nodded.

He dropped the biscuit into the bowl and set it aside, wiping his sleeve across his mouth. "Why? What is he doing there?"

"So, he is your son?"

"Yes." He frowned, his eyes darkening.

"Apparently, his grandmother is ill. Smallpox. Jacques, why did you never say you had a son? A family?"

"Smallpox?" Jacques's shoulders seemed to sag, a great sadness filled his eyes. After a moment, he asked, "How did he get to you?"

"A man brought him. He said they were Ojibwe. He was looking for you. You never told me you have a family."

"Is he okay? He's not sick, too, is he?"

"He's fine. He is with Catherine and Minette right now. Scared but fine. Did Armand know you have a family?"

Jacques let out a breath. "He did."

"And yet, he never said a word to me?"

"I swore him to secrecy."

"But I am...I was his wife." The hurt in my voice must have been evident.

"Don't blame him. Armand was a man of his word. That's why he was so respected in the colony. He wasn't trying to hide anything from you. He just...never brought it up. Much as with you about your father."

Mulling his words, I gazed at this enigma of a man. He spent his days on the river during trading season. He refused to bow to colonial authority. And he would disappear for months at a time in the winter. Apparently living among the Ojibwe. Living with his own family.

"The boy...your son...Miigwan...he said his mother died."

"A year ago." His eyes hardened now. "She was killed. In a raid. By the Iroquois."

I swallowed hard. The same people who had tried to kidnap me. Who mortally wounded Armand. "I'm so sorry."

He reached through the bars to touch my hand. "I've tried to spend as much time with Miigwan as I can when I'm not working the beaver routes. It's been hard for him. And now…with his grandmother sick…" His voice trailed off.

"He can stay with me and Catherine. At least until you are out of this place." I gestured toward his cell in disgust.

"I appreciate that, more than I can say. But I don't know how long it will be before they let me out. If ever. And if the Council finds out about Miigwan, they will just add it to my list of charges."

"I don't understand. It's not illegal to take a Native woman for a wife." In fact, in the early days of the colony, before the recruits began to arrive, it had been encouraged. "Were you not married to the boy's mother?"

"We were married, but not in the Church."

In the realm of King Louis that was a sin. And illegal.

"Yours was a *marriage à la façon du pays*?" A common-law marriage, the wedding likely an Ojibwe ceremony.

"Makade refused to convert," he said. "She had no interest in living among the French. She felt strongly about her people and their beliefs. I respected her for that."

"But the King's government doesn't.

He grasped my hands. "Talon's men. They'll send him to the Jesuit school. They'll force the Ojibwe out of him. I promised Makade I would never let that happen. Sylvienne, promise me you won't let them take him."

He stared into my eyes, his own pleading, until I nodded. "I promise."

His relief, evident on his face, overwhelmed me. And made my heart ache for him all the more.

"Jacques, there is something I must say. Something I will likely regret. But I'll regret it all the more if I don't."

He gazed at me intently, his eyes questioning now.

"You know I cared deeply for Armand. And that I would never, ever have betrayed his love for me or broken our commitment to be faithful to each other. But…" I drew in a ragged breath. "Somewhere along the way these past two years, I…" My voice became barely a whisper, the words caught in my throat. "I think I've fallen in love with you."

He laid a hand against my cheek. "I've loved you from the first moment I saw you."

It was true then, what Armand had told me. I closed my eyes, feeling the warmth of Jacques's fingers on my face, his thumb tracing my lips.

His voice cracked in a whisper of despair. "But damn my soul to hell, Sylvienne." He pulled his hand away. "He's barely been in the ground a day, and here I am desecrating the memory of a man I loved above all others."

"He knew. And he loved you all the more for it."

"That I had fallen in love with his wife?"

Now I touched his face. "That you would never have acted upon it. Nor I. That's why you stayed away, isn't it? All winter and through the spring All that time I thought you were afraid of being arrested."

He kissed my fingers, then pushed them away. "You should go."

While I hated to leave him there, I was relieved to escape the awful prison. Stepping out into the sunshine, I squinted against the intensity of the light after the dimness of the cell block, the intensity of my joy at Jacques's words against the grief in my heart for Armand.

A soldier waited near the door, startling me when he spoke. "Madame Gervais, Intendant Talon requests your presence at the residence. I am to escort you."

Talon? What could he want now? Obviously, "request" was a polite way of putting it, or he wouldn't have ordered an "escort" for me.

CHAPTER THIRTY-FIVE

Intendent Talon stood when I entered his office. He invited me to sit, indicating a damask-covered armchair in front of his large, ornate desk.

The Chevalier de Lorraine, slouched in a matching chair, jumped to his feet and offered an abrupt bow. He took my hands. "My dear girl, I am so sorry about your husband. But…you do have a penchant for dire circumstances."

Pulling my hands from his grasp, I said, "Thank you. I suppose." I turned toward Talon. "You requested my presence?"

"Yes. Thank you for coming." He looked at de Lorraine who had re-seated himself, his eyebrows arched expectantly. "I would like to have a private conversation."

"Of course. I will take my leave." He rose. "I told that houseboy of yours I would give him a lesson in pairing wines with various meats. Though I doubt there is anything that will compliment roast bear or moose." He bowed again and left.

Talon hid his exasperation poorly. He came around the desk and took the seat de Lorraine had vacated. We sat facing each other.

"Again, I offer my sympathies regarding Captain Gervais. He was a good man. An extraordinary man, if truth be told. His death will be an immense loss for our community."

"It is kind of you to say so."

He cleared his throat before beginning again. "The news of your relationship to the King, I must confess, came as quite a shock."

"That I am his daughter? Or that I am *une bâtarde*?" I asked looking directly at him.

"I treated you poorly when we first met. I apologize for any discomfort I might have caused."

"It would seem it shouldn't matter whether or not I am of royal blood to be treated with respect."

Ignoring my comment, he reached for something on his desk. "I thought perhaps you would be interested in a letter from your father. Delivered by de Lorraine."

"A letter? Why was it not given to me immediately at the luncheon that day after he arrived?"

"I suppose he could have. Should have. Regardless, here it is now."

I took the letter from him. The seal had already been broken. There was no point in complaining about that now. Silently, I read the words, written in the familiar hand of my father, the King of France.

My Loving Daughter Sylvienne,

I have dispensed the Chevalier de Lorraine to bring you home. All is forgiven. It is safe for you to return now. I have signed a decree legitimizing you as my true and legal daughter.

Grimacing, I had to force myself not to crumple the letter and throw it into the fireplace.

You will be happy to know I have several possibilities for a good match for you. I acknowledge the Duc de Narbonne was a poor choice. Together we will choose your new spouse. You will be given a title and appropriate lands on the day of your wedding.

Affectionately,

Louis, your Father

Obviously, the King knew I was already married. He had sent annulment papers. Not that they were needed now. However, he had no way of knowing I'd been widowed a second time. Nor that I had a daughter of my own now.

I had dreamed so long of returning to France, but now...now New France was my home. Here I lived among people who cared for me not because I had access to the king or could provide political or financial advantage, but because I was me. I realized I did not wish to live anywhere but here. The things that once frightened me—the wilderness, the Native people, the lack of "civilization"—now enthralled me. I wanted to raise my daughter here.

"I have no interest in returning to France. I've already informed de Lorraine. He will have to go back without me." I started to rise, the letter dropping to the floor.

Talon put out a hand to stop me. He retrieved the letter and folded it carefully as he spoke. "One does not refuse a request from the King."

"So my mother once told me." I lifted my chin defiantly. "If he wishes to compel me to comply, he will have to order you to put me in chains."

Talon sat for a long moment, tapping the arm of his chair with the letter. "I would not wish it to come to that. I have a proposition to make."

My brow furrowed. The word "proposition" made me wary, but I sat back anyway to hear him out.

"As Intendant, I have final jurisdiction over all civil court proceedings."

I waited for more.

"Despite what I said that day at the governor's chateau, I have never believed Jacques Farley to be guilty of that which the governor accuses him."

"Then why is he imprisoned?"

"Politics, my dear. Politics. His trial is scheduled for the morrow. He will be found guilty and sentenced to hang."

I gulped. He wasn't trying to frighten me. What he said was a simple fact. My hands clenched. "What has Jacques Farley's situation to do with the King's request?"

Talon rubbed his hand across his knee. "The Chevalier de Lorraine delivered a letter to me as well. A letter from the Crown recalling me to France."

This was a surprise. Talon was a highly regarded administrator here. He would be missed.

"If you will go back with me, willingly, on the next ship out. Perhaps even reconsider my proposal of marriage, to take place after we have arrived in France, I will free Farley and prepare a writ pardoning him from all transgressions against the crown."

My breath caught in my throat. Had I heard him correctly? Then a realization hit me. "Once you are gone, the governor or the new Intendant will simply reverse your order."

"I can make it binding."

"You…you would do that? Pardon Jacques?"

"I would."

"Why? Why would you offer such a pact?'

"I have long wished for a position in King Louis's court. Perhaps…Minister of Finance."

"But you have served the King well here. You have brought his dream of a thriving colony to fruition. I'm sure you have earned a good position."

"Yes, but one misstep is all it would take to reverse everything I have sought to attain for myself."

"And returning without me would be considered such a misstep."

He inclined his head in acknowledgement. The silence between us grew long, but Talon waited without further comment, his hands resting motionless on his knees.

My hands twisted fretfully in my lap. I was being given an opportunity to save Jacques from the hangman, to allow Miigwan to grow up with a father. But it meant returning to the country that had rejected me. To a father who professed to love me, but who saw all his children as pawns in the game of political chess. And what of Minette? Would I dare take her across the ocean at so young an age? Could she survive such a voyage? A voyage that had sent Hannibal and Claire into the depths of the sea? Jacques's life saved at the expense of everything I held dear. Was there any way out of such a quandary?

Summoning a determination I didn't feel, I said, "I want Monsieur Farley's pardon in writing. Signed and witnessed."

"Of course."

"And to see him set free before we leave."

"That can be arranged."

I shifted my eyes from his face down to my shaking hands.

CHAPTER THIRTY-SIX

"Are you purging the garden of carrots?" His voice startled me. I had a strong sense of having heard those words before, in another garden, in another time.

"Not carrots." I shaded my eyes as I looked up at Etienne. He was rubbing LeDuc's ears. "Beets. They have to be pulled before they get woody." In fact, I had been digging in the garden to quiet my nerves and to think through what I must accomplish in the next few days.

"I see. Well, can you spare a few minutes?"

Climbing to my feet, I brushed my hands against my garden apron, willing my heart to quiet itself. I hadn't seen him since I had introduced him to his daughter the summer before. He looked tanned and healthy. The scar near his left eye had faded to a pale reminder of a past brush with death. "Would you like to come inside and have something to drink? Beer? Wine?"

"Beer would be nice. Where is Minette?"

"Catherine took her and…a friend." I wasn't ready to get into an explanation of who Miigwan was, and why he was living with us. "Into the village to visit with the convent sisters."

"That's too bad. I had hoped to see her."

He followed me inside, LeDuc close on our heels. He sat at the table, and I poured a mug of beer for him.

"I wish to extend my condolences on the death of Captain Gervais," he said. "Sincerely so."

"Merci. I appreciate that."

He rolled his mug slowly between his hands. "But Sylvienne, in all honesty, I have to tell you, I am...conflicted." His voice rose now. "How could you put yourself in such danger going with Claudette and that god-awful husband of hers? You could have left Minette motherless."

"I thought you were dying." My voice was small in the face of his sudden anger.

He reached out and laid his hand on mine, his voice tender now. "And that very act moves me in a way I have no words for. That you would put yourself at risk for me."

Looking into those blue eyes of his, I knew he understood. And even without his saying so, I knew he was grateful.

He took my hand and kissed it. "There is something I wanted to talk to you about.

"Etienne, wait." I pulled my hand away. "I need you to know I love you. But..."

"But...?"

"Well, I..." I clasped my hands tightly in front of me.

He smiled warmly. "You don't have to say anything. This must be a difficult time for you. With the kidnapping and everything that followed. And it's so soon after the death of your husband. I understand."

My shoulders relaxed, and my whole body felt relief. He wouldn't expect a decision from me immediately. He had the patience of a saint. I didn't deserve his love.

He took both my hands in his. "I wanted you to know I...I want to get married."

My shoulders sagged. "Oh, Etienne, please. I...I can't. It's too soon after Armand..."

He looked at me, confusion furrowing his brow, but only for a moment. Those intense blue eyes crinkled in sad amusement. "It's not you I wish to marry, my dearest Sylvienne. Though I will always love you."

"Not…? Someone else?"

"There is a young lady I much admire. Well, more than admire. Her name is Kanti."

"A Native?"

"Metis. Her father is the new surgeon at Fort Ville-Marie. He is from Rouen. Her mother is a baptized Cree."

"And you…" I shook my head, trying to understand what he was saying. "You love her?" The same words he had asked me when he'd learned of my marriage to Armand.

He grinned like a schoolboy. "I do. Desperately. Sylvienne, I never thought I could love anyone but you. And I haven't stopped loving you. But with Kanti, it's different. A different kind of love. I don't know…a homemaking kind of love, perhaps? I'm sorry. I don't mean to hurt you."

"You haven't. I've…I've been nothing but trouble for you."

"Trouble is a kind word for it." His eyes crinkled again, teasing. "But I do think in truth I will always love you."

"And I you." A simple statement, but his eyes told me he was glad for it. I entwined my fingers with his. "Etienne, I think we can't control who we love, who our hearts wish to be with."

"You're not upset with me?'

I shook my head. I was relieved and happy for him. But I wasn't ready to tell him about Jacques. Our feelings for each other were too complicated to express to someone else, even to Etienne, who of all people likely would have understood.

"Will you be all right?" he asked. "You've been widowed twice now."

With a rueful sigh I said, "Yes, I'll be all right. Tell me more about her. Kanti. How did you come to know her?"

"I was in Trois-Rivières. I was supposed to meet with Robert Gravel about consigning some of my shoes and boots to his store. When we learned about the attack on Gravel, I offered to help look for his wife. I didn't realize she was the same Claudette from Amiens. Or that you were with her. But Captain Gervais said I should escort the surgeon's family back to Ville-Marie to ensure their safety. That's how I got to know Kanti."

I smiled, stroked his hand. "That's a wonderful story. She's lucky you were assigned to escort her family."

He hesitated a moment. "What about Minette?"

I looked into his eyes. "I'd like her to know her father."

"I'd like that, too."

"There will be no secrets from her," I said.

"None?" He smiled, his eyes challenging me. "Will you tell her about her grandfather?"

I thought of all the stories my mother had told me of her life at court, letting me believe they were nothing more than fairy tales. I wouldn't do that to Minette. "When she is ready to hear it."

Catherine walked in at that moment with Minette and Miigwan in tow. The boy grabbed Catherine's skirt and moved behind her at the sight of Etienne, his eyes suddenly filled with fear.

"Catherine, this is Monsieur Damise," I said, picking up my daughter. "Minette's father from France."

Catherine's eyes widened. "Bonjour, monsieur. I believe we met once before."

"When you first arrived," I said to Etienne. "I brought you home to meet Minette."

"I remember," he said to Catherine. "Though I don't believe we were properly introduced."

I'd already told Catherine that Armand was not Minette's father. In fact, most people in the colony assumed it to be the case, since I was so far along when we married. They admired Armand all the more for his willingness to marry me, a pregnant widow, and provide a home for my baby. Only Catherine and Perrette knew my late husband in France was not Minette's father, either.

"And this is Miigwan. He's staying with us for a while."

Etienne smiled at the boy and held out his hand. Catherine pushed Miigwan into position, and the boy warily shook Etienne's hand.

"Good man," Etienne said.

Miigwan offered a shy smile.

Etienne stayed to share our noon meal, playing with Minette and Miigwan while Catherine and I prepared the food. Afterward, he said, "I came here mainly to tell you my news. But I also have business in town. At the Chateau Saint-Louis. I have an appointment to interview for a seat on the Sovereign Council."

"I know. Intendent Talon mentioned it to me."

"You know him? I could use another reference."

"You won't need my reference. You will be a good fit on the council. Your business acumen and common sense are much needed."

A smile lit his face. "Do you think so? I've worked hard to make my mark in the colony, even though I haven't been here very long."

"I know you have. The intendent is of the same mind."

"So, what happened to Claudette?" he asked.

"She has been arrested. There will be a trial. When you have been oriented to your position on the Council, you will have to help decide what consequences she will face."

Etienne left soon after, but he was back just two hours later. "I am the new Sovereign Council Member," he announced, pleasure and his pride shining in his eyes.

"Congratulations!" I threw my arms around him. "Your new wife will be pleased."

"Perhaps not. This means I must divide my time between Ville-Marie and Québec."

"You'll find a way. And the Council will be the better for it. Did you see Claudette?"

"No," he grunted. "She wasn't there." Consternation and anger marred his happy countenance.

"They let her go?"

He shook his head. "She escaped. Apparently, she bribed one of the guards. I'll be damned if I am going to let her get away with what she did." He started for the door.

"Where are you going?"

"To find her. Perhaps wring her neck."

"Etienne, let it go. Talon's men will find her. I'm sure of it."

"You were almost killed. My name was used in their ruse. I will not let it go." He stormed out, and I chased after him.

When we reached the lower village and approached the Gravels' store, I could see that the single display window was shuttered. The door was locked, the stoop unswept.

Etienne banged on the door, but there was no response. A glance up at the apartment window above caused me to shudder with apprehension. It looked dark, empty, like the maw of an abandon wolf's den. Etienne banged again with his fist.

The butcher's wife stepped out of their shop across the lane. "She's not there. No point in keeping up the racket."

"Where is she?" Etienne asked.

"She was in jail. But that didn't last long."

"Where is she now?"

"Took off on that ship of theirs. The new one that dead husband of hers just bought. Before he died, of course."

"What?" I stared at her disbelieving.

"She ordered the captain to pull anchor and set sail. She told my husband some crazy nonsense, saying she herself owns the ship now, and she can do with it what she wants. Said she's planning to sell it when they get to wherever it is she's going."

"Back to France?" I asked.

"Some place she called the West Indies. Never heard of it. Plum crazy, if you ask me. People say it's because her husband was killed by them Iroquois. But everyone here has lost someone somehow. I lost two husbands before I married Monsieur le Boucher. You don't see me running off back to France." She shook her head in disgust and waved a hand as if to dismiss the notion before heading back into the shop. At the door, she stopped and turned back toward us. "And if she thinks that boat captain will let her sell that ship out from under him, she's even crazier than I thought. Ach! Wait, I have something for you." She disappeared inside.

Etienne and I looked at each other puzzled. A moment later the butcher's wife was back with a sealed letter. "She told me to give this to you."

"Me?" I took the letter from her and tore it open.

She hovered as I read it silently, craning her neck to get a look, even though I knew she couldn't read. When I refolded it with no comment, she shook her head and went back inside, mumbling.

"What is it?" Etienne asked.

"From Claudette." I handed it to him. We moved away from the butcher shop, and he read it out loud:

Sylvienne, I know who you are, and I know of the price on the shoemaker's head. I am happy to keep quiet, but you will have to reward me to do so. Send the money, the same amount as his bounty, to me in Martinique in the French West Indies. If I don't hear from you within three months' time, I will petition the Crown and get the bounty from the King in exchange for the shoemaker's whereabouts. ~ Claudette

Etienne snorted.

"What will we do?" I asked. "How can we possibly come up with that amount of money?"

"It won't be necessary. I doubt she will make it in one piece to where she thinks she's going. She has dangerously miscalculated the loyalty of her ship's captain and crew."

"And if she does survive?"

"New France is a very large place. Larger than all of Europe, I suspect. Easy to lose oneself in." He put an arm around me. "I'll worry about that when and if the time comes."

What he didn't realize was that her threat was just one more thing for *me* to worry about with Jacques awaiting the hangman, Miigwan at my house, and Intendant Talon bargaining to free Jacques if I would return to France with him.

CHAPTER THIRTY-SEVEN

Stones. Filling my pockets. Dragging me under the water. Can't breathe.

In a panic, I pushed myself up, gasping. My body soaked with sweat, I sat up in bed, my heart beating wildly from the awful dream. I reached for Armand, but of course he wasn't there. With a groan, I glanced out the window. Still dark. But I was afraid to go back to sleep. Wrapping myself in my quilt, I sat by the hearth, LeDuc at my feet, until the sun came up.

Jacques was adamant he had not traded nor had negotiations of any sort with the British. However, he admitted to selling arms to the Wendat and the Ojibwe traders. That didn't help his case. He told the tribunal that the tribes needed a way to protect themselves against the Iroquois. As Jean Talon predicted, he was found guilty of high crimes against the King and sentenced to hang.

Catherine's face drained of color when I told her of the judgement against him. She begged to go see him, but Jacques said he did not want her anywhere near the prison. My heart broke listening to her sobs of grief.

I didn't say anything to Catherine about my pact with Jean Talon. Nor to anyone, not even Jacques. A ship was due to leave the following week. There wasn't much time, and I had much to put into place.

My first visit was to the notary to draw up papers giving Titus permission to live at the house I had inherited from Armand. I included a clause stating that when he raised enough money to purchase the seigneury, Titus was the only one it could be sold to.

When I told him about it, his eyes got misty. He confided in me that he planned to ask Catherine to marry him. As distressed as he was to learn why such good fortune was coming his way, he promised to use the house to give her a good home if she agreed. I asked if he would keep LeDuc, and he assured me he would be honored to. Shadow, unfortunately, would have to be returned to the fort. As Armand had told me, she was the property of the King and did not belong to us. Titus said he would return her for me.

Next, I went to the Ursuline convent and met privately with Sœur de Sainte-Agnès. I told her I would be leaving and going back to France in a week's time. She expressed both shock and dismay. I asked her not to tell the other sisters until after my ship had sailed. I did not tell her I would be traveling with the Intendant. He had his own announcement to make, and I wanted no part of it.

I gave her money to ensure the convent's expenses were covered for the year ahead. Tears filled her eyes when she accepted my donation. When I first arrived in Québec, I had been dismayed to learn I would be living in a convent. My memories of being cast out by the nuns of the convent school in Amiens still rankled. But over time, I came to be a member of this unique community. The sisters of this convent and the girls they tutored were far different from those I'd known in France. My heart was heavy when I walked through the convent's palisade gate for the last time.

That same afternoon, I trudged over to the Hôtel-Dieu, to say goodbye to Sœur Helene and the Augustine nursing sisters. The hospital had given me a sense of purpose when I was floundering. And it had been my beloved Armand's last place on this earth. After many hugs and many more tears, I had one more task I wished to do. Stepping into the chapel, I crossed myself in front of the altar, then turned to the alms box next to the votive candles. I pulled from my skirt pocket the pouch of coins I'd collected as payment during my tenure as substitute scribe and dropped them into the wooden box. Then I lit a candle for the repose of Armand's soul.

The next day, I took Minette with me to see Jeanne and Michel. My good friends, the first I had made in this new world, were distraught beyond words when I told them I would be leaving. I did not tell them why the King was calling me home, just that I had no choice in the matter.

When I arrived back at the house, Catherine confronted me, angry tears in her eyes. "There are rumors you are going back to France. Please tell me it is not true."

"Catherine, have you spoken to Titus?" I asked.

Confusion filled her eyes. "He has...he has asked me to marry him."

"And what was your answer?"

"I told him I will. But...if you go, you will miss our wedding."

Wrapping her in a tight hug, I said, "The thought of missing your wedding breaks my heart. But it cannot be helped."

I sat her down and explained everything that was going on. She was beside herself. "No, no, no. You cannot do this."

"It is the only way. You don't want Jacques to hang, do you?"

She shook her head, tears running down her cheeks.

"Will you keep Miigwan until Jacques is free to fetch him?"

"Of course."

"Good. There are some other things I need you to do for me. And you will have to act quickly. There isn't much time before the ship sets sail."

She clasped my hands tightly. "I will do everything you ask."

"Help me saddle Shadow. We must go to Cécile. I must speak with her before I leave Québec."

Eventually, I sought out Etienne. He had been meeting with various council members to orient himself to his new duties. I found him in an office at Château Saint-Louis going over paperwork. He told me of Talon's stunning announcement that he was returning to France on the next ship out.

"Etienne, I will be going with him."

"What?" His eyes narrowed in disbelief. "You're joking. Don't say things like that."

"It's true. It's difficult to explain, but it has to do with a friend. A good friend. Jacques Farley."

"The coureur des bois? The one sitting in the garrison prison awaiting the hangman? I understand he tried to help your husband when he was hurt, but—"

"Please, he is a man who desires freedom. Much as I remember your yearning for freedom when you were summoned to work at Versailles."

He let out a long sigh. "And would it be true to say you and he are…closer than just friends?" When he saw the look in my eyes, he blurted out, "Oh, Sylvienne, what could you possibly be thinking?"

"The intendent has offered me an opportunity to free Jacques."

He groaned. "But it requires that you return to France with him. Damn! I'd hoped it wasn't true."

"You knew already?"

"Talon has kept pretty quiet about it, but I did hear mention King Louis has formally requested your return. That's why that pissant lover of the prince was sent here, isn't it?" He looked out the window at the river filled with ships at anchor and canoes and barges making their way up and down the busy waterway. "So, you will go back?"

"I don't have a choice."

"On this side of the ocean, you always have a choice."

"Talon has said he will pardon Jacques if I go with him."

He scoffed. "It seems rather ironic—I traveled to the far side of the world looking for you, and now that I've found you, you're telling me you're going back."

"Don't be angry with me." I touched his sleeve. "You have someone here you care about. You told me yourself. Someone you love more than you could ever love me."

His smile was sad. "Maybe not more. But equally. I will grant that."

"She will make you happy in ways I never could."

"Honestly? I believe you on that point." He leaned over and kissed my cheek.

Reflexively, I brought my fingers to the spot his lips had touched. After a moment, I said, "Etienne, I need your help."

He gave me a sidewise look. "You want me to use my new position on the sovereign council to influence the trial of a man accused of crimes against the Crown?"

"No! I would never ask that of you."

"Then what?"

"I need your help in a different way. You know people throughout the colony, you have business contacts. There are some things, some arrangements that have to be taken care of before I board that ship. And you are the only one I can trust." I grasped his hands. "Etienne, please. I am desperate to keep Jacques from the hangman."

His eyes hardened for the briefest of moments. Then they softened. "Just as you kept me from being arrested that day at Versailles."

Suddenly I couldn't speak. Words wouldn't come.

His gaze held mine for a long moment before giving me that crooked smile. "I may regret it…but tell me."

CHAPTER THIRTY-EIGHT

Once all the arrangements were made, I needed to visit Perrette. This would be the most difficult of all my pre-travel tasks. I asked Titus to row Minette and me out to the island.

Perrette was surprised to see us but quickly invited all three of us into the house for lunch. After putting food on the table, she immediately took Minette onto her lap to cuddle and feed while we ate and chatted.

When our lunch was finished, Perrette sent Minette to play with her children. That's when I told her and her husband of my predicament, Jacques's trial and his sentence, Talon's proposal. They both looked at me, shocked.

"You can't be serious," Perrette said. "There must be another way to keep him from the hangman."

"There is no other way. And Perrette." I closed my eyes for a moment, willing the tears away. "I cannot take Minette with me."

She stared at me, aghast. "What are you saying? You…you would leave her behind?"

"Only until I can return for her. She is too little for such a voyage. And I don't know what I'll be facing." I hesitated, my eyes filling with tears. "Perrette, will you keep her for me?"

Perrette put her hands over her heart. "Dear Sylvienne, I don't know how you can bear to even ask this. But of course I will. We will." She looked over at her husband. He nodded in agreement.

"She will be as my own child until you return," she said.

I called to Minette and pulled her onto my lap. I held her tightly, Perrette and I both crying. Finally, I sent Titus and Perrette's husband to fetch the travel chest from the boat, the travel chest I had carried all the way from France. In it I had packed everything Minette would need.

I did not tell Jacques why he was being pardoned. And Talon had the grace to keep his promise not to tell him either. There was no point in creating undue histrionics. I had made the necessary arrangements, and I was confident in my decision.

It wasn't until I boarded the ship that they brought Jacques to the landing. I watched as they unshackled him. The guard pointed to where I stood on the deck then handed him my note. Even from the middle of the river I could see his confusion. He looked up suddenly, cried out, "Sylvienne! No!!" He dropped to his knees.

Talon and the Chevalier de Lorraine stood on either side of me as the captain gave the command to weigh anchor. The ship drifted downriver. Soon he ordered one of the jib sails unfurled. We picked up speed, the current taking us around Île d'Orléans via the deeper southern channel. Québec disappeared from sight. My hands tightened on the gunwale.

"I'm sure this is difficult for you," Talon said.

I took a breath to calm my heart. "More difficult than you can know."

We passed the eastern tip of the island and sailed out into the wider river, dotted by smaller islands. I found myself gazing down at the dark water, shivering at how cold it looked.

"I am impressed," de Lorraine said. "You do not weep. The royal blood must run deep in your veins."

Scanning the bank of the river, I noted the number of islands we passed. "What makes you think royals do not weep?"

"I think not bastard royals, at any rate," he answered.

Talon gave him a disparaging look. "Life hardens us from the moment of our births."

"That is certainly true," I said.

A group of Wendat men in canoes—I counted five of the craft—waved from just beyond a small rocky island. Talon and I both held our hands up in greeting.

"Dirty sauvages," de Lorraine said with a sneer.

To keep from slapping him, I swiveled away from the rail. "Is something wrong with that sailor over there?"

"Where?" Talon asked, turning to follow my gaze.

"Over by the quarterdeck. On the other side of the main mast."

He rushed off to see what the problem was.

I dropped a glove.

"Ah! Let me, madame." With a flourish, de Lorraine bent over to retrieve it for me.

Grabbing the gunwale with one hand for support, I planted my foot on his backside and pushed him over.

As he went sprawling along the deck, I turned and stepped up onto a sideboard and threw my leg over the rail. I pulled the other over. *Don't look back.* But I did. De Lorraine had scrambled to his feet. Talon was running toward us, panic contorting his face. Looking down, I gulped. The river, blackish green, moving, always moving, mocked me, dared me, welcomed me.

"Sylvienne!" Talon screamed. "No!"

I jumped.

"What the hell?" De Lorraine's voice was the last I heard.

The shock of the cold water panicked me. My skirts swept out all around, dragging me down. I pushed against it with my feet and hands, bobbed my head up gasping for breath, but was drawn under again, the current taking me fast. Fighting to keep my head out of the water, I shrieked and grabbed for a tree branch hanging out from the bank. The current was too strong and pulled me away, leaving bloody scratches on my hands and arms. Just as I thought I was going to die, a hand reached down and grabbed me by my hair. I thudded against a canoe, banging my head. But I could breathe.

Two Wendat men grabbed my arms and hauled me into the craft. One shouted at the others in the canoes surrounding us, and they began to paddle against the current, taking me back upriver. I gave a silent prayer of thanks to God. And to Catherine and Cécile, who helped organize the rescue party. My body trembled, and my teeth chattered.

"You are safe," Haro'nu said. He wrapped a blanket around me.

"*Tiawenhk*," I said. "Thank you."

"I am honored to help a friend of Ora'wan. Cécile." He smiled.

"Will they catch us?" I pulled the blanket tighter.

He shook his head. "The current has a mind of its own, and the wind is against them. They cannot sail upriver today. Not for several days. By that time, they will be at the great salt waters. No point turning back then."

I closed my eyes in relief. When I opened them, we were in the shallower northern channel alongside Île d'Orléans. Haro'nu and his men steered their canoes to the mouth of a small channel on the northwest side of the island. There stood Perrette and her husband, and with them Etienne holding Minette. Haro'nu beached our canoe. I climbed out and ran into Etienne's arms, crushing Minette between us.

"The canoe you requested has been requisitioned and filled. Haro'nu will take us to a landing on the far side of the cape to pick it up."

"Will he be —?"

"Your friend Titus will transport him and the boy."

Perrette hugged me. "I have dry clothes for you," she said.

She and I went off to a bushy area for a bit of privacy, and she helped me out of my sodden clothing and into a practical, clean wool dress. We hugged again, tears flowing down our cheeks. I promised to write, to find a way to get letters to her.

"Etienne, how can I thank you?" I said to him.

"Thank me when you are safe. We need to go now." He and Perrette's husband carried Minette's travel chest and put it into one of the Wendat canoes.

Etienne and Minette climbed into Haro'nu's canoe with me, and our small fleet pushed off. The men paddled past the mouth of the Saint-Charles River. The buildings of lower Québec came into view. Above them, I could see the Château Saint-Louis and the fort next to it. And above that the convent and the hospital and the church where I had married Armand. The wooden merchant buildings that made up the lower town didn't look as ramshackle to me as they did when I first arrived over two years ago. They looked busy, lively, built of fortitude rather than stone.

We skirted the half-dozen ships moored in the middle of the river, then kept going until we reached a small settlement called Sillery. Haro'nu told us how the Wendat and the many nations of the Algonquin people used to summer there to fish for eels.

"They don't anymore?" I asked.

"Not since the settlers brought the sickness from across the salt waters. Some of our people converted to Christianity, and their families settled here. But their numbers are dwindling. The others moved on to take advantage of the French desire for beavers." He pointed to a spit of land jutting out into the river. "I think your friend awaits us there."

My heart did a flip at the sight of Jacques standing at the river's edge. Behind him were Miigwan, Catherine, and Titus. A dog bounded back and forth between them, barking a welcome. LeDuc!

Haro'nu steered our canoe up to the small landing. I climbed out of the canoe and sloshed through the water to throw myself into Jacques's arms. He kissed me until I thought he would swallow me whole.

"Damn, woman!" he said, when he finally released my lips. "What the hell were you thinking?"

"That I couldn't let them hang you."

"She has a bad habit of rescuing men from the clutches of the law," Etienne said coming up behind me, Minette in his arms. "For a change, she needed rescuing herself. You must be the infamous coureur des bois." He held out his hand to shake. "Etienne Damise."

"Jacques, this is my…my dear friend, Etienne."

"The bootmaker." Jacques took Etienne's hand in his own firm grip. "Your name has become quite well known in these parts."

Etienne nodded his appreciation. "I've outfitted a canoe for you. The larger one there." He pointed to one waiting near the small fleet that had accompanied us since my rescue.

"Etienne, I—"

He put a finger to my lips. "Don't thank me." He buried his nose in Minette's hair before saying, his voice husky, "Take care of her. That's all I ask. And come back when it's safe."

"You put all this together for us?" Jacques asked.

"She was never going back to France," Etienne said. "Catherine called on Haro'nu to make sure she survived the short trip downriver. My job was to make sure you have what you need so she and Minette will survive the trip with you upriver."

"I'll keep them safe. Miigwan and I will." Jacques pulled the boy over to his side.

"There is a trading post on an island where two of the large inland seas meet," Etienne said. "The Ojibwe call it Big Turtle, I think."

"Michilimackinac. I know of it," Jacques said. "I've been there. There's talk of building a fort on the mainland in a year or two."

Etienne nodded. "There are people at the trading post who will welcome you. I've packed boots into the canoe for them." He grinned and slapped Jacques on the back. "It's not a good idea to arrive without gifts."

Jacques shook Etienne's hand again, then pulled him into a brusque hug. "Merci, mon frère. Merci beaucoup."

Haro'nu told us he and his men would accompany us as far as Ville-Marie. There we could find another group to join for the next leg of our journey.

Catherine and Titus hugged each of us goodbye.

"I'll take care of the house. *We'll* take care of it," Titus said, placing a protective arm around Catherine.

"I know you will," I said. "I have something for you." I pulled a silk pouch from the travel chest I had used for Minette's things. In it was the gold wedding band that held such bad memories for me, but which would start a new life with new, loving memories with Catherine and Titus. I gave it to them. Catherine exclaimed over its beauty. Titus then pocketed it to keep it safe until their ceremony. I would hang on to the braided gold ring, the one from my royal father, a bit longer. I still wore the silver ring Armand had placed on my finger when we wed.

"I have something for you, too," Catherine said, smiling a bit sheepishly as she handed me Armand's toque, the hat I had knitted for him myself. "I thought you might want it. For the winters."

My eyes welling with tears, I hugged her again. "Will you tell Jeanne and Michel I am safe?"

"I will. And the sisters at the convent and the hospital. They will finally be able to stop saying their rosaries for you."

"What will you do now?" I asked Etienne as he walked us back to the waiting canoes.

"I have business with the council. We have to get ready for the new Intendant. And the governor is fuming over your friend's pardon. I need to make sure it sticks. Then I'll go back to Ville-Marie."

"And marry Kanti?"

He laughed. "Yes. I will marry Kanti."

I threw my arms around him. "I am so happy for you."

"And I for you." He ran his fingers through Minette's curls. "Perhaps Kanti and I will take a trip to Michilimackinac one day."

"We would love that." I kissed him one last time. Not a lover's kiss, but one that lingered, the memory of his sweet lips never to be forgotten.

My small family and I settled into the canoe. I sat in the middle with Minette on my lap and LeDuc at my feet. Jacques took up position in the back as always. Miigwan sat in the front. Despite his young age, the boy picked up his paddle with confidence.

Etienne and Titus pushed our canoe out into the river, then stood with Catherine waving and yelling "Bon voyage!"

I pulled Armand's toque over Minette's curls to keep her head warm and wrapped my arms around her. Jacques angled our canoe to face into the sun-dappled current. With strong strokes he set us on our way to our new future.

THE END

AUTHOR'S NOTE AND ACKNOWLEDGEMENTS

Braving the Dawn: A Novel of New France arose from my passion for genealogy—discovering my ancestors and my heritage. Writing this book gave me the opportunity to engage in another of my passions: historical research. *Braving the Dawn* is not a story about my ancestors, but rather it was inspired by them. It is the story of what life might have been like for some of my 7th and 8th great-grandparents who emigrated from France to New France (Canada). The story is wholly fictional, a product of my imagination, but the research that went into making it as authentic as possible was very real.

Braving the Dawn continues the story of Sylvienne after she boards the ship at the end of *Courting the Sun: A Novel of Versailles*. That book chronicles her adventures leading up to and after she receives an invitation from King Louis XIV to attend his court in Paris and at Versailles.

The genesis of both novels is that King Louis wanted his own colony in the New World. While he had acquired plenty of land in New France, most of the French inhabitants were soldiers, fur traders, a few farmers, and even fewer families. Louis devised a scheme to recruit young women to sail to Canada and marry eligible men. Offering to pay their passage and provide dowries and trousseaus, he even promised bonuses if they had ten or more babies. In the ten-year period from 1663 to 1673, roughly 750 women took him up on his proposition. These women are referred to today as *les Filles du Roi* (Daughters of the King). At last count, I discovered that twenty-three of my many French-Canadian ancestors were Filles du Roi.

The driving question in my first novel, *Courting the Sun*, was what would cause a woman—despite the monetary incentives—to leave everything and everyone she knew and traverse a dangerous ocean to marry and raise a family in an untamed land filled with wild animals and unfamiliar Indigenous people. While many women joined the program for relief from poverty, because they were orphans, or had no prospects for marriage, or perhaps they simply craved adventure, I created an entirely different reason for Sylvienne, which plays out in *Courting the Sun*.

Sylvienne is fictional, loosely inspired by my own Filles du Roi ancestors. And I do mean loosely. To my knowledge, none of my ancestors lived the life that Sylvienne did at Versailles.

Armand, Jacques, Etienne, and Claudette are also fictional, as are most of the minor characters in *Braving the Dawn*. However, the ship Sylvienne sails on, *la Nativité*, is named after a real ship that carried the Filles du Roi to Québec in 1672. The women in the group she travels with do not represent actual historical Filles but rather are named after various of my own ancestors.

Gouverneur Général Daniel de Rémy de Courcelle, Father François de Laval, Soeur de Sainte-Agnès, Intendent Jean Talon, and the Chevalier de Lorraine are real historical figures. I have fictionalized them to serve my story. To the best of my knowledge, Jean Talon never married; however, the suggestion that he may have been more interested in men than in women in this rendering is fictional.

The inspiration for Jacques Farley was my own 5th great-grandfather, Jacques-Philippe Farley. He was a voyageur and legal fur trader, rather than a coureur des bois, who plied his trade between Montreal and Fort Michilimackinac in what is now Michigan. However, my Jacques-Philippe lived in the century after *Braving the Dawn* takes place. It was his father, Antoine Farley, who was born in Ireland and traveled to

Québec via France. The fun part of writing historical fiction is being allowed to take bits and pieces of historical facts and reconfigure them into fictional characters, storylines, and plots.

I did strive for authenticity when describing the settings for *Braving the Dawn,* as well as in portraying the lives of the Filles du Roi, the other French colonists, and the people of the First Nations of Canada. I am an avid researcher and try my best to be historically accurate.

The nuns of the Ursuline Monastery of Québec did welcome the young female recruits as they got off the ships, got them ready for married life in New France, and facilitated their meeting eligible men. The convent was founded in 1639 under the leadership of Sœur Marie de l'Incarnation to educate both French girls and the girls of the First Nations. Sœur de Sainte-Agnès was the first Canadian-born leader of the Ursuline convent. The monastery complex has grown over the years and today can be toured virtually or in person.

The *Hôtel-Dieu de Québec,* the hospital run by Augustinian nuns, had already been in existence for thirty-five years by the time the story of Sylvienne takes place. However, it was first established just outside Québec in a settlement called Sillery. In 1644, because of repeated attacks by the Iroquois, the sisters moved into the village of Québec and began construction of the hospital that still exists today. My ancestor, Antoine Farley, can be found in the record as having been a patient there.

Intendent Jean Talon did build a commercial brewery, *La Brasserie du Roy.* However, it was not very successful and closed after only four years of production.

The lower village of Old Québec is a popular tourist destination now. A fire in 1682 destroyed the original ramshackle wooden buildings. Many of the current stone buildings in the lower village date from the time of rebuilding after that fire.

I tried my best to accurately represent the people of the First Nations of Canada who lived in the area—particularly the Huron/Wendat and the Ojibwe. The French colonists generally got along with and respected the First People. They were trading partners, and before the Filles du Roi arrived, French men were encouraged to marry Indigenous women. The nuns and priests learned to speak the local languages, and Sœur Marie de l'Incarnation, founder of the Québec Ursuline convent, wrote French/Huron-Wendat and French/Iroquois dictionaries. However, the Iroquois never took to the French, and in fact were aggressive against other First Nations who were not of the Iroquois Confederacy, especially the Huron/Wendat.

Québec was quite small in 1672, probably only about 1,200 people. Montreal (then known as Ville-Marie) was even smaller. However, both grew quickly in the years during and after the arrival of the Filles du Roi. In fact, the population of the entire French colony tripled during that period. It seems King Louis's recruitment program was a success.

~

I am forever grateful to Reagan Rothe and the entire team at Black Rose Writing for their support and expertise in bringing to publication *Braving the Dawn.*

Merci beaucoup to my ever-supportive critique partners, Lucy Sanna, Carol Larson, and Anne Keller; to my editor, Mary Joy Johnson; and to my friend and mentor, Christine DeSmet, for challenging me to rise above the acceptable and to dig deeper into my creative psyche. You set a high bar. I hope I achieved it.

A special shoutout to Joan Fernandez, Dawn Hogan, and Cam Torrens who served as early readers and gave me invaluable feedback. And to my siblings: Darrell, who advised me on muskets and knives; Jim, my go-to guy about snowshoes; David for his knowledge of hatchets and knife making; and Jean who cheered me on every step of the way.

As always, I am indebted to my daughter Erin and son Joshua, their spouses, Jonathan and Hana, and my grandchildren Cameron, Zen, and Lilyenne for being my first fan club.

And finally, I can't say enough about my husband, Mark, who has patiently supported me in countless ways as I journeyed through the 17th century, researched, wrote, and continue to promote my books. I couldn't do it without you. You are my Etienne, my Armand, my Jacques. *Je t'aime*.

ABOUT THE AUTHOR

Award-winning author Peggy Joque Williams writes historical fiction inspired by her discovery of her 7th- and 8th-great grandmothers who emigrated from France to Canada in the 17th century as *Filles du Roi*. Her heroine's story, while fictional, is rooted in her deep research about her French-Canadian and Ojibwe ancestors of that era.

A retired elementary school teacher, Peggy is an alum of both Michigan State University and the University of Wisconsin. She loves spending time with her three grandkids, especially when she can get them to help out in her garden. She volunteers in their classrooms, helping kids with reading and math. Peggy lives with her family in Madison, Wisconsin.

Visit her at www.peggywilliamsauthor.com.

OTHER TITLES BY PEGGY JOQUE WILLIAMS

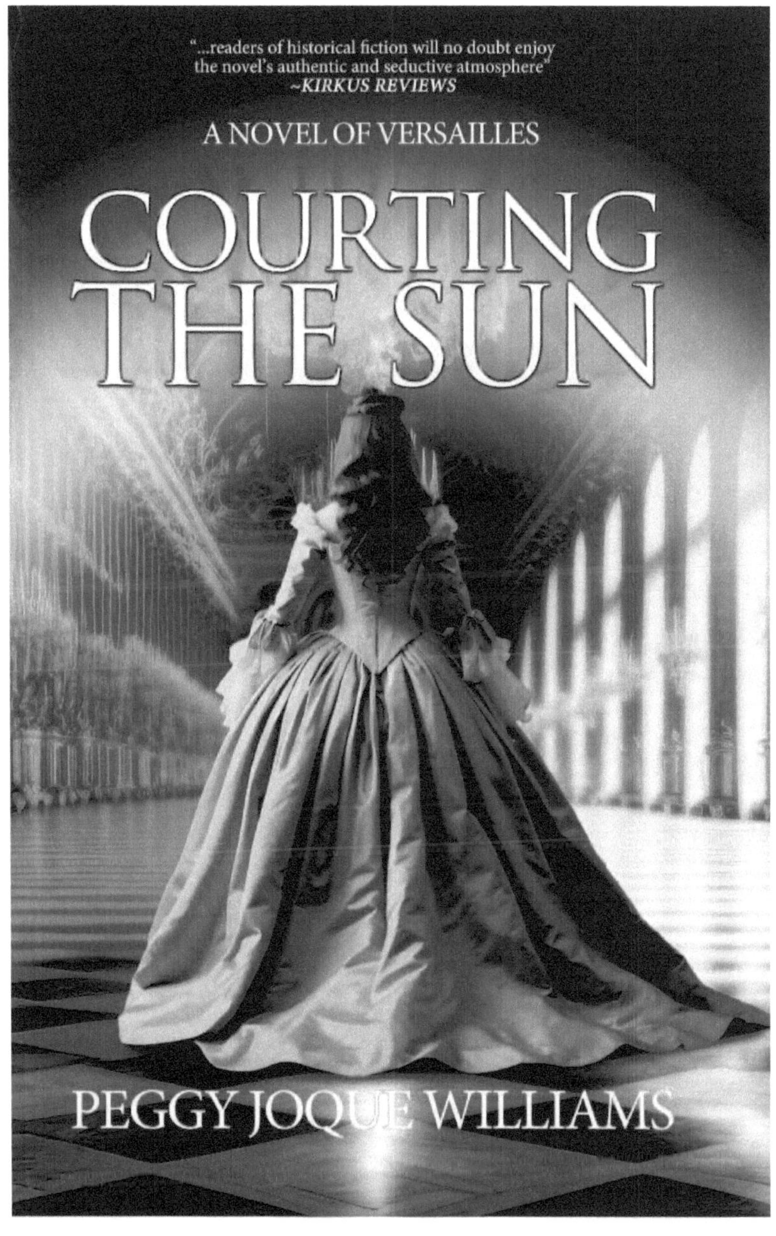

NOTE FROM PEGGY JOQUE WILLIAMS

Word-of-mouth is crucial for any author to succeed. If you enjoyed *Braving the Dawn*, please leave a review online—anywhere you are able. Even if it's just a sentence or two. It would make all the difference and would be very much appreciated.

Thanks!
Peggy Joque Williams

We hope you enjoyed reading this title from:

www.blackrosewriting.com

Subscribe to our mailing list – *The Rosevine* – and receive **FREE** books, daily deals, and stay current with news about upcoming releases and our hottest authors.
Scan the QR code below to sign up.

Already a subscriber? Please accept a sincere thank you for being a fan of Black Rose Writing authors.

View other Black Rose Writing titles at
www.blackrosewriting.com/books and use promo code
PRINT to receive a **20% discount** when purchasing.